Wilson, William
    Every man is my father.

DATE DUE		
Sept 8	Mar. 21	FEB 18
Sept 29	Mar. 29	
Oct 9	Apr. 25	
Oct. 16	JUN 17 1974	
Oct 23	JUL 21 1975	
Nov 1	SEP 22 1976	
Nov. 8	OCT 7 1976	
Dec. 8	OCT 21 1976	
Dec. 26	NOV 3 1976	
Jan. 28	FEB 28 78	
Feb. 1	JUN 1 1982	
Mar 8	SEP 2 1982	

EVERY
MAN
IS MY
FATHER

EVERY MAN IS MY FATHER

William E. Wilson

Saturday Review Press

New York

Library of Congress Catalog Card Number: 72-94799

ISBN 0-8415-0239-0

Saturday Review Press
380 Madison Avenue
New York, New York 10017

PRINTED IN THE UNITED STATES OF AMERICA

Design by Tere LoPrete

For JAY BAILEY WILSON

Contents

Author's Note

THE first successful ironworks in America, established on the Saugus River in Massachusetts more than three hundred years ago, are today completely reconstructed and restored. Seven waterwheels demonstrate for modern tourists the operations of the blast furnace, the forge and finery, and the rolling and slitting mill of this Colonial foundry. Among the original buildings that remain in the neighborhood are the Ironmaster's House on a hill above the ancient works and the "Scottish House" nearby, which was the home of sixty of the several thousand Scots that Oliver Cromwell captured at the Battle of Dunbar in 1650 and shipped to America and elsewhere to work off the indenture of eight years that he imposed on each of them.

In the summer of 1964, I visited the Saugus Ironworks Restoration for the first time, hoping to discover whether my first American ancestor of the Wilson name, one of the Scots taken at Dunbar and sent as an indentured man to New England, was among those who lived in the Scottish House and worked at the ironworks. Apparently he was not. But another discovery was in store for me that day at Saugus—the theme of a novel. That day I began to imagine a Scot among the prisoners of war at the ironworks and what might have happened to him in his cruel involuntary bondage in a strange land; and thereafter I created in my mind his descendants, men and women of the American Revolution and the Era of Good Feeling in the early years of the nineteenth century, of the Civil War period, and on down to our present time.

So this novel began. Most of it was written in the brick farmhouse built in 1830, where I live in Indiana, although it was both begun and completed on Longboat Key in Florida. In the course of the years intervening between the fall of 1964, when I started the book, and the spring of 1972, when I finished it, I took time out to write a history of my native state and some magazine articles and short stories and to travel about America and to Scotland and France; but all the while I was carrying the novel in my head and on notes stuffed in my pockets.

Every Man Is My Father is an imagined story of an imagined family, with only a few real people in minor roles; at the same time I have tried to make it a true story of what Americans were thinking and feeling during the four centuries that we have inhabited this land.

GOOD DEEDS: Fear not, I will speak for thee.

—Everyman

SUPPLY CLAYBURN: . . . in this country, we have inherited the whole damn'd hu-
man race, Clayburns no better
than the rest; in America, Sam,
every man is our father.

—Every Man Is My Father

Part One

JOHN CLAYBURN

ca. 1630–1705

WAKING at dawn under Doon Hill on Dunbar's field on the third day of September in the Year of Our Lord 1650, I believed for a long time that the voice I heard was the loving cry of the lass in my arms and I had no thought of giving over. On and on the voice cried at my ear—"John! John!"—and in my passion I called back, "My love! My love!" until at last I came full awake and learned how cruelly sleep was cheating me.

There was no lass in my arms. Naught lay beneath me but a fold of my Scottish soldier's plaid rolled into a wench's shape, which I was hugging like a ninny. Worse still, by the antics of my dreaming my plaid had got kilted high above my haunches and in the frosty chill of dawn my naked arse was colder than a paddock in a pond.

"John—!"

The voice became a shouting, thunderous, no lassie's, unmistakable.

"John Clayburn—!"

"Ay—?" said I at last, rolling over on my back and blinking my eyes against the sun. "Ingram Moodie is it?"

Ingram Moodie it was, standing above me, his round face gray as porridge.

"John, the Sassenach are coming!"

What happened thereafter happened in an instant. Ingram Moodie was gone, vanished, vapored in a ball of fire that was the sun just then appearing upon the sea nearby, and in his place stood one of Oliver Cromwell's devils with a sword held ready for thrusting through my heart.

"Hoolie, man!" I cried out. "Have a care!"

Behind the threatening devil and between his spraddled legs

I saw the rest of them, and I thought for sure they were the last of mankind that I would ever see upon this earth. All ten thousand of them I swear I saw through that devil's legs, charging straight at me across the burn that ran below the hill. Cromwell's whole army I saw in one glance, cavalry and infantry together, guns, claymores, pennants aloft, while at my back I knew Doon Hill was so steep that no man in my sudden need could clamber up it even were there not an Englishman standing over him with a sword to keep him down.

"Hoolie!" I cried again. "Think on the widow you will make in Edinburgh, man!"

At that, my enemy touched his swordtip to my breast with the icy prick of death, and thinking on my sins, of which a Scot has ever more on his conscience than most men if only because he has more conscience, I tried to bring to mind a prayer I had learned in the kirk. But before a prayer could come to me the sword's thrust stopped upon my ribs and the swordsman broke into a laugh. Tossing back his shaggy head, he bellowed, his ragged mouth as black and windy as the pass at Killiecrankie.

"Is that what you would do battle with?" he jeered, pointing at my middle with his sword.

I sat up, looked down, and saw what he was pointing at.

"Ochane!" I cried, and covered my nakedness with a corner of my plaid, as soldiers drape a fieldpiece with a banner for parade.

"Ochane!" my enemy cried after me in mockery; and when it was all too plain that my plaid had ceased to be a banner and become a shroud, he laughed and said, "Your artillery retires!"

I sprang to my feet in anger; and he brandished his sword again and cried, "Hold! Stand where you are or I will run you through!"

Weaponless though I was, I scorned his sword and, throwing the length of my plaid across my shoulder, stared him down.

Cowed, he said, "You have won a stay of death, man. If you will go peaceably with me," he said, "I will turn you in as prisoner of war."

Only then did it come to me that the swordsman had been speaking all the while in my native tongue. No Englishman was he. A traitorous Scot he was. In my extremity I had not noted it before.

"Base hireling!" I shouted at him and snatched his weapon from his hand; and I would have killed him on the spot if, in that moment, another enemy had not leapt upon my back and pinned my arms behind me.

"March!" this one said to me in English; and I had no choice but to obey.

For a long time we marched, the three of us, amongst a milling of men beneath Doon Hill, the English devil with a sword at my back and the false Scot capering alongside taunting me in our own tongue about the sight that he had seen, until at last the Englishman, understanding none of it, tired of the hireling's chatter and drove him off.

Not long thereafter we came upon Ingram Moodie, who was marching like myself and thousands more, brave Scots all of us, but caught napping beneath Doon Hill at the rising of the sun. With an Englishman's sword pricking at his arse, Ingram pranced high and faster than ever was his wont. All asweat he was, no longer porridge-gray but ruddy from his exercise. I was overjoyed at seeing him alive and called out, "Ingram! John Clayburn here!"

When he saw me, his face came even more alight. Yet when we were abreast of one another, still dogged by our guards, he grew sly and winked and asked me, "Did the lass too escape unharmed?"

"What lass?" said I, forgetting what had gone before.

"Why, the lass you lay with in your sleep. Where is she now?"

Ingram and I had been friends forever. Born in the same village, we had played shinty on the haughs together when we were lads and later hunted MacDonald reivers amongst the crags. While there was still down upon my cheek I had streaked off to Edinburgh after Ingram, who was older than I, and there we had chummed together until my Dorcas and I were wed. I loved Ingram Moodie like a brother; that I did. But at that moment on Dunbar's field I would have boxed his ears for his impudence and knocked his bonnet from his head if there had been no English devils at our backs with swords.

"Och, Ingram!" I said, sadly. "Had the lass been of flesh and blood and not a shadow of my dreaming, I would not have run away and left her under Doon Hill as you left me, your own true friend, in no condition to do battle."

"Ay," said Ingram. "In no condition to do battle; that you were. And in no condition for running, either, on three legs and short of breath before you started." Thereupon he crooned, in mockery of me, "Oh, my love, my love!"

I would have given him a chop on the ear then indeed, English sword or no, had he not immediately turned solemn and pointed straight ahead.

"Look, John—yont the burn! Och, it is lucky for you that you could not run, and for me that I did not! Look yonder, man!"

We had come upon a hillock that gave us a view of the plain stretching from Berwick to the sea; and when I looked where Ingram pointed, I saw that the plain was black with running men, and after that I saw how those who ran were chased by Cromwell's men and, when they stumbled, still drugged with sleep, helpless, their weapons left behind, how Cromwell's men cut them down without mercy. It was like a rounding up of rabbits on a moor. A shame to noble Scotland it was. And yet, I think, a worse shame to Cromwell. Slaughter it was; not soldiering. In that one September morn, I learned later, three thousand of David Leslie's Scottish men were murdered so and five thousand wounded, Cromwell himself losing less than a score. Five thousand other Scots, like Ingram Moodie and myself, escaped unscathed but were taken prisoner.

Of all of these, I like to think, I was the only one saved from the slaughter by a lass. I like also to believe it was my Dorcas I was dreaming of on that September morning, that it was my good wife who saved me from being murdered by the Sassenach; but I learned long ago that what a man likes to believe and what is true are often not the same. It could be that the companion of my dreaming that morning long ago beneath Doon Hill on Dunbar's field was any lass that I had loved before I knew my Dorcas or maybe all my former dearies shaped together into the one perfect creature that every man will dream of now and then; for there is no foretelling who will come to pleasure a man in his dreaming, young or old, nor very clear remembering of her after. Indeed, upon a cold porridge for supper or a toss too many at an inn, I am sure I have had in restless sleep such drab and droop-rumped wenches as, next day, seen with both eyes open, would have left me hanging. Yet, whether it was my Dorcas or another, a lass it was, a female, who saved my life that day more than half a century ago.

Of such matters a man does not speak amongst his children, and so my own and their children and their children's children have never heard how I awoke that morning under Doon Hill when I was young and lusty. Nor have they surmised much of what happened in the years that followed hard upon that day. For this reason, they write pridefully now in their Bibles: *John Clayburn, Scot, fought with honor at Dunbar, 3 September, 1650, taken prisoner of war by O. Cromwell,* thus planting for themselves in this new land a family tree, with myself, although I am not yet arrived at my three score years and ten, the root of it.

After Dunbar, the English drove us captured Scots like turkeys down among the barren hills of Lammermoor, through the Middle Marches, an interchange of bog and shingle, southward against the sun—ay, ever against the sun—and on across England. The wounded and the lads who were too young for soldiering they sent home, but five thousand of us unscathed Scottishmen they drove southward thus, fearing we might fight for the king again if they freed us.

"March!" the Sassenach commanded.

And we marched.

Against that southern sun.

Through villages and towns I had heard about but never seen till then we marched—Belford, Wooler, Gateshead, Newcastle-on-Tyne. By day, it was castles, cots, colleries and foundries that we saw, our bodies asweat in that dry and hot September, and farms and marketplaces too, our bellies empty. By night, our bodies cold, we watched the kilns of charcoal burners glow amongst the distant hills.

"March!"

And on we marched.

Ever against the sun.

"Keep a calm sough," Ingram Moodie counseled at my side. "Keep a calm sough, John Clayburn."

That was his Scot's way of saying I should hold my tongue and not complain, although he himself talked thirteen to the dozen all the way, pretending that our journey was but a lark and he was overjoyed to see the world at last.

'Twas no lark for me, and so I told him. When he marveled at the strange land all about us, I asked him what was this to see.

What was there worth the looking at in this drear and dreadful England? I was hungry, I said. I was blinded by the sun. I was hot. I was cold. I wanted my Dorcas. Maybe, I told him, because he was not so young as I was he felt naught that I was feeling. Maybe, I said, more blood flowed in my veins than flowed in his, because my hair was red whilst his was pale as straw and sparsely flat upon his head like bracken drying on a boulder.

"Whisht, man!" he said, to silence me. "Keep a calm sough."

And afterward it was himself, not I, who kept on talking.

We swam the Derwent and a hundred times, I swear, forded or swam the knotted meander of the Wear; and those who could not swim were drowned. Afterward, upon dry land, "March!" it was once more. Days upon end, that was the only word we got from our captors save their cursing.

We lived by our own forage, which on English moorlands was not enough to keep a Scotsman's goat alive; and by the time we came to Durham, where the church stands that is more castle against the Scots than house of God, we were famished and crazed by thirst, our throats choked with dust, our feet bare and sore, and our sunken bellies gnawing at our hearts like rats. Some indeed had died already, and others we carried. But there, at Durham, after we had crossed the bridge and filed through the marketplace and down a narrow street to the other side of town, a sudden cry of joy went up from the vanguard of our column.

"Water!" the men began to shout.

When Ingram and I reached the spot where the shouting came from, we saw below us a wide blue lake in a broad valley.

"Water it is!" said Ingram.

"Water!" all behind us began to cry then in a chorus; and our ranks broke.

"Halt!" was the English answer to our rejoicing; and some of them fired their guns, first above our heads, and then, lowering their gunbarrels, dropping a dozen or more of those who clamored at our rear.

Heedless of the command, the rest of us ran down the hillside like a drove of wild-eyed Highland cattle with the hoose.

"Water!" we all cried, running.

But at the valley's bottom, what had seemed from a distance like a blue mountain tarn was not water after all. The glare of the sun and a rising mist together with our own thirst had deceived us. What lay before us was a field of cabbages.

For a moment we were dismayed. But only for a moment. Soon another cry of joy went up. Finding cabbages was like finding ale instead of water. We had drink and nourishment together.

The sound that rose thereafter from that field of cabbages is one I shall never forget. The teeth of nigh five thousand starving Scots sinking into those juicy globes was like the splash of surf upon a sandy shore, a rush of mountain water in a rill in spring. Ay, sweeter than a pibroch from Scottish pipes it was.

Many of the men knelt in the field and praised God as they ate, not waiting till they were done before they said their grace, as is the careful Scottish custom. They praised the Lord unmindful that their jaws were dripping slaver in His sight. Little wonder was it that He sent a pestilence upon us for their disrespect within an hour.

Ay, no longer than an hour it was before those cabbages began to colic us. Before we reached the Tees, which bounds the north of Yorkshire, they had gone through us like millwater through a sluice and we were straining our very gullets through our guts and out our arses.

And marching all the while.

For it was "March!" the English shouted at us still, giving us neither rest nor physic for our sickness.

"March!" they said.

And we marched, holding our guts in writhing agony, too weak to lift our plaids behind us nor heed the plaints of splattered comrades in our wakes.

"March!"

And we marched.

Still against the sun.

Had our captors but given us respite for a day and let us crawl away mongst the bracken to live out our grinding agonies, each alone, as sick animals will do, many might have weathered their misfortune.

But "March!" it was always.

And we marched against the sun.

And many died.

My recollection of the days that followed on that frolic in the cabbage field at Durham is of a loathsome stink and a never-ending pain, although Ingram and I had been less greedy than most and were not amongst the worst aggrieved. Very soon after the pestilence came, some began to fall in the road. At gun's point then the Sassenach made us roll them into the ditches alongside and leave them there to expire in their own filth. Before we came to Nottingham, five hundred were left to perish so, and in the days that came thereafter sixteen hundred died in all. When at last we reached London gate, no more than half of us remained from the five thousand that began that turkey-run at Dunbar.

Londontown itself we never saw, because at the Thames side, without the walls, the English herded us into a great pen so new that it could have been built only against our coming. There we stood like steaming cattle in the sun, and within an hour of our arrival men came out from the city to appraise us, like drovers gathered at a fair to buy.

Ingram Moodie, who had a way of learning things before all others, told us that Cromwell was asking twenty pounds a head for us as indentured servants. Most of us, Ingram added, purse-mouthed, were worth little more than ten, so weakened were we by the pestilence of Durham. Indeed, he thought some of us were worth no more than five. In all this reckoning, Ingram spoke as if it were himself who would be losing in the bargain and not the city men who came out to look us over.

" 'Tis robbery!" he said, shaking his head, as if he were not one of us.

Some days, to speed their business, our captors herded out men in lots and stood them up to auction by the gross or hundred.

"Five hundred pounds!" a London man would shout.

"Six hundred!" cried another.

"Six and ten!"

Then Ingram, looking over our comrades, who stood hangdog in the dust, would wag his head and mutter, "Fools! That runty lot is worth three hundred and no more!"

As soon as a price was agreed upon, the city men called up the bullies they had hired for their purposes, all armed with spontoons, and drove our comrades off. Then Ingram would wag his head again and growl, "As bow-houghed, runnygut, and spavined a drove of wretches as I have ever seen! And three Mac-Donalds in the lot!" Ingram was ever a hard man against Mac-Donalds.

Slowly our numbers in the camp diminished thus, but neither Ingram nor I was taken at the first. Ingram soon learned the fate of those that were bought. Some, he said, were bound for the north of Ireland, some for Virginia, some for the Barbadoes, all as indentured servants.

"Cromwell will scatter us round the earth," he explained, "so that we can never reunite against him."

The men remaining in our company groaned and vowed they would not go.

But Ingram said we had no choice.

One day, after giving the matter long thought, I told Ingram I intended to escape and return to Scotland and my Dorcas.

"Escape—?" said Ingram. "And how will you escape, man?"

"I do not know yet," I told him, "but I will devise a way."

"And if you succeed," he said, "how will you then reach Scotland?"

"I will walk," I said. "I walked from Edinburgh to Dunbar with David Leslie and thence to London with the Sassenach. I will walk back again."

"Ay, and be discovered along the way for what you are," said Ingram, "as plain to see as a daisy on a dunghill."

I thanked him for the compliment but said I would cast off my plaid and my bonnet, steal the clothes off the first Englishman I met on the road, and pass for one myself thereafter.

"And when the time comes for speaking," Ingram said, "what will you say and how will you say it? It is a long way back to Scotland without once asking the road."

"It was yourself who taught me the English tongue in Edinburgh, Ingram Moodie," I replied.

"I taught you the English words," he said, "but I could not teach you the English way of speaking them. Only an Englishman knows that. The first time you open your broad Scot's mouth, John Clayburn, all the world will know you for what you are, English duddies notwithstanding."

Unable to endure the thought of slavery in a foreign land

without my Dorcas, I made plans then without Ingram's help.

First, I offered an English soldier half my plaid if he would look the other way and let me climb the wall and flee. He seemed a kindly lad, English dog though he was, and took my plaid between his fingers to examine it. Although it was covered with filth from long marching and no washing, it was plainly good Scotch wool.

"All of it," the soldier said at last, "and I'm your man."

"Nay," I replied. "My offer is but half."

"All of it or none," he said.

That would have left me nothing to cover me and winter coming, and so I told him.

"Then climb the wall and run in your breech-clout, Scot!" the soldier said.

I saw then that he had been ill-willed from the start and was only tormenting me, the way a cat plays with a mouse; for even an Englishman knows that no Scot wears his breeks in battle. Beneath my plaid there was naught but my naked self, as I had been taken prisoner at Dunbar.

Thereafter, I plotted with some comrades to dig a tunnel out of the pen. We would dig at night. With our bare hands we would dig, having neither dirks nor shovels nor other implements of any kind; and with our bare hands, we pledged, we would kill any English dog who tried to stop us.

But at the end of one long night of digging we made no more than a scratch upon the hard-packed earth by the wall; and the next morning I took Ingram aside and said, "I have decided not to run away without you, Ingram. You and I must stay together at all costs."

He gave me his fat smile and said, "There is sense in your head now, John Clayburn. You have the right of it now. Keep a calm sough."

Our turn at the auctions came the very next day. One hundred and fifty men were wanted, "well and sound and free from wounds," as the proclamation read. Ingram told us those chosen in this lot would be sent to labor in the ironworks of New England for indentures of eight years.

"*New* England—?" one man in our company said. "Where is that? Is not *one* England enough to satisfy the Devil?"

The man was a MacDonald and, unwilling to converse with

him but also unable to hold his tongue, Ingram said to me, as if it were I who asked the question, "New England is a country in the New World. It lies across the sea and is a land of rocks and forests and cold winters and is populated by Roundheads and naked savages."

"I will not go," said the MacDonald.

"Nor I," said I.

Ignoring the MacDonald, Ingram looked at me, purse-mouthed.

"And what will you do instead, John Clayburn?"

"I will hang myself," I said.

"A man does not take upon himself his own predestination," Ingram said gravely. "Anyhow, 'tis better to go farther than to stay here and fare worse," he said, and walked away.

I was sick of his proverbs. I wanted nothing to do with his New England and its rocks and Roundheads and naked savages. But I knew that he was right about predestination.

The men who came out from London that day prodded us from head to foot, rolled back our eyes, and counted our teeth, as if we were Scotch ponies up for sale. Being strong, big-boned, and of a favorable appearance, I was amongst the first chosen. But Ingram had a wen he could not hide. Although he set his bonnet firmly on it like a hen upon an egg, the buyers ruled him out.

Ingram was black-hearted then. Glum as an owl he was. All scowls and sulks, he paced up and down with his hands clasped behind his back and finally went apart and sat upon a stone.

But he was never a man to be long daunted. When the English lined up those they had chosen for the final counting, although he stood among the rejected, he was once more smiling his fat smile and watched us with a look of calculation in his eyes.

An English officer came along our line reading off the names.

"John Clayburn."

"John Clayburn it is," I said.

Immediately afterward I felt a nudging at my ribs, and there was Ingram, standing in the line beside me.

"They'll find you out, for sure!" I said.

"Whisht, man!" he whispered, his finger at his lips. But as soon as the English officer was beyond hearing, he spoke up boldly. "One hundred and fifty men are to be sent to New

England. They will not reckon us up again until our journey ends. By that time surely some will have died, and they will be pleased to have me in the place of one of them."

"And if none should die?"

"Then you and I shall heave a MacDonald into the sea on the last night of the voyage," he said.

Och, Ingram was indeed a hard man against MacDonalds! But so in that time long ago was I, for I thought only then how it would be more convenient for us both should one of the Mac-Donalds amongst us be predestined on that voyage to fall overboard of himself.

The ship awaiting us in Blackwall Reach was called the *Unity*. She was hardly bigger than a cockle, and when we boarded her she lay tossing at her moorings in a jabble of waves and windy rain, the first rain to wet our skins since we left Dunbar. Her master's name was Augustine Walker, and as we came aboard we had a view of him standing on the deck. A gaunt, ill-favored man he was and one with never a care for his passengers, as we would soon discover. He stowed us below at once, cheek-by-jowl, with hardly room to scratch ourselves, and there for nine long weeks we were to tumble about at the mercy of the winter sea, breathing our own foul breath and the stench of our own foul bodies except for the one hour each day that the seamen led us up to the deck for exercise. In all that voyage we had only hardtack, dried fish, and moldy cheese for our diet.

I was the stronger of us two and did not suffer from the hardship as Ingram suffered. Yet he bore the confinement better than I at the first, his head being full of mathematics to entertain him with visions of the fortunes we would make in America.

"You will send to Scotland for your Dorcas," he said to me, "and I shall marry a Puritan lass or maybe an Indian maiden if she be fair and a chieftain's daughter, and we shall live like lords on fine plantations in Massachusetts."

"I shall be all of thirty when our indentures are done," I answered him. "An old man I shall be, Ingram Moodie. And you will be older still."

He paid no heed and talked on about his dream while I no more than half-listened to him, beginning as I was to wonder whether I might go daft before we reached New England's shores. Some of our number were by then already mad, stark staring mad. Before we had crossed but half the sea, men began leaping about in our midst in the crowded hold, screeching and tearing their hair, until the master put them in irons and stowed them in the bilge. Would I, I was asking myself, soon be one of them?

Finally, one day, I interrupted Ingram's prattle and ventured on the subject of my anxiety.

"Ochane!" I sighed. "It is not easy for a man to be thinking ever upon the lasses and have no opportunity."

Ingram Moodie gave a start.

"Thinking of the lasses, John?" he said. "Thinking what?"

"Why, of lying with one in love," said I. "What else?"

My answer seemed to take him by surprise. He looked at me as if I were a woman with child asking for strawberries in dead of winter. He laid a hand upon my arm.

"You must keep a calm sough in that matter, John," he said. "There's naught to be done about that in our present circumstances. There's not a lass aboard this ship, and there will be but few in New England—and those mostly spoken for."

"I know that," I said. "But that makes the thinking harder to bear."

"Then think of something else, John."

"I can think of nothing else to think of," I replied.

He stood in meditation for a moment, and at the end all he could say was, "Keep a calm sough!"

Unburdening myself thus to him eased the load of my thoughts somewhat, but thereafter Ingram seemed unable to forget my trouble. He came back to it often.

"How goes it with you this day, John?" he would ask me, with a worried look, as we walked the deck.

"Like a pony with the spavin," I would say.

"Losh, man!" he would cry then. "What a pity it is so much on your mind!"

"Like a gander with the spraddles walking in the dew," I would tell him the next time he inquired.

"Och, it is indeed a burden to you!"

"Like a hen with an egg I am," I would say, "and no nest to lay it in."

"It pains me to think about it, John Clayburn."

"Then maybe," I said to him finally, " 'twould be better if you did not ask me about it again."

After that, Ingram remained silent about my trouble and I learned to live with it; but I noticed that he was silent on all other subjects too and to the end of the voyage went about with a burdened look of his own while sighing aloud sometimes, "Ochane!"

When at last the end of our voyage came, Master Walker allowed us to come up early on the deck, and as the *Unity* entered the harbor of Bostontown Ingram and I stood together at the rail on the windward side. Finally we saw the town, dead ahead on a hill under a pall of gray sky. To me it was nothing compared to Edinburgh seen from the Firth, and I said so. Anyone, I said, who had sailed the Firth of Forth and gazed up at Arthur's Seat against the sky could think but little of this place, and Ingram could do no more than purse his lips and observe that it was solid earth at least.

But when we dropped anchor and two agents of the ironworks came aboard, Ingram's spirits began to rise, for here once more was an occasion for him to display his superior knowledge. We heard the agents announce themselves to the ship's master as Joshua Foote and John Becx. One was English, lean and fair, but the other, short and dark, spoke the English tongue as if a frog croaked in his gullet, and Ingram whispered amongst us that this was a Hollander's way of speaking. When the master pointed at our woeful company, Ingram was pleased to see how vexed the agents were and said he had warned that they would rue the day we were bought in London.

Savages we must indeed have seemed to those two gentlemen in fine cloth with silver buckles on their shoes. We were greatly reduced in numbers by deaths at sea, many were mad, as I have already reported, and all the rest of us were verminous and sick and required physic. One, a Davidson, believed sick, was delivered to Foote and Becx dead, like a parcel, and they had to purchase a winding sheet from Master Walker and drop the poor man in the harbor before anyone could leave the ship.

Ashore, the two agents of the ironworks tried to question us, and at Ingram's prompting many of us replied, "Ha niel Sassenach," whether we could speak English or not, until Master

Becx, the dark one, turned purple and swore he would have justice from the Company's men in London who had cheated him, and Master Foote, the pale one, turned paler still and wrung his hands and moaned like a cow in the lane at milking time.

"Ha niel Sassenach."

It was a credit to Ingram's thinking. In a small way it was revenge for the English order, "March!" at Durham.

Becx and Foote culled out the most unfit amongst us and stood them to one side while a notice was posted that these would be sold at auction by the waterside on the morrow.

"They will draw no more than a pound apiece," Ingram whispered gleefully. "None of us is worth the expense they have been to. It serves them right."

As he spoke, however, I noted that he was holding his bonnet tight upon his wen.

Those of us the agents thought the best, some sixty, including Ingram and myself, were marched through Boston's steep, snow-drifted streets and off across the frozen marshes of a river that I later learned to call the Saugus. This was in the bleakest, stoniest country I had ever seen until that day. A wilderness it was, which made the crofts of Scotland seem like the Garden of Eden and even England less than a wasteland, with no wide moors nor crags and summits like those we knew at home and yet with trees taller than any I had ever dreamed of. A cold unnatural country it was that would take me many years to learn to love.

In the gloaming of the woods we came at last to a broad house that was only half-built. A scaffold still stood all around it, and an overhanging upper story gave its face a most unwelcoming scowl. Here our new masters packed us in worse than we were on the ship, a dozen to each small room, and set armed guards at the doors.

All in our room grumbled, and even Ingram agreed that, whipped as it was by the winter wind, our "Scottish House," as the English called it, was no better than a coop for keeping poultry in till it was sent to market. But the burden of the voyage was gone from his mind now and his head was once more full of mathematics. Smiling into our sullen faces, he said, "We're the cockies of the flock they drove from Dunbar down to London. We will outlive our captors in this new land. No Scot was ever long disadvantaged by the weather, and we shall one day own the earth we stand on."

"This weather is nothing like our Scotland's," said one of our number dourly and, so speaking, wrapped his plaid round his chest and up about his head and turned his back upon us, standing face to the wall, his brow resting upon an upraised arm. A Campbell this one was, a great, glum, hooded falcon of a man, with legs as thick as tree trunks and pads of black hair upon his knees like sporrans.

"Ay, it is cold here," Ingram agreed cheerily. "Even for a Sinclair down from John of Groats it might seem cold in this New England at the first. But—"

Whatever consolation he had for us thereafter was lost in the sudden cry of a MacGillivray at the door: "Look! They have brought usquebaugh with our porridge!"

At that Scottish word for whiskey all turned toward the door —even the Campbell; ay, the Campbell first of all—and saw a lad coming in with a pot of porridge and a jug as well.

The nearest snatched the jug from the lad and the next the porridge, and we all sat on the floor and passed the two around.

Somehow the Campbell had the jug first, and when he took his draught, he made a dour face.

"It's like naught I've ever had in my mouth before!" he cried. "Cruachan!"

But, being a Campbell, he did not spit it out.

"Dunmaglass!" roared the MacGillivray when his turn came. "A Douglas! A Douglas!" gasped a Douglas, choking; and then a Cameron shouted, "Sons of the hounds, come here and get flesh!"

But each one swallowed manfully.

When Ingram had his turn his cheeks flamed red and tears streamed from his eyes; but afterward, wiping his mouth, he tried to smile and said philosophically, "Nay, 'tis not usquebaugh, but it does have spirit in it."

For myself, I thought it tasted in its afterglow of fruit, apples maybe, not of malted barley surely.

We drank it all and quickly; and at the end, whatever it was, there was not enough of it to get twelve Scotsmen full. We were left all glum once more and sat leaning on our elbows, staring at the cold porridge without a word.

All glum and wordless we were except Ingram Moodie. He, undaunted by disappointment in the brew, tried to lift our hearts with talk about the wonders we would see in the New World and the fortunes we were sure to make. On and on he talked till I, his best friend, could endure no more of it and shouted, "May the Devil colic your belly again, Ingram Moodie, as the cabbages did at Durham! Whisht, man! Whisht!"

But Ingram only smiled his fat smile and talked on.

Finally, the Campbell rose from where he sat and crossed the room and stood above Ingram, towering like Ben Nevis.

"Did you not hear the man ask you to be quiet?" he said softly.

But Ingram talked on. Rising to his feet, he peered round the Campbell's bulk and addressed me as if I were the only one in the room.

"Whisht!" the Campbell said; and then, with Ingram still a-jabber, he began to shunt him toward the nearest wall. Arms akimbo, legs aspar, taking a step and waiting a moment before he took another, the Campbell moved like an avalanche. All the while, Ingram kept peeking at me under one of the Campbell's arms and then under the other, still talking thirteen to the dozen, until finally the Campbell had him between the wall and his own great chest and belly. There Ingram disappeared altogether, his voice became muffled and finally stopped.

After a long while, the Campbell stepped back and I was surprised to see Ingram still alive, against the wall. But he was not talking.

"I have not laid a hand upon you, Moodie," the Campbell said, peering down at Ingram gloomily, "for you are a Scot like me, though not a Campbell. But I tell you, man, I will have silence when I am melancholy."

For the rest of that night Ingram Moodie said not another word, and there was silence enough in the room for the melancholy of us all.

The next day the Company of Undertakers of the Ironworks of New England learned truly what a bad bargain they had

made with Cromwell at the Thames side. Early in the morning
after we arrived at the Scottish House, where they had locked
us in for the night, they called us out of that cold barracks and
after a ration of porridge that would not have satisfied a mouse,
marched us through the woods to the ironmaster's house. This
house stood upon a hill above the ironworks, black and many-
gabled, with steep rooflines that made it look like a huddle of
witches in peaked hats. Under the overhang of its second story
we waited in a snowfall, pressing ourselves against the walls as
tight as clapboards while, one by one, they called us in for the
master to interrogate us.

Below the house was the iron furnace. It was not in blast, the
river and the sluices and waterwheels being thickly clogged
with ice. Across a high and narrow bridge, the charge-hole
yawned at us, round and black as a cannon's muzzle, and behind
and below it the houses of the furnace and the forge and rolling-
mill squatted silent, snow-covered and cold against a gray sky.
Except for their grumblings, the men were silent too, even
Ingram Moodie, who was perhaps mindful of the Campbell still.
As for the Campbell himself, he scowled at everything and nothing all at once and, at one point, caring not who saw him, lifted
his plaid and pissed, plentiful as a horse, in the snow.

At last, a bony bleak-eyed fellow with the cut of a Scot to his
jaw called out from the doorway of the house, "You with the
blaze under your bonnet!"

He meant my red hair of course; and I said, "Ay, man."

"John Clayburn is it?"

"None else," said I.

"Do you speak English?"

"Ha niel Sassenach."

Eyeing me with suspicion, he motioned me into the house.

Inside, he led me through a narrow hall and into a spacious
keeping-room where the master sat in a carved chair beside a
fireplace. The fire lighted up his face and showed it to be sharp
and shrewd but not unkindly. Like Master Foote and Master
Becx, he wore a long coat and black hose and silver buckles on
his shoes.

"John Clayburn?" he said, reading from a paper; and that
being my name and he having it writ there before him and I
having already answered to it outside, I found no reason for
answering again.

"Are you John Clayburn?" the Scot asked me in my own tongue.

"If it is written on the paper and I am not still outside where you called me so, then John Clayburn it must be," I said.

In English the Scot assured the ironmaster that John Clayburn it was.

"He speaks no English?"

"He says not, sir."

The ironmaster sighed, and there was a deal of delay thereafter. He turned and tapped his fingers on the table top beside him, picked up a rushlight, studied it round and round, set it down, crossed and uncrossed his slender legs with a soft whisper of the fine cloth of his breeches rubbing together, and scratched his knobby chin so hard that it took on the rosy glow of a pear in late summer. Behind him a pale light shone through the panes of a leaded window and built a halo round his head. This made no saint of him, for no saint would have been a party to bringing me to America, far from my native land and my Dorcas; yet I could not prevent a liking for him growing in me as I waited. I could see that he was weary of his business and perplexed, a good man at heart, at least as good as it was possible for an Englishman to be.

At last he spoke to me again through the Scot who had brought me in.

"Have you ever worked in a forge or finery?"

I shook my head.

"Can you make charcoal?"

"In a land where peat is plentiful," I said to the Scot, "who has need of charcoal?"

"A wood-cutter then," the ironmaster said to the Scot. "Can this man fell trees?"

To this I answered there was naught but whins in my native glen.

The Scot explained my answer, addressing the ironmaster as Master Gifford; and Master Gifford sighed again and shrugged, and the Scot shrugged back at him.

The Scot said to me then, "Master Gifford would know whether you have been a merchant or a merchant's apprentice? Do you have skill in mathematics? A clerk is needed in the company store."

At once I knew where Ingram's lot was going to fall. In our

village he had kept the drover's accounts when we stole Mac-Donald cattle and ran them into Aberdeen to sell. In Edinburgh he had been a clerk in a draper's shop. He was a canny one at ciphering. But my own head was not long enough for trading, and so I told the Scot.

"Perhaps we can put him in the stables with the smith," the ironmaster said; but I told the Scot it would be an ill day for any nag I nailed a shoe on.

Once more Master Gifford tapped his fingers on the table top, looking now as if he found no good in me at all; and yet I believe he approved somewhat my lank and bony frame. I was a well-made lad, tall and strong—and comely too, or so my Dorcas used to tell me. After a long time, the ironmaster sighed and wrote something on his paper, gave it to the Scot with a shrug, and dismissed me.

In the hall I asked my countryman what had been decided; and he turned his bleak eyes upon me and said, "They will try to school you."

"At what?" I asked.

"At the ironworks."

"They will rue the day," I said.

"Ay, that they will. I am sure of it," my countryman agreed.

Afterward, I sought out Ingram Moodie in the yard to tell him of my fate and inform him that a clerk was needed in the company store. But Ingram had already learned that for himself.

I waited in the snow for Ingram while he took his turn in Master Gifford's house, and when at last he came out I knew by the look of him that matters had turned out to his liking.

As we walked together back to the Scottish House, he fairly danced through the snowy woods, as happy as a lass with a new jerkin, and I was as pleased as himself over his good fortune until he told me that he would live in the loft above the store and must move that very day from our barracks. Then I grew as glum as the Campbell had been the night before.

Even worse news awaited me at the Scottish House. There I learned that many others were departing that day to work on farms and at the collieries and in the woods roundabout, and I would henceforth share the room with but two others: the hoodie-crow of a Campbell and, to the horror of both Ingram and myself, a MacDonald.

"Keep a calm sough, John," Ingram said, as he told me good-bye. " 'Twill be practice for learning to live with the Devil, should you prove not to be of the Elect."

The next morning the three of us, the Campbell, the Mac-Donald and I, traveled together the three miles through the woods to the ironworks, the Campbell striding ahead in a tene-brific silence, leaving the MacDonald and myself in company like two strange dogs who have a mind to romp, being both hardly more than puppies, yet each wondering whether a play-ful nip might inspire a vicious bite. All I learned of the Mac-Donald that morning was that he bore the Christian name of Alan and was two years my junior.

At the ironworks, the master finer, whose name was Jenks, sent the Campbell to the rolling-mill, the MacDonald to the docks, and me to the forge room, where I was put in the care of a hangdog Englishman named Quentin Pray. He was a wee man, spindly but gutty, who took a surly view of me from the start, for a long time staring up into my face with spittle drool-ing from his chin and the smell of spirits strong upon his breath.

"They say you speak no English," he said finally.

Thinking my chances at the forge might be better if I under-stood what was said to me, I told him I had learned a mite of the language in Edinburgh.

"Good!" he said. "I will teach you to work."

Yet in the end he taught me nothing, for he knew no better than to point and grunt and curse, telling me what to do but never telling me how to do it. The little I learned I learned by my own mistakes.

Throughout the winter, this man Pray was ever a burden to me as company, as were most of the others in the finery, Eng-lishmen all. There was one named Nicholas Pinnion and an-other, John Turner, and although they were always at odds between themselves, they were ever united against me. In the town of Lynn, where they lived, they fought and cursed each other publicly. One night, John Turner stabbed his daughter-in-law and the next day at the forge boasted of it, swearing by the eternal God that he would kill John Gorum, a carter, who, Pray told me, was the lass's lover. Another time, John Turner's wife was called to court for saying she would fornicate with any man who took her fancy and the authorities of Massachusetts could be damned. Often these Englishmen were fined for breaking one another's heads and making filthy speeches, and their wives were fined for wearing silver lace and silken hoods; but none of them was ever locked in prison or put in the stocks for these offenses, because the ironworks could not spare their skills.

The morning after Mistress Turner made her boast and the court set her free with only a fine, Quentin Pray spoke of it while we were working over the bellows with beeswax and thread. His head that day was tied with a dirty rag from fighting the night before, and his foul breath struck me hard in the face.

"Now, there is provision for you, Clayburn," he said, "if you are feeling the need."

"Provision?" I said.

"John Turner's wife."

"I do not understand," I said.

He looked at me askance.

"Don't tell me Scots aren't made like other men! Meet me tonight in the town and I'll take you round to Mistress Turner as soon as old John has gone to bed with his jorum. It won't cost you a farthing."

I was wanting a woman then as I had wanted one aboard the *Unity*, but I said no. I spoke so mainly because of my Dorcas, but I was thinking also that the likes of Quentin Pray were not to be trusted. He or John Turner, or both of them maybe, would have murdered me in Mistress Turner's bed for my plaid.

Indeed, we Scots walked ever carefully in those days amongst the Puritan laws, for the English were watchful of us and mistrusted us because we spoke a strange tongue amongst ourselves and professed a faith that differed from their own. Perhaps we were virtuous because we had no choice. It was drink that most commonly caused trouble among the workers of the ironworks, and although Scots have stronger heads for drink than the English, we were also on short rations.

In spite of the company of Pray and his kind, the first month at the ironworks passed for me without great hardship, and the second and the third. So long as the river remained locked by ice, my work was little more than puttering round the furnace at Pray's side, laying trenches for the pigs and sows that would

be molded when the ironworks was in blast. What I did mainly
was to fetch tools on command, and once I learned the names
for them, I could do that without much bungling. We mended
the leather bellows, built a new sluice for the overshot wheel,
hauled the Nahant rock and coral that would be used for flux,
cleaned out the charge-hole, and dug paths and cleared the
wharf at the riverside after each fresh snow.

This last occupation was the one that I liked best, for it gave
me the company of Alan MacDonald in my work. We had become friends, and every morning when there was new snow on
the ground, we walked from the Scottish House to work behind
the gloomy Campbell as merry as two schoolboys.

"When we return to Scotland," Alan said on one such morning, " 'twill be a strange sight to see a MacDonald and a Clayburn arm in arm."

"Ay, that it will," I said. "Our countrymen will be full of
wonder when we lift a pint of ale together instead of lifting one
another's cattle."

" 'Tis skirts we'll lift then, man; not cattle," Alan said. "We'll
lift the lassies' skirts and make them lie aspar, share and share
alike."

"Nay, friend," I said. "You forget I have a wife in Scotland."

"Losh, I did forget, John! Forgive me, man. But 'tis a pity, a
great pity that you cannot join me in such excursions."

A pity it seemed to me then for a while thereafter. I loved my
Dorcas, but in such need as I was, she seemed sometimes far
away.

One morning in March when I arrived at the foundry on the
Saugus I saw that the river had thawed and the mill wheels were
turning, and that day Quentin Pray, loitering at the foundry
door, told me my task would be to help him carry loops of
molten iron from furnace to forge.

"You'll learn what work is now, you Scots bastard," he said.
"You'll learn or get killed in the learning."

All that day the cauldron roared at one side of the room, the
bellows soughed and panted, the cams of the axles of the big
wheels clanked and thumped, and the great hammerhead
banged on the anvil, scattering fire and brimstone all about. In

the thunderous noise I could hardly keep my wits about me, and when the day was done I was so worn by weariness that even the Campbell noted my condition and, slowing his pace, walked with Alan at my side.

The next day was even harder than the first, but the following day I began to grow accustomed to the noise, and the day after that was easier still. But on the fifth day, when I saw Quentin Pray at his loitering post by the door, I had a premonition of disaster. Although the heat of the furnace had not yet struck Pray's face, his eyes were bleared and his cheeks blotched turkey-red. From the way he slouched against the wall like a half-filled sack of grain, I knew that he was still drunk from his dissipations of the night before, and I was afraid.

He spat at my feet as I passed him.

"It's pots and kettles for you today," he said.

Pots and kettles meant ladling molten iron out of the live furnace and pouring that devil's brew into the clay molds we had made. Before that day I had worked only at the troughs for pigs and sows and merchant bars, carrying iron that was hot but already firm and manageable to the forges and the hammerhead. But this day, Pray told me, I would use the long-handled ladle for the first time and swing raw iron about while it was still flowing. This task had previously been Pray's, but apparently Jenks, the master finer, had seen that he was too unsteady to be trusted with it.

And that he was. He should not have been allowed to work at anything that day. Laboring at the troughs that morning while I labored at the molds, he swayed and staggered like a blind pony, and soon my foreboding of disaster came true. Within an hour, as I was carrying my hissing ladle to one of the molds, Pray lurched against my elbow. The long handle twisted in my grasp, and molten iron splattered and danced across the clay floor about Pray's feet and mine.

I leaped in time to be spared the worst of it, but Pray was not quick enough. The rest of my days I shall hear his screams. He stumbled across the room and fell in a writhing heap beside the hammerhead, his voice rising in a high, continuous, womanish screech until at last it stopped when his wits left him. Thereafter came a smell of burning flesh to my nostrils where I lay by the door beating out the charred fragments of my plaid.

The men gathered round Pray, and finally two of them carried him off to the village. It was only after that act of mercy that anyone thought of me. Jenks came then with the others and stood above me and, after a brief inspection, slapped grease upon my burns.

"Can you stand, Clayburn?" he asked.

I got to my feet and was surprised that I could.

"Can you walk?"

I took a step forward, like a man trying out new shoes at the cobbler's.

"Go at once to the company store and fit yourself with something to cover your nakedness," Jenks said.

One of the men laughed then, and I looked down and saw what there was for all to see. To be sure, it was not so vaunty as it had been that day at dawn under Doon Hill, but I told myself I was lucky it was still there.

Turning my back to the men, I started toward the door, but there I stopped and looked back at Jenks over my shoulder.

"Quentin Pray," I said. "Will he live?"

Jenks nodded.

"For that I am thankful," I said.

Jenks glanced at the men and then turned back to me.

"I am not sure that you should be," he said. "I will speak to Master Gifford to learn whether there is some other work you can do for the Undertakers. Your life will not be worth a farthing here when Pray recovers."

Thinking of what Jenks had said, I hobbled halfway up the hill toward the company store before it came upon me that I was going to see Ingram Moodie there. I had not exchanged words with him since he left our house in the woods three months before.

Ingram greeted me from amongst his bales and boxes as if I were a stranger come to trade, and thinking how success had changed him, I was at first dismayed until it came out that he had not recognized me against the light of the door.

"John Clayburn is it?" he cried out joyfully when he saw who I was and, coming round his counter, shook my hand.

"John Clayburn it is," said I, "and in sore need of duddies, Ingram, as you can see."

He squinted at my burned legs and cried, "Losh!" while I told him about my misadventure at the mill. "Losh!" he cried again and again, plucking at the charred remnant of my plaid as I spoke. "Good Scotch wool!"

Turning his back upon me finally, he hauled down from his shelves a pair of workman's leather breeches such as the colonists wore; but when he laid them on the counter between us he held one leg of them tight in his fist as though he was loth to part with them.

"Good Scotch wool and ruined!" he said again, as if to reproach me for carelessness with my plaid. "And do you know that on the morrow you will limp like a horse with the spavin, John Clayburn, and when Quentin Pray is well again he will murder you if he can?"

"Ay," I said. "But Master Jenks is going to speak to Master Gifford in my behalf for a change of my labor."

Ingram's eyebrows rose.

"Master Jenks is it now?" he said. "Nay, it is Ingram Moodie who will speak for you to Master Gifford. How would it please you to work for a settler in the woods?"

"At what?" I asked.

"At farming. Or perhaps at cutting wood for charcoal at his kilns. Colliers have the best of it hereabouts. They are paid five shillings a load for charcoal, and in a year some earn more than Master Gifford himself. Did you know that, John Clayburn?"

"Earn it they do indeed," I said. "I have seen them hauling in their loads at the mill. Black with soot as the Old Clootie they are. But you know that I have never cut wood bigger than a cudgel to beat off MacDonald dogs with, Ingram."

"You could learn."

"Ay, with an ax in my hand," I said, "I would surely not be so clumsy as I am with bloomer's tongs. Will you recommend me for such work, Ingram?"

Ingram pulled at his lower lip in meditation, still clutching my new breeches with his other hand. When he spoke at last, he did not answer my question but asked me another.

"Do you still have that old complaint that troubled you aboard the *Unity?*"

"What complaint is that?" I asked.

"A yearning to lie with a lass."

His words angered me.

"That is no matter for a man's friend to be prying into, Ingram Moodie," I said. "I yearn for a lass no more than any man would yearn for one in my condition, no more than you would yourself had you more blood and less mathematics in your veins. It is no business of yours to ask."

Ingram seemed not to hear my reproach.

"It is true you write to your Dorcas often," he said gravely; and more angered than ever, I asked him how he knew that.

"By Master Gifford's order, all letters to and from us Scots now pass through my hands for sorting," Ingram said. "I have seen your letters to Dorcas, and I also know that no letter from her has come to you yet."

"Ay, it has been a long time of waiting," I said woefully.

Minded suddenly of my new breeches in his hand, Ingram instructed me to come behind his counter and try them on; and while I was doing so, he said, "Yesterday a collier came into the store asking for just such a man as you. He needed a strong man, he said, and honest and right-living. He wanted no drunken rascal who would run away or idle at his work. I thought of you at once. He said he would pay handsomely against an indenture, two shillings a cord for cutting and a shilling a day for work on his farm. He had gone to the iron-master's house first, but Master Gifford was away in Boston. I told him to return today. I will speak to Master Gifford in your behalf, John."

"You do that, Ingram," I said, "and I will be thankful."

But Ingram seemed to hesitate at that point.

"You must remember that the Undertakers rent your services to such a man for two years, the term being subject to renewal, and all that time you would be accountable to the collier, not to Master Gifford, should you have trouble."

"I will have no trouble," I said. "Save for this forenoon's misfortune with Pray, I have had none, and I will have none in future. You know well, Ingram Moodie, I am not a man who sticks his horn in the bog."

Ingram looked purse-mouthed, frowning and biting his lower lip; but at last he came out of such musing and smiled, as if it both surprised and pleased him to find me still there behind his counter in my new breeches.

"I will do it for you, John," he said. "I will. You are just the man for it. I will speak to Master Gifford this very forenoon before the collier comes again. His name is Horrock. He is an Englishman."

"Englishman or no," I said, "I will work diligently for him."

"See that you do, John. And see that you write often to your Dorcas and pray that you will hear from her soon."

I knew not what writing to Dorcas and praying for a reply had to do with it; but I had no intention of not writing to her and I could pray as well as Ingram Moodie, and I said, "That I will, man."

Ingram then showed me where to sign in his book for my new clothes, and I hobbled back to the ironworks.

That very afternoon Master Gifford sent for me to come to his house. By that time the burns on my legs from my ankles to my haunches had drawn the skin so tight that I could hardly stagger up the hill, but I was so near bursting with joy at the prospect of quitting the finery that the pain seemed nothing at all.

"How do you fare, John Clayburn?" Master Gifford asked me.

"Sore and lame in the legs, sir," I said, quick with my answer, "but nothing more."

"You have learned English since I saw you last."

"Ay, sir."

" 'Twas fast learned."

"Ay, sir," I said.

The ironmaster sat, as I had seen him the first time, in his carved chair by the fire in his keeping-room, but this time, opposite him, side by side on a settle, were a man and a woman. The man was a giant, thick as an oak in the chest and shoulders, bearded, red-eyed, a great black devil covered with soot. He held a gun upright between his knees, like a staff, and kept his high-crowned felt hat square upon his head to show that he was his own man, even in the ironmaster's house. His muddy stock-inged legs stuck out straight before him, as if their muscles were too stout for him to bend his knees with comfort. Beside the man's burly bulk on the settle, the woman looked like a child, a wee slender wish of a lass in a jerkinet and a full skirt that touched the floor and hid her feet. Her snow-white hands were folded in her lap like nesting birds, and her head was bent so modestly that I could not see her face for the broad brim of her Puritan bonnet, which was of felt, like her husband's.

When I came into the room the man looked me fiercely up and down, and after the ironmaster finished speaking with me he gave a grunt and spat into the fire.

"Good!" Master Gifford said, as if his visitor's grunting and spitting expressed approval of me.

The giant on the settle spat again.

"I have excellent reports of this man's character and disposition," the ironmaster said to his guest then. "He was burned at the forge this morning through no fault of his own and not severely, the master finer tells me. Nevertheless, I shall reduce the indenture fee by a shilling to compensate for any physic that may be required or any slowness at his work while he is mending."

The ironmaster's disregard of my presence as he spoke made me feel like a measure of oats that Ingram Moodie might haggle over in his store.

"You have observed that he speaks English," the ironmaster continued, this time giving me a sidelong glance, "and that is more than most of these Scots do. Nevertheless I will take the shilling off the fee."

In response to these words the collier's beard split crosswise like a wound, baring a blood-red cavern of mouth and teeth as white as bones. With his eyes fixed narrowly upon his opponent in the bargaining he leaned forward and held up three smoky fingers, speaking not a word.

The ironmaster picked up the tongs by the fireplace, took a coal from the fire, and relighted his pipe.

"One," he said through the smoke that wreathed his face.

The collier's red-and-white grin widened. He bent farther forward and thrust the three blackened fingers out before him like a devil's pitchfork until they almost touched the bowl of the ironmaster's pipe.

"One," Master Gifford said again.

The fingers remained where they were.

"Not three certainly," Master Gifford said, crossing his legs.

The collier did not move.

Master Gifford sighed and laid his pipe on the table at his side.

"Two," he said. "I will take two shillings off for the injury, but no more. Four pounds eighteen shillings is what you must pay in advance for the two years of indenture. No less."

I could not help wishing the collier would bring the ironmaster further down, for there was no belittling the pain in my legs. I knew well that in my condition I was no bargain, and the greater the reduction of the price the greater might be the collier's leniency with me till I recovered.

But four pounds eighteen shillings it was to be. The collier was satisfied. With a click of his teeth he snapped shut the great wound in his beard, nodded agreement, leaned back in the settle beside the woman, and closed the three fingers into a grimy fist on his thigh.

At that point, Master Gifford turned to me and spoke as if I had not been present all the while.

"I have just leased your services for two years to Benjamin Horrock, the collier, subject to renewal. He and Mistress Horrock will take you home with them this day."

"Ay, sir," I said.

When her name was spoken, Mistress Horrock turned her head, and the face that was lifted up to me was young and fair, the fairest I had seen since I left Scotland, the pale cheeks faintly flushed by the firelight and the blue eyes big and round and dark as thistle flowers. In spite of me, my heart leapt as if she were my Dorcas.

Benjamin Horrock's house was hidden deep and snug in a clearing in the forest. The days of late March still growing early dark, we did not come upon it till after several hours of walking along spongy paths in the gloaming of the woods between bogs where skunk cabbages were first beginning to show, giving off a smell that minded me of Durham. Single file we walked all the way from Master Gifford's witch-peaked house. To the Scottish barracks first we went where I had lived for three months and where now I gathered up my few possessions, and then on through the deeper woods to the Horrock cottage, Horrock himself ever in the lead, carrying his gun, then Mistress Horrock, then myself, none speaking a word to another. From time to time, Mistress Horrock turned her head and gave me a troubled look from under the broad brim of her hat, for I limped and staggered like a spavined horse, as Ingram had predicted I would; but she spoke not a word, and her husband never turned his head nor slackened his pace.

Before we came to the house, I smelled the woodsmoke from its chimney on the freshening wind of the spring night, and when at last I saw the keeping-fire of its hearth glowing through two narrow windows in the dark, I thanked God, for my legs were now so swollen and the skin so tight upon them that I could hardly take a step without a cry of pain.

Of a sudden then it seemed to me a bonny night. With the bog behind us, the air was clean and fresh, and stars were out overhead. Frogs skirled in the ponds, each taking a turn, piping merrily. I was free of the ironworks. I was going to fare better from now on. For these blessings I thanked my Maker as I staggered forward.

At the house Horrock opened the door and went in first and, after him, his wife, while I, remembering my place, waited outside. I leaned against the clapboards of the wall till Horrock came into the light of the doorway again and beckoned me in with a grunt that sounded like an angry pig.

Inside the house I saw a tidy keeping-room furnished better than any cotter's that I had ever seen in Scotland, although not so fine or large as Master Gifford's. A long plain table with four chairs about it filled the center of the room, and in one corner was a bed with a curtain that could be drawn to hide it and in another were a chest and a cabinet and a writing-stand. Above the ingle hung another gun like the one Master Horrock carried, and at the fireplace there were kettles and pots and pans such as we made at the ironworks and an iron skillet for frying which stood on legs. It was plain to see that Horrock had made a good thing of his life in the woods and also that Mistress Horrock kept his house well.

When I entered she had already removed her bonnet, and I was startled to see how black her hair was, black as a crow's wing and fitting tight against her head like a cap, with moist ringlets at her temples. Across the room, Horrock was setting his gun on the other rack above the ingle, and afterward he took up a jug from the hearth and tossed off one long draught. He offered me none and, instead, as he wiped his beard with the back of his hand, grunted and motioned to me again, and I followed him out of the house and helped with the chores as best I could.

In a shed at the back of the house were a cow to be milked and two oxen to be fed, poultry to be watered against the morrow, and firewood that required splitting and cutting to length. I worked in the dark while Horrock carried a lantern that gave but little light. He spoke not a word to me but, like Quentin Pray, only grunted and pointed, showing me what to do but never saying how he wanted it done. But I will say for him that, unlike Quentin Pray, he did his own share.

When finally we came back into the house Mistress Horrock had set three bowls of steaming cabbage soup on the table along with a joint of venison, and at the smell of the cabbage my gut all but colicked as if the Durham pestilence were upon me again. Mistress Horrock stood silent behind the table, eyes lowered, waiting for Horrock to sit first; but before he sat, Horrock showed me my place by picking up one of the wooden bowls she had set on the table, handing it to me, and pointing at the stool by the fire. After we were all seated, I with great difficulty on the low stool because of the pain in my legs, he sliced venison for himself and then for his wife, giving none to me, and began to eat.

The two of them ate in silence, as did I of course, although it is not true to say that I ate; I pretended eating. Whenever one of them glanced my way I raised my spoon to my lips, but I held my breath and could not sup from it. Empty as I was, the smell of cabbage sickened me, and I held the bowl as far away from my nose as I could. When my master and his wife were all but finished, he noticed that my bowl was still full.

"Eat!" he roared at me. "Eat, you stupid Scot, or you'll have no strength for the morrow's work!"

I was so startled that I almost dropped the bowl, for it was the first time I had heard his voice in speech. It was as if an animal had spoken. It was more like the bellow of a bull than speech, however. His words began somewhere deep in his chest, like thunder behind a hill, and rumbled up and out through the crevice in his beard.

"Eat, man!"

Without thinking, I replied in my own tongue that I was not hungry, but that I doubted not Mistress Horrock's soup was very good nonetheless.

The Englishman scowled at me, uncomprehending, and to my great surprise Mistress Horrock told him what I had said, leaving off the latter part of it and blushing prettily in the place of the compliment I had paid her. So she was a Scottish lass, I said to myself. I should have known as much from the first, so bonny she was.

Horrock stood up, swinging a leg wide over the back of his chair and farting as he did so, and in two strides he was above me snatching the bowl from my hands. Its contents he poured into the iron pot that hung from a crane in the fireplace.

"We speak English in this house!" he growled at me. "None of your Scot's gibberish, do you understand? You will speak the English tongue here, or none at all."

"Ay, sir," I said.

He turned to his wife.

"And you will speak English with him whether I am present or not. Is that clear?"

Mistress Horrock bowed her head in agreement.

"Now," he said, turning back to me, "on the morrow at the kilns the same rule applies. I allow no Scot's gibberish there either."

So I was to work at the kilns on the morrow, thought I.

"Ay, sir."

"Now, get you to bed."

He pointed at a peg-ladder on the wall, and I rose and pulled myself painfully up into the loft. There, groping in the dark, I found a pallet that had been laid for me, and I fell upon it with a groan.

Below me I heard Horrock's voice again. "For every word you speak to him in that heathen tongue of yours, I will give you five strokes of the rod, and for every word he answers I will give him ten." Whether Mistress Horrock replied or not I do not know. Either her voice was too gentle to carry to the loft or I was already asleep when she spoke.

No lasses pleasured my dreaming that night, fair or homely. Instead, I was plagued by a constant pricking of a sword at my backside, which had got burned along with my legs, and ever there was an English voice at my ear that growled and rumbled, first "March!" then "Eat!" But I was not on the field of Dunbar beneath Doon Hill nor on that wild turkey-run down to London nor yet in Master Horrock's keeping-room gagging over a bowl of soup; I was at the ironworks on the Saugus.

All that night, with a swordpoint at my blistered arse, I worked at making iron; not only sows and pigs of iron, although those I made along with the rest, nor only pots and kettles either; pots, kettles, anchonies and merchant bars I made along with pigs and sows and flats and rods, the whole product of the ironworks. From the charge-hole at one end of that hellish place to the creaking overshot wheel at the other, where the rolling and slitting mill stood, I scurried and toiled at sword's point all the night through; and each time that I woke fitfully in the night I was so drowned in sweat that I was sure I had pissed upon my pallet.

When finally the light of morning starred the shingled roof above me, the first sound I heard in my waking was Benjamin Horrock's great voice booming up at me.

"You, up there!"

I was in such a state of misery that I could not answer at once.

"You!"

"Ay, sir," I said; but so faintly that he could not have heard me.

"You, up there! What is it they call the Scots bastard?"

"Clayburn," I heard his wife's voice say.

"You, Clayburn! Come down, man! It's past daybreak!"

"Ay, sir. I am coming."

I started to sit up then but discovered I could not. My legs were as stiff as rods, and with each effort to bend them a flame of pain shot up to my backside.

"You, Clayburn!"

"Ay, sir. I hear you, sir."

With great caution I turned over on my face and tried to draw my knees up under my belly, hoping to rise in that fashion. But I could not.

"Come down! Come down!"

"Ay, sir—if I can heave myself off the floor."

I tried again, in vain.

Horrock began to use vile language.

"I cannot bestir my legs," I called out to him, remembering to say the words in English. If he had beaten me that morning, I would have died.

There was a stamping across the room below, a great thumping of boots, oaths shouted, and a chair turned over. Finally, where the ladder came up to the loft, no more than a yard from my face on the pallet, I saw Horrock's shaggy head thrust through the hole in the floor. Glowering there beside me, it was like the head of an unholy John the Baptist on a platter.

"Get up!" He shouted in my ear.

I tried once more. Nothing happened. I lay still. Sweat dripped on the pallet from the end of my nose.

"I cannot bend my knees for the burns," I said.

Cursing me roundly, Horrock reached across the narrow space that separated us and, grasping one of my legs, dragged me off the pallet. I gave a screech of pain. Afterwards, to keep from cursing him back in such good Scotch oaths as would have made his own in English sound like a granny's prayer in the kirk, I bit my lip until blood salted my mouth.

With more oaths, Horrock pulled himself up into the loft, knelt at my side, grasped my new breeches at the waist, and yanked them down from my arse to my ankles. It was like peeling back the skin itself, and I screeched again and this time, not caring what he did to me, lashed him with oaths in my own tongue.

Whatever it was that he saw on the backs of my legs, he became convinced that I could not rise; for he gave a grunt of disgust and, without re-covering my nakedness, got up and lowered himself through the ladder-hole without another word.

I heard him below then, talking to Mistress Horrock, and in another moment her head rose through the hole in the floor, so close that I felt her soft breath upon my face. At my unexpected nearness she gave a little start and drew back. When, next, she saw my burned legs and haunches, she uttered a little cry, putting her hand to her mouth, as if my pain were hers.

"Come down, woman! I've no time to waste!" Horrock bellowed from below; and at that she disappeared.

"He is most badly burned," I heard her say.

"Ay, more than two shillings' worth, I fear," Horrock replied. "I have made a bad bargain."

More oaths followed, and more thumping of boots about the room, until, of a sudden, Horrock was gone. I knew it was Horrock who went out because of the slamming of the door and the silence in the house thereafter, and soon I heard him outside cursing the oxen and driving them off into the forest.

I hoped then that Mistress Horrock would appear through the hole in the floor beside my head, and the thought of her coming comforted me. But I waited for her in vain. Instead of the soft sound of her feet on the ladder-pegs and the sight of her wee hands peeping like mice over the edge of the hole and of her black ringlets and her wide, troubled eyes, there was a long silence, until finally I heard the door open again, softly this time, and softly close, and I was left alone in the house.

How long she was gone I know not, for I heard not her returning nor saw her the second time come up through the ladder-hole at my side. Indeed, by the time she came I was half-delirious, comprehending only slowly that her gentle hands were drawing my breeches the rest of the way down and off my legs. Although I knew that my backside was bare to her gaze, I felt no shame and was conscious only of being comforted, like an innocent babe whose mother tends him.

Soon after, there came upon my legs a delicious coolness from my backside down to my ankles. With the easing of the pain, my head cleared and, opening my eyes, I saw her kneeling above me. Beside her was a heavy firkin that must have caused her great effort to carry up the ladder and lift over the edge of the hole in the floor, and from this firkin she was taking out black muck and moldy leaves, which she laid in dripping poultices over my burns.

"I am most thankful to you, Mistress Horrock," I said.

"Whisht!" she said.

"You are a blessed angel out of heaven."

"Whisht!" she said again. "Go back to sleep, lad."

At her command, I closed my eyes and slept.

The next time I woke, she was there at my side again, but this time only her bonny head and shoulders showed through the hole.

"No," she said, when I tried to rise. "Lie still. Are you able to feed yourself?"

She lifted over the edge of the hole a steaming bowl with a spoon in it, and there was the fragrance of Scotch porridge in the air.

"Ay," I said, and drew the bowl toward me, heaving myself up on an elbow, my legs paining me now less sorely.

After I tasted the porridge, I told her it was the best I had had since Scotland. Without thinking, I spoke in my own language, and she shook her bonny head at me.

"You must not speak that language in this house. You heard what he said."

"I forgot," I said. "But we are both Scots, and he has gone from the house. I heard him drive the oxen off this morning."

"He has gone to the kilns. The furnace at the foundry is in full blast and there is constant need of charcoal."

"Then we may talk as we wish."

"He has forbidden it," she said firmly.

"Tell me in English then," I said in English, "what the healing poultice is that you have put on my legs. The pain is all but gone."

She thought upon my question a long time and finally admitted she could not name the poultice in English and then, smiling, boldly told me what it was in our own Scots tongue.

"I took it from the bog. There is a healing in the leafmold. It is what my mother used to do when we were babes and burned ourselves at the ingle."

"In Scotland?"

"Where else?"

"I knew you were a Scottish lass."

"What else?"

"Where did you live in Scotland?"

"In Edinburgh. But eat, John Clayburn. You had nothing for your supper yesterday, nor yet this morning any breakfast. Hold your whisht and eat."

I swallowed several spoonsful of the porridge before I spoke again.

"I lived in Edinburgh before I joined with David Leslie's men against Cromwell. I ran away to Edinburgh when I was but a lad."

"You are no more than a lad now," she said.

"I am a man," I said, and started to tell her I had a wife; but for some reason I said, instead, "You have not asked me where I lived before I ran away to Edinburgh."

She did not ask me then; so I told her.

She was quiet for a long time, watching me eat the porridge; finally she said shyly, "My mother came from that place."

I took another spoonful of porridge—the last—and asked her mother's name.

She seemed loth to tell me and lowered her eyes to the bowl, which I had set on the floor between us, but the bowl was empty and there was naught for her to do but scrape the spoon about in it idly.

"She was a MacDonald," she said, at last.

I was of a sudden moved to laugh, but I did not and said, "I hold naught against MacDonalds."

Her dark eyes flashed.

"And why should any man?" she said fiercely.

I laughed then, and so did she.

"How were you christened in the kirk?" I asked her.

"My name is Ann."

"It is a bonny name—Ann."

She gave a sudden look of fright and changed her speech to English.

"You must never call me by that name, even when we are alone."

So timorous she was, peering over the edge of the hole at me, that I laughed again.

"Nay, Mistress Horrock," I said. "Never fear. I am your servant. I know my place."

Her mouth quivered, and a white arm came farther out of its sleeve. Her hand seemed to want to touch me.

"I did not mean it that way. I was thinking of my husband."

"Whisht," I said, and reached my hand over and laid it gently upon hers. She drew her hand away. But not so quickly, I thought, as she might have done.

"You must sleep again," she said.

She took the bowl and the spoon and disappeared, but I could still feel the touch of her hand beneath mine.

The next day was the Sabbath, and Mistress Horrock and her husband being gone most of the day to the church in the town of Lynn, I had two days of rest before I went with my master to the kilns in the woods. Still lame I was, and sore, though greatly eased by the poultices; but I would have sung a Scottish song that Monday morning had not Horrock been with me, dour and silent as he goaded the oxen through the woods. The dawn of that day promised fair weather, and I believed my worst woes in the New World were over. At least, that devil's warren of forge and finery were behind me, I told myself, and I was going to work under an open sky.

But in that belief I was mistaken, as I soon discovered when Horrock and I came to the end of our morning's journey. Until that day I had never seen colliers' fires except from a distance, when we were making our long march from Dunbar down to London. Above the clearing that Horrock and I finally came upon there was no sky at all. Instead, there was a thick pall of smoke that shut down upon us closer than the ceiling of a Scotsman's cot in the Highlands, and the clearing was as murky as the ironworks on the Saugus. I had exchanged one devil's warren for another.

"You'll work among the wood-cutters for a start," Horrock said, stopping and surveying the clearing with the pride of possession in his gaze; and for a moment my hopes revived. But I was wrong in that too. As I gazed at the scene before me, I saw the wood-cutters at work beyond it, and heard them too. If anything, high in the trees, they wore the shawl of smoke more thickly about their shoulders than the colliers below them. On three sides of the clearing, enlarging it as they worked but never escaping the outward-rolling billows of smoke, the wood-cutters brought down trees with a rumble and crash like the Lord making thunder amongst His angry clouds.

"Hoolie!" I said to myself. "You'll come away from here, John Clayburn, with a face as smutty as Quentin Pray's and taste smoke with your porridge the rest of your life!"

But to Benjamin Horrock I said, "I'll learn and not grow gutty at it."

For reply he only grunted.

The kilns in the clearing were cone-shaped piles that reminded me of Indian wigwams we had passed on our way from Boston to the ironworks after we came off the *Unity,* and it was

plain at once that Benjamin Horrock was the sachem of the tribe
that labored amongst them. At sight of him all conversation
ceased, and the sooty workmen scurried about their tasks with
a livelier spirit, eager to impress him.

At a cabin in the middle of the clearing Horrock turned the
oxen over to a man who stood waiting.

"This is where I live," he said to me then. "You do not come
here unless you are asked. And whatever you may see here you
do not speak of after. Do you understand?"

I did not understand his full meaning, but I nodded.

"I am not a man who sticks his horn in the bog," I said.

A dozen kilns crowded the clearing, three of them a-building,
the rest finished and burning, one indeed already reduced to a
mound of charcoal, which four men were loading into carts. At
the unfinished kiln, a collier was scraping up turf from a circle
that was marked round an upright pole, which, as I reckoned
after study of those already finished, would be the center-pole
of its flue, or chimney, when it was done. At another, a man was
stacking logs upright against such a pole, laying on the pieces
end to end, and chinking them with sod to preserve the draught
when the fire was lighted. At still another, where the piling of
wood was completed and the kiln stood ten feet high at least, a
workman applied wet leaves and muck to the surface, not unlike
the poultices Ann Horrock had laid upon my legs. This layer of
leaves made a skin round the cone of the kiln to keep the flames
inside.

But the flames did not always remain inside, as I learned when
Horrock began to curse the man at the next kiln we came to.
This collier was atop his smouldering wigwam doing a strange
dance, which, I saw when we came closer, was his way of stamping out little tongues of fire that licked through the leaves and
muck and threatened to change the whole pile into a bonfire.

"If you fall through and burn to death, it will serve you right,
Fanshaw!" Horrock shouted up at the man. "I told you when I
left that you were building it wrong."

"Nay, it was built right, sir," the man Fanshaw replied, without interrupting his capers. "The wind shifted in the night and
burned it faster on one side. When I stamp out the weak spots
all will be well, sir."

"You were tupping that Indian wench again," Horrock said,
"and failed to see what was happening."

"Nay, I kept an eye on my fire too!" Fanshaw protested.

Horrock led the way then beyond the remaining kilns to a place where men were cutting down trees, stacking wood in cords, and loading carts to haul them to the colliers. From amongst these workers a brawny man with one bowed leg came forward at sight of us. Up close, I saw that he was not so old as his limping gait at first made him appear, a man of two score years perhaps, no more. In his smoky face a pair of large, round, yellowish eyes shone like two moons in the night.

"Here's the new hand for you, Merkle," Horrock said. "A bloody Scot with burned legs, as I told you Saturday, but strong and says he's willing, if I understand his heathen way of speaking. Show him what to do."

"That I will, sir," Merkle said.

Without another word, Benjamin Horrock turned on his heel and was soon vanished in the smoke, and for a while the man named Merkle said nothing and only stared at me like an owl studying a mouse that it intended to swoop down upon and eat at its leisure. But when he spoke at last there was that in his voice and even in his round, yellow eyes that told me we would be friends if I was fair with him and performed my share of the work.

"What do they call you?" the man named Merkle asked.

"John," I said. "John Clayburn."

He seemed startled and pronounced my name after me wonderingly, as if John were the most uncommon name in Christendom.

"Why, that's my name too!" he said at last. "John Merkle I am."

He held out his hand, as if to let me know that sharing the name made us friends at once.

"Fair fall to you," I said. "John is a good name."

Beneath the trees where he and another man had been working, John Merkle showed me how to tie an end of rope about my waist so that it would neither slip nor bind and, with many warnings of the dangers I would encounter, sent me up among the branches, into the lower ones at first, and gradually up and up. What kind of tree it was I knew not. It could have been a linden because of the yellow flowers that had begun to show, but there was no smelling of flowers up there in the smoky sky. Whatever the tree was, it was taller than any I had ever climbed, and it was wreathed like a crag in a thundercloud.

From the ground, Merkle and the other man, whose name was Smith, directed me where to tie another rope around each limb that I came to, so that they could swing the smaller branches free when I cut the limb off. After the limbs were all stripped from the tree and the butt stood naked like a mast, I fastened the free rope as high as it was safe to do—ay, higher even—and shinnied down to earth. At once Merkle and Smith set to work on the butt with axes, while I leaned my weight into the rope's end to guide the fall. Afterwards we split the butt into eighths and quarters with maul and adzes.

Such was my work all day. Mindless of my sore legs, I learned to scramble about in the trees like a squirrel, tying, chopping, sawing, and ever dodging the backlash of branches, till my hands were as black as Merkle's and my face also, I am sure. The smoke that poured up from the kilns so enflamed my eyes that all I saw looked red as well as murky. It was aching work, and by nightfall I was clawed and bleeding, my hands blistered, my body covered with bruises, and my burned legs beginning to stiffen again. So blasted with weariness was I that I could hardly lower myself from the last tree I readied to bring down.

Merkle was generous with praise of my work, and his good will and the ration of spirits that the men received with their suppers restored me. While we were eating and drinking, a wee sprig of a lass came out of the woods and the men at our fire greeted her with a cheer, as if her coming was to be expected at that time. She returned the greeting with a curtsey, like a grown lady. Then Merkle picked her up and swung her about to the accompaniment of her shrieks and laughter, planting kisses on her rosy cheeks and leaving there dark circles of smudges, which the men teased her for.

"This is my daughter, John Clayburn," Merkle said. "Her name is Ann."

"Ann—?" I said, with the same wonder in my voice that had been his when I told him my name was John.

"Ay, Ann," he said. "She comes to see me every evening. Although our house is two miles away in the woods, she knows no fear."

"Ann," I said again.

"Ay—Ann."

" 'Tis a bonny name," I said.

After little Ann was gone, other wood-cutters came and joined our group, and it was plain that John Merkle was much admired amongst them. Crouching on their hunkers round our fire, they talked mainly of the day's work and of their homes in England. A few among them were Scots, and we stayed mostly silent and to one side, unwilling to expose our speech to the laughter of the English and loth to speak our own tongue amongst ourselves for fear of stirring up resentment.

Upon one subject all were agreed, Scots and English alike; it was better to cut wood than to tend kilns.

"A collier is never his own man till the charcoal is made," Merkle said to me. "It is so even for Horrock himself. Once a kiln is fired, it becomes his master and there is no leaving it until the last of the charcoal is cooled at the bottom. I have heard Horrock in the middle of the night cursing and giving orders, and I have seen him climb atop a kiln himself, no better than the next man, and tread about upon it to search out the soft spots where the live fire could break through and send up all his work in flames. Ay, 'tis a hard life."

I had learned by then that Horrock held a grant of rights to all the forest to the south of our camp and leased shares of it to other colliers, taking a fee from what they earned.

"He is a rich man," Merkle said, "but he labors as hard as the rest."

At that point, Smith, Merkle's helper, a young fellow with a laugh like the braying of an ass, spoke up from the other side of the fire.

"Ay, but Master Horrock's bed makes his labor worth his pains. I'd not complain of fire or smoke if every night, at work's end, I could sink my ax into the fork of that sweet sapling of his. No labor that!"

Smith rose to his feet then and began to swagger about the fire with a hand on his crotch, walking with legs aspar and leering. The men laughed. But I could not abide his speaking so about my mistress and acting so lewdly, and when he passed me, I stood up and gave him a blow across his foul mouth.

In a trice Smith snatched a brand from the fire and came at

me with it; but in the same moment John Merkle snatched up a bigger one and thrust it in Smith's face, driving him off.

"Hold your tongue, you fool!" Merkle said to Smith, still brandishing the torch at him. "One day Master Horrock will break that wagging jaw of yours." He turned to me then, as angry as he had been with Smith. "And as for you, John Clayburn, we'll have no brawling in this camp. Hold your peace hereafter, do you hear?"

"I will hear no man speak so of my mistress!" I cried, so overwrought that the words came out in my own tongue.

Not understanding, Merkle and the other English looked at me askance. My countrymen, my fellow Scots, had by that time all vanished and heard not a word of what I had said.

"Get to bed!" Merkle said. "All of you!"

When I rose the next morning at dawn from my sleep, I learned that I had misconstrued Smith's antics of the night before and, at the same time, understood at last the full meaning of Benjamin Horrock's orders to hold my tongue in regard to anything I observed at his cabin in the camp. Across the clearing, at the fire before his cabin, I saw an Indian wench, young and lithesome, and Horrock himself, approaching her from behind, laying a hand in the parting of her backside in the fashion of a man who knew his way there well.

I was still staring at this sight when John Merkle came out of his hut and looked where I was looking.

Merkle spat on the ground at our feet.

"Come, John," he said then. "There is another day's work to do."

Once a man is torn away by the roots from the place where he was born and is knocked about hither and yon, he acquaints himself quickly with each change of his fortunes. So at least it was with me. I was hardly a week in the wood-cutters' camp when the clearing where we worked became my home; hardly a fortnight was I in that place when the ironworks on the Saugus—and, ay, the house in the woods where Ann Horrock lived—seemed as far away as Edinburgh.

My days wheeled about with a sameness that made me feel I had never done aught but wood-cutting. We rose at dawn and

were in the trees before the sun's rays touched below their
highest branches. We worked till the sun was overhead, at
which time we stopped for our noonday meal. Then up again
till time for a ration of spirits and supper.

Each night was the same as the first one, save that Smith and
I fought no more and nothing was said again in our camp about
Horrock and his Indian doxy. Usually wee Ann Merkle came
through the woods, but sometimes not, Merkle seeming to know
the order of her coming. Sometimes, but not often, Horrock
himself strolled over from his cabin after supper and stood by
our fire in silence, watching us as if he were studying to decide
which one was the worst. On these occasions, our talk died.

The Merkle lassie and I became friends, and I taught her to
dance a Scottish dance and sing a Scottish song, with Merkle's
permission.

"So long as it is not the Sabbath Day," he said, "I do not
object. I care not a whit for the Puritans' other prohibitions."

Ann called me "Master Clayburn," my being an indentured
man meaning naught to a child.

"Master Clayburn, will you marry me when I grow up?" she
asked one night; and all the men laughed and she became shy
after.

"That I cannot, lass," I said, "for I have a wife in Scotland.
But I will take you home with me and acquaint you with all in
my clan who are not yet wed."

The lass grew bolder then and said that perhaps one of my
clan would serve as well, provided his hair was red like my own.

"And her live on porridge and bannocks the rest of her days!"
said Merkle. "Not my Ann! She will marry Governor Win-
throp's son, or something better."

"Better to be the wife of a poor Scot than to wed a rich
Englishman," I replied.

"Ay, I will become a Scot," Ann said, mimicking my speech;
and all the men laughed, Merkle included.

With custom all things become familiar and are accepted, and
so, in time, the sight of Horrock's Indian wench going and
coming about her duties like a wife no longer troubled me.
Indeed, I soon learned that it was common amongst the colliers
and some of the wood-cutters to keep such women in their
service. "Squaws" they were called. Merkle himself had none

such, nor the envious Smith, but there were many who had. I told myself that Horrock was no worse than most and it was no concern of mine what he did.

I thought I had forgot my resentment of Horrock's Indian connection until, one morning, a fortnight or so after my coming to the camp, I saw the absence of fire before his cabin and the departure of his Indian woman and knew that Horrock himself was gone. It was then that I discovered I had been reckoning each minute of the going and coming at Horrock's cabin more closely than I had thought, and I was disturbed in my mind by my image of him once more in the house in the woods in the company of Mistress Ann. Boldly—ay, wickedly too, with great shame to my conscience—I wished that it could be myself and not Horrock who was with my mistress in that house.

That same day Merkle stowed our tools in his hut at noontime, saying to me, "Master Horrock has gone home to plant turnips and I shall do the same, for our work here will be slack till his return. Would you come with me, John? Ann and her mother as well as myself invite you."

My impulse was to stay at the camp and sulk and idle by the fire, but I knew how sinful my thoughts might grow in my loneliness, and so I said ay and went with him.

The spring season had advanced and the dogwood was abloom in the woods, vying with white patches of snow that remained in sunless places. In front of Merkle's house were violets, blue and white, and little flowers of Mistress Merkle's planting that I could not name.

Wee Ann Merkle ran from the house to greet us and leaped first into her father's arms, then into mine, and as I held her so, planting sooty kisses on her cheeks and feeling the innocent giving over of her little body to my embrace, my darker passions seemed more sinful than ever by the contrast, and I was glad that I had come.

Mistress Merkle stood in the doorway watching us. She was a plain woman, with speech from London that I found difficult at first to understand. Aspar and akimbo, she stood in the doorway not unlike a man.

When the little girl grew weary of our kissing, I put her down; and Mistress Merkle said: "So you are John Clayburn, are you?

Ann talks of nothing but you. Perhaps you are as well-favored as she says, but I see nothing but soot and grime." She turned to her husband. "Go to the well and wash, the two of you, before you set foot in my house."

It was kindly said, and her husband and I obeyed her.

John Merkle showed me his place proudly: the house, prim and clean as any I had ever seen in Scotland; his hunting-gun, of which he was almost as prideful as he was of Ann; and after that the acres he had cleared. All the while his daughter tripped along behind, before, and around us with cries and chattering. The place was not grand, but there was love in every nook and cranny. From the scrubbed hearthstone, where Mistress soon had supper cooking, to the farthest corner of Merkle's fields there was love.

He told me he had lived on the farm since before the founding of the ironworks, coming to America with his wife, a free man, a year before Ann was born.

"In my heart I am a farmer," he said. "I am a wood-cutter only of necessity, for this land is rough and stony and unwilling and will not provide a livelihood by itself."

Mistress Merkle was like his land, I thought, rough and stony at least, though not unwilling, while little Ann was like the flowers that bloomed in her dooryard and in Merkle's woods. Yet he loved them equally.

"I gave thought once of moving to Virginia," Merkle continued, "but I am told there is no room in that country for a middling man like me. It is all great plantations there or poverty and nothing in between, and with no more room for a man's conscience than there is here in New England."

He paused and looked thoughtful, finally saying that one day he might move westward to the mountains, where a man was "most free of all."

"Maybe I will join you there one day," I said; and at once I was startled to hear myself speak so. When my indenture was finished, would Dorcas be willing to come and live with me here in the New World? I had never thought of it before.

The rest of the day I helped John at his planting, and after supper he produced a viola from a box and sat for an hour with his elbow jerking and the bow scraping while Ann and I danced our Scottish dance for her mother and they taught me an English song. I wondered that my host had courage to defy the Puritan fathers thus, even at so great a distance in the woods, and I said so.

"John Merkle is his own man and ever will be," Mistress Merkle said proudly, "and he is as right with his God as is Richard Mather himself."

I had no notion who Richard Mather might be, but I said, "As good as any Scot John Merkle is."

For a while after my visit with the Merkles I was merry at my work in the treetops, as merry as the birds, and I sang the English song the Merkles had taught me; but when the day came when I saw Horrock at last, striding across the clearing toward our campfire, my heart stopped singing and the old darkling thoughts returned.

"You, Clayburn!" Horrock said, with never so much as a glance at Merkle. "I am taking you out of the trees and putting you on a kiln."

"I know naught of firing kilns," I said.

"Fanshaw will teach you."

Fanshaw, I remembered, was the man I had seen dancing atop a kiln that first day when Horrock brought me to the colliers' clearing, the man he had accused of lying with an Indian wench when he should have been minding his kiln in the night.

"Fanshaw is a fool," Horrock continued; and ay, that he was, I knew, because I had heard the men speak of him. "But maybe you can learn as much from a fool's mistakes as from a good man's skill."

Another Quentin Pray for a teacher, I thought.

Horrock turned then to Merkle, who at the first had risen respectfully from his place by the fire when Horrock came up but, seeing himself ignored, had sat down again. He remained now crouched on his hunkers, looking up at Horrock.

"I need Clayburn at the kilns now," Horrock said.

"He is a good man in the trees," Merkle said. "He has learned fast and will be missed."

"Then he should learn fast at the kilns too. If he does not, I will give him back to you." He turned once more to me. "Come. You will sleep beside Fanshaw's hut tonight. Maybe that will discourage him from his weakness."

At this remark, some of the men at the fire laughed. But not Merkle. He had risen and was shaking my hand.

"Maybe Master Horrock will send me back," I said. "If I succeed at his kilns it will not be from trying overmuch."

"Nay, you will do your best," Merkle said. "It is not in you ever to do less."

Thus was my life altered once more. I moved my few belongings to the center of the clearing among the kilns, and the next day I was given a pick and shovel to work with instead of an ax and saw. Once more it was fire and brimstone for me.

Fanshaw proved to be all the fool that Horrock called him, and yet maybe not so much fool as frightened. I soon saw that he lived in fear, not only of Horrock and of the fire he worked with but also of the Indian squaw he kept—and ay, of himself too. There was no love between him and the squaw. She was as ugly as the sin they committed, and in his heart Fanshaw loathed her. Time and again he told me he would have driven her from the camp long ago had he but the will to do so.

"But I cannot, Clayburn," he said. "Fornication is my weakness. I take to it as some men take to drink."

All day Fanshaw's squaw sat on a stump by his cooking-fire, preparing his victuals, washing and mending his clothes, smoking a pipe, and waiting for the night. When his day's work was done, they ate together, myself to one side. Afterwards, moved by his ration of spirits, Fanshaw would curse the squaw, but she showed no feeling in her dark face and only watched him with flat beady eyes till he ran short of oaths. Then out from the many folds of her heathen dress crept a strong brown hand while Fanshaw watched with fascination, as though it were a snake, until it took him by that part of him that she fancied most. Thereupon a foolish grin came over Fanshaw's face and he allowed himself to be led, like a pony by its halter, into the hut. At the very last he would cast a despairing glance at me over his shoulder.

"Mind the kiln, Clayburn. And speak not to Horrock."

Speak not to Horrock indeed! As if Horrock did not know! As if the whole camp did not know! Among the colliers and the wood-cutters Fanshaw's "weakness" was famous.

"He is a gifted man," the men said, with envy in their voices even as they were laughing at him behind his back.

And that he was! I had seen his giftie once when he was

pissing into the fire of a kiln. A rung big enough to beat off bogles with it was.

"He is a man all grown to seed," the men said. "Poor Fanshaw."

But they were envious nonetheless.

Poor Fanshaw. His weakness and his giftie combined left him as helpless as a man far gone in drink.

In a short time I was doing most of Fanshaw's work as well as my own; for often, now that he had a helper, he allowed his squaw to lead him into the hut in midday, leaving me to tend the fire alone. Thus because of necessity and not because of Fanshaw's teaching I learned quickly the chores of a collier.

"You are a good man, Clayburn," Horrock said to me one day; but I took no pleasure in his praise, for I saw the speculation in his eye that told me he would burden me with more work the more skilful I became.

After a fortnight, Horrock said to me, "This day you will take a load of charcoal with my oxen to the ironworks, for I have started a new kiln and cannot leave it. You will deliver the charcoal to Master Jenks and then, with the receipt he gives you, go to the company store for supplies. You can pass the night there with the man Moodie or at the Scottish House in the woods. I will expect you back on the morrow at sundown." He paused and surveyed what he could of the sky. "When you return, we shall go together to my house for the corn-planting, if the weather dries enough."

My heart turned a somersault. I would soon see Ann Horrock again—if the weather dried enough!

"I begin to put trust in you, Clayburn," Horrock said.

At once I was ashamed of my thinking about his wife, and thinking of his Indian doxy did no good; I was a Calvinist in my conscience and ashamed.

Horrock gave me a pass to show that I was not fleeing from my indenture, and I loaded the ox cart and by noon left the clearing. It was the first time I had been away from it in two months, except for my short visit with John Merkle and his family.

The spring rains had all but drowned the cartway that cut through the woods, and the oxen stumbled and staggered in the mire, floundering at times to their knees, and I became wetshod before I had traveled ten rods from the colliers' clearing. But as I walked alongside the loaded cart, goad in hand, mud bubbling in my shoes like porridge in a kettle, I was as merry as a linnet and began to sing a Scottish song. There was no great sin, I told myself, in singing.

But there was a little sin in it, and letting a little sin into the heart, with a Scot, lets in a lot. I had hardly traveled a mile before I knew I must not allow myself to be so happy with Ann Horrock as the cause. So I tried then biding in my mind upon Ingram Moodie and built up a fancy of our meeting in his store that day or the next.

I would clamber up the hill, thought I, and stand in the doorway of the store until Ingram's round face broadened into a smile when he recognized me.

"John Clayburn is it?" he would shout.

"None other," I would reply.

We would fall then to talking of Scotland and old times in our own tongue, thirteen to the dozen.

Surely, thought I, he would have a letter for me from my Dorcas; but I would have to shout at him, "Give it to me, man!" before he would let it go from his hand. "Devil colic your fat belly!" I would have to shout at him, before he would give me my letter. "Hand it over!"

Ochane, thought I, what a tribulation Ingram Moodie could be at times; and before I finished building my fancy of our meeting, I was sore vexed with him.

But no matter how I tried to think of Ingram and of other matters, my mind came always back to Ann Horrock and I would grow merry again. Och, I was sinful! I believe I would fair have danced a minuet beside the oxen could I have lifted my shoes out of the mud in proper time.

"Think on Dorcas, John Clayburn!" I counseled myself.

And that I did. I swear I did. I thought about Dorcas and then about Alan MacDonald and even about the Campbell. But nothing availed. Always I came back to Ann Horrock and the thought of seeing her again, if the weather dried.

Strange it is what magic so frail a creature as a lass has upon a man, what she can do in his heart, once she has planted herself within it. No matter how much a man may love another, no matter what his conscience tells him, no matter how he tries to think of other things, the lass will remain ever in a cranny of his heart like a flame burning in the murk, blinking and beckoning, so that his inward eye turns ever back upon her, as if he fears that the flame will stop its burning even while he is telling himself that he wishes that it would.

Such was my state when I came to the fork in the cartway that broke off in one of its directions toward Ann Horrock's house and in the other toward the ironworks on the Saugus. The oxen, following their nature, turned into the path toward the Horrocks' home, and I was sore tempted to let them have their will.

"Hoolie, man!" I cried out at myself, even as I raised the goad to prod them toward the ironworks. "It is their doing; not yours!" Indeed, I allowed them to travel ten rods up the path toward Ann Horrock's house, saying to myself, "Maybe I should stop and ask if there is aught she needs from the company store. Maybe Master Horrock intended me to do so but forgot to say it." Finally, I was saying to myself that maybe he did say it and it was I who had forgot; and then it was that I knew it was the Devil speaking in my ear, for such a thing I could not have forgotten.

Dutifully I cursed the beasts and turned them about in their course; but when I had them headed safely toward the ironworks I walked backward beside them for a long while, peering amongst the trees in the hope that Mistress Ann might appear there, shining in the woods like a flower. For a long time I walked so, hoping, and finally when I gave up hope and faced about the way the oxen were going, I was glum and angry with myself.

"They have more sense than I have!" I said aloud. "I should have let them have their way!"

But I goaded them on; for turning back then and going to Mistress Ann's house would have been a sin of my own devising; not the oxen's.

Full dark it was by the time I came to the Scottish House, and therefore I decided not to go on to Ingram's store that night but to seek shelter with Alan MacDonald. The house was unlighted and no sound came from it, and I stood in the road a while wondering what to do, not sure that I should go to the stable without permission lest the English had some rule against it.

Finally, I raised my hand to my mouth and called out, "Halloo, the MacDonald!"

No light was lit.

No answer came.

I called again.

"Halloo, the MacDonald!"

That second time no answer came, and a third; and when upon the fourth time Alan MacDonald failed to answer, I said to myself, "What else?" and called, instead, "Halloo, the Campbell!"

At once a light shone in the room where Alan MacDonald and the Campbell and I had chummed during my days at the ironworks, and soon the Campbell himself was at the door below with a lighted candle in his hand.

"Whisht, man!" he said. "I heard you from the first."

"You heard me from the first?" I said. "You heard me from the first and did not answer?"

"It was not for me that you were calling, until the last," the Campbell said.

Without a word more, he stepped down from the door and lighted my way round the house to the stable, where he stood holding the candle while I unyoked the oxen and bedded them down for the night. After that, still not speaking, he led me back to the house and up the steep stairs to the room where I had once lived with him and Alan.

"Whisht!" was all he said then, pointing at Alan asleep on the floor.

All that while there had been nothing in the Campbell's face to tell me that he was either surprised or pleased to see me; and yet I do think he was pleased in his dour way, for it was in his own plaid that he made me roll myself for sleeping that night between himself and Alan MacDonald.

Next morning, Alan MacDonald's shout of joy when he woke and saw me beside him made amends for the melancholy welcome I had come by with the Campbell the night before.

"The Clayburn!"

"Ay. Himself," said I.

Wide awake at once, Alan fell to asking me a thousand questions and answered my own in turn.

Had I a letter from my Dorcas?

None.

Had I seen Ingram Moodie yet?

Nay, said I. How fared the man?

Still at his store, said Alan, snug as a mouse in a pail of oats, and hand-in-glove with Master Gifford.

What else? said I.

But was I not the same now with Master Horrock?

Aha! said I. And was Alan still at the docks at the ironworks or working elsewhere now?

Nay. Jenks had given him my old place at the forge.

Beside Quentin Pray?

Ay. At the man's side each day.

Losh! I cried. What a pity! And what of that drooling, gutty, foul-mouthed little Sassenach? Did he still suffer from his burns?

Alan MacDonald's face clouded then; but before he framed an answer to my question, the Campbell, dour by the door, said it was past eating-time, and we went below and took porridge with the other Scots. Later, while the Campbell awaited us in the road and Alan and I yoked the oxen and hauled the cart from the stable, Alan told me that Quentin Pray was ever threatening to kill me when he saw me again.

"You must have a care in that quarter, John," he said.

"I fear nothing from a coward like him," I replied. "He is but half a man."

"Ay. But he has the advantage of you, John. He is English and a free man and his work is needed at the mill, while you are a Scot and indentured. Should you overcome him, should you so much as give him a box on the ear in your own defense, he would have the better of you in the courts. You would end in the stocks, or worse. You must have great care in that quarter, John."

I thanked him for his warning and promised I would not fall into a quarrel with Quentin Pray if I could help it.

Afterward, the three of us marched together through the woods to the ironworks like old times, I at the off-wheel of my cart, goading the oxen, Alan at my side, the Campbell pacing gloomily three paces ahead. When we came to the yard of the ironworks, however, the Campbell marched not onward toward the rolling-mill without a fare-thee-well, as was his former custom, but stopped of a sudden and seemed by his stopping to intend that we do the same.

Alan MacDonald laid a hand upon my arm and I halted the oxen. In the same moment the Campbell raised his arms straight from his sides like the wings of a bird and, step by step, moved slowly forward, and at that moment I saw Quentin Pray.

Pray stood beyond the Campbell, glowering at us all, legs aspar, gutty paunch thrust forward like a dare.

I grasped the ox-goad tighter in my hand.

The Campbell continued to move forward slowly, arms still raised at his sides, walking straight at Quentin Pray without a word. Pray began to skitter and dodge, uttering not a word of his own, but to no avail; the Campbell kept coming. Never touching Pray with his hands, the giant of a Campbell swept him along at his will, first to one side and then to another, but ever toward the wall of the forge.

"He has a knife!" Alan MacDonald cried out; and indeed in that instant a knife flashed in Pray's hand.

But the Campbell moved on, undaunted, arms stiff as broom-handles, straight out from his shoulders, until finally Pray was against the wall.

"Hoolie, Campbell!" Alan cried. "Have a care for yourself!"

Pray could have stabbed the Campbell, but instead he let himself be pressed like a bug between the wall and the Campbell's belly, the Campbell towering over him, arms still out-stretched, never touching him with his hands, until at last Pray, breathless, his hands gone limp with terror, dropped the knife.

"Pick it up, MacDonald," the Campbell said; and Alan leaped forward and snatched the knife up.

"Give it to me," the Campbell said.

Pray began to scream and beg for mercy, and men came running out of the finery. The Campbell took one step backward, turned half about, and flung the knife into the air. It shimmered, somersaulting in the sun, and fell into the water beyond the docks.

"What goes on here?"

It was Jenks, the master finer, speaking, himself then coming out of the forge.

"I laid not a hand on him, sir," the Campbell said to him. "You may ask the others." And without another word and not a glance at Quentin Pray, who still cowered by the wall, he stalked away across the yard to the rolling-mill where his work was.

I saw nothing of Quentin Pray the rest of that day, neither while I unloaded my cart in trade for the receipt Master Jenks gave me nor when I walked up the hill to the store after.

But I knew nevertheless that I was not for all time shed of my enemy.

My meeting with Ingram Moodie was not as I had fancied it would be when I was forethinking on it on my journey from the colliers' camp. First of all, there was no surprise for Ingram in our reunion, for he had already heard of the encounter with Quentin Pray in the ironworks yard that morning and was standing in the doorway of his store waiting for me as I came up the hill.

"John Clayburn! Come in, man! Come away in!"

After we clasped hands in greeting, he drew me inside and closed the door, but we did no talking thirteen to the dozen about Scotland and old times, as I had fancied we would. Nor did Ingram stand mincing behind his counter with the purse-mouthed smile of a man who is about to sell a bag of last year's turnips. Nay; another stood there now to do Ingram's bidding.

No more than a lad this clerk was, coming and going at Ingram's beck and call. To Ingram's obvious delight, and to mine also, the lad was English. An Englishman taking orders from a Scot! Ingram ruled the room from a high stool at a desk in a corner, and there he perched, puffier than ever, like pussy on a post.

"You work at the kilns now, they tell me," Ingram said to me.

"Ay, I have become a collier."

"Good! Good!" Ingram said, like Master Gifford himself in his manner.

"It is better than the ironworks, even though there is as much fire and brimstone about as there was at the forge. But there is no Quentin Pray."

"Ah—Quentin Pray," Ingram said. "I must warn you of him."

"I have been warned of him. I have no fear."

Ingram frowned and smiled thereafter.

"Maybe he should be fearing you, John Clayburn. You have the sootie look of the old Hangie himself, though not yet so black as Benjamin Horrock." I had washed before I left the camp and washed again at the Scottish House, but I knew he was right; I was no snowdrop. "Yet Horrock is white enough," Ingram continued, "when he appears in church on Sundays with Mistress Horrock. What news is there of her, John?"

"None," I said. "I have not seen her these two months past." At once I became all business in my manner. "I bear an order from Master Horrock for supplies. But first I must ask is there a letter from my Dorcas?"

Ingram seemed not to hear the question.

"John," he said, looking closely at me. "John, I trust you are not. . . ." But there he stopped.

"Are not what?" I said.

Without answering, Ingram dismounted from his stool. Although we had been speaking in our own tongue, he tilted his head toward the English lad and, touching his finger to his lips, beckoned me outside. There, beyond the door, he cast sidelong glances all about before he spoke again.

"John," he said, seeming of a sudden as shy as an unbacked filly. "John," he said again, after taking a deep breath, "has aught grown in your heart for Mistress Horrock these past months?"

So overcome was I by his impudence and, at the same time, so fearful that maybe he had caught a glimpse of the wee flame in my heart for Ann Horrock that I could not speak at once. When finally I found my tongue, I said, with an appearance of calm, "Ingram, I am an indentured man and married, and Mistress Horrock is married too."

"But bonny," said Ingram.

"Ay," I agreed, "since you have made a note of it."

After that, Ingram would not look at me and turned and went back into the store, and I followed him. Inside, he handed the English lad my list. When he turned to me again, after the lad had disappeared into the warehouse at the back, we stood staring at each other, alone in that small room, like two bulls in a pen.

"Is there a letter for me from Dorcas?" I asked.

"Nay," Ingram said. "But this very day a letter did come for you which I forgot. The writing is a man's, I think. Wait, I will fetch it."

He retired to a great chest behind the counter and brought forth a letter in a writing that was strange to me. I tore it open.

May the band that gives you this have somewhat in its power to give you comfort as well. . . .

I knew at once what was to come thereafter, and I read on as if I had written the words myself. Dorcas was dead.

She had died in childbearing in December, and the babe too was dead. The scrivener that Dorcas's mother had hired to write the letter told me not whether the babe was a boy or a girl.

I stood like one struck a blow that fails to knock him down but leaves him hardly alive, upright but wooden as a post, dumb.

Of a sudden I had no wife, and I had had none for five months without knowing I was bereaved. Of a sudden I had no child, and I had never known that I was to have one. Of a sudden I had no home, although I had had none since that dawn at Dunbar under Doon Hill. And in that moment, Ingram seeming lost to me, I had no friend. I had nothing. But worse than all of that, I discovered of a sudden that I had no grief. I could not remember what Dorcas looked like. I could not believe that she was dead because I could not believe that she had ever lived. Worse still, for all of that I had no shame.

Without looking at Ingram I gave the letter over to him, and after he read it he softened in his manner and laid an arm about my shoulders. Then I felt lonelier than before.

"Weep, man," he said. "You will feel the better for it."

But no tears came to my eyes.

"Weep, man, if you can," Ingram said.

But there was no weeping in me.

"The cart is loaded, sir."

It was the voice of the English lad behind the counter.

Ingram and I both gave a start.

"I must go," I said.

Ingram chewed at his lip and said, "John, forgive me. I should not have said what I said. I know you are not a man who sticks his horn in the bog."

"Keep a calm sough, Ingram," I said.

Then, with the old kindness and love of our days together in

Scotland, Ingram did something that he should never have done, that I am sure he would not have done if he had thought long enough about it; he went behind his counter and came back with a flask of spirits and slipped it inside my blouse.

"Tonight, John," he said, "when you are alone by your fire in the woods at the kilns, this will comfort you. It will make the weeping come at last and comfort you."

I thanked him and left.

But neither I nor the flask reached the kilns that night. By the time I came to the fork in the path through the woods, the flask was empty and thrown away and the spirits it had contained were in my blood, and at the turning toward Ann Horrock's house I let the oxen follow their own will.

When she saw me, she uttered a wee screech and stood for a time after in her doorway with her hand over her mouth, saying nothing.

As for me, corky-headed I had been and staggering as I came up the lane to her house, my legs no more of a mind to go all in the same direction than a new-foaled pony's; but I had ever the thought of her to guide me while the sunset flamed like beacons in the windows of her house.

As soon as I saw her, however, I discovered that I was not so full as I had thought I was, and I knew that at the turning in the woods toward her house I had used more will with the oxen than I had wanted to believe. My legs were limber with drink, but with love and longing too.

"Where is Master Horrock?" she asked, first of all.

She could see the oxen where I had left them at the edge of the woods and was peering round me at them in the gloaming.

"I know not," I said.

"Has he come with you?"

"Nay."

"Where is he, then?"

"At the kilns, for all I know."

My tongue was like a swatch of woolen cloth in my mouth.

"Has something happened to him?"

"Nay," I said, angry with her because her concern was for her husband and not for me. "He's well enough, for all I know. He was well enough yesterday, when last I saw him."

"Yesterday—?" she said. "Where have you been since?"

"To the ironworks. He sent me there."

"But why have you come here?"

"I come from there."

That was no answer, and she knew it and said again, "But why did you come here?"

"The oxen took the wrong turn and I followed them," I said.

In the shadows her hands fluttered up to the white oval of her face like moths in the gloaming, and I reached out to catch them. She drew back.

"Och!" she cried. "You have been drinking!"

Maybe she had just then smelled Ingram's spirits on my breath. Yet after she spoke she seemed less frightened than she had been at first, although she still blocked my way in the door and did not ask me in. Woman that she was, she must surely have seen that more was working in me than Ingram's spirits; but woman that she was, she had to speak of the drinking first.

"You have been drinking," she said again.

"Ay," said I, recognizing the advantage she had given me. "Drunk as an owl I am."

I staggered a bit on the stoop to prove it. Of a sudden I had grown canny, reasoning that if I made the drink seem more than it was, I had good excuse for taking the wrong turn in the woods and she might have pity on me and admit me to the house.

"Drunk as an owl," I said again. "No less."

I fell silent then, fearing maybe I was overdoing it.

Her brow gathered in a worried look, and I reached out to stroke it smooth. But she escaped me.

"Something is wrong," she said. "Have you been hurt?"

"Na," said I. Then, remembering the letter in my blouse, I said, "Ay." Then reconsidering, I said, "Na," again. "That's the woe of it," I said. "I am not hurt, though I have cause to be. That's the woe of it. I am hurt, but I am not hurt."

She seemed to study both my words and myself at once, cocking her bonny head to one side and then the other like a bird. Finally, with a sigh, she stepped back from the door and bade me to come in. Indoors, she pointed at my stool by the fire, and I went and sat upon it like a schoolboy being punished in a corner.

"I'll warm some milk for you," she said. "Maybe it will sober you."

She closed the door and crossed the room to the fireplace. But for the fire on the hearth it was dark inside the house, and in her gray Puritan dress she was no more than a shadow, except where the firelight touched her face and the quick whiteness of her hands pouring milk from a jug into a pannikin. She set the pannikin by the blaze and turned and looked at me, the firelight falling aslant upon her deep eyes and kindling tiny sparks in them.

"Now, tell me what ails you, John."

"I am full," I said.

She shook her head in a small fury, making the dark locks dance at her temples.

"Nay!" she said. "You are not that full! Do not try to deceive me with that! What made you come here?"

"The oxen—"

"Tell me no more of the oxen! Tell me true, John."

"John," I said after her, gazing beamishly up into her face. "You called me John."

"Whisht!" she said.

"It is twice now that you have called me John. Thrice it is. More, if I count the wee screech you gave when you opened the door, for that was the same as calling my name."

"John!" she said, as if the name meant nothing, as if to say that John she had called me once, John she had called me twice and thrice and maybe more, and John she would call me till Crack of Doom if she liked, and I was to make naught of it. "Answer me, John!"

"Ingram Moodie gave it to me," I said meekly and let my head fall between my knees as if I could no longer hold it up. But as soon as she said after me, "Ingram Moodie?" I raised it up again and said, "You do not know the name of Ingram Moodie?"

"I do not know the name of Ingram Moodie," she said angrily. "I know only that you are being sly with me and pay no heed to my questions. John Clayburn, has something happened between you and Master Horrock?"

"The one who works at the company store," I said.

I saw her hands clench at her sides.

"The one who works at the company store," she said after me, mocking. "Who is he?"

"Why, Ingram Moodie," I said.

She was angry with me then for sure.

"All right," she said. "The man who works at the company store gave you the drink. The one with the wen. But I was asking about yourself and Master Horrock."

I could have reached out and drawn her to me in gratitude for her saying, "The one with the wen." She had remembered Ingram's wen but not his name. But I said nothing and kept my elbows on my knees and my chin in my hand, watching her.

Her back was toward me now, for she had remembered the milk and was kneeling once more by the fire. As she poured the warm milk from the pannikin into a wooden cup, I let my eyes rest on the curve of her hips where her skirt drew tight across.

"Hoolie, man!" I said to myself. "Keep a calm sough!" But to her I said, aloud, "Ann . . ."

Without turning round, she said, "I told you never to call me that."

"But you called me John."

She turned about then, with the cup in her hand.

"Here," she said. "It is warm enough, I think."

I did not drink the milk at once but sat with the cup in my hand, looking at her until I was sure the color in her face was her own and not the fire's.

"Ann," I said again, testing her.

This time she made naught of it, except to shake her head as if to say there was no hope for me. She stood up, clinked down at the table, set her elbows on its rim and her chin upon her hands, and frowned at me.

"Drink your milk."

I shook my head.

"I have no need of it."

"You are wight and wilful," she said. "As wilful as a child you are, John Clayburn!"

She spoke as if she despaired of me still, but at the same time she seemed ready to acknowledge an understanding between us, as if to say she had known all along about the flame in my heart for her and there was naught she could do about it.

"You have known about it all along," I said. "You know what is in my heart."

"Hold your whisht and answer my question," she said.

"What question is that?"

"About yourself and my husband, whether there is trouble between you."

"None," I said.

She studied me hard and finally gave a sigh.

"Good," she said. "But if ever there should be trouble, you must tell me."

"That I will."

"Good," she said again. "Now, drink your milk before it is cold."

I drank it dutifully.

When I finished, she fetched the pannikin from the fire and offered me more; but I said, "Nay, I have no need of it. I am not so full as I thought."

"Then you must go," she said. "It is wrong to tarry here. He will be expecting you."

"Who?" I said.

"Master Horrock."

"I had forgotten him."

She sighed as if she wished she could forget him too, and I stayed where I was.

"There is something I must tell you," I said.

"No more of the blaze that burns in you."

"Na. It is not of that."

I tried then to find words to tell her about the letter I had got at Ingram's store, but there were no proper words to say and I only sat and gazed at her in silence.

She was sitting once more at the table and tapped her foot on the floor.

"Hurry!" she said. "Tell me quickly. You must not tarry longer."

I drew the letter from my blouse and held it out to her.

"I can find no words to speak of it," I said.

She rose and lighted a taper at the fire and held it to a candle. Sitting down again, she began to read, and as she read I watched her face in the candlelight. She began reading impatiently, still angry with me and not expecting what she was to learn, but soon her eyes widened and her lips parted. She said nothing, however, reading on to the end. Thereafter she sat for a long time silent, looking over the paper in her hand as if there must be something more that she should read before she spoke. I waited. Finally, she shook her head back and forth and said, "Poor lad! Poor John!"

"Ay, poor John!" I cried out bitterly then. "Poor John it is! You have the right of it. But only because poor John feels no proper grief! That is why I came here, drink or no, oxen or no, Master Horrock or no. That is why I am here. Poor John's wife and babe are dead and yet poor John feels no grief. It is because of you."

She stood up quickly.

"You have no right to say that! It is not fair to speak so! I have done nothing to—"

But she broke off there and of a sudden was at my side laying a cool hand upon my cheek and saying again, over and over, "Poor lad! Poor John . . !"

Yet when I touched her hand she drew back as if my own hand burned her, and cried, "Na, John!"

"Not grief enough!" I shouted at her; and she retreated from me, stepping backwards across the room, letting her hand drift along the table's edge to guide her. "I loved my wife!" I cried out at her. "Ay, I loved her well. But Scotland seems ten thousand miles away and last September at Dunbar was a century ago and now there is you! A man should weep when his wife dies, but there is no weeping in me. What comes over me now, at last, is not for her. It is for myself. I weep now for myself alone. There is not grief enough inside me for both of us. I weep only for myself, because I am lonely, ay; but more, because I am a sinful man, because it is you I love, Ann Horrock! You!" I dropped my head to my knees and wept like a child.

For a long time I wept, with no comfort from her; and when at last I raised my head, I thought she was gone from the house, until finally I saw her in the shadows at the other side of the room by the door. She must have stood there all the while I was weeping, unable to leave the house nor yet to come to me, her hands at her sides, flat against the door, seeming not to press against it but to cling to it, as if she were holding herself apart from me. Her face was white and her eyes large and dark in the shadows.

"I love you," I said.

She made no sound. She did not move.

"It is a wicked thing," I said, "but I cannot help it. I love you, Ann."

There was a long silence between us thereafter.

"You must go," she said at last, in a voice that was deep and strange; but I remained where I was, with my elbows on my knees, staring at my hands, which dangled loose between my legs.

"I cannot go back to the kilns with this within me," I said.

"Na, John," she said. "You must go back, and we must never speak again of what is between us."

I stood up.

" 'What is between us,' " I said after her. "You said 'between us,' Ann!"

I started across the room toward her. Although she could easily have fled through the door, she only moved along the wall away from me.

" 'Between us,' " I said again.

Then I stopped where I stood.

"Ann, if you tell me to go now," I said, "I will go. I will not go back to the kilns. I will never go there again. But I will never come here again, either, to trouble you. If you do not love me, say it now."

She turned her face away and did not move from where she stood clutching the pegs that led up the wall to my loft.

"It is the drink in you," she said. "We must not talk like this."

"I am not that full. You said so yourself."

My head was clear and I knew all that I was saying. True, my tongue had been loosened by Ingram's spirits and I was saying things I could not have said, would not have dared to say, without those spirits in me. My tongue and my Scot's conscience had been loosened together. But I was not drunk.

"You love me, Ann."

"You must go."

But this time, even as she spoke, I had her in my arms and was kissing her and she was kissing me, clinging to me even as she was saying I must go; and in no time after that I was lifting her lightly and thrusting her up through the opening into the loft and climbing up after her. There, gradually, her protests weak-

ened and finally stopped as we lay together on my pallet. Thereafter it was no longer nay but ever ay at my ear.

"Ay, John!" it was. "Ay, lad!"

"Ay, quick, John!" it was. "Do not tarry!"

"Ay—so—lad!" it was. "Leeze me on thee, lad!"

"Ocheye . . !"

And after that, "My jo!" it was. "My love . . !"

In my proper marriage bed with Dorcas and, before that,
frolicking with lasses on the braes of Scotland, I had no occasion
to discover what a daunting creature in transgression a virtuous
married woman could become. But now at last I knew. Love
with Ann Horrock in the loft that night was no unbridled,
bungling, youthful folly such as a lad and lass are driven to in
green desire, nor yet was it curbed by the bit of custom and the
harness of law and respectability such as restrain a man and wife
in bed. Wild and fresh as a lad's and lass's love was ours that
night, and solemn as marriage it was as well; but canny also it
was and wanton as whoredom, for we knew our way well at
what we were doing. Every moment of our loving was measured
by time that had been lost till then and by the knowledge that
there was no time to waste in the present. In those swiftly flying
hours on the pallet in the loft Master Horrock's wife and I
practiced together the whole lesson of love.

But a Scotsman's heart is like the land he was bred in, now
sunny and warm, now dark and cold, and it makes of him, in the
end, a perverse and tumbled creature, the worst enemy of his
own pleasure at the same time that he is as clever as Satan in the
pursuit of it. When the doing on that pallet was finally done for
the last time and the weariness of love came upon us, Ann and
I slept, as men and women do on such occasions; but on waking
in the dawn there was not for me the sweet and sad contentment
that love earns for most men. Nay; there was not that quiet
melancholy time when a man is wont to lie upon his back and
think on his mortality and that of the loved one who lies sleeping at his side, when he tenderly cherishes the memory of his
joys with her and yet mourns the fleeting nature of them. Instead, when I woke and saw daylight winking through the shin-
gles overhead and, turning, marveled at its dappling of my mis-

tress's hair like glow-worms caught in the murky web of night, dour Calvin came into my conscience and began to cry out against what I had done.

I sat up and, clasping my hands about my knees, said aloud, as though I had just then discovered it, "I have sinned!"

My voice awakened Mistress Ann, and she looked up at me, rubbing her eyes.

"What is it, jo?"

"Nothing," said I.

She sat up at my side, unabashed at being bared to the waist above the coverlet we had drawn over us in the night, while I, as if I had not had the knowledge of her I had taken that very night, turned my eyes away in modesty, seeing nonetheless, before I did so, how her nipples stood up in the cold as pert as lasses at a looking-glass.

"Morning has come," she said, yawning and stretching her arms above her head.

"Ay; so it has," said I.

My tone of voice must have frightened her. She dropped her arms and leaned hard against me and whispered, "Is aught amiss?"

"Nay," said I.

"Have you heard a sound outside?"

"Nay. There's naught outside to fear. It is what is here within that I am fearful of."

She leaned forward and, turning her head, looked up into my face. Her eyes were dark with sleep, her mouth in a pout.

Outside, a cock crowed. But the hour was well past dawn.

"You do not love me, after all?" she said.

"Ay, I love you."

"But it is a long face you are making, lad."

"I am only thinking," I said.

"And what are you thinking?"

"I am wondering what manner of man I am."

She kissed my cheek and patted the place after.

"A good man," she said. "That is what you are. A good man, John. You have proved it. You should have no doubt of it. Say you love me."

I looked down at her solemnly and said, "I love you," as a man must at such a time, though in his heart there may be the blackest doubt of everything, for it means much to a woman at such a time to hear the words.

"Then why are you sad?"

"Because a love like ours can lead only to grief," I said.

She drew her knees up under her chin and thought a long time on what I had said.

"You have the right of it," she said at last. "In the next world it must lead to the fires of hell, and maybe to as bad in this. But I care not, so long as it leads again to such loving as we had last night and you do not change in your heart."

Whereupon she began to stroke my thigh, her hand under the coverlet, till finally I had to capture it in mine and hold it quiet.

"It is a great sin we have committed, Ann Horrock," I said, all solemn.

With a face as solemn as my own, she nodded in agreement; but she kept her gaze on our hands, knotted now and lying atop the coverlet.

"Ay, it is that," she said. "But what we have done we have done." She looked up at me of a sudden, her face brightening with discovery. "It is only I who have committed adultery, John. It is only I who am married. If there is a burden of guilt to bear, my heart can bear it for both of us. I have no regrets."

With that, she turned to what she had been thinking on before, and her hand began to struggle in mine like a netted bird.

I marveled at her. She who had been the timid one at first was now the bolder of us two. At the same time, I began to discover that it was not of sin that I had been thinking, after all; for if her hand did not cease struggling in my lap, I would soon be ready to sin again. It was not sin but only the consequences of sin that I was thinking on. I was as willing as my mistress to burn in hell for such pleasures as we had had and could have again together. I doubt that any man, even a Scot, with a woman at his side ready to his touch and desire growing in him, regrets aught save that which he may have failed to do. Nay, it was not the punishment in hell that I feared as we sat there together on my pallet, her hand ever more eager to free itself for further venturing; it was the earthly punishment awaiting us that I feared—for myself, ay; but worse, for her, if we were discovered, as I was sure we would be in the end.

I tried to tell her this. By the laws of the land, I said, a bondservant cuckolding his master would be whipped, most certainly imprisoned, maybe hanged, and for all of that I cared naught; but the pillory awaited a woman taken in adultery and, after that, perhaps the stake. That she should pay such a price for our love was more than I could bear to think on.

But it is hard for a man to talk so to a woman who has thoughts such as were playing in my mistress's mind at that moment, and I spoke poorly. At the end, she only laughed and said she cared not and told me to hold my whisht.

"Thou art as dour as thou art doughty," she said, laughing. "Loose my hand, lad."

I let go her hand and she drew down the coverlet.

"My great lad!" she said. "Your words and your thinking do not match! Leeze me on thee once again!"

She threw herself back upon the pallet, drawing me down upon her, and I gave over.

"Och!" she cried. "I love thee . . !"

After, we slept again.

Ann it was who woke first the next time, and when my own eyes opened she was gone from my side. Hearing footsteps below, I rose on one elbow and looked down through the hole above the peg ladder. There she was, in the keeping-room, already dressed, setting out dishes upon the table. She had livened the fire and laid on fresh logs.

"Come," she said, when she saw me watching her. "Come away down. The morning is half gone."

I dressed and joined her in the room below, where already she had cooked a porridge and was spooning it out. We ate it sitting side by side at the table, our hands clasped together, calling one another endearing names. But she seemed in great haste nonetheless and kept saying, again and again, "We have no time to waste. We must not dally."

I supposed that I would go back to the kilns now, and I wondered how I was going to face my master when I returned, how I would explain my delay. I knew that I could not run away as I had talked of doing the night before. I must remain near at hand to renew our love-making whenever the occasion came again, and I believed she had the same in mind.

But that was not at all what she was thinking. When we finished our porridge, she pushed back the two bowls, took my hands in hers, and told me.

It was flight together that she proposed.

"But they will find us sure," I said, "and bring us back. Better that I should return to the kilns for a while and give some excuse for my absence. I will say that I was full yesterday and fell asleep in the woods on the way back from the ironworks. We cannot leave like this, without plans or preparations, without a place to go to. We must wait till we are ready for such a journey."

Her lips drew tight and she shook her head.

"Do you think I would have skill in deceiving my husband while we waited? Do you think we could stay apart from one another, you and I? Nay; I love you too much, and even a man like my husband would see it."

"Then I will go alone," I said. "I will run away, and one day I will send for you."

Again she shook her head.

"That would be worse still. I cannot live without you. He would soon see what was in my heart. We must go together."

I stood up and clenched my fists.

"I will kill him," I said.

To bolster my intent, I thought about Master Horrock's squaw. He did not deserve to live. It was himself who had sinned, before ourselves and more than ourselves. But she only laughed at me and said, "You are not the one for that, lad," and I knew she had the right of it.

"Let us wait until tonight, at least," I said. "After dark."

Once more she shook her head.

"Tonight will be too late. He will have come looking for you by then. We have no time to lose. We must go at once."

"But where? I do not know this country. Nor do you."

She only shrugged and said after, "Does it matter where, so long as we are together? We will go where there are no white men but only Indians. They will not punish us for our sinning. We can travel far before winter comes again. Anywhere, if I am with you, lad."

It was a woman's way of thinking. For myself, I thought only of the darkness of the forest and the horrors that men said the Indians committed. But I remained silent, for I saw of a sudden that she was right, woman or no. We had no choice. I could not leave her to suffer the fate of discovery alone, and if I stayed at her side the chances of discovery would be even greater. I remembered then that John Merkle had spoken of the mountains of the west, the royal province of New Hampshire. Men were free there, John Merkle said, and not so numerous. There might be a new life for us in New Hampshire without the dangers I foresaw elsewhere. I wished John Merkle were at my side to counsel me. But a man bent upon fleeing with another man's wife has naught but his own counsel to guide him.

While I was thinking thus, my eye fell upon Master Horrock's gun above the fireplace, and I said, "What is the value of it?"

"The value of what?" Ann said.

"The gun. If we flee into the woods I will have to take it, and someday I must send him back the value of it."

Her gaze went to the rack above the fireplace for a moment.

"You have a tight conscience," she said; and then she began to laugh, and after a while, seeing the humor of it, I laughed too. The thought of stealing my master's gun had troubled my conscience more than the stealing of his wife. With our laughter Ann and I sealed the bargain between us. We would run away together. "I am sure he prizes the gun more than he prizes me," she said. "Come! We must gather our plunder."

There was but little for me to gather in the loft, and I was down from it again quickly with my belongings wrapped in a short length of plaid that was still left to me from Dunbar. In the keeping-room I found Ann awaiting me in her bonnet and shawl, while at her feet was a small trunk with a handle to carry it by. With my rolled plaid under my arm, I picked up the trunk and started toward the door.

"You have forgotten the gun," Ann said.

"Ay, the gun," I said.

I set the trunk down, dropped my bundle on the table, and took Horrock's gun from the rack. I was turning about with it in one hand, ready to wedge the rolled up plaid under my arm again and pick up the trunk, when of a sudden there came a pounding at the door.

Ann, halfway across the room to the door when the pounding

came, jumped back against me and uttered a cry that was surely heard outside.

"Whisht!" I said.

For a long time we stood together, frozen, staring across the room at the door, neither of us knowing what to do.

The pounding came again.

Although we had forgotten to bar the door for the night, the latchstring was inside. But for that very reason, whoever was outside knocking would know there was someone in the house. If it was Horrock who had knocked, as I deeply feared it was, he would also know that I was with his wife, for I had left the oxen in the clearing, still hitched to the cart, and they would not have strayed from their home. If we did not answer the knocking soon, Horrock would break the door down, and if we dropped the heavy bar in place to prevent him, the sound of it would be a confession of what he must already be expecting.

I tiptoed to one of the small windows beside the door and took a careful glance outside. Because the view was narrow I could not see Horrock on the stoop, but in the clearing I saw something I had not expected. Four men stood in a circle round an object on the ground. I recognized one as Fanshaw. The others had their backs to me. Whatever was in their midst I could not see for their crowding.

Ann came to my side and strained on her toes to see what I was looking at.

"Who are they?" she whispered.

"Men from the kilns," I said, and drew her back.

"Why did he bring them?"

"I do not know."

At that moment the knocking came again and this time, with it, a voice.

"Mistress Horrock."

It was not Benjamin Horrock's voice. It was John Merkle's. Not knowing what else to do, I opened the door. John Merkle's body blocked the doorway, and for a moment he did not move or speak. I knew that he was seeing first me, then Ann Horrock behind me in her bonnet and shawl, and afterward my rolled plaid on the table and Ann's little trunk on the floor. And all the while there was the gun in my hand for him to see as well. Our purpose must have been as plain to him as it would have been in large letters posted on the gallows.

John Merkle spoke finally. "Benjamin Horrock is outside. He was burned last night at the kilns. He was stamping out a fire and fell through. He was badly burned but we got him out in time. He is conscious."

Without a sound Ann darted past me and tried to elude Merkle in the doorway, but he caught her and pushed her back into the house.

"Nay, Mistress Horrock, you must not go out there yet." Holding her firmly by the arms, he looked at me helplessly over her head, his eyes saying to me, "What am I to do?" But I had no answer for him. Finally he said, "There are men from the kilns with him. Fanshaw is one of them."

"Ay, Fanshaw," I said.

"And Smith."

Smith. That was worse. I said nothing.

"You must not be here when they bring Horrock in, John," Merkle said.

Ann began then to understnad his meaning and gave over struggling against him. She turned about and faced me.

"John! Quick! Go out the back door!"

"But the oxen," I said. "The men have surely seen the oxen."

"Ay; that they have," Merkle said.

"Och, who cares about the oxen?" Ann cried. "Go and circle through the woods and come back by the path at the front with a tale that will explain them. Circle round and come back. That will give John Merkle and me time. . . ."

Already I had turned and, leaving Horrock's gun by the wall, was departing through the door at the back.

Following Ann's instructions, I went round through the woods deep enough to remain out of sight till I was able to return by the path at the front of the house, and in that time I invented the lie I would tell. I would say that on my way back to the kilns in the dark of night I had gone in amongst the trees to relieve myself and when I returned to the cartway the oxen and the cart were gone. I would say that I had spent the morning hours searching and only within the half hour had found the tracks that led to Master Horrock's house.

But when I returned to the house the men were so eager to tell me what had happened that there was no need at first for speaking of the oxen. They had taken Horrock into the house and were waiting in the clearing for Merkle to come out and return to the kilns with them. "Burned to a cinder Horrock would have been, Clayburn!" Fanshaw said to me, over and over. "Burned to a cinder had I not been near the kiln when he fell in. . . ." When finally I gave my lie about the oxen, they seemed hardly to listen—even Smith, although, as always, I did not like the look upon his face.

Ann and John had put Horrock to bed behind the curtain, and when I went into the house I noticed that my plaid and Ann's trunk were out of sight and Horrock's gun was in its rack above the fireplace. Throughout the confusion of my return and the looking after Horrock, John Merkle spoke not a word; but when he was departing, while we two were alone for a moment, he said, "I think the men believed you, John."

"I am ever awkward at lying," I said.

"And at sinning," Merkle said.

I gave him a questioning look.

"Long before I saw the oxen in the clearing," he said, "I knew you would be here. When I learned that you had not returned from the ironworks at the time agreed upon, I knew you were here. That is why I left the men with Horrock in the clearing and came to the door alone. John, your long Scot's face gives away too clearly what is in your heart. I hope the others have not seen it."

At that moment my heart was so filled with black despair that I could not speak. Merkle and I moved together slowly to the edge of the clearing and stood there silent while the men went on into the woods. Then Merkle laid an arm kindly across my shoulders.

"It is not always a blessing to be young," he said. "God have mercy on us all."

He limped off into the woods then, and I stood watching him. In the air there was the softness of spring and in the trees birds lilted, but in my heart there was a winter weariness.

Knowing not what to do else and being told to do no other, I stayed on at the house in the woods and performed at first such simple chores as my mistress would have done had I not been there, as indeed she had done in the past when Horrock and I were at the kilns together. While I worked thus, she sat ever at her husband's side within the house, going out only to gather leafmold in the woods for poultices of the kind that had healed my legs when first I came to the house.

When she went into the woods I could have followed her, and indeed I told myself each time that I should not waste the days by holding back; but she went always with her head bowed and gave me no sign to follow, and I resolved to keep a calm sough. By speaking too soon, while she was in the first agitation of her husband's burning at the kilns I reasoned that I might scathe my case with her. It was better to wait and learn first whether Master Horrock would live or die. We could not run away together and leave him helpless, and there was that in Ann's eye which told me she had too much on her mind now for further loving.

In those first days we sat sometimes together at meals in the keeping-room, Ann at table and I once more on my stool by the fire; but there was little we could say to one another, save her asking if I cared for more porridge and my asking how her husband fared, for always he was there a few feet away moaning on his bed behind the curtain. More often Ann was behind the curtain with him in those days, and I ate alone. At night I tossed restlessly on my pallet in the loft where but a short time before we had loved so tenderly.

But such a state I could not endure for long. True, I was an indentured man and helpless, how much a slave in a foreign land I had not known until that time. I loved my mistress and was loth to leave her although there was no joy in our company for either of us in our condition. But a Scot is soon troubled by idleness because he finds it unprofitable and, hence, a sin. One day, therefore, I said to Ann: "Until your husband is recovered there is no one to tell me what to do except yourself. What I am doing now is boy's work, and it will profit Master Horrock more if I return to the kilns." I hoped with these words to startle her out of the dream she lived in, and that I did; she lifted her face to mine with a deep troubled look. I went on quickly: "Before

I went to the ironworks with the charcoal, Master Horrock spoke to me of corn-planting if the drying weather held. It has held, and maybe corn-planting is what he would have me do now, if he has the strength to speak his will."

We were at breakfast in the keeping-room, and after I spoke she went behind the curtain to her husband's bed. I waited, listening to the murmur of her voice and her husband's mumbling, until finally she came out and said, "Ay. He wants you to plow with the oxen, harrow out the roots and stones, and plant the corn after."

"I learned plowing in Scotland," I said. "That I can do if you will show me where it is to be done. But the planting of Indian corn is another matter. You will have to show me how to do it."

She crossed the room and stood by my side in the doorway pointing out the corner of the clearing where the plowing was to be done, and as she spoke I took her hand in mine and she did not withdraw it. But her hand was as cold as a paddock and her fingers as stiff as a bundle of twigs in my palm.

"I love you," I whispered to her then; and I would have whispered more but for the terror that came into her face as she glanced toward her husband's curtained bed.

I spent that whole day behind the plow, stopping only once to watch her when she came out of the house and went into the woods for poultices. She did not raise her head or give a glance in my direction, and I did not follow her. "Hoolie, man!" I said to myself. "She is frightened and perplexed. Keep a calm sough." At noon when I returned to the house for dinner she remained behind the curtain with her husband, having put my victuals on my stool for me to find. That night at supper I was again alone.

The next day began the same. In the forenoon I finished the plowing and commenced the longer task of digging out roots and stumps and the stones that are as thick in this New England soil as currants in a Scotsman's bun. For that task I used a grubbing hoe and sometimes an ax. It was aching work, and when sundown came and the chore was not yet done I was sick of it and grateful for the gathering darkness that made me leave the rest for the morrow.

Ann was at table that evening when I entered the house. She had put a blue ribbon in her hair, and I hoped it was for me. But when I spoke to her I spoke for her husband behind the curtain as well as herself, as usual. "Tomorrow I may start the planting if it does not rain, but I do not know the way of it."

Prim as a schoolmistress and never looking in my eye, Ann explained how she had helped her husband with the task, how to mound hills and plant the grains, the measure that must lie between the hills and the depth the grains must go, and how, after the planting was done, I must tread the earth down with my feet. She stood up then and, lifting her skirts an inch above the floor, showed me how it was done, raising her little feet one after the other and setting them down in the same place, side by side. At the end she blushed, clinked down at the table again, and said, "It is like an Indian dance." Then she looked up at me, and for a time our gazes tangled like the tendrils of a vine. I formed the words "I love you" with my lips, and at that moment Horrock stirred in his bed and quickly, to fill our silence, I asked in a loud voice how her husband fared that day.

She answered in a strong voice of her own that a physician had come that day from the ironworks and bled him while I was at work in the field.

"And what did he say of Master Horrock's state?" I asked, with a black hope in my heart.

"That the leafmold has done well for him but he broke his hip in the fall and may long be confined to a chair."

"And so will be here in this room," I said to myself, "here, in his chair, between us! Ay, *between us!*" But I said naught of this aloud, and Ann continued speaking.

"It was Ingram Moodie who brought the physician, coming here himself to speak for Master Gifford about the kilns."

I looked up of a sudden from my thoughts.

"Ingram Moodie—?"

"Ay," she said, a strange small smile upon her lips. "The one who works at the company store."

"The one with the wen," I said.

That night I tossed more restlessly than ever on my pallet, and before I slept I resolved that on the morrow I would talk with Ann when she went into the woods.

That next morning was a morning made for love. Spring was everywhere when I struck off from my labors into the woods after Ann. Before me flocks of yellow finches flashed among the greening trees like bolts of sunlight while above my head other birds sang vauntily; a quilt of flowers spread out beneath my feet, and the south wind was so soft upon my cheek that it minded me of my mistress's hair. I all but danced along the forest path, humming a Scottish air and thinking on the joy it would be to have Ann alone unto myself once more. No calm sough kept I that morning as I followed her into the woods, my heart pounding like a drum.

I found her stooped at the edge of a bog filling a basket with the healing leafmold, and approaching her softly from behind I lifted her up of a sudden to her feet and, turning her about, kissed her hard upon the mouth.

"Ocheye, my darling!" she cried out after, and returned my kiss.

But soon, when my hands began to wander, eager, down her back and cupped her haunches like two plump partridges in my palms, her lips were quick away from mine before I could prevent her. She leaned back, looking up at me, her face as bleak as New England winter, and shook her head.

"Na, na!" she said. "We must not!"

I held her head gently in my hands and whispered loving words close to her ear, but she only stiffened more and tried to push me away.

"Thou art mad," she said. "We must have a talk together."

She pushed me down upon a log and sat herself upon another and looked at me with eyes all sadness and loving, dark and round as thistle flowers, but her lips pale and thin, full of grim determining; and when finally she spoke again, she seemed to read her words as from a prayer book.

"We cannot go on like this."

It was naught that I had not myself thought many a time during the days just past. "Ay, lass," I said. "You have the right of it. We must find a better way to be alone together. But let us talk of that on the morrow."

"On the morrow, lad," she said, "you will be saying on the morrow once again." She shook her head; and then as if she were saying something she had just reasoned out for herself, she said, "John, it is a sin we have committed."

Her words astonished me, but only because I had heard them before, from my own lips. "Ay," I said, knowing not what else to say. "You have the right of it again, lass. But what we have done we have done. We must not scathe ourselves now with regrets."

"Na, na," she said, shaking her head again, but speaking gently, "you do not understand my meaning. It is more than just the sin itself that I am thinking of."

Ay, the consequence, thought I. But we had talked about that too on my pallet in the loft. Was she forgetting how willing she was then to burn in hell for love?

But that was not what lay hidden in her thoughts.

"It is my sin I am thinking of," she said. "The nature of my sinning has been changed."

This time I was lost. We had sinned but once and never since; so how could the nature of that sinning have changed? "What we reckoned on my pallet in the loft," I said, "we must reckon still. I see no change."

"The change is that my husband needs me now."

Och, adultery was adultery, thought I, and is ever so, whether the cuckold be burned and helpless in his bed or is fornicating in the woods with an Indian squaw. But I knew that such an argument would avail me naught with her, and I said, "Ay, he needs you now. You have the right of it. We cannot run away till he is healed. But while we wait, my love. . . ."

Without speaking further I rose to take her in my arms again.

This time, she not only pushed me away; she began to weep, tears pouring down her cheeks like mountain rills.

"Have you no mind for what I am trying to say to you, John Clayburn?" she cried out amongst her sobs. "It is God's judgment upon me. Can you not understand that?"

So it was God's judgment now, was it? Would God take unto Himself in His judgment such an ally as Benjamin Horrock? I wanted then to tell her about Horrock's squaw; but she was such a wee thing, weeping there on her log again, that I had not the heart to speak so and hurt her more. I saw too that John Calvin was working in her conscience now, and I knew the agony of that. Maybe John Calvin would have been working in my own conscience at that moment if, in my desiring of her, there had been any conscience left in me for him to work on; but a man in my condition at that moment, even a Scot, has no conscience.

"Hee, balou, my darling!" I said. "Do not weep so. I cannot bear it."

I lifted her into my arms then thinking only to comfort her, and there were no protests from her this time. She clung to me, soft and weak, until finally the comforting ended and the loving once more began.

"We must not!" she kept saying to the last. "We must not!" But we did.

While we were lost in loving, a veil of clouds spread over the sky that had been so fair earlier in the morning, the woods filled with a deep gloom, and by the time I returned to my labors a light rain had begun to fall. I set to work fast, but soon the soil was mire, clinging to my hands, my hoe, and my shoes, and there was no more that I could do that day. Nor would there be aught the next day, I reasoned, nor the next; for the rain came down steadily with a sure intent to give the land a drenching. I stored the hoe in the shed and hung the sack of grain in a dry corner and went to the house, taking off my shoes on the stoop before I entered.

Ann was at her spinning wheel in the keeping-room and continued at her task without turning her head. I stood in the doorway looking at her for a moment, holding my shoes in one hand with the other resting on the door's latch. It was a happy household scene, and I forgot in that moment that Master Horrock lay in the bed behind the curtain. It was as if I were the master of the house, returning from my labors, and this was my wife awaiting me.

"It is raining hard," I said. Ann glanced at me and returned to her work. "There will be no more planting of corn for a while."

"You can finish tomorrow," she said.

"Nay; on the morrow it will be worse. The earth will be like porridge. Since there is naught else to do here, on the morrow I will go to the kilns to see how matters stand there."

Ann turned full about then, her eyes wide, her mouth agape. My words had startled her but I am sure my manner of speaking had startled her even more. I had not asked her whether I should go to the kilns nor asked her to obtain Master Horrock's permission; I had told her what I would do, as if she were indeed my wife and had no authority to say me nay.

Before Ann could speak, Master Horrock's voice came from behind the curtain, and we were both startled then.

"Clayburn."

It was the first time he had spoken to me since his burning at the kilns. In all our days of living thus strangely together in the house no sound had come to me from him save his moaning and mumbling. His voice was no longer the old bellow and was hardly more than a whisper.

"Ay, sir. You fare better, sir?" I said.

"Ay," he replied from behind the curtain. "But God knows when I can work again, and the men at the kilns need looking after."

"Ay, sir. I was telling Mistress Horrock I should go there on the morrow. It is raining and the corn-planting must be delayed."

"Ay, go. Go now."

"This day?"

"Ay. The men need governing. Act for me there."

I saw Ann clench her hands into little fists, but I said, "That I will, then, sir. I will go at once."

"Come here, Clayburn." I moved toward the bed-curtain, but he stopped me. "Don't draw the curtain. I cannot stand the light." There was but little light in the room, and I knew it was not that but my seeing him helpless on the bed that he could not abide. "You will be in charge," he said, from behind the curtain. "Tell Merkle. You will move into my cabin." With his squaw? I wondered; and he answered my unspoken question with a single word. "*Alone.*" There was a silence then for a moment. "Alone," he said again. "Do you understand?"

"Ay, sir," I said.

Thereupon I did something on the wish of the moment that startled myself this time as much as it startled Ann; I set down my shoes and, striding across the room, laid a hand upon her shoulder. "Fair fall to you while I am gone," I said to her; and Horrock, thinking my words were for him, said from behind his curtain, "Ay."

"I shall return as soon as I can and plant the corn when the weather dries," I said to her; and Horrock said, "Ay," again.

"Until that time, I will send a man each day from the kilns,"
I said to her, "to learn if you have need of me; and if you have,
I will come myself at once."

"Ay," said Horrock.

"Thus I will be thinking ever of you and your fortunes while
I am away," I said to her; and Horrock, still thinking my words
were for him, said, "Good."

Then, heedless of Horrock's presence but a few feet away, I
bent over and placed a kiss upon Ann's startled, open mouth.

"Fair fall to you," I said again; and returning to the door, I
pulled on my shoes and, without looking back, went out upon
my journey to the kilns.

I found all in disorder at the kilns. Or such, at least, was the
tale that Fanshaw gave me as soon as I arrived.

"The men are slacking at their labors for want of their pay,"
he said.

"And for want of Horrock here to oversee them," I said.

"Ay, that too. There is no one to rule them. And amongst the
wood-cutters it is the same. Merkle has fallen from a tree and
done injury to his back and gone home, leaving MacGillivray in
charge."

"Is he hurt bad?" I asked, anxious for my friend.

"No bones broken," Fanshaw said. "He should be back soon.
But meantime, MacGillivray being a Scot, the men are making
trouble for him, Smith chief of all."

"Ay—Smith. That is to be expected. But what about yourself,
Fanshaw, with Horrock gone? Are you laboring at your kilns as
you should?"

Fanshaw lowered his eyes.

"I would drive her into the forest," he said, "had I but the will.
The savage wench!"

I could not help laughing at him.

"You should set yourself as an example to the men, Fanshaw,
working here beside Master Horrock's cabin."

"That lies not within my authority any more than it lies
within my power," Fanshaw said. "It is you now, Clayburn,
who must set the example. But it will be hard for you, a foreigner and an indentured man."

"The men will learn that it is ever ill taking the breeks off a Scot," I said. "Meantime, look to your kilns." I pointed at the heap of embers that glowed in the rain under a shelter of thatched poles beside his hut. With care they would soon be charcoal, but without proper governing they would burn to ashes. "Meantime, for myself, I will do naught about the men till the morrow and will build a new kiln of my own to set torch to if the rain has slackened by morning. First things first, man," I said. "We will act as if there has been no interruption in the work and no change in the overseeing of it. We will begin our own overseeing by setting an example. There is no good idling here in the rain asking for trouble."

Fanshaw stared at me as if he had never seen me before.

"Ay, sir," he said, at last.

Following my own counsel, I set to work at once in the rain laying up a new kiln with the wood stacked to hand beside Horrock's cabin. The whole afternoon I spent at the task, keeping an eye on Fanshaw's labors nearby to make sure his squaw did not persuade him to yield to his weakness in the midst of them and thus ruin his charcoal, and at the same time watching the other colliers roundabout without ever looking directly at them. They stood mostly idle at their kilns, watching me, and once or twice several of them huddled in council, arguing amongst themselves, no doubt contriving a rebellion; but none came forward to cause me trouble. I suspected it was only the weather that dampened the fire of their resentment of my presence, but I was grateful for the reprieve and told myself that the longer they delayed the less danger there would be of an uprising against me.

It was after nightfall when finally my kiln was built and ready for the morrow's firing. I went then into Master Horrock's cabin and ate the supper his squaw had prepared for me on a crude hearth of stones.

The Indian lass made no answer to my greeting when I came in, and she spoke not a word while I ate. Yet all the while, sitting in a corner, she stared at me. After I finished my meal, she washed my wooden bowl and then came and stood beside me with her eyes fixed upon me in a steady gaze once more. My head was full of the problems that would confront me on the morrow, and only half-mindful of her I pointed at the doorway.

She went out into the rain without a word and rolled up in her blanket beyond the door. At the same time I went to Horrock's bed.

First things first, I told myself as I lay waiting for sleep; and it seemed to me that the first matter of all was the colliers' pay. I dared not go myself to the ironworks to draw money from Master Gifford, for by my going I would leave my station at the kilns unattended and postpone other problems. Indeed by going away so soon I would make those problems worse. For a time I wondered how the collecting of the money could be achieved, until it came to me that by morning Fanshaw's charcoal would be ready. I would send him. The mission would give him an importance in the colliers' camp, which was what he needed if he was to be of further help to me; at the same time it would relieve me of his complaining voice in the first day of my duties. And he could stop at the house in the woods, according to my promise to my mistress.

After the colliers' pay, the next among my problems was to end the rivalry between MacGillivray and Smith, if indeed such rivalry as Fanshaw saw existed; for without a steady supply of wood from the wood-cutters there could be no steady production of charcoal at the kilns. I wished there were some way I could rid the camp of Smith altogether, for I liked not the look of him, but I supposed it was better to have him close at hand where I could keep an eye on him. I would visit John Merkle at his house in the woods as soon as possible to seek his counsel. I would go on the morrow if I could. Until then, I supposed there was naught I could do about Smith and MacGillivray.

All problems solved thus in some degree, I was left with only thoughts of Ann in my head as I fell asleep.

How long I slept I know not, and when I woke I was dreaming that I was once more at Dunbar under Doon Hill. But at Dunbar what I had believed was true was a dream, whereas now what I thought was a dream proved true. The company in my bed was no plaid rolled beneath me in a wench's shape, as it had been that September morn under Doon Hill; it was indeed a lass.

"Rain," I heard a voice say at my side.

Springing up, I lighted a brand at the embers of the fire and, turning, saw Horrock's squaw lying naked in my bed.

"Rain," she said again, pointing at her wet clothes and her blanket, which were strewn on the floor beside the bed.

I cannot say that I was truly angry or that I turned away in disgust; for the Indian lass was young and beautiful, her skin glowing like copper in the light from my torch, her arms upraised and ready for my embrace. What is more, in my sleep she had made me want her, and standing there before her in the middle of the room I was still wanting.

"Come," the lass said, holding out her arms. "Like red hair."

Still drugged with sleep and in my state of wanting, I moved closer to the bed, and when I was near enough she reached out and took hold of me as I had seen Fanshaw's squaw take hold of him.

I stepped back then, freeing myself from her grasp.

"Nay," I said.

And yet I could not help speaking gently, for the lass was but a heathen and knew not right from wrong—and, ay, she was bonny and I was still wanting.

"Na, lass," I said, gently.

She frowned and pointed boldly at my wanting member.

"Red hair likes," she said.

I started to explain to her that what a man liked and wanted in his sleep, unknowing, was beyond his control. But it was no good trying to say it in the infant language that white men speak with Indians, and I stopped in the middle of it and said, "Get up!"

Instead of obeying, the lass closed her eyes and turned her head from one side to the other.

"Get up!" I said again.

This time she obeyed me and stood naked and unabashed before me.

I backed away and pointed at her clothes on the floor.

Without a word she began to put them on.

When she was clothed, I pointed at her place outside the door.

"Rain," she complained then pitifully, and I relented and pointed at a place within the door.

Again she obeyed, rolling herself in her blanket and lying on the floor with her back to me contemptuously.

After that, I went back to bed.

But now I could not sleep. The Old Hangie had got in bed with me—ay, Satan himself. I could think of nothing but the lass lying on the floor across the room. The desire in my unruly body took possession of my mind. I tossed and turned, and I heard the lass turning too. In her blanket on the floor she rolled back and forth and, from time to time, gave little moans of agony. I tried to think of Ann. "I love you," I said over and over in my thoughts. But it was not Ann who was in the cabin with me, and the words got mixed with my thinking on the Indian lass. I told myself there was no hope for Ann Horrock and me, an indentured man. What difference would it make if I called the Indian back to my bed? Who would know? Nay; who would know that I had not done so? In the morning the men in the camp were going to believe I had fornicated with her whether I did so or not.

Finally, I swung my legs over the edge of the low bed and sat staring at the lass in the dim light. She stared back at me like an animal, her eyes black beads in the firelight.

"Red hair likes now?" she asked, after a while.

"Ay," I said, startled both by the sound of my voice and the word I had spoken.

She started to rise from the floor, but I was on my feet before her, startled again at myself, knowing but not believing what I was going to do.

"Come with me," I said to her.

She followed me out into the dark. The rain had slackened. In the camp a few fires were burning low, but there was no one in sight. I led the lass to Fanshaw's hut and at his door called out his name.

"Fanshaw! Clayburn here!"

After a while, he appeared at the door, rubbing his eyes.

I pointed at Horrock's Indian.

"She will sleep with your squaw in your hut," I said. "You will come and stay in Horrock's cabin with me."

"I'll not do it," Fanshaw said.

I saw the look in his eye and said, "Nay, Fanshaw, it is not what you are thinking. It is because I have not the strength to stay away from her if she remains with me. Come."

"You are a fool, Clayburn," Fanshaw said.

"I would be a fool if I did aught else," I replied, and rudely pushed Horrock's Indian past him into the hut. "You may remain here with them both if you like," I said.

"I am not that much of a fool," Fanshaw said. "Horrock would kill me."

"Then you would have him kill me instead?" I asked.

He shook his head.

"Then come," I said. "There is no other way. I wonder Horrock did not think of it."

"Horrock is the fool," Fanshaw said. "Why do we think of him?" But he followed me.

Back in Horrock's cabin, I handed him the Indian's blanket and pointed at her place inside the door.

"Tomorrow," I said, "you can bring your own bed from the hut and give the blanket to the lass."

He threw the Indian's blanket disdainfully into a corner and lay down by the door without it. I went back to Horrock's bed and soon thereafter I heard Fanshaw snoring. I have no doubt that I was soon snoring myself. Yet I dreamed restlessly the night through.

I began the next day by writing a message to Ingram Moodie and, giving it to Fanshaw, sent him off on his mission to the ironworks, instructing him to stop at Horrock's house both going and coming to learn whatever might be needed there. "Tell Horrock," I said, "that you have moved into his cabin with me." He could lodge with Ingram Moodie in his store on the Saugus, I told him. The journey was a reward for the loss of his squaw, I said, and if he performed the mission well I would have further use for his assistance in the management of the colliers' camp.

A greater transformation in a man in so short a time I have never witnessed. Fanshaw stood upright, no longer sniveling and whimpering and bowing and curtsying. Yet he was respectful to me withal. "Ay, sir," he said, and went off happily into the woods with his load of charcoal.

Although the rain had all but stopped, my fresh-built kiln glistened too much with wet, and I decided to postpone the firing of it and go amongst the men instead to explain to them

Fanshaw's mission and assure them that their wages would soon be in hand. Some of them proved surly; others eyed me with suspicion; still others with contempt; but a few, asking after Horrock's condition in tones that told me they hoped never to see the man again, seemed ready to abide my presence. I soon discovered that, after their wages, it was my treatment of Horrock's squaw that troubled them most. At first I wondered if they were sharing the evil thought that had passed through Fanshaw's head when I told him to come to the cabin; but I knew they could have no great scruples on that score, for many of them were guilty of the practice themselves. From one of them I finally learned that they feared I would eventually try to drive all squaws out of the camp, as if I fancied myself a great reformer, like Roger Williams in Rhode Island. When I let it be known that I had no such intention, they relaxed their belligerence toward me somewhat thereafter.

That evening after supper I sought out MacGillivray at the wood-cutters' camp. He had been amongst the Scots who shared our narrow room in the Scottish House in the woods the first night after we disembarked from the *Unity*, and I remembered him from that time. He was an ox-built man with neck and shoulders that could have borne a yoke and drawn a cart, yet long in the arms and legs for his size. The whole of him minded me of one of the bundles of iron rods that were shipped on Saugus boats from the slitting-mill of the ironworks.

We began by speaking together in our own tongue, for Smith was standing by.

"There is amongst the men one who is more troublesome than the rest," I said. "He stands not three feet away at this moment."

"Ay, that one!" said MacGillivray. "A clootie that one is, Clayburn! But have no fear of him. Already I have given him a chop or two that he will not forget."

"Keep a calm sough, man," I said.

"Och, have no fear of that either, man! No more than a wee chop now and then would I give such a man. A real crunt would finish the likes of him, and I am not one for killing."

I spoke next in English, for Smith to understand, so that he would know MacGillivray was in full charge.

"I go now to John Merkle's house in the woods. I shall spend the night. But when Fanshaw returns on the morrow with the men's pay, I shall be here again. I want you to help me hand it about."

I started then through the dark wet woods to Merkle's clearing, but on the path in the way I met Merkle himself coming back to the camp. He was not yet enough recovered for his work, he told me, but he believed his presence was needed amongst the wood-cutters.

"When I left I foresaw trouble between MacGillivray and Smith," he said, "but MacGillivray was the only choice I had. MacGillivray sometimes wants brains to match his brawn, but Smith—"

"Smith wants thrashing!" I said.

"Ay, true, John. But this is no time for that. In all circumstances there is a time for words and a time for blows, and the one is never a substitute for the other. But try the words first always. It is because you came early to blows with Smith that he is a dangerous man now. He wants careful handling at this point."

I knew that he was thinking of the day he had come with the men bringing Horrock home after his burning. Smith had been among them, and Smith hated me. As Merkle and I walked through the woods, it was like having an older brother at my side, a brother who loved me and wished me well and was wiser than I.

"I am glad you are returning," I said. "Your presence will be a great help to all of us."

At the wood-cutters' camp I left him and went on alone to Horrock's cabin. It was late and very dark. No one was about save two or three colliers dozing by their kilns.

In my absence Horrock's Indian lass must have tended my fire, for it was still glowing dully on its heap of stones when I entered the cabin. I sat down beside the fire without troubling to stir it up; my head was so full of what John Merkle had said to me that I had a mind for naught else. I had begun to see how his words applied not only to my governance of the camp but to the governance of my love for Ann Horrock as well. Say *loving* for *blows*, in Merkle's speech, and *silence* for *words*, and it made the same sense. Had I loved Ann only in purity of thought and deed, the future would not now be causing me so many uncertainties. If Horrock lived, I could have lived on with him and his wife in such a state to the end of my indenture. It would have been no state of bliss, true, but there would have been no deceit or injury to my conscience. If Horrock died, our love, unblemished by the memory of adultery, would have led to a marriage of innocence and joy.

Ay, it was the sinning that John Merkle had brought me to consider again, and I saw at last what Ann meant when she said, "The change is that my husband needs me now." Was a change beginning to grow in my own heart now because I was standing in Horrock's stead in the camp, filling his need of me? "But, och, I love her!" my heart cried then. "And she loves me!"

"You said you would spend the night at Merkle's house."

The words were spoken at my back, and I swung about and saw a man sitting on the edge of Horrock's bed behind me. The man was naked, yet with his hat set on his head. The rest of his clothing lay on the floor halfway between me and him. Behind him there was someone in the bed. I saw vaguely that it was a woman. Absorbed in my thoughts when I came into the cabin, I had failed to see the two of them in the murky light, and I had sat myself down at the fire between them and the door, blocking their escape.

"Smith!" I said, anger rising in me and taking the place of my astonishment.

"Ay, it is Smith," Smith said quietly. "And here is Horrock's wench."

He turned then and spoke to the lass in her own tongue, employing a talent I did not know he possessed. She rose from the bed obediently and, sitting beside him, began to dress herself.

"Since you had no use for her," Smith said, turning back to me, "I thought it a shame to let such tupping go to waste."

I stood up and advanced toward him. It was all I could do to keep from striking him across his foul mouth.

"Let the wench go," Smith said, quietly again. "We will talk as men afterward."

As he spoke, he gave the lass, dressed now and ready to depart, a smart slap across her rump, like a man starting a pony from a pen. She crossed the room without looking at me and went out.

I longed to take Smith by the scruff like a dog and throw him out after her, if not for his fornication, at least for the impudence of his trespass. But I recalled Merkle's counsel and stayed my hand.

At once I was glad I had done so, for it struck me then, in the look of Smith and his manner, that there was more in his being in the cabin than lying with my master's Indian. I sat down again, deciding to hold my whisht and wait him out. Nonetheless, I ordered him to put on his clothes.

" 'Tis no way for a man to sit before another," I said. "Have you no shame?"

Smith laughed and took up his clothes from the floor and drew on his breeches and his shirt, as cool as a man who had only taken a swim with a chum.

"Take off your hat," I said.

He hesitated but finally took it off. He came then to sit across the fire from me, and when I saw him maneuver for a place nearer the door than mine I moved quickly and forestalled him.

"I am glad you returned, Clayburn," he began, once he was settled, speaking as if all that had gone before meant naught. "The wench was not worth a whole night. It is better to have a talk with you now."

I settled forward on my hunkers with my legs ready like a catapult beneath me should he make a move I liked not. My arms hung loose between my knees.

"Talk, then," I said.

"It is the wood-cutters' camp I would talk about, and you may not like what I say at first. But hear me out."

"Talk," I said.

"It is about MacGillivray," Smith said. "I like him not."

"MacGillivray is a good man."

"A Scot," Smith said, spitting in the fire. "I want his place."

"His place—?"

"As master of the wood-cutters—till Merkle returns."

"Merkle has already returned this night," I said.

This news threw Smith's demand out of kilter, but he recovered quickly.

"In that case, he said boldly, "I want Merkle's place."

I stared at him.

"As master of the wood-cutters? Are you daft, man?"

He gave no sign that he had heard me.

"Merkle has done injury to his back, and he was lame and a poor woodsman to begin with," he said. "He is an old man and finished."

His speaking so about my friend enraged me, but again I recalled Merkle's counsel and held myself in check.

"If that is all you have to talk about," I said, rising to my feet, "then our talking is done."

My manner seemed not to cow him, for he moved not and stayed squatting by the fire.

"Maybe. . . ." he said.

"That is final," I said. "Now, go!"

He did not move a muscle.

"Maybe, after all," he said thoughtfully, "I should not take Merkle's place at once. Maybe you do not have the authority to get rid of him. So only give me MacGillivray's place at this time, as the next in order, and promise me I will have Merkle's place should anything further befall him in the trees."

I liked not these words and wondered whether Merkle's fall during my absence had been of Smith's doing. Merkle had told me nothing about the accident, and I had not thought to ask MacGillivray how it happened. But to inquire now of Smith or accuse him would open new paths for talking, and of that I had no intention.

"Nay," I said. "And there is an end of it. If Merkle ever leaves, it is MacGillivray who will take his place." I could not then withhold what I was thinking. "And should aught else happen to John Merkle in the trees, have a care, man, that you are not nearby when it comes about."

At that, Smith rose, and I stepped aside to let him pass.

But it was not his intent to leave the cabin.

"Maybe, Clayburn," he said, leering at me across the fire, "maybe a man in your position should reconsider."

"In my position—?" I said.

"Ay. A man who stands in his master's place. An indentured man, too, a bondservant."

"I have Master Horrock's commission to act for him."

"In all matters—?"

"In all matters."

Smith grinned at me, his lewd mouth twisting to one side, a menace in his eyes.

"Think well about it, Clayburn. Do you mean what you say? Would you like it known abroad that you act for Master Horrock in all matters? Would you say the same before Master Horrock himself?"

"I act on Master Horrock's own order," I said. "If you ask him, he will bear me out. Now, go, Smith. We have done talking."

Still he did not stir from where he stood across the fire from me.

"Nay. I think we have not done talking," he said. "I think that before you say again I am not to have MacGillivray's place or Merkle's, you should tell me whether you act for Master Horrock in the woods too."

I was puzzled. "In the woods—?" I said. "You mean here, at this camp?"

"Nay, nay," Smith said impatiently. "At Horrock's farm. In the woods by the bog. With his wife. As you were acting only yesterday morning with her, before you came to the camp."

Smith had no need to speak so plainly. Before he finished I knew all that he meant. He had been there in the woods the day before and had seen us, had watched us. The thought of him hiding amongst the trees and watching Ann and me in the act of love sickened me. But in another moment I was in a fury and springing across the fire at him. Had my first blow struck him it would have killed him, I am sure; but he was ready and leapt aside. When I came up against the cabin wall behind him and turned about, a knife was already flashing in his hand like a brand snatched from the fire.

"Nay, Scot," he said, grinning at me. "Easy! Easy, you bloody fool! You do not want this in your gullet, do you? You want to live for more of the tupping you had yesterday in Horrock's woods. Easy, man! Think! All you need to do is say I can have MacGillivray's place now and Merkle's when he quits, and I will put the knife away. You do not want to die, do you, with such a wench as you have got? Think about her, man! If I kill you, they will do nothing to me, for I will tell them what I saw in the woods and say I fought for Master Horrock. Think about that. You would not want the wench in the stocks or burned at the stake, would you? Say the word, Scot, and I will put the knife

away. Maybe I can help you afterward. Maybe you need someone like me. Think about that. I am clever, Clayburn. Maybe I
can help with Horrock. Eh—? I have other weapons than this
knife. There's fire, if you haven't the nerve for it but want to
marry her. He is helpless in his house. Together we could go a
long way."

Smith so convinced himself by his own speaking that the
knife loosened in his hand, and I sprang again, coming at him
from below and grasping his wrist, so that the knife thrust
upward over our heads. We fell, hugging each other with our
legs, and rolled through the fire and across the room and back,
our shirts and breeches a-smoulder in smoke and dust.

A long time we struggled so, rolling back and forth, first
myself on top, then him. He had the knife at my ribs once, and
I felt it enter my flesh and blood trickled down my side like
sweat. But I bent back his arm then, and finally, on top of him
again, with my knee in his groin, I twisted the weapon from his
grasp, and it fell to the floor. Thereafter, it was but a matter of
strength between us, and I was the stronger. I beat his face with
my fists till his head looked like a bladder of haggis, and when
finally his wits were gone I continued beating him and stopped
only a moment short, I think, of beating him to death.

I picked up his body then. Limp as a half-filled sack of oats it
was as I slung it across my shoulder and carried it in the dark
across the colliers' clearing to the edge of the woods. There I
threw it into the brush like so much offal. Afterwards, I returned to the cabin, washed my wound, picked up the knife
from the floor and, hiding it under a stone, threw myself on
Horrock's bed. I was a-tremble then with my wrath but with my
conscience also, for I knew that I had come within a breath of
killing a man.

The next day my wound was sore, but it was hidden well
beneath my shirt and I made myself move straight and sure as
I went about my duties, firing my kiln and paying off the men
with the money Fanshaw brought from Master Gifford at noon.
I could only hope that Smith was holding his whisht, explaining
his bruised face with a lie.

At nightfall, John Merkle came over from his camp to mine

and squatted on his hunkers beside me where I sat watching my
burning kiln. For a long time he did not speak.

"Have you seen Smith?" he said finally.

"Smith—?" I said. "Was he not at the wood-cutters' camp
when I came with their pay?"

"He has not been there all this day," Merkle said.

"Smith—," I said, musing.

"Ay, Smith."

"I have not seen him this day," I said, with as much indifference in my voice as I could muster.

Merkle was silent. I kept a calm sough, but I was not calm
within. Finally Merkle left, and I sat there wondering had I
murdered Smith. After a while I got up and went to the edge
of the woods where I had thrown his witless body the night
before. I found naught in the dark. Nor was there aught to be
found the next morning when I looked again. "Dead men do not
rise and walk away," I said to myself all that day, as I went about
my work. But all that day, and the next day and the next, I was
sore troubled, wondering where Smith had gone and what his
wagging tongue might be saying, if indeed it still wagged at all.

"Smith has not returned," John Merkle said each day. "Have
you seen him?"

"Nay, I have not seen him."

"It is strange. I still have his pay in hand."

I could not look at him.

Smith did not return to the camp, and for a long time I
worried whether he was dead and I was a murderer or whether
he was alive and telling what he had seen in the woods. But after
a while, when nothing happened and the word I got each day
from Horrock's house gave no hint of trouble in that quarter,
I reasoned myself out of my anxiety. Were Smith dead, I told
myself, I would have heard of his dying. In that sparsely settled
country such news traveled fast. Yet were he alive and talking,
surely I would have heard that too. I concluded that Smith had
fled to Rhode Island or the mountains of New Hampshire,
where many went in those days to try a new life, and I accepted
his disappearance as a blessing.

After the colliers and wood-cutters had their pay in hand, matters went better amongst them, so well indeed that when a train of loaded ox carts was ready for delivery to the ironworks and the camp was in need of supplies from the company store, I decided that my surveillance of the camp could be spared for a while and I would make the journey to the Saugus myself, taking Fanshaw with me to drive the empty carts back so that I could stop and stay a while at Horrock's farm on our return.

John Merkle, I could see, was deep troubled by my decision, but when he protested I had an answer for him.

"With you in charge and that troublemaker Smith vanished, naught can go wrong."

"It is not of the camp that I am thinking," he said.

I saw his meaning but pretended not to and said, as lightly as I could, "I go to Horrock's farm because there is none but me to finish planting his corn, and that is already overdue. I shall return as soon as it is done."

Never once had we spoken of that day when he brought Horrock home from his burning and found Ann and me locked in the cabin together, and our long silence made it easier now for me to speak with such mendacity. Yet I am sure Merkle saw the blaze for Ann still burning bright in my heart.

"Have a care, Clayburn," was all he said.

On our journey, Fanshaw and I stopped for the night at the Scottish House in the woods, and I saw Alan MacDonald again and the Campbell. They were the same, Alan full of quips and merriment and the Campbell ever as dour as bald Cruachan in the snow. The next morning we went all together to the ironworks and I had no time with the two of them alone.

When Fanshaw and I halted our train of ox carts in the yard of the ironworks and Alan and the Campbell went on to their work, Quentin Pray was standing slack in the doorway of the forge. He grunted and spat at my feet as I passed him, but I paid him no mind and he said naught and made no move toward trouble.

Ingram Moodie, in his store, where I went at the last without Fanshaw to make my purchases for the camp, seemed no longer his old self, although I could not say how it was that he had changed, save that he was more pleased with himself than ever.

"Master Gifford likes the reports of the work you are doing

at the kilns," Ingram said. "And so does Master Horrock. We hear naught but the best of you."

There was that in the way he said "we" that told me he thought himself one of them.

"You have seen Horrock?" I said.

"Ay, I went once with Master Gifford to his house in the woods."

"And how does he fare?"

Ingram sighed and looked as if what he had to tell me could only fill me with sorrow.

"He is changed," he said. "He sits all day now in a great chair. You will hardly know him when you see him next."

"He could change but for the better," said I. "And as for knowing him, I wish I did not."

"Na, John," Ingram said. "You must have more kindness in your heart. He is grievous hurt. He will be ever confined to a chair." Ingram turned about then and retired amongst his shelves at the rear of the store, returning with a jug. "Give this to Master Horrock," he said, passing the jug across the counter to me. "Drink is now his great comfort."

"A giftie from you, Ingram?" I said, unbelieving.

Ingram looked perplexed that I had asked. "Nay," he said, after a time. " 'Tis a standing order with Master Gifford to send him spirits when I have the chance."

I took the jug and started across the room intent upon going out to oversee the loading of supplies into an ox cart by the English lad; but Ingram stopped me when I reached the door by asking, "John, know you a man named Smith?"

I remained at the door with my back to him.

" 'Tis a common name," I said.

"He worked of late at the colliery."

"Ay; I know him."

"What do you know of him?"

"Naught that is good."

"He chums with Quentin Pray now," Ingram said.

So Smith and Pray together it was now, I thought. Ochane! But I kept my voice low and quiet when I spoke again.

"Two of a kind they are," I said, and waited, my back still turned to Ingram.

"Pray says he found Smith wandering in the woods, his face

a pulp as purple as a prune, his wits half gone. Pray took him to his house and gave him a home." He was silent a moment. "I think you should have a care in that quarter, John."

I turned half-about.

"Does Smith speak ill of me, like Pray?" I asked.

"It is a great mystery hereabouts," Ingram said. "There are those who think Smith is bewitched. He does not talk but lives in Pray's house like a strayed cat. He does no work, save for exercise in Pray's garden."

"He will poison Pray's cabbages by his presence," I said. "May the Devil colic them both! He does not talk, you say?"

"He says naught to anyone who passes Pray's house. Why Pray keeps him I know not. He makes a great mystery of the man. Some say he is a bogle Pray caught in the woods and Pray keeps him to work magic with. Lights burn late in Pray's house, and men come and go there, but none says aught. It is a great mystery. I remember that Pray said he would kill you, and now Smith coming from the colliery makes me wonder."

I liked not the sound of it, but there was naught that I could do. Nor could I tell Ingram about Smith, for somehow I no longer trusted Ingram, friendly though he seemed. When I returned to the camp I would talk to Merkle. Meantime, I knew naught but to shrug and say, "Maybe Pray has stuck his horn in the bog, taking a stranger into his house. Maybe he has stuck his horn in the bog and cannot pull it out."

"Ay; that could be it," Ingram said. "Maybe it is Pray who is bewitched, not Smith."

I went out into the yard then to oversee the loading of my cart, and Ingram followed me, all business.

Returning that day toward the kilns, I bade Fanshaw farewell at the fork in the cartway and walked alone toward Benjamin Horrock's house. I liked not what Ingram had told me and knew I would have been wiser to go straight to the camp and seek John Merkle's counsel. But I had not seen Ann in a fortnight and could abide our separation no longer.

In spite of Smith and Pray, in spite of my neglect of the need for Merkle's counsel, and with all the cares that filled my head, how different it was this time when I took the turning in the forest path to my mistress's house, how different from the way it had been that other time returning from Ingram's store more than a month before. The blaze for Ann in my heart burned just as strong—ay, stronger—but with a difference that was like the difference between the season of that other walk through the woods and this one. That earlier season was the frail infancy of spring, when the new leaves of the trees and the birds on their branches were still uncertain of the morrow's weather and knew naught but the day at hand; but now summer had come in, the leaves hung full and sure from their branches, and the birds sang with a wiser consideration of their melodies. Ay, I was a man now and Ann's lover; whereas, before, I had been but a timorous lad.

As I entered Horrock's clearing, my mistress herself came to the door of his house. She was bonnier than ever, and the blaze in my heart flared up and consumed me. But before I could speak she signaled me with a tilt of her head that Horrock was in a chair in the keeping-room behind her and could hear all that I might say.

I did not stumble on the stoop and stammer in my speech as I had done that other time, but bowed and said, "Good day, Mistress Horrock. I am returning from carrying loads of charcoal to the ironworks and fetching back supplies. I have sent Fanshaw on with them, and being mindful of the planting of the corn and other necessities of the farm, I have come to give what help I can, for all goes well at the colliery." I held out my hand then boldly like a free man, and before Ann knew what she had done she took it and curtsied; and then I said good day to Master Horrock, stepping into the house past her.

Ingram Moodie had the right of it; Master Horrock was grievously changed. He sat now in a chair instead of lying abed behind the curtain, but there was naught else to be said for his recovery. No man who had known him before his burning would have recognized him but for his being in his own house and in the company of his wife. A singed and beardless monster of cicatrix and fire he was, his once great burr-thistle bulk shrunk to no more than a sack of useless bones in a loose skin, his face twisted and shriveled and drawn, as scarlet as the blazes that had burned it. Had he been any man but Benjamin Horrock I could have wept at the sight of him.

"Clayburn," he said in a thin voice that whistled in his parched and shriveled throat like wind in a dry reed, "the corn wants planting and the roof leaks and there is mowing to be done."

"Ay, sir," I said. "I saw foggage in the hedgerows as I came out of the woods, and the hay is high in the meadow."

"And there is the cleaning of the stable," Horrock complained, "and the cow is sick. An overweight of work lies all about, and all this long time and no man to do it." All the while he spoke, he seemed not to be able to look at me, and his eyes swam ever about like two carp in a pool.

"I would have come sooner, sir," I said, "had there not been so much work at the kilns."

He went on complaining. Yet, withal, he spoke in complaint of his own incapacity and not in reproach of me.

"Have no care, sir," I said. "I will do all while I am here."

I was minded then of the jug in my blouse, and I took it out and gave it to him. To my surprise he offered me a drink after he took a great draught for himself.

"Nay, sir," I said, casting a sly look at Ann from the corner of my eye, "I have not the need of spirits that I once had, although I am still a Scot and naught else has changed in me."

Ann turned away quickly. Meanwhile, a burned-out smile crossed Horrock's ragged mouth, and he shook his head at me despairingly as he took another draught from the jug.

"Good!" he said, after. "Now we shall go to work."

What he meant was that I should carry him out into the clearing where he could watch me while I mended the roof; and that I did, Ann following after us with his chair. He was as light as a child in my arms, but he grunted and growled like a bear, beseeching me to have a care with his broken hip. Once he was settled, however, he looked as happy as a man could be in his condition and said it was the first time he had breathed aught but the air of the house since his burning at the kilns.

Ann would have lingered in the clearing with us, standing as close to me as was seemly, but Horrock ordered her indoors to attend her woman's duties, saying, "A woman is in the way when there is man's work to do. Eh, Clayburn?" He looked thoughtful then; and after Ann was gone, he said, "Save maybe if the woman is an Indian wench. Squaws ask no questions and give no advice. Fanshaw told me my Indian wench now lives in his hut with his squaw and Fanshaw himself has moved in with you. Is that true?"

"Ay, sir," I said. "I arranged it on the first night of my return to the kilns."

"I am sure it was not because of any fancy you had for Fanshaw, Clayburn."

"Nay, sir," I said. "I have no fancy for that practice."

"Ay, I am sure of that," Horrock said, and chuckled. "You are an honest man, Clayburn."

I felt shamed and could not look at him. I fell to wondering then was he indeed enamoured of the Indian lass. Or had he been only jealous of my opportunity with her, being himself no longer a man? I thought of Smith. What if I told him Smith had tupped his squaw? It would serve him right—and Smith too. Still, he had called me an honest man and I was ashamed and of a sudden could not think of him with aught but pity. It is ever grievous tragic to see the wreckage of manhood.

After a time of silence, we fell to talking of the leak in the roof; and after that I set to work, Horrock watching me from his chair below and Ann not coming again out of the house while we were working together so.

And so it was the whole time that I remained at the house in the woods; so passed each working day from dawn till sundown; a whole week passed so. After breakfast I carried Horrock out of doors, and he sat close by where I worked, beneath the eaves of the house while I mended the roof, beside the cornplot while I loosened the soil again for planting, in the shade of a tree while I mowed hay and cut the foggage by the stone walls that I still called hedgerows in the manner of my native land. We cured the cow of her indisposition, and after that, under Horrock's direction, I cleaned out the stable, Horrock telling me his own way of digging a middlin-hole at the bottom of a dunghill, which, I told him, was not our way in Scotland but maybe no worse.

By the third day, working nights after supper, I had fashioned for him a rude chair with an axle and wheels on each side. I put knobs on the wheels for him to turn them by. We kept it outside by the door, and thereafter there was no need for Ann to follow us out of the house each morning carrying his chair from the keeping-room. Thus, unwittingly, by making the wheeled chair I robbed myself of even that small portion of her company.

In this machine Horrock was able to move somewhat about the farm at his own will, but if the way was rough or uphill I had to push him. He took great pleasure in my invention and sported about the clearing like a lad on his first pony. At noontime, Ann brought us out our dinner to eat wherever I was working, and I saw her briefly then. When the three of us supped together at night, Horrock talked ever of the day's work and of what was to be done the next day, and Ann and I held our whisht, silent over our porridge at opposite sides of the table, I being no longer banished to the stool. After supper I climbed to my pallet in the loft and slept restlessly in spite of weariness from the day's work.

Not once during those days and nights was I with Ann alone, for she went no longer to the bog for poultices. Even had she done so, I could not have followed her because Horrock was ever at my side. As the days passed I saw how she grew unrestful, and I was myself the same. From time to time in Horrock's presence we caught and held each other's gaze, but as soon as it came upon her what she was doing she turned away with a look of fright. All this while the blaze burned in my heart, and yet within me there began to grow a liking for Benjamin Horrock that I could not deny.

"Hoolie, man!" I said to myself, when thoughts of Ann came too strongly over me. "Keep a calm sough. The time will come. But, meanwhile, it is a sorrowful thing that has befallen her husband. Help him all you can now, so that when you finally run away with his wife your conscience will not hurt so much."

Horrock treated me with great consideration in those days and talked to me with an ease uncommon between a free man and a bondservant. He was a lone man, he told me, and had been lone all his life, an orphan lad in London at the first of his life, apprenticed to a blacksmith and finally running away to sea when his master's beatings all but lamed him. In Boston he left his ship and there he met Mistress Ann, who was a bondservant with a family named Snow. He set himself up as a smithy in Boston and took part in several other ventures, and soon he had enough money to buy her out of bondage and marry her. All this I learned from him and more as I worked under his overseeing. In New England, he told me, he grew to be the burr-thistle of a man that he was and also prosperous; but now, he said, all strength sapped from him, he was but a dried stalk in a field. I think he feared the years that were left to him as a child fears the night, for it was more like a child than a master that he clung to my company in those days. Had he been a Scot and not an Englishman and not Ann's husband, my pity for him could have grown into a friendship.

At last the day came when I had done all that needed doing except the planting of the corn, and that task I could perform in a few hours the next morning before I set off for the kilns. I was loth that day to speak of departure; yet there was that in me, a Scot's sense of the rightness of things, which made me feel I must bring the matter up if Horrock failed to mention it himself, unhappy though I was at parting from Ann without once being alone with her. I waited until eventide, choosing a time when I was corning the oxen in the stable and Horrock sat outside in the slanted rays of the sun by the door and could not see my troubled face.

"On the morrow," said I to him then, "I will plant the corn, and thereafter I must return to the kilns."

From without the stable there came naught but silence for a time, and I began to wonder had he heard me.

"Nay," he said finally. "The morrow is the Sabbath Day. Should the Puritans learn that you had planted corn, they would put us both in the stocks." I wondered at his unexpected concern for the Puritans' opinion. That was not his nature. With his next words I was even more surprised than before. "On the morrow, Clayburn, you will take your mistress to church."

I could hardly believe I had heard aright. A day's reprieve he had given me, and now the promise of Ann's company, alone. Take my mistress to the kirk? Go into the woods with her, and no one to say us nay? Was this our time then, come at last, if she could be persuaded? My heart leapt, and the blaze in it burned like witch's fire in the woods, all topsy-turvy.

"A woman needs to go to church now and then," Horrock was saying. "Not for the religion of it but for society. A woman needs society from time to time, as a man needs fornication.

Walking in society quiets a woman, as exercise quiets a mare after breeding. Remember that, Clayburn, should you ever marry."

"Ay, sir," I said, thinking that I had never before heard him speak with consideration for his wife, although even in doing so now he was likening her to a brood mare.

For a long time then I was silent, thinking of the morrow, until finally Horrock called out, "What are you doing, Clayburn?"

"I have finished," I said.

"Then come and carry me into the house."

In the keeping-room Ann was bending over a pot at the fireplace. As Horrock and I came in she glanced at us aslant.

"Supper is ready," she said, plainly all innocence of what awaited us on the morrow.

I feared that Master Horrock might tell her at once, and I dared not face her in his presence when she heard.

"I must bring in the last of the hay from the meadow before dark, on the chance of rain," I said.

To my great relief Horrock agreed. "Ay, supper will hold," he said. By the time I returned he had told her.

I saw it at once in her face. Her cheeks were flushed and her eyes shone in the firelight. What was more, when we sat down to supper, she ducked her head prettily over her porridge and would not look at either her husband or me.

As soon as Horrock was settled at table he began to talk of our going to the church together, plainly pleased with his generosity and his understanding of women. He seemed to me like a gawky youngling unable to let good intentions stand for themselves.

"Clayburn, I told you a woman needs society now and then," he kept saying; and each time I was afraid he would continue in the vein he had followed at the stable door and compare Ann to a brood mare. But he did not speak so, although it was all too plain that he had taken several draughts from his jug while I was in the meadow. At table he kept it close at hand. "See how Mistress Horrock's face is flushed with pleasure," he said. "Ah, they are like children, Clayburn. Remember that when you marry. They must be humored now and then to keep them happy." Then he would laugh and reach for his jug.

His talking and drinking were a protection for Ann and me,

for we were not required to speak. As we were getting up from the table, however, he laid his big burned hand heavily on Ann's arm.

"You are happy, wife?"

"Ay," Ann said.

"No doubt it is from thinking that none of the women at the church will be dressed finer than yourself. But have you thought of that poor Scot of ours? How will he appear in such an assemblage, dressed only in his apprentice rags? Nay; you should be thinking of him too, should you not?"

From Ann's puzzled face he looked to mine and back to hers again and laughed and slapped his thigh.

"The Scot will wear my clothes," he said then. "I have no further need of them. I shall never wear them more."

I was astonished beyond believing.

"They will be too large for me," I heard myself protest.

Horrock nodded and took another drink.

"Larger than they should be," he said, "ay, in the shoulders and the bottom. But my goodwife is a fine seamstress. This night she can bring all down to your measure, I am sure."

At that Ann uttered a little cry, and I stared at him. For some reason, I liked not the look that had come into his eye. But there was no protesting against his wish, and after supper Ann measured me for the cutting down of his Sabbath clothes while he sat in his great chair and drank more and laughed and slapped his thigh.

The next morning as I was leaving the house with Ann, Horrock called after me, "The gun, Clayburn."

I stopped in the path and turned back, puzzled. Trussed up like a very laird in Horrock's finery, I walked as stiff as a soldier. Ann had gone ahead and was already at the edge of the clearing.

Horrock sat grinning at me from his great chair in the keeping-room, a jug between his knees to comfort him in our absence. All morning he had been merry. Before prayers he reminded me again and again of the need of women for society, and after prayers he said to us both over and over how, at the church, we would show the Puritan fathers that Benjamin Horrock was his own man. Had I thought upon his words I should have liked them not; he was using us for display—his lady and her manservant—to please his vanity. But I was thinking with impatience only upon the time when Ann and I would be alone together in the woods and gave him no consideration.

"Take a gun with you, Clayburn," Horrock said when I came up to the door.

"But the Indians are peaceable now, sir," I said.

"For a turkey, if you see one, for our supper."

I hefted down the gun that was on the rack. The other stood at the fireplace, close to Horrock's hand. As I went out the door, I did not look at him, but I felt his eyes upon my back and heard him laugh.

In the forest, Ann had stopped just beyond view of the house.

"My love!" she cried, running to me; and soon, locked in our first long kiss in many a day, I forgot all else and thought only of the moment, until she stopped me.

"Na, na, lad," she said gently. "Not now. Not here. We have all the time in the world for that now."

Did she then need no persuading to run away this time? I was so startled that I drew back somewhat and looked down into her upturned happy face. She saw my question and cried, "Och, my love, 'tis God's will now! He has no more need of me."

"Ay, that it is, that it is," I said; but I faltered in my speech and stood like a milestone in the path, until her arms loosened about me and fell to her sides.

"What is it, lad?" she said. "Is aught amiss?"

To tell true, I did not know. There was something amiss within me, but I knew not what it was. She was willing to do what I had believed I would have to persuade her to do, and now of a sudden, without reason, it was I who required persuading.

She had stepped back and was scanning my face.

"Have you had a change of heart?"

"Na, na," I protested, but weakly.

"You are loth?"

Ay, of a sudden I was loth; but I had not yet come at the full reasoning of it.

"Why?" she said.

Thereupon it came to me.

"He is as helpless as a babe," I said.

Anger rose to her eyes.

"A babe is it?" she cried. "You are the babe, John Clayburn! Not Benjamin Horrock! He is no babe, that one! Ochane!"

I had not the least understanding of what she meant. She gave me a long look of waiting and afterwards turned and started slowly down the path. I followed her, speaking her name, and she stopped.

"I love you," I said.

"Yet you are loth to run away."

"Ay, I seem somewhat loth."

"Because of him."

I nodded.

She bit her lip and seemed to choose her words carefully. "It is the very thing I said, John. Can you not see it? You are the babe. Not my husband. He is evil and scheming. He knows you are a man of conscience, and although he is not such a one himself, he knows how a good man's conscience works. There is naught but goodness in your heart, John, and he knows that." But her words were to me only riddles, and I frowned.

"Och, you cannot see it!" she said. "Can you not understand that he has cozened you with kindness this past sennight, and again this day with our freedom to go to church together, even with one of his guns in your hand? He has used you. He was sure this would happen to you."

I thought upon her words a long time, till finally, seeing the light in them, I cried out, "Och, I have been a fool!"

"Nay, not a fool, jo," she said gently. "Only too good for your own good, for the good of both of us. But have no more conscience in the matter. I have none now. He is as healed as he will ever be and has no need of me. Heartless he is and needs no one. Neither me nor you. No one. He has played with you as a cat plays with a mouse. At this very moment, he sits there in the house with his jug, sure of himself, knowing perhaps what we are saying to one another, for I think he has guessed what has happened between us." I remembered Smith and thought Horrock perhaps had more than guessed. "He is an evil, spiteful, scheming man, John Clayburn. You need have no thought for him."

"My love," I said, and took her in my arms again.

But this time something else stopped me, and once more I knew not at first what it was. Certainly no longer was it pity in my heart for Benjamin Horrock, for she had persuaded me to see clearly how he had cozened me, and I believed he was sitting in his chair in the house, as she described him, gloating over what he had done, sure that his wife was safe with my conscience.

Yet if he was indeed gloating, as she said, he had the right of it; for when I kissed her that second time the wanting went strangely out of me. Ay, my manhood deserted me as soon as my lips touched hers and left me slack, like a bag emptied of oats, and I stood limp in her arms.

"It's his duddies," I said to her in woeful explanation.

Ay, stiff and starched between our two loving bodies, Benjamin Horrock's clothes had of a sudden become himself, a hollow ghost of himself, true, but nonetheless himself, between us; and myself within those clothes, naked and defenseless and not my own man, was no man at all.

Ann knew what had happened to my body, but that sudden failure of my manhood was beyond her woman's understanding. No matter how I tried, I could not explain it to her. "Ochane!" she cried. And "Fool!" And asked me was it more crime to steal a man's clothes than it was to steal his wife? Had I such low regard for her that a swatch of cloth was worth more than she? Och, what a child I was! And all the while, I could only say, "A man must be his own man in matters of this kind," and I sounded more foolish than ever. "Then go back," she said finally, "and take his clothes off and put on your own! Are you afraid? You have the gun." But she knew as well as I that such a course would be fatal to us both. It would be no time then till a posse of men filled the woods in search of us. Tears crowded her eyes, and she turned and walked swiftly away from me toward the kirk.

I followed, calling her name from time to time, but I was still no man inside Master Horrock's clothes and my voice said so. She paid no mind, and in the end I fell back a few paces from her. All the way we walked thus, Ann neither speaking to me nor turning about, and it was not until we reached the kirk that I saw her face again. I could not believe my eyes; there were no tears upon her cheeks and her chin was tilted high. To all who saw her she was Master Horrock's goodwife come to worship, guarded on her way by his manservant, no more, no less.

She joined the congregation, and I sat in the rear with the indentured men and women. For two hours I sat sweating in Benjamin Horrock's fine clothes, listening not to the sermon but only looking at the back of Ann Horrock's head, stiff and pert above one of the pews at the front of the church, and thinking how I had once held it cupped in my hand while I told her that I loved her. I wondered would I ever hold it so again. All the while, I heard the whisperings and titterings of other indentured folk about me, and I blushed and sweated more.

When at last the service ended, I went outside, and there I had to walk what seemed a very Indian gantlet of men from the ironworks: Master Gifford and Jenks, the master forger, Nicholas Pinnion and John Turner and John Gorum and many others. They stared at me but said naught. I was grateful that Quentin Pray appeared not among them, nor his new chum Smith. But that was only a small comfort to me. At a distance I saw Alan MacDonald and the Campbell watching me, wonder and amazement in their eyes at my fine dress, and Ingram Moodie too, looking, I thought, somewhat askance. I nodded and they nodded back, but they were all three herded with the Scots and could not come to my side.

Ann and I walked home through the woods ten paces apart, she in the lead and I following. Once or twice I spoke her name but with only half my heart, for there was still no manhood in me. Halfway home, she stopped for reply and said, "John, we must think no more of running away. In the kirk I thought about it, and you had half the right of it in being loth in my husband's clothes. It was his devising, as I said. I am sure that he knows, and this was his way of taking vengeance. But it was God's devising too. God put the scheme into my husband's head to use as punishment upon us for our sin. The rest of it—our living on together as we are until your indenture is fulfilled—will be our penance." I was as stunned then by the way she spoke the words as I was by what was in them. So God's will it was again! I thought it blasphemy. God would not use such a man as Horrock for His divine devising. And as for penance, I thought it penance enough for me to see her as she was this one time, this lass who had loved me dearly, and all that lost forever now between us. I needed no more penance than this one moment of seeing my mistress standing before me looking as old as the oaken tree behind her, no beauty remaining in her form and face, all spirit gone. "Ochane, my love!" I cried. But for answer she only turned and quickened her pace. My own I could not quicken, for I knew that if I overtook her, her arms would hang at her sides as stiff as wands and they and Master Horrock's clothes would hobble me again.

She arrived at the house ahead of me, and when finally I came there, having forgotten about the turkey Horrock would have had me shoot, she had already retired behind the curtain in the keeping-room, to change no doubt from Sabbath dress to that of every day. Master Horrock sat facing the door in his great chair, his other gun across his knees. I wondered at it being there but concluded he had sat so for the sport of shooting a turkey himself if one came into the clearing. Because he snored loudly I thought not to disturb him and stood the gun that I carried against the table beside him instead of going round him and hanging it on the rack where it had been. I climbed to the loft as quietly as I could and, in a few minutes, was down again, dressed in my own clothes.

I had no choice but to run away alone. God's will or no, penance or no, I knew that I could not live another day in the company of the two of them. I would run away to New Hampshire and start a new life for myself, trying to forget what had been between Ann Horrock and me. Maybe someday. . . . But that hope, I told myself, I must save to contemplate when I was gone.

I tiptoed past Horrock, stopping once, thinking to take up the gun I had left against the table, but in the end deciding not to. I wanted nothing of his in my flight, since I could not have his wife; not even a gun. I crept on past his chair and out the door into the noonday light and started across the clearing on the run; and I was in the middle of that open space when I heard a shot behind me and a ball whistled past my head. I dropped to the earth then for my own protection, remembering the other gun I had left to his hand, and crawled—ay, fairly galloped on all fours—toward the woods.

"Stop!" I heard Horrock's reedy voice call after me; and I looked back then for an instant and saw him half out of his chair with the other gun raised in aim at me.

I flattened and Horrock fired and missed again. Then I sprang to my feet and ran once more.

I went first to John Merkle's house for food, having not that day eaten since early morning. Merkle was not at home. Although it was the Sabbath Day, he had gone to the kilns to survey the next day's work. It was Mistress Merkle and her daughter who greeted me, and I said I could not wait for Merkle's return. I told Mistress Merkle naught save that I was hungry and had need of food for a journey, and she gave me cold journey-cake and a flask of spirits, asking no questions, her plain face asking me none either.

When little Ann heard me speak of a journey, she clapped her hands and begged me to take her with me, until finally her mother quieted her.

"I shall tell my husband you were here," she said to me.

"Maybe it were better he did not know."

She shook her head.

"John Merkle is your friend."

As I was departing from the house I looked longingly at John's gun over the fireplace, but it was his hunting gun, his great pride, and I dared not ask for it, and Mistress Merkle did not offer it to me. Thereafter, with a kiss for wee Ann, I returned to the woods.

Much as I needed sustenance, it was a grievous error for me to go to Merkle's house, for going there delayed me and took me off my western course, leaving me longer than I should have tarried in the neighborhood of the ironworks and giving time for someone—would it be Ann herself, with her new Puritan conscience and thoughts of God's will, I wondered—to sound the alarm that I was in flight. By the time I had traveled less than an hour from Merkle's house, the woods began to fill with men in search of me.

Puritan authorities they were, sheriffs and bailiffs and such, with guns and an eagerness for the bounty that would be upon my head. I encountered the first of them face to face. A villainous-looking man he was, under a peaked hat, with a jaw jutting from under it like a forge beneath a cowl. Thinking there was not yet time for anyone from the Saugus to come after me, I was still walking openly through the woods when I came upon him in a glen. He seemed to rise in my path from no-where.

"Halt," he said, "and give me your name."

I should have lied to him. Merkle I could have said my name was and he would have known no better, for it was plain he had no image in his mind of the man he was hunting in the woods. But so startled was I that I could think of no name but my own. So I answered not at all and, turning, fled.

The man gave a shout and fired his gun. The shot shattered a tree's branch above my head.

I outran him then, himself being burdened by the heavy gun and stopping to reload it. I lost the sound of his crashing through the brush behind me and, soon thereafter, lost the sound of his shouting as well. I ran on and on and would have kept on running had I not seen another man, dressed and armed the same as my pursuer, stalking along a ridge above me at some distance away. If he saw me, the word would soon spread through the woods that I was there. I threw myself into the bushes, where at once I found myself tumbling down a sharp decline.

When I stopped rolling downward I lay still, panting. I prayed that my pursuers had not heard my fall, and apparently they had not, for there was no sound from them. For a long time I lay where I was, concealed by bushes and tall ferns, conscious for the first time in my life how loud are the noises in a wood-land, especially when a hunted man lies breathless. Birds sang; animals scurried about; insects chirped and buzzed; the wind sighed; water gurgled somewhere in a stream nearby; and the branches of trees rubbing against one another in the wind groaned like men in agony.

After a long time, sure at last that none of the sounds I heard was made by my pursuers, I crawled carefully down the decline farther until I came upon a hollowed place beneath a bluff that overhung the stream. There I fashioned a kind of nest, gathering brush and ferns. I covered myself in this hiding-place, thinking how well it was to be near water to quench my thirst if need be, for the day was growing hot.

On into the waxing hours of that afternoon I lay in my cov-ered hollow, listening. Insects stung me; mosquitoes swarmed about my head; a snake slid near and slithered away; wee animals, so tame I could have touched them, came and looked at me and went away; one—a weasel, I think it was—nibbled at my shoe. But I lay still.

From time to time I heard voices in the woods. Two men met once on the bluff above my head.

"I know the man. He has red hair."

I did not recognize the voice.

"He had but a short start ahead of us. Master Gifford and Jenks, coming home from the church through the woods, heard Horrock's gun and were at the house soon after the Scot fled."

So it was not Ann who gave the alarm. For that I was thankful.

"Horrock said the Scot stole his clothes and a gun and the two of them went brazenly off to church, like man and wife, in defiance of him. He said he would have stopped them if he could have got his other gun in hand in time."

So it was indeed of Horrock's devising, as Ann had said; but also to have excuse for murdering me when I returned from the church with her, and perhaps to have her put in the stocks after.

"When Gifford and Jenks came to the house, the wife was gone too, they say. Horrock said he would have killed her on the spot as she fled, but both guns were by then empty. He fired twice at the Scot."

So Ann had fled too. Where? Into the woods, after me. But where was she now, the wee helpless lass?

"I fear there will be no finding them," one of the men said, "if they are not found before dark."

I prayed then for an early dark. I prayed for Ann. It was all I could do to lie still, although I knew that I must.

When nightfall came at last, I stood up, stiff from lying all afternoon in the hollow. But I had no more than risen when I saw men with torches in the woods. Above the narrow clough, where the stream ran, the flares were like witch's fire amongst the trees. I crept to the top and watched and listened to make sure as best I could at such a distance that Ann was not a captive amongst them; and then I groped my way down again through the murk to the stream. Drinking from it, I discovered the direction of its flow, and knowing that all water in that country ran eastward in the end, I began to move along the bank against the current. If I moved ever against it, I told myself, it must eventually take me to the mountains. I prayed that Ann would have the same sagacity as mine.

I walked as quietly as I could, ever fearful of loose stones and snapping twigs. When my feet struck one such, I stopped dead still for a time. My progress was wearying in its slowness and anxiety. What was more, there was the knowledge that the course I took was hazardous. In the daylight I had observed high hills and bluffs on each side of the stream, and if I encountered pursuers there, I would be helpless, trapped. But away from the stream I might walk only in circles in the woods. I reasoned too that Ann's instinct might tell her to do as I was doing; if she was not already taken, here was the only place where I might hope to encounter her. Yet I had little hope of that and little heart now for my flight.

A long time I walked so in the stream's clough, and I was at last beginning to think I was safe when of a sudden I heard stones falling into the water behind me. I looked back and saw the light of torches, not bright blazes of them but a paler light that fingered the walls of stone and clay that formed the gorge, a light that had its source in torches round a bend behind me in the stream. In the same moment I heard voices echo in the gorge and knew I was followed not by one man alone but a company of them. I laid myself flat against the far wall of the bend and held myself waiting till I could see them. They were all men; no lass amongst them. Then I ran.

Stumbling over the rough wet earth but by some miracle never falling, I ran and ran till the light on the walls of the clough behind me began to fade and the voices grew fainter. My heart raced in my breast and my lungs were swollen like a piper's bag at call-to-arms. But I ran on.

So I ran for a long time, desperate, headlong, until of a sudden I came up against something immovable in the dark. Soft it was, like clay, but hard also, like rock. Such indeed I might have thought it was had I not heard in the same instant a grunt, as from a man whose breath is knocked out of him. It was indeed a man, and there was wind in it, and after it grunted, the wind came out of it in a wheeze, like bagpipes emptying. Then two thick arms encircled me.

I struggled, but the body was a wall. Nay, an avalanche it was, forcing me backward, until finally I heard the body's voice say,

"Campbell here, Clayburn. Have a care." Together then we stood in the dark clough hugging one another, like schoolgirls, to keep our footing on the slippery bank of the stream.

"I have him here," the Campbell said in a loud, hoarse whisper; and afterward I heard others moving toward us in the dark.

"Here," the Campbell said hoarsely.

"John Merkle here," said one of the men; then another, "Alan MacDonald"; and still another, "Ingram Moodie." And then came Ann Horrock's voice, "John! Och, John!" I let out a cry of joy.

"Whisht!" and "Hush!" the men all said together.

"Follow me."

It was John Merkle again.

"This way."

We formed a procession in the dark clough, I knowing by their voices that the Campbell and Alan MacDonald were on either side of me, John Merkle in the lead with Ann, and Ingram Moodie in the rear. Thus we headed upstream and walked fast.

"I have hunted this country," I heard John Merkle say. "There is a cave not far."

Behind us the light from our pursuers' torches began to flicker again on the walls of the gorge, but we walked fast and they came no closer. Soon it seemed to me they were once more fading, and I could hold my tongue no longer.

"Ann—?"

"Ay, John."

"Whisht, man!"

That was the Campbell, pressing hard against me. At my other side Alan MacDonald grasped my arm. "Whisht, Clayburn!" he said.

But now it was Ingram Moodie who could not keep silent. At my back, he whispered, ever full of information: "She went straight to John Merkle at the camp. We met them in the woods."

"Whisht!" the Campbell said again.

Both Ingram and I were silenced then; but no words could quiet the happy pounding of my heart.

We had marched but a few paces more when other lights

appeared. This time they were ahead of us, and we stopped. Pursuers were coming at us now from both directions. We were trapped in the clough. As the new light grew brighter I saw for the first time my friends' faces and my Ann's. Hers was drawn and frightened, looking back at me. I saw that John Merkle carried a gun. The others were armed with clubs. Ingram's was as long as a staff. I reached forward, grasped Ann's hand, and drawing her toward me, kissed her brow. "Keep a calm sough, lass," I whispered.

"This way," Merkle commanded.

The Campbell moved sideways, pushing me against Ann. Alan MacDonald took my arm again and drew me after him. My other arm was linked in Ann's, and we went together.

"Och, my love!" she whispered.

Merkle seemed to have vanished; but soon we heard him call again, "This way! Here!" and we moved toward the sound, Ingram Moodie at our heels. Together, one by one, we crawled into a shallow cave not unlike the one in which I had hidden earlier that day.

"Farther!" Merkle commanded in the dark; and we moved cautiously back into the hollow.

"Have a care! There's a fall!"

There was indeed. Even as he spoke, the wet earth gave way beneath our feet and we slithered and slid into a hole.

"Ochane!"

It was Ann.

"Are you hurt?"

"Nay."

It was more like a trench than a cave, no deeper than our shoulders, and as soon as we recovered our footing we stood peering over its edge, like soldiers behind a breastwork. All but Ann. She alone amongst us was not tall enough to see over the lip of the trench as the light of the torches came nearer, from both sides now. I held her close, under my arm, pressing my cheek upon her soft hair.

"Down!" Merkle commanded; and we squatted low in the trench, while he alone remained standing with his gun resting across its rim.

Outside, we heard the two pursuing forces meet with shouts and cries. Merkle, peering over the edge of the hole, whispered, "There are a score of them, all armed."

The men outside held a council.

"They are not upstream," said one of them; and I recognized the voice of Quentin Pray.

"Nor downstream either," said another; and I believed it was Nicholas Pinnion, although I was not sure.

Then Smith's voice rose above the rest, unmistakable. A high-pitched drunken yammering it was. "Tupped his master's wife he did! I saw them. We'll burn the Scottish whore and hang him on a tree!"

I felt Ann shudder in my arms. I held her close and stroked her hair gently; she began to sob, and I laid my hand softly over her mouth.

"Let's try the upland to the north."

"They'll not go there. It's too open."

"South then. In the bog."

"Ay, that's the place!" It was Smith again. "In the bog! That's where she whored with him! We'll catch them there!"

"The bog, then?"

"Ay, the bog."

In all the voices there was an idiot sound, the sound of spirits coursing in the brain. I knew they were all ready to burn and hang if they found us. I put both arms about Ann's shuddering body and tried to comfort her, shuddering myself.

Full as they were, the men took no precautions to search the cavernous walls with their torches but stood and shouted at each other so loud they could be heard a mile away; and when finally they clambered up the slippery bluff, they passed but a few yards from the hole where we were crouched and did not see us. The last words we heard as they plunged into the woods above us were Smith's again: "We'll burn the Scottish whore and hang him from a tree!"

"My love," I whispered. Her frightened breathing stroked my neck, but she was no longer sobbing. "My love, my love. . . ."

A long time after the men from the ironworks were gone we waited. Long after no more light from their torches touched the treetops over the bluff and their voices had trailed off into silence we waited in that cave, the six of us.

Finally someone touched me on the shoulder.

Merkle it was. I knew him when he spoke.

"Come."

We climbed out of our hiding place and slid down to the stream's shore where a short while before our pursuers had stood in drunken council. In the murk my friends gathered round us, Ann and me, silent until Merkle spoke again.

"You are safe now, I think," he said. "There will be no more of them. The officers of Lynn gave up their search at sundown, and the mob from the ironworks are too drunk to come so close again. But the officers' search will begin again on the morrow. So have a care."

"I shall be ever grateful to you, John Merkle," I said.

"Nay, John Clayburn," he replied. "It is to Campbell and MacDonald and Moodie you should be grateful. When my good-wife came to the camp and told me you had set out upon a journey, I did nothing. I thought you could best manage for yourself, fleeing from naught but bailiffs and such. But when the lass came to the camp and I was taking her home to Mistress Merkle, we came upon Campbell and MacDonald and Moodie in the woods and they told us Pray and Smith had raised a mob. I thought better of my own counsel then, and we formed a party to search for you."

"I shall be ever grateful to all of you," I said.

"It was naught," said Alan MacDonald, laughing merrily after. "It was like old times, and no more. In Scotland, I have often hunted Clayburns in the woods."

The Campbell spoke not, but he shook my hand.

Then Ingram Moodie said, "It is better to go farther than to stay here and fare worse"; and for a moment I feared that he meant to accompany Ann and me; but it proved that he was only reciting one of his proverbs.

In the dark I felt something cold touch my hand, and thereafter I found myself holding Merkle's gun.

It was his hunting gun.

"You will have need of it," he said. "Have a care of it." I felt him then lay a hand upon Ann's shoulder at my side. "And you, lass, have a care ever of my friend. He is a good man, even though he is a sinner like us all. God be with you both."

Of a sudden after that my friends were gone in the murk, and Ann and I were alone in the clough and on our way together to freedom from all that had held us in bondage on the Saugus, freedom to love without dour Calvin darkening our conscience and eventually to wed, freedom to labor and build for ourselves and not, as slaves, for others, freedom to bring into the world children who would themselves be free.

And all that we did. We settled in New Hampshire, Ann and I, and when word came from John Merkle that Benjamin Horrock had died, we were wed; and now pridefully our children and our children's children write in their Bibles: *John Clayburn, Scot, fought with honor at Dunbar, 3 September, 1650, taken prisoner of war by O. Cromwell; sent to America as an indentured man against his will; married first, in Scotland, Dorcas Bowen; married second, in New Hampshire, Ann Horrock; married third, in Massachusetts, Ann Merkle* ... thus planting for themselves in this new land a family tree, with myself the root of it. Ay, all that we did, my first Ann and I, living in harmony in the mountains of New Hampshire until she died.

Ay, it is of this second goodwife of mine and myself that I have told this tale, setting down such things as a man cannot speak of to his children—nor to his third wife either, although I am sure she has guessed most of them. Of such things an old man must speak, however, to warm his flesh as near to the hot truth of his youth as he can come. Of such things an old man must speak over and over, if only to himself—and set them down in writing too, if he had the skill—else he may cease to believe, in the lonely westering of his years, that he too once ran with the rising sun.

Part Two

SUPPLY CLAYBURN

1750–1835

Ohio Valley Magazine of History
Vol. XLVI No. 4 December 1913

SUPPLY CLAYBURN LETTERS[1]

Contributed by the Hon. Thomas Bradford
Clayburn[2]
Edited by Diomedes F. Click, Ph. D.[3]

1819

Dunbar, N.H.
May 13, 1819

Samuel Clayburn, Esq.
Red Bank on the Ohio River

My Dear Sam, —I believed that you were dead!
Ay, Son, I was convinced that you were killed in the recent

---

[1]Supply Clayburn was born in Woburn, Mass., in 1750. At the age of twenty-three he moved to Dunbar, N. H., and took up land claimed in 1656 by his great-great-grandfather John Clayburn. He fought at Bunker Hill, was a member of the U. S. House of Representatives, served nine years as a Selectman in Dunbar, and prospered as a farmer until his death in 1835. Nine of his letters addressed to his son Samuel have been preserved by the Clayburn family and are published here for the first time, some in their entirety, others excerpted as indicated by ellipses (. . .). An unabridged edition of the letters with full notes is in preparation for future publication by the editor.

[2]Appreciation is here expressed to the Hon. Thomas Bradford Clayburn of Crescent City, Judge of the Circuit Court of Liggum County, for his suggestions in editing the letters. Judge Clayburn is a great grandson of Supply Clayburn.

[3]Diomedes F. Click, editor of this magazine, is Professor of History at Crescent City College. He is the editor of *Hello, The Boat: The Journal of Herman A. Tutweiler, Merchant and Flatboatman, Written on a Journey down the Ohio and Mississippi Rivers in the Winter of 1841 with a Load of Hogs, Ginseng, Beeswax, Whiskey and Hoop-poles.* Crescent City: 1909. 22 pp., and the author of three articles published in this magazine.

conflict, called by my Federalist neighbours "Mr. Madison's War,"[4] for which, with no word of farewell,—bravely, it is true, but with no regard for a Father's convictions and counsel or a Mother's loving heart,—you left this house six years ago to become a soldier. I have also been compell'd, during the winter months just pass'd, to harbour the further sorrowful belief that no male of the Clayburn name would, in future, hold title to these New Hampshire lands, which Clayburns have owned for five generations and upon which, forty yrs ago, with my own hands, I built the dwelling[5] in which I write these words; for at the outset of this letter, it is my sad duty to inform you that both of your brothers have died in yr absence.[6] John was struck down October last in his 33*d* year by the great oak that he was felling in the meadow. Tom succumbed to a fever at the same age 3 yrs ago. Both were without male issue. Meantime, I hasten to assure you that yr sisters live in excellent health: three of them now married, and only Agatha, who has inherited the Clayburn nose, remaining at home.

Now, by receipt of yrs of Ap 3*d*, from a place you call "Red Bank on the Ohio River,"[7] which does not appear on any map that I possess, I am comforted by the assurance that I have not only one remaining male heir of the Clayburn name, but Two: Yourself and the Son just born to you. Praise be to God!

Praise be to Him a thousandfold if you will but tell me in yr next that you will return to New Hampshire; for I have grown old in yr absence and shall achieve my 3 score yrs & 10 in the forthcoming year. However, from the nature of yr letter, I draw small confidence that I shall know the joy of yr returning. Andrew Jackson for President, indeed! Was it for the rule of the rabble and not the rights of man that I & others among yr forbears fought the English tyranny at Lex'ton & Concord & Bunker's Hill? You were ever an unreasoning and headstrong lad, and I must conclude that you remain so still. Furthermore, yr present situation appears so well established that I can not,

---

[4] The War of 1812. Reference is to James Madison, fourth president of the United States (1809–1817). The war was unpopular in New England.

[5] The house still stands but is no longer in the Clayburn family.

[6] Supply Clayburn had seven children: Thomas, John, Suzanna, Naomi, Agatha, Abigail, and Samuel.

[7] Now Crescent City.

in clear conscience, urge you to abandon yr prospects as partner with yr wife's father in the building of steamboats on the Ohio River. Instead, I must congratulate you upon a wise marriage; for did not I myself, in my first marriage, half a century ago, do the same as you, when, returning from the action at Charlestown,[8] I won the hand of my Captain's daughter and, with it, accretion of substantial acreage adjacent to that which I already owned? And did I not remain thereafter in New Hampshire and never return to my Mother's home in Massachusetts, but bring her here to live with me and my Bride? And now, in my second marriage, have I not also prosper'd, yr Mother's father leaving to me his farm in Dunbar, which I sold at good profit?

Nay, Sam; you have my blessing. A good wife is worth her weight in Gold; but a good wife who improves her husband's prospects as well is worth her weight in Diamonds. True, the name LaMar, which you tell me derives from S. Carolina in yr wife's instance, has a ring to it more Foreign than Scottish; but if the lass loves you and remains dutiful and in good health and you thrive in her father's business, I shall find no fault with yr marriage.

But, Sam, you tell me little more of my Grandson than his name, that he is strong and cries lustily, and was born Feb'y last "at a time of exceeding high water in the Ohio." Do you attach significance to that last, as did the character in Shakespeare's play,[9] who boasted of claps of thunder and bolts of lightning at the hour of his birth? The Bard said it was no more than if his mother's cat had kitten'd, and I am of the same opinion. Twenty yrs ago, when you were yourself born in this house in the course of a snowstorm in the month of April, I made nothing of the circumstance, snowstorms being no more uncommon in that month in this clime than floods in Feb'y in the Western rivers. Indeed, on this very day in May, as I write to you, the north side of the big boulder in the meadow is still white with snow. If the skies had rained fire and brimstone at the time of yr delivery from yr Mother's womb, I should have made nothing of it, Sam; for you were born in the same fashion as all mortals; a breech presentation, it is true, but disastrous neither to yrself nor yr Mother, nor otherwise noteworthy. Sam, yr letter would have

---

[8]The Battle of Bunker Hill.
[9]See *Henry IV, Part One, III, i.*

pleas'd me more if you had given the date of my Grandson's arrival in this world, instead of describing the altitude of the waters in the Ohio on that occasion. It could be that he drew his first breath on the birthdate of that great and noble man, The Father of Our Country, and you have not thought to tell me.

Sam, you should at least have considered yr Mother's feelings in yr manner of reporting the birth of my Grandson. It is important to a woman to have some account of an infant's physiognomy and parts; yet you wrote naught of such matters. You said that he is strong; ay, but are his limbs well form'd and is his head large and fully rounded, like a true Clayburn's? Has he the Clayburn Roman nose? Will he be tall, like all Clayburns? Has he the red hair that appears from time to time in the Clayburn family; or is he dark, like yourself, or fair like me? If you have neither the time nor the talent to venture upon descriptions such as a fond grandmother languishes to read, surely yr Amelia has sufficiently recover'd now from her lying-in to put pen to paper.

At this point, I hasten to assure you that yr Mother, about whom you had the grace to enquire, is in good health and excellent spirits and, at this writing, sits at my side before the fire altering a straw colour'd gown of which she is extravagantly fond. As for myself, although you had not the grace to enquire, I am in good health also, in spite of my years, and this very morning set my hand to the laying up of stones in the wall that encompasses the meadow, applying to the task, I feel compell'd to add, more vigour and skill than was exhibited by yr sister Abigail's husband, Ethan Townsend, who walked his boundary with me on the other side.

Henry—.

The name savours of an English heritage and is, therefore, not one that a Scot might favour; yet it is sound enough to last the boy a lifetime, if he use it well. Think on it, Sam; a ripe old age will allow him to witness the arrival of the 20th Century![10] *Henry Clayburn*—. The more I repeat the name to myself, the better it strikes my fancy. True, it is a departure from the customs in christening practiced by your progenitors; but I remind myself that you have married a lass from the South and there may have

---

[10]Henry Clayburn died in 1891.

been some outlandish influence from that quarter, as there was in my own naming, my Mother being of Puritan upbringing, and not Presbyterian, like the Clayburns.

My Mother gave me the name Supply because I was a posthumous son and she expected me to "Supply" the place of my father in the councils of the family, as a pastor is said to "supply" in the pulpit in the absence of another. Both my Father, Sam'l III and my Grandfather, Sam'l II, died in the year that I was born. I can not say what wisdom I "Supply'd" in family councils in my earliest years; for I have no recollection of them until the winter day when I stood at a window of my Mother's house in Woburn and gazed out upon an ox sunk to its belly in snow, whilst an uncle,—Andrew Cutter, I have been told since,—who was himself visible only above the waist, prodded the beast with a goad.

As I wrote the words foregoing, I thought I could hear you say, as you used to say too often for my patience when you were a boy and I was endeavouring to store your mind with Clayburn lore, "You have already told me that, Father." Alack, an old man repeats himself often, Sam, a father especially, as you will do yourself one day when this young Henry is older, not so much in forgetfulness as in the necessity to assure yourself that what has happened in yr life has truly happen'd & a desire to perpetuate yourself in the memory of yr progeny. It is the duty of a son to hold his tongue and listen, even when he has heard it before; for that is how we learn, through repetition. Besides, with yourself gone from under my roof these many years & no word from you, whether you were dead or alive, how can I remember what I have told you and have not told you of myself and past Clayburns? How, indeed, can I be sure that you ever listen'd to me? And if you did listen, how can I know what you have preserv'd in memory, diverted as you have been by yr adventures in the War, and living in the Wilderness on the Ohio River, amongst Indians, & Southerners as well, & no books at hand and no Bible, with inscriptions to remind you of Clayburns?

Be patient, Sam. Too often the past is lost because we do not hear when we are young, & when we are old and recognize the importance of our elders' words to the proper governance of our lives, those who were familiar with the past have departed for that land with which there is no communication. Be patient with yr Father, Sam'l, and preserve such recollections of his as this one of the ox in the snow, trivial though it may seem to you now, so that one day yr Son may match it with recollections of his own; not of oxen in snow, to be sure, but perhaps of the steamboats that you now build on the Ohio River with yr wife's Father. Thus will he discover how our great Country changes as time wheels forward, how it moves toward perfection, whether there be Monroes and Adamses in the President's House in Washington City, or Jacksons or Clays, as you in the West would have it. . . .

Would that I had now in my possession, to pass on to you and to my Grandson, the writing that our ancestor John Clayburn undertook in his old age, in which he recorded memories of his youth in Scotland, his part in the Battle of Dunbar,[11] for which he named this New Hampshire town, and his first years in America at Saugus in the Colony of Massachusetts, where that villain Cromwell sent him as a prisoner of war and bondservant to labour in the ironworks. John Clayburn was the first of our family in America, and his writing could tell us much about those early days; but according to our family's legend,[12] his memoir was destroyed by fire when my great-grandfather, Sam'l I, returning from a campaign against the Indians, found his dwelling in Woburn infested by rats and, with more impatience than good judgement, burned the house to the ground to rid himself of the vermin.

Great-grandfather Sam'l was said to have been a taciturn man as well as impetuous; and whenever thereafter he was asked about his Father, whether, for instance, John Clayburn kill'd his share of the Sassenach[13] that day at Dunbar, he could only reply, "Such is my recollection of the writing"; and when enquiry was made about the widow, Ann Horrock, whom his father married and who was Sam'l's own Mother, he could recall nothing save that his father call'd her "bonny." Ann Horrock died on this farm in 1658, giving birth to Sam'l I; but because no likeness of

---

[11]Oliver Cromwell defeated David Leslie's Scottish army at Dunbar, September 3, 1650.

[12]The family's legend was apparently erroneous. A manuscript said to be the memoirs of John Clayburn was deposited in the Boston Athenaeum in 1850 by Dugald Cameron of Boston, a descendant of John Clayburn, on the condition that it should not be made available to scholars until 1950.

[13] Gaelic word meaning Saxon, used by Scots to designate Englishmen.

her was ever drawn and nothing more than the record of her marriage to John Clayburn stands in Clayburn Bibles and her son Sam'l was wanting in speech to tell what he remember'd, we know naught else of her than that she was "bonny." What a pity!

Ay, what a pity that her son did not remove his Father's writing from his house in Woburn before he burn'd the dwelling down that day. Clayburns know but little of John Clayburn himself beyond what their Bibles and town records can tell them: that he was first married in Scotland to Dorcas Bowen, who died in Edinburgh soon after he was sent to America; that he was then lawfully married to Ann Horrock, a widow; that himself and five other men were granted this New Hampshire townsite by the Royal Government in Boston in 1656; and that, after receiving his homelot and certain fields, he resided here only two years, removing with his infant son after his wife's death to the town of Woburn, in Massachusetts, settling there on land adjacent to that of one John Merkle, who was his ancient friend, and there marrying John Merkle's daughter, who also bore the name of Ann. . . . "You have already told me all this, Father!" Ay, Sam; but I am telling you again, and now you have it in writing. . . .

. . . Time passes, and the oil in the lamp burns low, with yr Mother already asleep in her chair. I will give you now, in brief compass, our news since yr departure 6 yrs ago, with more at a later writing, if you answer. I am still a Selectman in the Town of Dunbar, as I was when you left. Two yrs ago, New Hampshire separated the authority of the Church from that of the State, and in that same year I was elevated from Deacon to Elder in our Congregation. Parson Petty continues in our pulpit and continues to preach badly and overlong. Yr little dog Snap died in the year following yr departure, of snake bite, we think, contracted in the woods. In the same yr, in Boston, I had the wen removed from my head without untoward consequences, though great soreness. We now have 12 cows, 1 bull, 34 sheep, 9 swine, and 4 horses, 2 of them for the phaeton in which I travel to Boston each year to oversee my affairs in that City. Yr mother will be 49 yrs of age next month. Yr sister Agatha is now 26 and still without prospects. In April of this year, I mended the roof with some help from Sam Richardson, who still lives down the

road. He fell to the ground the second day and broke his leg; and
although he fell by his own carelessness, I paid him nonetheless
a bushel of apples from the fruit cellar. Mary Simon, who was
our bond-girl when you were at home, has had a baby with no
father in sight. The MacGregors moved to Ohio a year ago, and
the Cooks intend to follow them by-and-by, MacGregor owing
Cook money. Last fall, our cider fetched twice the customary
price, as it has now become known as far away as Derrydale that
I add no water to it, as do most. Potatoes, however, were down
2¢ the bushel and hardly worth the digging. Ethan Townsend's
horse has the glanders, and I have forbidden Abigail to visit in
this house until it is cured, or dies. She talks to her mother each
day from the road.

> Yr Loving Father,
> Supply Clayburn

Dunbar, the 7th Oct

Dear Sam—

. . . . Yr bro-in-law, Ethan Townsend, learning of yr whereabouts from Abigail, talks now of nothing but moving to the
Ohio Country; but I doubt that he will do so, having only the
voice for such a venture; not the gumption. . . .

Our Revolution, whilst it freed us from the tyranny of the
English, has robbed us of the authority of parents in our land,
making Youth headstrong and restless. Too many, like yourself,
flee from the discipline of their fathers for the license of the
Frontier, whilst their sisters, remaining at home, demonstrate
their independence by reducing their clothing to a scandalous
bare minimum, in the current imitation of the fashions of Ancient Greece, violating all rules of decency and hazarding their
health. What is worse, their mothers encourage them by following their example, regardless of shape or size.

I give you lines from an editorial in the pages of the *Hampshire
Gazette*, which lies before me:—

"What sight can be more preposterous than that of a short,
thick, broad-shouldered, fat female in a spencer? Short women

destroy their symmetry, and encumber their charms, by all redundancy of ornament; and a little woman feathered and furbelowed looks like a queen of the Bantam Tribe. Thus, while the sylph-formed maiden may be allowed to float in gossamer" (I part company with the editor here.) "the more matured and portly female should adopt a fabric better suited to her size, her figure, and her time of life." (Here, I tell yr Mother, I subscribe to the editor's opinion *in toto*.)

I give you, further, lines from the *Connecticut Courant*, which I read in the past summer and put to memory for the frequent reproof and edification of yr sisters, especially Abigail:—

> "Doctor, I have lost my health
> Where, O where my vigor?
> No faithless swain, no act of stealth,
> Reduc'd me to this figure.
>
> "Plump and rosy was my face,
> And graceful was my form,
> Till fashion deem'd it a disgrace
> To keep my body warm.
>
> "I sacrific'd to modish whim
> (What belle can e'er forsake it?)
> To make myself genteel and slim
> I stripped me almost naked.
>
> "And naked thus I must remain
> Till fashion weds with reason—
> God grant they may united reign
> Before the frosty season."

Sam, are women in the West such fools these days as they are in New England? Write and tell me that it is not so, that yr Amelia keeps her body modestly covered. . . .

. . . Ethan Townsend's horse has recovered from the glanders, & none in the family has come down with it, thanks to my precautions. Abigail comes once more to the house every day to borrow from her mother's larder. Ethan has had my harrowing rake since last spring without returning it. Otherwise, all well.

What is the news of my Grandson Henry Clayburn?

Yr Father—
Supply Clayburn

1820

Dunbar, N.H.
Feb'y 10, 1820

Sam'l Clayburn, Esq.
Crescent City on the Ohio

My Dear Son,—In the reading of yrs of Jan'y 3*d* just receiv'd, in which you recount the re-naming of yr settlement on the Ohio River and yr part therein, I was twice disappointed.

First, I like not the new name "Crescent City." Second, when none of the preponderance of Southerners in yr councils came forth with the names "Jefferson" or "Madison" or "Monroe,"[14] nor even the name of yr Father-in-law LaMar, though he be, as you report, the town's leading citizen, why did you not yourself then step forward with the name "Clayburn"? In all humility, of course, because in this country, we have inherited the whole damn'd human race, Clayburns no better than the rest; in America, Sam, every man is our father. Why did you not, Sam? "Clayburn on the Ohio." I like the ring of it. . . .

If modesty prevented yr making such a proposal, then why did you not offer "Adams" or "Stark" or "Allen"? All of them good New England men, and two from New Hampshire. Have you forgotten your origins, Sam? Could you not at least have proposed, discreetly and in all modesty, the name of yr native New Hampshire town "Dunbar" and thus have honour'd not only this place but also the battlefield in Scotland where yr ancestor fought with valour nigh onto 2 centuries ago? On maps

---

[14]In Ohio there are both counties and towns named Jefferson, Madison and Monroe. Indiana has counties bearing those names and towns named Madison, Jeffersonville and Monroeville. Illinois has counties named Jefferson, Madison and Monroe and a town named Madison.

of the Western Country there are already Bostons and Spring-
fields and a Worcester, although the orthography of the latter is,
I note, incorrect;[15] but no New Hampshire names that I can
find: no Jaffreys, no Keenes, no Nashuas. Why not, then, a
"Dunbar"? But Crescent City—! Could not yr fellow townsmen
conceive a more substantial name than that? I like it not.
'Twould have been better to allow the town to remain honest
"Red Bank," as it was, than to adorn it with such plumage.

Ornamental naming is not inappropriate for girl-children.
Their patronymics vanish with marriage, & such prettifying
encourages swains to indulge in flights of poetic fancy, thus
aggravating their own passions, as the scents of flowers attract
and excite bees; but a town, Sam, is male, not female. A town
requires a name that is solid and enduring, as a boy-child is
named John or Sam'l or Supply. Even Paris was named for a
man, although the weakness of the Son of Priam for the opposite
sex and his profligate misuse of the sturdy apple may account
for the effeminacy of that place. Like a man, a city must stand
strong against its neighbours, else it perish. I am told that Boston was once called Trimontaine. Think on it! Think what
would have been the fate of that City if its original nomencla-
ture had remained attached to it. In such case, I daresay, Ports-
mouth would now be the principal harbour of New England,
—to the greater glory of New Hampshire, it is true, but to the
lasting shame of Massachusetts. . . . No; honest Red Bank was
better. . . .

I am pleased to learn that my Grandson Henry Clayburn (It is
a good name.) grows apace and cries less and a brother or sister is
already on the way. May it be a brother! Clayburns have been over-
bless'd with female children in the past two generations. . . .

I remind myself that today Henry Clayburn is one year old.
Soon he will follow you about wherever you go and ask questions of you by the hogsheadful. Answer him with care, Sam.
And listen to him in return; for you will discover that wisdom
comes often from the mouths of babes, and what he says may be
for yr edification. When you, at four years of age, first remarked
the difference between our bull and the cows in the pasture with
the observation that "a cow is but a bull turned wrong side
outwards," I punished you for speaking so; but afterward I

---

[15]Possibly a reference to Wooster, Ohio.

privately debated with myself whether Our Maker did not indeed have something of that sort in mind when He created Eve from Adam's Rib; and I wish'd then that I had enjoy'd the benefit of yr observation in my earlier years when yr sisters were infants in this house. At that time I might have treated them with a more Christian patience if I could have reminded myself that females are but creatures like ourselves turn'd wrong side outwards and therefore not responsible for their irrational behaviour. (In yr reply to this letter, you would favour me if you made no allusion to the foregoing; for yr Mother reads yr letters as well as myself, & sometimes Agatha, who is still *Unwed.*)

... I am spoken of here to stand for election to the House of Representatives in Washington in the Fall. I have now attain'd my 3 score yrs & 10, but no matter. Ben Franklin served his country well beyond that age.

Yr aff'n'te Father,
Supply Clayburn

Dunbar, Sep 6

Samuel Clayburn, Esq.

My Dear Sam'l,—The Federalist Party having all but disappear'd from the political scene and yr Western Breed of Republicans mustering no partisans amongst our New Hampshire people, my candidacy for a seat in the House of Representatives goes unoppos'd &, like the President of the United States, I am assur'd of election. Rumour has it that Gov. Plumer harbours a secret hostility in his heart toward Mr. Monroe, and this may account in part, alongside the absence of contest, for the general apathy toward the election that prevails here, although I am told it is so elsewhere. Indeed, one might think we were living four years hence and not in the current calendar year; for all political comment now abroad ignores this election and concerns itself with the hopes of yr Clays, Calhouns, Crawfords & such in 1824, though no mention here of Andrew Jackson. . . . [16]

---

[16]James A. Monroe was unopposed in the election of 1820; but in the Electoral College, Governor William Plumer of New Hampshire, though pledged to Monroe, voted for John Quincy Adams.

In a previous letter, I reported to you that yr sister Agatha had, at last, a suitor, one Wm Smith, from over Nashua way. He is a widower with six children, and for that reason I held expectations that he wd prove ardent. But not so. He appears now to have abandon'd his suit, for we have not seen him in this house for six weeks. Whether he suffer'd a change of heart or was discourag'd by a refusal yr Mother can not ascertain from her intercourse with Agatha, the latter remaining silent on the subject and seeming indifferent toward Wm's retirement from the field of courtship and intent now only upon her novel determination to become a teacher at the Academy, if she can gain employment there. As for this last, it does not altogether meet with my approval, there being no female teachers in these parts and myself in agreement with the Lexicographer[17] in thinking that a woman teaching, like a woman preaching, as he says, resembles a dog walking on its hind legs, inspiring wonder not so much for doing it well as for doing it at all. However, Agatha and yr Mother compose a majority in this house, and I may be over-ridden at the last. 'Tis less difficult to be a candidate for Congess than to oversee the machinations of two females in the same household. Yet, Agatha's employment at the Academy would ease somewhat the burden of her keep and might prevent an ultimate languishing for want of a husband. . . .

Yr Father,
Supply Clayburn

1821

"Roman Mess"
City of Wash'ton
Dist of C
Nov 21, 1821

My Dear Sam,—Arriv'd here Tuesday last, bringing with me yrs of 12 Sep to answer, which I now do forthwith.

The journey requir'd 10 days of travel &, excepting for a rest

---

[17]Samuel Johnson, 1709–1784, English writer and lexicographer.

in Philadelphia to recover from an attack of Gout, was without
incident & less hazardous than I had been led to expect it would
be by yr bro-in-law Ethan Townsend, although why I should
have given credence to his dire prophesies I know not, he pos-
sessing always a more copious supply of opinions than knowledge &, in this instance, having no more experience than myself
to go by. . . .

The least inhabited section of the journey is from Phila to
Baltimore & beyond. Through New England, N.Y., & Pennsylvania, we travell'd at all times over good roads, past cultivated
land or woodlands cleared of underbrush and well cared for; but
the State of Maryland, excepting along its waterways, can boast
of little besides swamp & dismal wasteland of thick growths of
trees of no value, with vines entwining all, like snakes. Yet the
roads from Balt're to Wash'n have been newly paved and, I must
acknowledge, are less painful to the traveller than are our pikes
in New Hampshire.

I have install'd myself here in a boarding-house that calls itself
"The Roman Mess," because it stands near the Tiber Bridge
below the Capitoline Hill. It enjoys a convenient proximity to
the street that connects "The White House," as it is now called,
with the Capitol. This street is referred to here as "The Avenue," although it resembles nothing more than a bog in rain and
a river of dust in dry weather, bordered by a few houses like my
own, but more often by the shanties of workmen and stragglers
come to the Capital for alms, and still more often by wastes of
empty lots, all gone to swampy undergrowth, & is therefore no
great tribute to the State of Pennsylvania, for which it is named.
Cows, chickens, & pigs wander unrestrained amongst its hummocks and hollows & even on the lawn of the President's abode,
which is poorly fenced; moreover, it is not uncommon for
snakes to invade houses along its course, regardless of the distinction or importance of their occupants. Few sidewalks are
paved anywhere in the City; indeed, save in the regions round
The Wharf, The White House, & The Capitol, there are no
streets at all & one finds oneself in a "countryside" where one
is easily lost, with only stone markers for guides, most of them
hidden in brush and weeds, where it is expected that there may
be street-corners in future. No lights; & many Senators and
Representatives carry sidearms.

A score of Members of the House of Representatives reside in the house where I live. Most of them are New England men like myself; but I, alas, share my bed with a Rep from the new State of Indiana, who, like myself, arriv'd late and had small choice in the matter of quarters. He sleeps in his drawers and, because he is given to the consumption of whiskey in great quantity every evening after supper, resorts frequently to the chamber-pot throughout the night, thus disturbing my slumber. The "Roman Mess" is run by a "lady" from Virginia. Such, Sam, is the appellation for all females in this part of the Country, at risk of a duel otherwise. This "lady" is assisted by several slave girls and women and an ancient black man with no teeth, whose speech is to me wholly incomprehensible. The first morning after my arrival, this Blackamoor entered our bedroom unannounced, before either the "Gentleman" from Indiana or myself had risen from our bed, and, bowing ceremoniously, whilst he tugged at his grey wool as though it were a cap, said something which had to be interpreted for me by the Gent from Ind, who, having spent his boyhood in the South, understands the *lingua* of Africans. He said the black man had warned us we would miss breakfast if we were not downstairs at the ordinary[18]in 5 minutes, a bell having been rung to summon us for the last time 10 minutes before. It was then not yet 7 o'clock.

We dress'd in great haste & without washing & went downstairs, arriving in time to be served, but only to discover, for my part at least, that the meal would have been better miss'd than eaten: Eggs but half cook'd & Pork swimming in Grease, lac'd with Hominy Grits, which they cook somewhat like our Journey Cake but serve by the spoonful and coarser; & all cold withal. I took hope from a belief that the inferior quality of the repast was a result of the "late" hour of our arrival at table; but in vain; the next morning it was the same; and dinner and supper not much better; All swimming in Grease; Meat, pork mostly; Potatoes, yellow & call'd yams; a vegetable much fancied here, call'd Oker,[19] which is small & podded & covered with a thin slime, like a snail, & looks like one; Dried Peas, etcetera, & more Grits, which they also fry and serve with a yellow mo-

[18]The long table at which meals were served in boardinghouses.
[19]Okra.

lasses made from Sorghum. The Gent from Ind thrives on such provender, eating more than his share at each meal; but already I have discover'd that my bowels are not imbued with the same fervent degree of Patriotism as my heart in my determination to serve my Country at all hazards & at night I now vie with my bedmate for the use of the chamberpot.

If yr Mother were here, she would surely insist upon an inspection of the kitchen, of which I have a sufficient view from my position at the ordinary; and the pots and pans being presided over by an enormous black slattern of unsavoury appearance, I have no doubt her inspection would terminate our residency in this place. Therefore, it is not my intention to invite yr Mother to join me here, this session or next; for I am convinc'd that all messes are alike & I have no thought of buying property in this town on such uncertain tenure as a seat in the Congress affords. Indeed, most men in Wash'ton are without wives or families for the same reason, few Senators or Representatives having the means or the temerity to speculate in the brick houses that are being built in rows on what is call'd "The Hill," where the Capitol stands, a neighbourhood said to be less malarial than the rest of the "City," which I doubt. No member of the Government stays in Washington longer than is necessary, even The President. . . . Except for a morning of duck-shooting in the marshes along the Tiber and another in a region of the "City" known as "Foggy Bottom," I have taken no pleasure from my residency here. . . .

Congress will meet in a few days. I am told, however, that its main business is accomplished at night in the parlours of the messes, the sessions on "The Hill" being largely wrangling & speech-making prior to the voting pre-ordained by decisions arriv'd at in the boarding-houses. . . .

I write this letter at my desk in the House Chamber, which has been decorated with a new Brussels carpet, red settees, a silk canopy over the Speaker's Chair mounted by a gold Eagle, and gold curtains, all too Frenchified for my tastes and ill designed, I think, for the legislative deliberations of a Republic. I daresay, however, that the mud and dust carried in on our boots from the "Avenue" & other "streets," compounded with the tobacco juice that is spouted wantonly from the lips of yr Gents from the Western States, will soon reduce the hall to a more Plebeian aspect. . . . With the dispute over the slavery in the new State of Missouri now at last settled & Florida at last relinquish'd by Spain, the session forthcoming should be quieter than those just past. Let us hope we can concern ourselves with less troublesome matters, such as improvements in our canals & rivers and roadways. . . . Sam, you should rejoice with me that we have such a man in Washington as Mr. J. Q. Adams, whilst I rejoice with you that there is also yr Mr. Clay. . . .[20]

Yr Mother informs me by recent post that Agatha is content in her work as a teacher at the Academy & nothing more said of Wm Smith. . . . Perhaps my Grandson Henry Clayburn will someday be President of the United States. Why not?

Yr Loving Father, who now signs himself
"The Hon. Supply Clayburn, M.C."[21]

1822

Wash'n Jan 7 1822

Son Sam'l,—The Gent from Ind has left our Roman Mess for another, which is on Capitol Hill and more to his liking because there he will be amongst his own kind, Western men; and I now share my bed with a more congenial companion, although he comes from Connecticut and would sometimes argue with me that General Israel Putnam was a greater hero at Bunker's Hill than Colonel John Stark. . . . [22]

My letter to you of recent date may have suggested erroneously that this Capital is without elegance; but such is not the truth, Sam, as witness the levee, or "Drawing Room," as Mrs. Monroe would have them call'd, which I have just attended at The White House. . . . I travell'd in the stage, which plies twice daily between The Capitol and Georgetown and plunges amongst the holes and hummocks of Pennsylvania Avenue like

---

[20]The treaty with Spain, in which Florida was ceded to the United States, was in part the work of Secretary of State Adams of Massachusetts; the Missouri Compromise was principally engineered by Henry Clay of Kentucky.

[21]Member of Congress.

[22]Putnam was from Connecticut, Stark from New Hampshire.

a cow afflicted by the hoose.[23] At the start, we were an exclusive company atop this diligence, all Gentlemen from New England, until the Gent from Ind, who was unaccompanied, saw us from below and, joining us, was thereafter ever at our elbows. . . .

The new appellation for the President's Palace derives from the coat of glistening white paint that has been applied to the stone facing of the edifice to conceal scars left by the fire the English vandals set when they occupied the City in our recent conflict with them. No ravages of the conflagration remain visible anywhere, either within or without the domicile of the President, all repairs having at last been completed; indeed, plans are now in progress for addition, in near future, of a Portico to grace the front of the house and a Pavilion & Wing of magnificent proportions at its Eastern end. The interior furnishings remain somewhat sparse, Mr. Monroe being compell'd to supply them out of his own pocket, and are more French than American and therefore, in my opinion, unsuitable to the residence of the Chief Executive of a Republic, but can be excus'd on the grounds that the President was forc'd to employ such furnishings as he already possess'd, articles acquired in Europe in his travels during previous Administrations:[24] heavy gold chairs cover'd in Crimson cloth, gold eagles, ormolu clocks (sans the nudities that I have noted in the adornment of such clocks elsewhere, even in Boston), gold candlesticks, and the like; all, I am told, of the Empire design.

Mr. Monroe and his Lady greeted the guests in the Oval Room, he with an informality that was nonetheless dignified and graceful. The President is a tall man, as tall as myself, and sturdily built, though not stout. He has a long face and cleft chin and a long nose, set between large grey eyes that give him a gentle aspect; not dour. He speaks with a Southern softness that is pleasant to the ear, & converses in French as well as English, as I heard him do when a member of the French legation was presented to him. He wears his grey hair full at the back, in the current fashion, but otherwise gives the appearance of a gentleman of the century just past, being one of very few men at the

---

[23]Scottish word for a disease of cattle that makes them stagger.

[24]Prior to his presidency, James A. Monroe was a minister in several European capitals, including Paris.

gala attir'd in knee breeches, silk stockings, and buckled shoes. In spite of such quaint dress, I remind you that he has a broader knowledge of our Country than any President who has preceded him, excepting G. Washington, having travell'd to Boston and other cities with the purpose of seeing as much as he can of the Nation he serves. Mrs. Monroe, a handsome woman but somewhat haughty in manner, wore a turban. As for the rest of it, yr Mother or Abigail, had they been there, could better describe the spectacle of the Lady's gold and white gown, & I can only tell you that it is said here Mrs. M. spends several thousand dollars per annum on her dresses, ordering them all from Paris. Her attire, and the President's, and many of the others were in striking contrast to the coarse hunting-coats and muddy leggings and boots worn by some of yr Western gentry, including the Gent from Ind, who complained that no whiskey was serv'd in the collation. A party of Indians was present also,—Creeks, I was told,—wearing headdresses. Servants pass'd through the rooms at all times, bearing trays of food and drink. I took four glasses of an excellent scuppernong wine & was at stool twice in the night. . . .

I trust my Grandson and his sister are well.

Yr Father,
Supply Clayburn

1823

Dunbar, June 4,
1823

Sam'l Clayburn, Esq.
~~Red Bank~~ Crescent City on the O. Riv

My Dear Sam,—What is a half-horse half-alligator man[25] that you mention in yrs of Ap 27 just receiv'd? Have you no gaol in yr settlement for the incarceration of such . . . ? You write also of "planters" and "sawyers"[26] in a manner that is not familiar

---

[25] Keelboatmen.

[26] A planter was the riverman's name for a log up-ended in the water; a sawyer was a log horizontally afloat.

to me. Sam, I trust yr speech, as it was taught to you by yr Mother & in yr years at the Dunbar Academy, has not been corrupted by the presence of Southerners and other such in yr environs. . . .

Yr Mother is well, as am I. Agatha still teaches at the Academy. No suitor in sight. We have not seen Suzanna and Naomi in some months, they living at a distance in Massachusetts with small infants & one of our carriage horses lame in the left foreleg. . . . Abigail now wears her hair in the new style, fastened up in loops at the back and on the top of her head. From Philadelphia last spring, on my return from Wash'tn, I brought to her a "three-story bonnet" of the latest fashion, red, white and blue, which, I tell her, when worn with her striped skirt and short spencer, gives her the appearance of "Uncle Sam" from the back side. She has long argued that women are the equals of their husbands; and I tell her that now, when she is dress'd for church in her new bonnet, she is at least taller than Ethan. At the risk of inflating her vanity, I could truthfully tell her that she is also more intelligent than her husband; but that I do not. . . .

Does my Grandson yet have a small horse or pony to ride . . . ?

Another girl-child. . . . What a pity! Yr Mother sends her love to Amelia & the infant, as do I.

> Yr Loving Father,
> S. Clayburn

1824

Dunbar Sep 1

Sam'l Clayburn, Esq.
Crescent City

My Dear Son,—It is grievous news to us that yr wife's Father was drown'd in the river August last & now a great responsibility that you must operate the boat-building *solus* & not yet 25 yrs of age. But you are a Clayburn & I have no doubt of yr capacity for such. Remember to conduct yourself with discretion in all matters financial. I send you herewith, for yr perusal, the *Autobiography* of Mr. B. Franklin. . . .

Yr Mother complaining so much of being alone in this house, save for Agatha, who is all day at the Academy, and Abigail's husband proving incapable of the proper management of the farm in my absence, although that absence occurs only in winter, I have this day given notice that I shall not stand for re-election to the Congress to serve a third term, offering as my reasons my age (74) and the press of my private affairs. Furthermore, between us, it is my opinion that, being an avow'd advocate of the candidacy of J. Q. Adams for President, I wd have small chance of re-election. . . .[27]

Was Mr. LaMar's property, besides the boatwrighting establishment, extensive; and are there other heirs in addition to yr wife & self? Our condolences to Amelia. Does Henry grow apace?

Yrs,
Supply Clayburn

1825

Dunbar, N.H.
June 21, 1825

My Dear Sam'l,—Return'd from Boston yesterday, where I was present at the Fiftieth Anniversary Celebration of the Battle of Bunker's Hill and the laying of the corner-stone of a Monument that has been designed for that place, & findings yrs of June 1, answer forthwith. . . .

Sam, I wish you could have been there! The day was clear & cool and thousands stood along the streets to witness the parade from the State House in Boston to Bunker's Hill in Charlestown and later attended the ceremonies that follow'd. First came the

---

[27]John Quincy Adams was elected in 1824.

Military, with a band playing; then 200 Veterans of the Revolution, foremost amongst them about 40 who had fought at Bunker's Hill, which included myself. Although I could have walked the whole distance with no fatigue, many were infirm or maimed and we rode in barouches. Following us came the Masonic Fraternity and other societies in splendid regalia, heralding the celebrities of the occasion, who came next, amongst them Gen. Lafayette, who assisted at the laying of the stone, and Hon. Daniel Webster, who delivered an eloquent address, from which I copy here the concluding words:—"Let it rise till it meet the sun in its coming; let the earliest light of the morning gild it, and parting day linger and play on its summit." Afterwards, we entered a tent that covered one acre of ground & sat down to a sumptuous repast at 12 long tables on which were assembled plates for 4000 guests. Think on it, Sam! Toasts were drunk and more speeches made, and after these ceremonies, the Veterans of the Battle were allowed to go up, one by one, and shake the hands of Mr. Webster and the Great French Hero.

It happened that when I was presented to Gen. Lafayette, there was some delay in the line for reasons which I could not ascertain &, left alone in my company for several minutes, the Gen made conversation by asking me where I resided. When I told him New Hampshire, he said, "Then you were with Stark's men in the Battle?" "That I was. At the stone wall on the beach," I told him proudly. "Ah, yes," said he. "Where the British light infantry made their first assault." Immediately thereafter, however, the Gen proved himself less conversant with American geography than he was with the disposition of troops at Bunker's Hill; for he asked me then if I enjoyed the acquaintance of Col. William Barton. Col. Barton is a Rhode Islander and played no part in the Battle of Bunker's Hill, but only joined the Continental forces in Cambridge some days after the action. However, I did not correct the General's misunderstanding of our geography & told him, instead, what by sheer accident I knew about Col. Barton: namely, that he is now virtually a prisoner in our neighbouring State of Vermont, detained there in the town of Danville in his old age, 300 miles from his Rhode Island home, because of an inability to pay court costs in a suit he brought to clear title to a township he had purchased in good faith from Vermont some years ago. When I reported Col. Barton's predicament to Gen. Lafayette, the good General express'd great astonishment and indignation that the brave Colonel should be so mistreated by the Country he had valiantly serv'd in its time of need.[28] Sam, if you remember yr American History, as you learned it at the Academy and yr Father's knee, you will recall that it was Col. Barton, with 40 picked men, who rowed in the darkness of night across Mount Hope Bay and captured the English General Prescott,[29] taking him in his nightshirt. Gen. Prescott was later exchanged for our own Gen. Charles Lee,[30] who was then being held by the British in N.Y. State. I have no acquaintance with Col. Barton, but his detention in Vermont has long been a scandal amongst Patriots in New Hampshire.

When the French General asked about my part in the Battle of Bunker's Hill, I told him proudly that I was at the stone wall on the beach; but afterwards, when I went with Amos Barkeley down to the bank of the Mystic River to see again the spot we had defended on that hot June day fifty years ago, we could not find it. All changed! Streets and houses all about! No stone wall left! No hayfields! Earlier in the day, when, riding in the barouches provided for the transportation of the Veterans, we crossed Charlestown Neck, we had encounter'd a similar unfamiliarity. All changed! Nothing the same!

As you should know, Charlestown sits on a peninsula that is almost an island, connected to the mainland by the Neck. Fifty years ago, on that hot June 17, we cross'd Charlestown Neck about two o'clock in the afternoon under a blazing sun, with cannonballs from the British ships screaming over our heads and chainshot hissing everywhere. There was not a bush or a tree on that narrow Neck of land, which was no more than 30 yards in width, and nothing else to shelter us either from the sun or the shot from the British guns; yet we marched, Sam, *in step* and *slowly* all the way, never turning our eyes toward those who fell beside us as we marched. Afterward, I heard Captain Dearborn say that, marching in the van at Colonel Stark's side, he

---

[28]General Lafayette later visited Colonel Barton in Vermont and paid his indebtedness. The township the colonel had purchased is now Barton, Vt.

[29]Major-General Richard Prescott was in command of the British forces occupying Newport, R.I., at the time of his capture, July 10, 1777.

[30]General Lee was captured by the British in New Jersey in 1776

asked for permission to quicken the step of the men, so that their exposure to the British shells in the hazardous crossing of the Neck would be shortened; but Stark replied, "Dearborn, one fresh man in action is worth ten fatigued"; and so the *slow but steady* pace was continued, until we were finally across the narrow Neck and up Bunker's Hill, where we joined Old Put.[31]

From Bunker's Hill, Col. Stark saw at once a hole in the American lines that sorely needed filling; otherwise, when the action began, the British would surely round our left flank and attack Prescott's men on Breed's Hill from behind.[32] Just to the left and the rear of Prescott's breastwork on Breed's Hill, Connecticut riflemen had already manned about 150 yards of rail fence, but there were not enough of them to extend the defence over a low bluff and down to the lapping waters of the Mystic. There, on that narrow expanse of shore, the British could penetrate unopposed. When he saw what must be done, Colonel Stark made a brief speech about his intentions; and after we gave him three rousing cheers, he led us along the Connecticut line, detaching some of our men amongst those troops that were already spread out too thinly behind the rail fence; and then over the cliff and down to the water's edge with the rest of us, where he told us to lay up a stone wall and extend the line to the water. This we did; & because there were not enough stones for our purpose lying about, at the last we stuffed the crevices and raised the level of our breastwork with hay, which had just been cut and lay in windrows before us. Thus, to deceive the British more than as a protection to ourselves, we gave the wall the appearance of a thickness, height & strength that it did not actually possess. When we had finished our work, Colonel Stark himself climbed over our wall and, pacing off some 40 yards in front of us, drove a stake into the ground as a marker, afterwards instructing us not to fire until the first redcoat had crossed it.

On Breed's and Bunker's Hills, Gen. Putnam is said to have told the men not to fire until they saw the whites of the Britishers' eyes; but Colonel Stark told us to wait until we could see their gaiters plain and then fire at their legs, knowing well that

---

[31] General Israel Putnam.

[32] Breed's Hill, commanded by General William Prescott, was the focus of the British attack.

in the impatience of our firing and re-loading, once the fight had begun, we would let our muskets buck and send our aim upward, directing our lead fatally into British bellies.

For an hour, we lay then waiting behind our wall of stone and hay, whilst the British guns set the Town of Charlestown aflame to our right and raked Prescott's redoubt on Breed's Hill before and above us. Old Put came and went on his horse, brandishing his sword, threatening laggards, and urging all to stand firm; but we put our faith in the quieter words of Colonel Stark and Major McClary.[33] Behind the wall, my friend Amos Barkeley lay at my left, and on my other side was a lad of no more than 15 who talked to anyone who would listen, about his mother. He was worried about what she would say to him when he returned to the farm in the New Hampshire hills, where there was hay to cut and corn to plant when he ran off to go to war. The day was exceeding hot, and our throats were parched, & by three o'clock most of us had emptied our canteens, contrary to orders; but our captains quieted our complaints by telling us that the men in the redoubt on Breed's Hill had labour'd the night through at building their fort and had since withstood the British bombardment for eight daylight hours, without relief or refreshment. We were content then with our lot, and ready for Gen. Howe when, at last, he came.[34]

But when at last he came, it was not as I had expected. His Redcoats seemed at first too beautiful to fire upon, like peaceful men dress'd for parade, like dolls, like women almost, in their clean red-and-white uniforms, their hair curled and powdered, a splendid sight, marching in orderly ranks toward us, first through the uncut grass and finally coming into full view into the field that had been mow'd, their gaiters chalked as white as doves in the stubble, their bayonets shining in the sun, all eyes steadily ahead, as if they saw us not, so sure they were that we would turn and run before them. But the moment those Redcoats reached the stake our colonel had set up, I saw how their bayonets, leveled at us now, were meant for our destruction; and at command, I fired with the rest.

---

[33]Major Andrew McClary. After the battle, he was killed while returning across Charlestown Neck to reconnoiter the position the British had taken on Bunker Hill.

[34]General William Howe. He was in command of the British troops at the Battle of Bunker Hill and personally led their assaults.

Sam, in an instant, there was a sheet of flame and a roar of thunder from our stone wall like nothing I have ever seen or heard before or since, and afterward a cloud of black smoke so thick that all before us was lost in it. All I remember of the moment after our first firing was one Redcoat's screeching scream of pain pitched high above the rest and the boy beside me puking in the grass as he re-loaded his Brown Bess.[35] When the smoke cleared, we saw, not 40 yards before us, what we had done: bodies piled as thick as sheep in a fold, arms, legs, red and white, shakos rolling on the ground, and some bodies floating in their own blood in the waters of the Mystic by the shore. Sam, it was a dreadful sight, and I have since wonder'd often that men can make soldiering their profession.

But already more Redcoats were advancing toward us, the same as before, climbing over their comrades' bodies when they came to them, as they had climbed over the walls in the field, as indeed they would be climbing over our wall of stone and hay in another minute, if we did not stop them. This time they were firing their guns at us, but all too high, their ill-aimed bullets ripping through the tallest branches of the trees behind us like hail driven on the wind. So again we poured our lead into their ranks in one great blast, piling more dead and wounded on the others that had fallen. But still they came. Above the screams from that writhing pile we could hear the commands of their officers and the report of their guns and the rattling of bullets in the branches overhead; and we fired back, aiming blindly, but low, into the billow of smoke that our muskets had belched out upon the field; fired; re-loaded, while our comrades fired in turns of three, by Stark's instruction before the battle; and fired again; until finally we stopped them, and the next wave wheeled toward the rail fence above us, where our comrades waited with the Connecticut men. There, the result was the same: our comrades did what we had done, and the bodies piled higher, until at last those that were left alive turned and fled. *British soldiers,* Sam! British *Regulars,* running away! Running, Sam, *running,* like frightened boys! We could not believe our eyes; and, like boys who had won a game, we shouted in our victory.

Thereafter, Gen. Howe re-organized his troops in the tall

---

[35]Name given to their muskets by Continental soldiers.

grass and set about to storm Breed's Hill; and once more, for a while at least, it was the same as it had been before our own guns. The Redcoats advanced and were cut down like the wind-rows amongst which they fell, advanced again, fell, and advanced once more, until finally Prescott's men on the hill had exhausted their powder and ball and could only club the enemy with their rifle butts when at last they swarmed over the parapets. Prescott's men had to abandon their redoubt then; and we too, below them, at the rail fence and the river's side, had to retire, else we would have been outflanked and helplessly cut off from the main body of our Army.

But we retired *in order*, Sam, dropping back to other walls and fences, firing as we went, giving cover to the men fleeing down Breed's Hill toward Bunker's with their empty guns; and when we came to Charlestown Neck again and took the road back to Cambridge, our pursuers dared not follow further and stopped on Bunker's Hill, where they stood watching us depart. We were victorious that day, though we lost the field we fought for.

Sam, you too have seen the British run. Someday you must tell me what happened at the Thames.[36] Was it as brave a day as June 17, 1775? Sam, you must come home soon. And bring the boy. . . . [37]

> Yr Loving
> Father

---

[36]Battle of the Thames, fought in southern Ontario, October 5, 1813, in the War of 1812.

[37]This may have been the last letter Supply Clayburn wrote to his son, Samuel. He suffered a stroke the following winter, and although he lived for another nine years, he was confined to a chair in his house in Dunbar, partially paralyzed, and eventually became blind, unable to see either his son or his grandson when Samuel brought young Henry to Dunbar in 1830 to enroll him in the Dunbar Academy. After his grandfather died in 1835, Henry Clayburn returned to Crescent City, studied law, served in the American Army as a lieutenant in the Mexican War, and later became the Mayor of Crescent City.

Part Three

HENRY CLAYBURN

1819–1891

THE FIRES
OF ANGER

Being the True history of what Happened in Crescent City, 8 & 9 July, 1863, based upon Testimony taken and Evidence examined by The Author, Who has Recorded here not only What Happened to Himself but also What he Conscientiously Believes Happened to Others when He was not Present.

by

HENRY CLAYBURN
Att'y-at-Law

*Published By The Author
Thomas Wilcox, Printer, Willow Street and
Main, Crescent City*

1869

I was the first to see the Confederate raiders. I was standing on a bluff above the river several miles upstream from Crescent City when I discovered them leading their horses, one by one, down the steep bank of the opposite shore, and in the vast and vacant immobility of the July morning it was this motion that first attracted my attention.

I was the mayor of Crescent City. My hair and moustache, once black, were beginning to gray, but because I was then but forty-four years old my face was probably still youthful, a long Scotch face, beardless and tanned by the sun the color of walnut stain. My eyes have always looked dark because they are deeply set under heavy brows; but they are gray, not black. I wore that day a new fawn-colored broadcloth coat that hung from my shoulders straight to my knees, a light checked waistcoat, and bluish-gray trousers tucked inside soft black boots. As I watched the opposite shore of the river, my hands were crushing a round-brimmed hat that I held behind my back.

After I detected the presence of the raiders, I traced their serpentine course down the face of the cliff, in and out among the driftwood, and along the water's edge, until I saw, half-concealed in a clump of willows, the steamboat on which they were embarking. I was sure then that they were Confederates; for Union troops manoeuvring along the Ohio River far behind the front and in no need of secrecy would not have chosen such a hazardous spot for a crossing.

My first impulse was to return to Crescent City at once, but I forced myself to remain motionless under the pin-oak where I stood on the bluff until I had estimated the number of men and, gauging the river's depths and currents, had guessed the point

below me where they would land. After that, I studied the
fieldpieces the raiders were lowering over the cliff and concluded they were three-inch Parrotts. With the guns and the
horses, according to my calculations, six hundred men would
have to make at least six crossings, and each crossing would
require at least an hour. It would be afternoon before they could
attack the city in force. After arriving at this conclusion, I
delayed a minute or two longer to survey the river carefully in
both directions, making sure that there were no other points of
embarkation; and only then, stepping cautiously backward, I
left the spot under the pin-oak and, as quietly as I could, faded
into the thicket of redbud that edged the woods behind me.

As soon as I reached the shelter of the larger trees beyond the
redbud, I turned about, pushed my hat down upon my head, and
strode forward rapidly; but even then, headed homeward and
contemplating the uncertainties that awaited me in the town of
eleven thousand people of which I was the mayor, I was able to
preserve a certain deliberateness and calm, reminding myself,
although there were no Union Regulars in Crescent City to
defend it against a Rebel raid, Regulars could be summoned
from Offitt, forty miles away and, meantime, there was a Federal
gunboat at the Crescent City wharf and there were also the
Home Guards. And yet, while I thought of Regulars, gunboats
and Home Guards, another part of my mind was confronting
the imponderables of panic and possible treason in the town. I
had lived in Crescent City all my life, but I could not guess how
its men and women—how the Home Guards themselves—
would meet the ordeal of invasion. It was a border town, with
a border town's division of loyalties. Indeed, I was not altogether sure of myself; for I knew that I was a man of thought,
not of action, and I did not wholly believe in the rightness of the
war.

Halfway between the river and the River Road, when I came
to a clearing where there was a graveyard enclosed by a low
dry-wall of gray stone, I slowed my pace and looked first at the
cluster of markers over the graves and then at two chimneys that
rose above the trees on the next ridge.

"They will see the chimneys and go there first," I said to
myself.

I could feel the muscles of my jaw tighten in restraint of a smile as I thought of my first wife's father, Reuben Draper, who was buried beside her in the little cemetery. If Nancy's father were alive, I told myself, he would feel no hesitation such as I was feeling. He would not be pondering the imponderables; he would be up on that ridge this morning with his old Kentucky rifle, as impartially ready to fire at Hobson's Union men as John Hunt Morgan's Rebels, not because of any theories about slavery or secession or the rightness of war, but simply to protect his horses.

But that day the Rebels would find no horses on the Reuben Draper place. As I plunged into the woods again and began to descend the ravine on the far side of the clearing, I regarded with pleasure my image of their chagrin. They wouldn't even have the satisfaction of burning down Reuben Draper's house in reprisal for their disappointment. The house had burned six years ago, soon after the old man died, and there was nothing left on the ridge but the chimneys that would draw the Rebels there and a crumble of vinegrown roofless brick walls.

In spite of my anxieties, I let my mind dwell for a moment upon the night of the fire six years before. "You, there—! Jack Clayburn—!" I had cried out at Nancy's and my son when I first saw the boy dismounting among the men in the barn lot by the cistern. "I thought I told you to stay in town with Bradford and your stepmother!" As I scolded him, I had been moved not so much by anger at being disobeyed as by a sudden upsurge of other emotions. Jack was only fourteen that year, and in the light from the burning house his face was the image of Nancy's. "Yes, Papa," the boy replied. "But I came anyhow. It's my grandpa's place, —— it, sir!" A roar of laughter rose then from the men who were forming a line from the cistern in the barn lot to the house; and afterward, while Jack was tying his stepmother's carriage horse to the rail fence, they shouted at me, "It's his grandpa's house, —— it, sir!" in high falsettos that mimicked the boy's voice.

At the bottom of the ravine, I emerged from the woods upon the River Road and turned north toward the town. The road, narrow and winding, no more than a wagon trail, rose sharply to the second ridge behind the river, widened as it passed the weedy ruins of the Draper place, and thereafter stretched for a mile or two along the undulant spine of the ridge like a snake in the sun. At one point on the ridge, I had to pause and get my second wind, and I stood looking down upon the red and white houses and buildings of Crescent City that encrusted the outer edge of one of the river's long loops like jewels on a golden hairpin. Behind the town, the ridge swept round in a protective curve, a wall of green woods broken only by the new black hole of the railroad tunnel to the north and the dry yellow cut of the canal that had been abandoned within a year after it was dug. Above the ridge, the sky burned in a blue flame. There had been no rain for two weeks, and the woods and the town were as dry as tinder. It was a perfect day for house-burning, if that was what the raiders had in mind, I thought, and the thought put an end to my rest and I started walking again.

From the crest of the ridge, the road dipped into the valley and ran a brief course between corn fields that were creased by sunbaked creek beds where willows and alders were a dusty green and ravaged sycamores rose like spectres against the sky. Larks chimed in the fields and yellowthroats rasped out their monotonous switching song in the sumach at the roadside. At the bridge over Bug Slough, a copperhead dangled like a rope of tarnished gold from a rotting guardrail; and wondering why it was abroad so late in the morning, I looked at my watch and was surprised to discover that it was not yet six o'clock.

Beyond the ridge, a road wound up through the corn from the Sykes farm in the river bottoms and merged with the widening River Road, and a mile and a half farther on, the River Road itself jogged round an abandoned sawmill and became abruptly Outer Audubon Street. Before me then, the tree-shaded street stretched away in empty Sunday-morning silence for six or eight blocks until it was lost in the center of the town. By the time I reached this point, I knew what I had to do for the town's sake, and keeping to the grass beside the plank sidewalk in order to make as little noise as possible, I ran the rest of the distance to my house.

It was a new house then and the finest, I thought, in Crescent City, a tall austere house of brick with iron grillwork on the two galleries that spread across the full width of its façade; and yet, as I hurried up the stone steps and unlocked the door, I suffered again, as I always did when I came home to it, the pang of regret that Nancy could not have lived to see it built, and wondered again, as I always did at such moments, whether she in that other world of hers knew of its achievement and, if so, whether she was jealous of the wife who now lived there. But in almost the same moment, I heard a sound of hoofbeats far off in the street whose length I had just traversed, and all such thoughts vanished from my mind as I stopped and listened.

In the next moment, the sound emerged more clearly from the early-morning stillness, and I identified it as the approach of a single horse just beyond the sawmill. I smiled at my moment of apprehension when finally I recognized the animal's familiar rack and knew it was Doc Pendleton's five-gaited saddler, Secesh. For confirmation I glanced across the street and saw that Doc Pendleton's stable door was open and Secesh's stall was empty. Doc, I concluded, was returning from a nocturnal expedition either professional or bibulous and most likely both. And perhaps, I added to my conjecture, amatory as well.

Inside the house, the front hall was dark, but the white balusters of the stairway gleamed in the shadows and splashes of light from the opaque glass of the door danced ruby-bright on the carpet of the stairs. I dropped my hat on a chair and climbed the stairs two steps at a time. From the long cool hall above, I looked in on my second son, Bradford, to make sure that he was in bed and asleep, and closed the door on him quietly. Then I went to the door of my wife's bedroom.

The sun slanted thinly through the closed shutters of polished ash, fell across the sheet of the four-poster bed, and pushed a crooked ladder of light up the bolster till it touched the tip of one loose strand of her reddish-golden hair and made it glow like a candleflame. She was as small as a child in the big bed, and when my presence in the doorway disturbed her and she frowned in her sleep, the troubled gathering of her brows seemed to me childlike too.

I heard Secesh rack past in the dust of the street outside and remembered then why I was standing in the door.

"Helen—" I said softly, and stepped into the room.

The horse I had heard in Audubon Street was Doc Pendleton's horse, but I would learn later that the rider was not Doc Pendleton. The rider was a young man, dressed in black coat and breeches that were of military cut and yet were not a uniform. Soft riding boots came above his knees, and he wore a soft gray hat with a flourish to its brim. Between the hat and the high tight collar of the coat, a small black-bearded face peered out, impudent and alert, with eyes as bright as a raccoon's.

The young man was obviously delighted with Secesh, a mahogany bay mare. She had broken into a brilliant rack of her own accord at the edge of town and was carrying him very high and fast and smoothly down Audubon Street. But his attention was not concentrated solely on his mount. He seemed delighted with everything about him. As he passed the houses of Audubon Street—first the log cabins near the sawmill, then frame dwellings set in large lawns surrounded by picket fences, and finally mansions of stone and brick, he cast sharp sidelong glances at them; and when he came to my house, he turned in the saddle and appraised it openly, smiling, as if he had never seen it before but knew of its existence and who lived in it.

The mare felt his motion and lost her gait, for she had turned her head toward the opposite side of the street, expecting to enter the lane that led to her stable. Her action brought the young man out of his contemplation of my house in time to hold her steady in her course down the middle of the street until they reached the intersection of Main. There he drew rein and sat quietly surveying the view in first one direction and then the other.

To his left, Main Street was a short steep incline of cobblestones that dissolved into sky a hundred yards away at a point where the levee dropped off precipitously into the river. Above the street's abrupt end, the tops of steamboat stacks were etched in startling black against the sky. From where he sat, the young man could not see the hulls or cabins of the boats nor the water nor the Kentucky shore beyond it but only the black smokestacks strung across the end of the street fencing the edge of empty space.

To his right, the young man had a clear view of the seven or eight blocks of Main Street that ran almost directly east from the river's crescent. After the street curved northward, it became a meandering trail through a bleak half-forest of stumps and dying trees, but even in the wide straight urban stretch of it that the young man could see, it hardly deserved to be called a street.

A heaving, cratered, yellowish waste of dust and chuckholes, it was nothing more than a vacant area between two rows of wooden banquettes; and an unreliable area, at that; for at one point, in front of the courthouse, it vanished altogether for a hundred yards along the hitching-rack where the stamping of horses through the years had dug a deep wide trench. On the west side of the street, reflections of the morning sun glared from gaunt, dirty, second-story windows above an unbroken row of tin awnings, where the day's heat had already begun its shimmering dance. The whole vista was empty and still and depressing, and because of the false fronts above the blank-eyed windows, it seemed two-dimensional and unreal, like a stage set deserted by its actors.

The young man sat in contemplation for a long time—ten minutes, perhaps a quarter of an hour—so long, in fact, that if he had not touched the mare's flanks just when he did, I would have seen him as I emerged from my house on Audubon Street a few minutes after I entered it.

Secesh carried the young man then across Main Street at a trot. There Audubon Street loses its dignity and becomes Lower First, a region of wholesale houses and chandler's shops. From the bales and boxes stacked along the sidewalk, all kinds of fragrances fill the air—coffee, tobacco, spices, grain—and the young man must have sniffed delightedly, for he had not savored such odors in a long time. At the intersection of Division Street, near the abandoned canal, in an ill-smelling district of mills and factories, he drew rein again and this time dismounted, tying the mare to one of the hitching-posts that marched along the edge of the plank sidewalk.

He began to walk toward the river, keeping close to the walls of the buildings, moving warily. At the corner opposite the railroad station, his caution was rewarded when a Negro girl appeared out of nowhere and stopped not far from where he had flattened himself against a wall in a littered doorway. The girl, whose name was Delphina, was barefooted and wore a starched blue dress, and when finally she flitted across the street, she looked like a blue butterfly in the sun. Leaping over the railroad tracks, she came to another halt on the station platform and stood there for several seconds in white-eyed panic, both hands pressed over her mouth, her brown elbows, bare below puffed sleeves, making bright golden angles. Again she failed to see the young man in the doorway, and in another moment she was gone, bounding along the railroad ties until she disappeared among the alders of Dove Creek at the far side of the trestle.

The young man waited motionless for a time after the phantom in the blue dress had vanished; then he peered cautiously round the corner of the building in the direction from which the girl had come. There was no one in sight. Water Street, like Division behind him, was empty and still. With a shrug, he stepped quickly away from the building and crossed over to the station.

On the station platform, he became cautious once more and crept under a window and looked into the waiting room before he entered the building. There was no one in the room, but at one end of it the door into the ticket office stood open and he could hear the chatter of a telegraph instrument. The sound seemed to amuse him, for he smiled, and with a kind of eagerness he sidled into the station at once, keeping his back to the wall until he was inside, and then glided noiselessly among the benches until he reached the open door. There he stopped again.

A blue-shirted telegrapher with a cap on the side of his head sat in the ticket office with his back to the door. Beyond him, a window looked out upon a short end of track, which was abutted on the levee by a pile of stones. Above the telegrapher's bowed head, the young man had an unobstructed view of the track's end and the levee, of Water Street and the wharf and the river.

The waterfront was quiet, but on the decks of some of the steamboats the young man saw a few men moving about. Their voices were faintly audible between the bursts of noise from the telegraph, and from time to time there was a splash as they threw things into the river. While he was surveying the window view, a light breeze came up, making the sun glint upon the ruffled water, and the smell of frying pork drifted up from the boats, mingling with the fishy smell of the river.

The young man shifted his gaze from the window to the narrow office before him. It was cluttered and dirty, the table strewn with papers, the floor giving off an odor of sawdust, lye-soap, and tobacco juice. Opposite the window that faced the river, a ticket window opened into the waiting room beside the door where the young man stood. Its frayed oilcloth shade was three-quarters drawn and lopsided across the wicket of iron bars. The man at the telegraph was fat and round-shouldered and gave off a strong scent of sweat and talcum powder.

He was pressing the telegraph key heavily in a plodding, methodical way, and as the young man began to listen to the sound the telegrapher made, the look of eagerness and impudence left his little raccoon face and he became solemnly alert. With a cautious movement, he laid the heel of his hand on the door frame and tapped softly with a spatulate finger, cocking his head to one side, like a musician tuning an instrument. After concentrating on this exercise for some time, the young man stopped and gave himself a little nod of approbation, slid the hand inside his coat, and drew out a large double-barreled revolver.

The young man's eyes were bright and merry again as he curved the spatulate finger round both triggers and pointed the revolver at the back of the telegrapher's head.

"Good morning, Charlie," he said in a quiet friendly voice; and as he spoke, he reached with his left hand and drew the oilcloth shade the rest of the way down across the ticket window and at the same time stepped into the narrow office and kicked the door shut behind him.

Meantime, in the house on Audubon Street, Helen opened her eyes immediately at the sound of my voice and of my coming into the bedroom.

"Where have you been?" she said.

In the middle of the night, when I left the big four-poster bed, she told me afterward, she had not wakened, but in her sleep thereafter she had been aware of my absence and now she was more relieved than startled by my appearance in the room. She asked me the question quietly, as if she had been sleeping with it on her lips and her awakening had released it; she spoke without reproof but with a profound and gentle concern, instead; and yet she did not wait for my answer.

"You'll get sick, Henry. This is the third night in a row that you've got up before dawn and gone prowling off in the dark. You need rest. Why don't you ask Dr. Pendleton for a powder?"

Her voice was full of love. She was worried about my health, the mess my clothes were in, and the dusty sweat that streaked my face, all of these at once. She was ten years younger than I was and, therefore, must have thought of me at times as old.

"Is it that hot out?" she said languorously. "You're all asweat. What time is it? Have you been running? Why?" She became solicitous once more and held out her arms to me. "Darling, I worry about you! Even if I don't wake up, I know you're gone and I worry about you in my sleep. I dream about you. Come back to bed."

She let her arms fall back on the pillow and studied me for a moment. I knew then that she was fighting off jealousy and suspicion. Some girl I had met in City Hall? A scarlet woman down on Water Street? Some woman I had loved before I brought her to live in Crescent City? Then she saw that I was reading her thoughts, and she laughed with me.

Afterward, she made a face at me and said, "All right. Where were you then?"

I sat on the edge of the bed. She pushed herself higher on the bolster, letting the sheet drop about her waist, and I kissed her shoulder.

"Don't," she said, pushing me away.

"Don't," I said, mocking her.

She frowned.

"You are trying to distract me. Where were you?"

"By the river."

"Of course," she said, "I knew that. Where else? You're always down by the river. But where by the river?"

"Upriver—near Nancy's old place."

As I spoke, I took her hand and began folding and unfolding my fingers over it thoughtfully without looking at her. She took her hand away and put it under the sheet.

"Oh," she said.

I laughed again.

"You aren't jealous again, are you?"

"Of course not! But going out there in the middle of the night —it's morbid!" I must have grown rigid, because she reached out her hand to me again. "I didn't mean it that way, Henry. I'm sorry. I do know why you went. You were looking for your youth, because finding it would mean freedom to quit being mayor and to join the army. Isn't that it? Isn't that what you want to do? But, darling, you should be content with the way things are, because Jack is doing that part of it—for *your* side of the family at least." She uttered a little laugh at the way she had put it and, leaning against me, began twisting my watch-chain round her finger. "Honey, if you'd only wake me up in the night when you're feeling this way—" She stopped in the middle of the sentence and, drawing back, looked up at me searchingly because I had not responded. "Henry, what is wrong?"

"There were Confederates crossing the river," I said.

"No!"

"About five hundred of them, I think. Maybe more."

"I can't believe it!"

"Morgan's men, I think—a detachment of them anyhow."

"But only yesterday you told me there were no Confederates within two hundred miles of Crescent City."

"These are calvary—raiders. No one can ever be sure where Morgan is."

"John Morgan?" she said, her face brightening.

"John Hunt Morgan."

"Why, then Cousin Stacey may be with them! We'll get to see him! He'll have news of my kin in Tennessee, and maybe—"

I got up and went to the window and stood with my back to her, and her words broke off abruptly. I opened a panel of the shutters and looked out at the sunlight on the maple leaves and heard a catbird chattering.

"That's odd," I said, half-aloud, to myself. "I heard Doc coming home, but Secesh isn't in the stable."

"Cousin Stacey was with John Morgan at Murfreesboro last year," Helen said. "You'll like him, Henry."

I turned about, shaking my head.

"You sound as if you thought these Rebs were coming just to make a polite visit, Helen."

She slid her legs over the edge of the bed and sat up, staring at me. "You don't intend to resist them, do you, Henry?"

I nodded.

She stood up and ran barefooted across the room to me, her hair tumbling about her shoulders. I caught her small, slim-waisted body in my arms and kissed her. "Baby, baby," I said, and kissed her again.

For a moment she surrendered; then she freed her mouth from mine. "Don't, Henry!" I must have frowned, for she said then: "Oh, I don't mean that! I liked that! I mean about the raiders. Don't try to stop them. Fighting won't accomplish anything. All you have is fat old men like Major Hefflinger and his Home Guards—and these men will be soldiers, Henry, Southerners."

I held her close, stroking her hair.

"It won't do any good," she continued. "You know that. And what if it isn't just a raid, after all? What if it isn't Morgan but Bragg and the whole army? What if it's the real invasion, Henry, and not just a raid?" She grew suddenly furious with me and disengaged herself from my arms. "What are you laughing at?" she demanded.

"You," I said.

"But it might be Bragg! It could be!"

"No darling, it isn't Bragg. Bragg will never get this far north."

"How can you be sure? Why are you always so sure about the war? You keep saying the South can't win, but we haven't lost a real battle yet. Even Shiloh—if Johnston hadn't been killed—and Grant and his butchers will be punished for that at Vicksburg. You wait and see!"

As she spoke, I stopped laughing.

"Don't talk like that, Helen," I said sternly. She burst into tears then and I relented and put my arms about her and rocked her back and forth gently. "It's all right," I said. "Only, I don't like to hear my son called a butcher."

She quieted and dried her eyes with the hem of her night-dress. "I forgot about Jack being at Vicksburg," she said. In the next moment, she was looking at me reproachfully. "But you might think of *our* boy, too, Henry."

"I am thinking of Bradford," I said. "He's one of the reasons I came home before I did anything else."

She was not listening to me.

"If you fight them, Henry, you know what Bradford may try to do. He isn't old enough, but he's old enough to want to."

I held her at arm's length and, looking down into her face, spoke solemnly.

"That's exactly what I mean. I came home to tell you to keep

Bradford in the house, and I have stayed longer than I should because I did not want to leave until I was sure of you. I can be sure of you, can't I, with Bradford? He is still a boy."

"I hope it *is* Bragg and he takes the city and the whole state!"

"I know, I know," I said. "But you are wrong if you think I feel that way, Helen. I'm the mayor of Crescent City and I have a duty to perform."

"But you're a Democrat!"

"That doesn't mean I'm disloyal. You sound like Asa Ross."

Her face contorted in disgust. "That man!" she said. "But, Henry, don't!" she pleaded. "Stay here with me and just let them come. You don't have to do anything, one way or another."

"I've stayed too long already," I said, and went out into the hall.

When I came back from my study, I knew that the black leather holster slung over my arm filled her with terror; but she said nothing, because, in her heart, she knew that what I had just said to her was right. I was the mayor and I believed in the Union, in spite of all my other misgivings. I had no choice. I am sure she would have ceased to love me if I had decided otherwise, Rebel though she was. And she must have been pleased that I had thought of *our* boy. I loved him as much as I loved Nancy's and my son, Jack. She knew that. She had known it all along.

At the last, however, when I started down the stairs, she ran out into the hall after me and, leaning over the railing, cried, "I didn't promise anything, Henry! I didn't promise anything!"

I stopped halfway down the stairs and stood still for a moment without looking up at her.

"I figured if you loved me, Mrs. Clayburn," I said, "I wouldn't need a promise."

"Oh, I do love you, Henry! I do!"

"Then everything will be all right," I said.

I started down the stairs again.

"Aren't you going to kiss me goodbye?"

I stopped on the last step and looked up at her.

"I wouldn't dare to, Mrs. Clayburn."

I began to fasten the holster about my waist under my coat. Watching me, she slid along the railing to the head of the stairs.

"You'll be sorry, Mr. Clayburn," she said. "When John Hunt Morgan takes the city, you'll be begging for my favors."

I blew her a kiss then.

"And I'd better get them, too, Mrs. Clayburn," I said, and went out the door.

When, returning from the river that morning, I unlocked the front door of my house on Audubon Street, the click of the big brass key had awakened my son Bradford; and when I paused in the upstairs hall on the way to Helen's bedroom and looked in upon him, he was not asleep, but only pretending.

He could not explain to me later why he had pretended to be asleep. Perhaps he had a premonition that the day was to be a day of adventure, for he told me there had been something mysterious and exciting about my long pause on the front porch after I unlocked the door and about the way I hurried up the carpeted stairs afterward. Perhaps he felt the need of that sly advantage over me, his father, that a feigned sleep gives to the dissembler; he was always a little awed by me in those days, I think, and resented being still a child now that my other son, Jack, had become a man and was in the Federal army. Perhaps it was only the caprice of a boy of thirteen; at that age a boy does many things that he cannot predict and can see no reason for after he has done them. Remembering that day, it is hard for me to think of him now as a man and himself the father of a son; Thomas Bradford Clayburn, my grandson! I do not yet feel old enough myself for that.

Whatever it was that compelled Bradford to lie still in bed that morning and keep his eyes closed, he abandoned the attitude as soon as I shut the door of his room. Leaping from the bed, he ran to the door, opened it again, and deliberately eavesdropped until he heard me tell his mother that Rebel raiders were crossing the river at the old Draper place. After that, he closed the door and dressed as fast as he could.

As soon as I had left the house and Helen had returned from the head of the stairs to her room, he tiptoed along the hall, down the stairs, and out the back door, grateful that Delphina, our Negro cook, was nowhere in sight. Outside, the magic of that beautiful morning must have touched him instantly and given wings to his feet as he ran down through the dew-drenched garden and the orchard and quickened his fingers as he saddled and bridled Dancer, his Welsh pony. It was all he could do to hold Dancer down to a walk as he rode through the alleys behind the sleeping houses on Audubon Street; and when he came to the jog at the sawmill and entered the River Road, it must have been the joy in his own body that sprang through Dancer as he let the pony go in a gallop.

Bradford was a tall, straight-backed boy, so tall for his age that Mollie Torr, who was thirteen too then, often told him he looked as old as the boys in Miss Laura Pendleton's high-school class. In every aspect except height, however, Bradford resembled his mother, not me. He had her fair hair and skin, her large blue eyes, and her fine straight nose. He had also inherited her romantic passionate nature, and that was why he was riding south on the River Road.

Because of his inheritance from his mother, it was inevitable that his sympathies, like hers, should be with the South. He had lived all his days in Crescent City on the north shore of the Ohio River and had never seen the Tennessee country for which she was always slightly homesick; consequently, the South inspired him with a stubborn rebellious loyalty, not only because he loved his mother but because, in all matters, he was convinced that the faraway was more beautiful than the near-at-hand.

This habit of mind must have interfered seriously with Bradford's devotion to Mollie Torr. He must constantly have pretended that she was not freckled and that her head was crowned with raven tresses instead of a mop that looked like shredded carrots. When Mollie ate the dill pickles she filched daily from the barrel in Grumby's store, he must have had to pretend that she was not a girl at all but a nursing colt, for otherwise the sucking noise she made would have been unbearable. In fact, Bradford's passion for Mollie in those days flourished best when she was not around. He did not know that one day she would be the most beautiful girl in Crescent City and he would marry her.

In a roundabout way, Bradford's flight from the house on Audubon Street, like his romance with Mollie, was inspired by his half-brother, Jack. Ever since he could remember, he had tried to do things as Jack did them, even practicing before a

mirror unobserved—or so he believed—Jack's manner of walking and standing with one leg thrust slightly forward and his
arms folded over his chest. When Jack became engaged to Laura
Pendleton, Bradford had swallowed his pride and, overcoming
his disdain of girls, plighted his troth with Mollie. Now, at last,
after almost three years of envy and frustration, he believed he
was going to become a soldier, too, like Jack—but a soldier in
a far more glorious cause. After all, had not their great-grandfather fought at Bunker Hill, their grandfather at the Thames,
and I, their father, at Chapultepec?

As he rode Dancer through the bright morning light, Bradford experienced, in advance and many times over, with varia-
tions, the adventure that lay ahead of him. He had no doubt that
General Morgan would make him an aide at once—perhaps a
captain with a company of his own. But he was afraid there was
going to be some difficulty over Dancer. The general would
certainly protest at first that a Welsh pony was not a suitable
cavalry mount and would request him to ride a horse into battle.
Bradford was determined to be firm. He would not abandon
Dancer. But for a long time he could not imagine how he would
persuade General Morgan, until he remembered that his mother
had said Cousin Stacey would be with the raiders. Cousin Stacey
would of course put in an appearance at the right moment.
Bradford had never seen Cousin Stacey and he could not
remember Cousin Stacey's last name, but he was sure he would
recognize his mother's relative at once. Cousin Stacey would
look something like Dr. Pendleton, who was Bradford's hero in
Crescent City, only he would be younger and handsomer and
more dashing; and he would intercede in the dispute over the
pony, convincing General Morgan that Captain Bradford Clayburn was a man of mettle and if Captain Clayburn preferred to
charge the Yankee redoubts on a Welsh pony, sir, he should be
allowed to do so, sir.

Soon after Bradford let the pony out in a gallop along the
River Road, the first test of his new mettle came to him unexpectedly. Down the road, over Dancer's plunging head, he saw
a man approaching him leading a horse, and it struck him at
once that the man's appearance was familiar and his behavior
odd. Instead of leading the horse along the road, the man was
walking it in the ditch, where his head and shoulders and the

horse's, plus the horse's rump, were just visible above the tall weeds. Bradford shifted his weight forward in the saddle and, relaxing the reins, led Dancer into a canter.

When he came closer, he saw to his surprise that the man was Dr. Pendleton and the horse was not the doctor's mahogany bay, but a black horse that he had never seen before. The horse wore a McClellan saddle and was lame in its right foreleg. Dr. Pendleton, too, seemed to be lame, for he lurched from one side of the ditch to the other. He was a short, sharp-featured man with coal-black, bristling hair. He had pushed his hat back on his head, and under the exposed coxcomb of pompadour his face was beet-red. Bradford could not tell whether the doctor's color was caused by the heat or by anger; but he was soon to learn that it was the result of both—and of something else besides.

"Give me your pony, boy!" Dr. Pendleton commanded, without so much as a "Good morning," as soon as Bradford came abreast of him. "Let me ride your pony, and you lead this —— nag into town for me."

Bradford had never heard the doctor swear before; and his voice as well as his language was unfamiliar, dry and harsh, as if he had been shouting.

"Where is Secesh, Doctor?"

"Never mind Secesh! Get off that pony and let me have him!"

It was then that Bradford realized there was something else wrong with the doctor besides heat and anger. He was drunk. Bradford had seen enough of the rivermen who loafed around the saloons on Water Street to recognize the effects of too much whisky even in a man whom he admired and could not imagine drunk.

"I can't let you have Dancer this morning, Doctor," he said.

The doctor belched and stood swaying in the weeds, scowling, taken aback and momentarily frustrated by the refusal.

Bradford remembered that the doctor had been drinking last night as he sat on the Torr's front porch with Mollie Torr's mother; but that had been only polite drinking, the kind his father did, although his father never drank in the presence of ladies. Bradford and Mollie, who were hovering in the grape arbor, had heard the doctor say, above the click and chatter of insects, "I tell you, Lucy, the high-handed and despotic acts of the present administration in Washington...." There was more, but Bradford could not remember it all. Only those words had remained in his memory, like an oration, making the blood course through his body, hot and proud. They were not the words of a man who had drunk too much. He must have done more drinking after he left the Torr house. Mrs. Torr sent him home at the same time that she sent Bradford home, and Bradford did remember that after he went to bed he had heard Dr. Pendleton ride out of his stable on Secesh and canter out Audubon Street past Mollie Torr's house and into the country. He supposed the doctor had got a call to a farmhouse up the river and felt sorry for him then, but now he wondered where the doctor had gone and what he had been doing in the country, whether he had gone to "that awful place on the river" that he had heard his mother whisper to her friends about.

"*Can't*, —!" the doctor said, finally. "Get down off that pony! Do you hear me?"

As the doctor spoke, he lurched up out of the weedy ditch still holding onto the lame horse's bridle. The horse, limping on the road after him, whinnied in protest and tried to hold him back.

"What do you mean—*can't*? What the — is wrong with you, boy?"

Last night, Bradford was remembering, Mollie had whispered in the grape arbor, "My mother thinks he's in the Golden Circle. He wants to marry her, but she won't because of that." He himself had not believed it. His father had said that no self-respecting Democrat would join the Knights of the Golden Circle. If a man felt that way about the war, Bradford's father said, he should come out into the open and join the Confederate army. Now Bradford was not so sure about Dr. Pendleton. Disheveled, red-faced and profane in the hot morning sunlight, he did not look respectable at all. Maybe that was where he had been, at a meeting of the Golden Circle. If so, he should welcome the news of the raiders' coming, and that might be the way out of the present predicament.

Bradford took a deep breath and drew himself up in the saddle.

"General Morgan crossed the river this morning, sir, up by the Draper place. "I'm on my way to join him. That's why I can't let you have Dancer."

The effect of his words was not at all what Bradford expected.

A look of enlightenment came into the doctor's face, but there was no pleasure in it.

"So that's who the young whippersnapper was!" he said. "Well, if that's what's up, there's all the more reason for getting these animals back to town. Come on, or we'll lose both of them."

Bradford had now backed his pony into the ditch at the other side of the road, but the doctor, dropping his horse's bridle, crossed over after him. At the doctor's approach, Dancer reared and wheeled about, and Bradford had to hold the reins with all his strength to prevent the pony from bolting.

"No!" he cried.

When Dancer reared, the doctor stopped at the edge of the road, but he began his approach again, walking cautiously.

"I'll give you a dollar," he wheedled. "Don't be a — fool, boy. I'll give you a whole dollar."

All the while, as he spoke, the doctor sidled closer, coming up on Dancer's near side, his hand outstretched. Dancer rolled his eyes and tossed his head. Bradford, stiff and tense in the saddle, tried to hold back the tears that he felt in his eyes.

"Come, boy. Walk this horse home for me, and I'll give you a dollar, a whole dollar," Dr. Pendleton said. "A whole dollar," he repeated; but all the while he spoke, his attention was concentrated on the pony's head and his right arm was rising slowly from his side toward the bridle and what he was saying was only a kind of chant. "A whole dollar. . . ."

"I'm going to join General Morgan, Doctor."

In the same chanting voice, Dr. Pendleton repeated the general's name after Bradford, slowly and contemptuously, "General Morgan —"; and to the end of it he added, as if it were part of the name, a short vulgar word, and with the utterance of the word he grabbed for the bridle. In the same instant, shocked beyond any concern for the consequences, Bradford turned Dancer on his hind legs so that the pony's pawing forehoofs struck out directly toward the doctor's head.

Without stopping to see whether Dancer's hoofs had knocked the doctor down, Bradford dug his heels into the pony's flanks and raced him pell-mell toward the bridge over Bug Slough; and he did not look back until the pony had charged across the loose planking. There was nothing to see then but a tumultuous rolling wave of dust that obscured not only the road but also the fields on either side. But Bradford believed he could still hear the doctor shouting Morgan's name with the ugly word attached to it, and he urged the pony on.

As I went out my front door and down the short brick path to Audubon Street that morning, I was resigned to being my own errand boy for a while, for I was sure the town had a stay of at least six hours before the Rebels could strike and I reasoned that it would be best to move quietly at first and not arouse the citizens to the danger until most of the preparations for their defense had been made. By mid-morning, however, I would need someone to do my legwork for me, and as I turned down Audubon Street toward Main, I considered the ideal qualifications for that duty.

Someone swift-footed and loyal, I thought, but also a person with no great sense of his own importance, a person who would not be diverted from obedience by his own notions about the way things should be done. It was ironic, I reflected, that the same independence of mind that makes for a successful democracy in peacetime can be its undoing in war; and afterward I found further irony in the discovery that my first choice for the job of messenger was Goosehead, the Negro janitor at the City Hall. Goosehead was swiftfooted and could be counted upon for unquestioning obedience. Fight fire with fire, I thought. When threatened by a force sweeping up from the empire of slavery, which you hope to destroy, seek out at once the nearest thing to a slave to serve you in your extremity. In your defense of freedom you will probably end by making everyone a slave of sorts, yourself included. Evil, too, is its own reward.

But that was not wholly just, I amended quickly, for Goosehead was far removed from abject slavery. Whatever his reasons, he would obey only because he wanted to. There were white men in the courthouse who couldn't cajole Goosehead into walking the length of a corridor to borrow a match for them or fetch a ledger. Ben Marvin was one of them. "*Him!*" Goosehead always said of Ben Marvin, and that was all. But that was enough.

Thinking of Goosehead, I glanced back at the summer kitchen

of our house and discovered what I half-expected to discover. No smoke rose from the chimney. That meant that Goosehead's wife, Delphina, had not yet come to work; and that, in turn, probably meant that Goosehead himself would be invisible all day. I was almost sure that Goosehead and Delphina already knew about the raiders. Somehow warnings of impending events reached Negroes long before they came to anyone else in Crescent City. While the white community was still unaware of imminent dangers—a tornado, a flood, a crime about to be committed while it was not yet fully premeditated by the criminal himself, a menacing stranger on his way to town but still far off among the hills along the river, or an incipient hysteria in the breast of some obscure and nondescript white female that could lead to lynching—the Negroes had full knowledge of it and had already vanished from the streets. It was not difficult to believe that Goosehead and Delphina had known about the raiders before I saw them that morning preparing to cross the river, perhaps before the raiders themselves, still deep in Kentucky or Tennessee, had completed their plans for the expedition.

That, I knew of course, was romanticizing, and as I passed Ben Marvin's house, next door to mine, I abandoned it for another of my vices, pride. Originally more finely proportioned than my own house—and not yet supplanted by the towering fashionable Tuscan villa the Marvins have built since on its site —Ben's house had been ruined by many ill-considered additions and sprawled on its lot like an aging slattern beside the graceful grande dame of Nancy's and my creation. It looked, I thought, like Ben Marvin's slovenly mind.

For a moment then, I weighed facetiously the qualifications of Ben Marvin's son, Rodney, for the job of errand boy. A pair of legs was all that was really needed. No head at all. And not much heart—at least until the shooting began, if there was to be any.

Fetch, Lieutenant! I said in my thoughts with a certain malicious pleasure, as I passed the house.

I would write to Jack down in Mississippi: "When you come home, we'll take Rodney Lycurgus Marvin hunting with us. He should be good at retrieving the birds. . . ."

Fetch, Lieutenant!

I was enormously, childishly, pleased by my image of the

young dandy—elegant and sideburned, like Ambrose E. Burnside, his commanding officer upriver in Cincinnati—doing something more appropriate to his talents than parading his pretty uniform up and down Audubon Street on what seemed to be an endless furlough from his desk in Ohio.

Fetch . . !

It was petty of me, and I knew I would not write the letter to Jack, because Jack would not join in my malice. Once when I had written to him on the subject of Rodney L. Marvin and the injustice of their assignments in the service, Jack had replied: "It takes all kinds to make a war, Papa. As I remember Rod Marvin, it's just as well not to send such fellows down here into action. Let them do what they can where they are. That is better than nothing. . . ." I had felt properly reproved then, and I was ashamed of my malice. I wrote back to him that what he had said was true for the Mexican War too, and I told him about the young Mexican cadets who had thrown themselves from the towers of Chapultepec, preferring death to capture, and how we Americans had found no joy in our victory and were almost ashamed of being alive when we came upon their young bodies sprawled under the wall, like boys dropped to sleep while at play, their bright red-and-gold shakos scattered among them like toy drums.

But that too had been a mistake, because it was irrelevant and because I knew that there was nothing that so bored the young as being told that you, too, had once had experiences like their own. For one thing, they never believed you. For another, remembering Chapultepec never brought me any satisfaction. That romantic episode of my youth, that thoughtless, animal adventure in violence, had seemed only shameful after it was over. Those Mexican cadets in the citadel, those lads of twelve and thirteen who threw themselves over the high parapets rather than be captured, were the real heroes of that occasion, not the seasoned and multitudinous victors. The only relevance in contemplating one war is not to compare it with another but to consider how it may be made the last one.

Yet here I was with a pistol at my side walking down quiet Audubon Street on my way to arming it for action! I determined that the remainder of my way I must stop thinking about youth and war and concentrate simply on the clamoring of my empty

stomach, which in the excitement of the morning's events I had
forgotten until I noticed the smokeless kitchen chimney of our
house. As soon as I could I would stop at the Pepper House
dining room or perhaps have something sent up to my office in
the City Hall. Meantime, I would cherish the discovery of my
stomach's hollowness as a reminder, in the face of the impending decisions and dangers, that what is there is often there only
because you allow yourself to think of it. *I think it; therefore, it
is*, I said to myself in paraphrase of Descartes. Maybe if I did not
think too much about the raid, it would never come to pass.
There were other directions that Morgan's men could take from
their landing place up the river.

I turned left on Main Street at the corner where the stranger
had sat astride Secesh only a few minutes before, but I did not
survey the view in every detail as the stranger must have done.
Like an actor who has played the same role countless times, I
was so familiar with the properties of that bleak little stage that
I would have known at once, almost without looking at it,
whether anything was awry. That morning nothing was. As
usual on a summer Sunday morning, the street stood deserted,
hot, and still.

I thought again of my empty stomach. I must not let myself
be persuaded by any of my own political judgments and opinions but must act upon the exigencies of each moment as it came.
The safety of Crescent City and not the sanctity of my own
views must be my concern. As mayor, I had no more right to
act upon my own dissent than I had at that moment to walk up
the street to the Pepper House and satisfy my hunger. I must
go first to the gunboat at the foot of the levee. *I think it*, I said
again to myself; *therefore, it is. I think it; therefore, it is right.*

As I descended the steep slope of Main Street toward the
river, I found myself hoping again that Helen understood how
I felt. She was wrong in saying that I did not believe in the war.
It was the perversion of the war's purpose that I disapproved of.
For a time I had thought that Lincoln was right. If I had lived
in Illinois, I would have voted for him when he ran against
Douglas for the Senate in 1858. I had almost become a Republican then, like Asa Ross. But since then I had been disillusioned
by Lincoln's surrender to the Radicals in the new party. I believed that Douglas, or even Breckenridge, might have kept the

country out of war, might at least have confined the war to a quick suppression of rebellion. I was for the preservation of the Union, but I was also for the preservation of the Constitution, which the new Republicans seemed determined to destroy.

Helen had understood my recent nocturnal wanderings. I did want to get into a uniform again and fight; not, as she thought, in the hope of recapturing my youth, but because fighting would be so much simpler than thinking and because I did not want my son Jack, alone, to make the sacrifice. If I could be at Jack's side . . . but of course they would probably put me in the Provost Marshal's office in Cincinnati with young Rodney Marvin! I could never be sure how much Helen understood beyond her perfect intuitive understanding.

I had never had that kind of understanding with Nancy, although the fault was my own more than hers, because when I married Nancy I was as young and innocent as she was. But from Nancy at this moment, I realized, I would have had something that Helen could not give me, a reinforcement of will, a heart for the day ahead that I could not honestly say I now possessed, in spite of my determination to resist the raiders. If Nancy were alive, I thought, she would be at my side at this very moment, in spirit at least, in the words she would have spoken before I left the house, at my side and striding even a little faster than I was as I descended the levee toward the wharfboat. She would have been there with me, whereas Helen could only remain behind, beckoning me to return to delights that Nancy and I had never had time for in the swiftness of our striding forward together. As Nancy had once inspired me to build the house on Audubon Street, so now Helen showed me how to enjoy it. I felt divided and disloyal.

Because it was Sunday, the wharfmaster was not on duty and I passed unchallenged through the long dark tunnel of the wharfboat, which was like a covered bridge, but when I reached the platform at the water side, a sentry in a new blue uniform barred my way. He had been lolling against a bollard beside the gangplank of the Federal gunboat, but when I came in sight, he stood up importantly, a youngster playing at the role of soldier, a boy of fifteen or sixteen, and not much taller than the Springfield musket he held at port arms.

"I'm the mayor," I told him. "I want to see Captain Price."

The soldier executed order arms, displaying a new corporal's stripe, and drew a whistle from his breast pocket with a flourish and blew for a messenger.

"Mayor of Crescent City to see Captain Price," he instructed the private who appeared at the top of the gangplank. But immediately afterward, finished with his part in the game of soldiering, he leaned against the bollard again and, grinning, said, "Hot, ain't it, Mister Mayor?"

I remembered how Jack had looked the first day he had worn his new blue uniform two years before. He had not told me in advance that he was going to enlist but had gone down to the Armory on Main Street one day and done it. Then he appeared in the office doorway at the City Hall, stepped inside, closed the door behind him, and saluted, grinning broadly. Like the soldier lounging against the bollard, Jack had abandoned the military pose as quickly as he had assumed it and, throwing a leg carelessly across a corner of my desk and selecting a cigar from my humidor—the first cigar I ever saw him smoke—said, with a happy twinkle in his eyes, "Well, Papa, I reckon Mr. Lincoln's Union is safe now." Afterwards, we sat and talked as one man to another; and for the first time I wished that I could wear the uniform, realizing, with a kind of premonition of what was to come, that going and doing would be much easier than staying and thinking.

Since that day, Jack had fought at Perryville and Shiloh and all through Grant's campaign to the gates of Vicksburg and had, no doubt, become a man much older than his years, a man much wiser than I in my contempt for the Rodney Marvins of this world, for example; but Jack had begun like the boy before me on the loading platform of the wharfboat, as all of them had to begin, novices, regarding war as a game and the Union for which they fought as someone else's, not their own, boys innocent of war's realities. You could not tell them about Chapultepec. Since the day Jack came to my office and smoked one of my cigars, the faces of new soldiers had reminded me of war's barbarity more profoundly than the wounds of veterans.

Although the chimney of our summer kitchen was smokeless, Delphina had appeared at our house on schedule that morning.

She did not stay to cook breakfast, however. Five minutes after her arrival, she left by the back door through which she had entered and ran thereafter, as if the devil himself were at her heels, through the dew-drenched back yards and the dusty streets of Crescent City.

If Helen, standing at the head of the stairs, had spoken the name of any other Confederate officer than John Hunt Morgan, Delphina would not have listened, for the war was a subject largely beyond her comprehension. But the name of Morgan was immediate and real. Her husband, Goosehead, had often talked to her about him. Goosehead said the white men at the City Hall called him Robber John and never spoke his name without spitting. Robber John was nine feet tall and sometimes carried his head in his hand so that he could see around corners, and if he ever came to Crescent City, Goosehead said, he would cut the throat of every free Negro in town and carry Amen back to slavery in the South.

As she ran through the empty back yards and streets, Delphina was thinking of Amen as much as herself and Goosehead. Amen was an old man, so old that Goosehead, studying him sometimes as Amen slept under the hackberry behind the cabin on Dove Creek, reckoned he might have fought with Joshua or seen Absalom hanging from the oak in the forest. But they could never find out how old or who Amen was, because he was stone deaf and said nothing understandable but the one word that had become his name. They did know—or, at least, they were fairly sure—that Amen was a runaway slave. They had found him squatting on their doorstep one cold winter morning, dazed, half-starved and half-frozen, and they had taken him in.

At first, Delphina had wanted Goosehead to tell Mayor Clayburn about Amen, in the hope that the Mayor would send him north on the underground railway to a place where he would be out of all danger, but Goosehead shook his head. "They's a law," he said, and nothing more; but Delphina knew what that meant. Like Goosehead, she supposed the Fugitive Slave Law was still in operation, in spite of the war and Emancipation, and like Goosehead, she regarded Mayor Clayburn and the law as one. Even so, if I had not had the pistol and holster that morning when I went out the front door, I believe that Delphina, who was hovering in the back hall, would have thrown herself on my mercy and told me about Amen at last. But Delphina's gun fright was as great as her fear of Morgan; so she ran toward her only other refuge—Goosehead and the cabin on Dove Creek.

When the stranger in the factory doorway on Division Street saw Delphina, her panic was at its peak, and she paused on the station platform only to decide whether to make one last dash across the trestle or to cut down into the alders on the near side of the creek and hide there a while, praying to the Lord to look after Goosehead and Amen without her help while she regained her courage. But with General Morgan on the loose, she reasoned, the Lord might be too busy that morning to listen to her and that would leave Goosehead and Amen not only unprotected but ignorant of their danger. Delphina was scared, but she was not a craven; she chose the dash across the trestle.

Once on the other side of Dove Creek and out of the austere world of white folks, Delphina felt better. The smell of creekwater and catfish breakfasts comforted her, and as she slithered down the clay bank to the lane that meandered, tree-shaded, along the creek, a sense of unwonted importance and power came to her. "Ain't nobody down here knows yet except me," she said aloud; and when she came to the cabin of the Quarter Browns, her next-door neighbors, she slowed her pace in order to relish her distinction. "Biggety ones ain't so big as they think," she said, glancing at the Quarter Browns' house. "Biggety ones going to learn something." She spoke loud enough for the Quarter Browns to hear if they were awake, which she was reasonably sure they were not; for in spite of their airs, they were low-down folks and never got up till noon on Sundays.

At her own house, however, Delphina's top-loftiness vanished when she saw Goosehead and Amen in the backyard. Goosehead was washing his face in a pan on the cistern box and Amen was standing by, bent almost double, drying his grizzled beard with a flour sack. At the sound of her footsteps at the side of the house, Goosehead straightened up, water glistening on his face like sweat, and stared at her.

"How come you home early?" he said.

Delphina stood in awe of her husband. A tall slat-thin man, he towered above her, and his narrow high-domed head, terminating the pole of his neck like the knob of an ebony walking-stick, bore a look of constant indignation. He was the fastest-running man on Dove Creek and he could read handwriting as well as print. Sometimes she marveled that he had ever conde-scended to marry a little sixteen-year-old girl like her.

"I come home," she said; and then, as she thought of the moment of her news, the air stopped in her lungs and she could say no more.

Goosehead waited a few seconds. Then he spoke with an elaborate patience.

"I see you come home, Delphina. Ain't nobody say you ain't come. Somebody say how come you come. That's all."

Delphina swallowed. Looking down at her loftily, Goosehead was waiting again. At his side, ignoring them, Amen continued to rub his beard. She moved closer to her husband and wrapped her fingers round his wrist.

"We got to hide him," she whispered, nodding toward Amen. "They coming after him."

"They," Goosehead said with a frown. "Who they?"

Delphina swallowed again. Speaking the name of Morgan was as terrifying as speaking the name of God or the devil. For them she usually ended by pointing up or down and saying nothing. But for Morgan there was no direction in which to point.

"Him," she said at last; and then, realizing that she still had not made herself clear, she added, "Him and them."

Goosehead shook his head in despair.

"Rebs," Delphina whispered.

Goosehead scowled.

"How many times I done told you ain't no Rebs round here?"

He shook her hand off his arm, took the flour sack away from Amen, and dried his face with it. He emptied the pan of water on the ground beside the cistern and handed the flour sack to Delphina. All the while, Delphina's throat grew drier and drier and time seemed to race past her head with a buzzing sound like a flight of bees.

"Like as not," Goosehead said, starting toward the back door, "you done busted some more of Mizz Clayburn's crockery and she got riled and sent you home. That's all. You scared to tell me. So you talking about Rebs."

Suddenly the dam of awe and terror burst inside Delphina, and she came out with the name.

"Morgan!"

She threw herself across the top of the cistern and began to sob like a whipped child.

"You ain't believe me!" she cried. "But it's him! It's Morgan!"

After a moment, she felt Goosehead's hand resting on her back. He did not speak or shake her or try to make her look at him; he just laid his hand on her back and let it grow heavier and heavier until finally there was no room beneath its weight for her to shake or tremble. When she turned her head at last and looked up at him sidewise and saw that he was not angry, she felt better and stopped crying all at once.

"Now, tell me, honey," he said, gently.

She tried to remember it all clearly, just as she had seen and heard it.

"I was in the back hall and Mayor Clayburn he come down the stairs and Mizz Clayburn she at the top talking to him snake-wild and then she say Morgan he done taken the city and she reckon the mayor he going to be powerful sorry about that and wish he was her favorite and then Mayor Clayburn say he going out and shoot him. Anyhow, he had a gun."

Goosehead waited a moment.

"That all?" he said.

Delphina nodded.

"You sure now? Ain't no more? That was when you run?"

Delphina nodded with greater emphasis.

"Mayor Clayburn had him a gun," she repeated; and then, as if the added information would confirm everything, "I ain't even started no fire in the cookstove yet."

Goosehead took his hand off her back and looked round the yard. Rising on her elbows, Delphina followed his gaze. The ragged weedy yard, long and narrow, backed up against a bluff of yellow clay. In one corner was a patch of corn and beans; in the other, surrounded by hollyhocks, a privy and a henhouse leaned toward each other. A black-and-tan rooster and two brown hens were in the garden.

"Can't put him in the backhouse," Goosehead said contemplatively. "If Robber John he have to go out back when he come, he find him."

The revelation that General Morgan was subject to the calls

of nature like anyone else reduced his stature somewhat in Delphina's imagination.

"We can hide him under the bed."

Goosehead gave her a scornful glance.

"Ev'body always look there first," he told her. He turned to Amen, who had not moved and was staring at the flour sack in Delphina's hand. "We going to hide you in the henhouse, Amen." The old man continued to stare at the flour sack, and Goosehead shrugged. "Ain't no use telling him. Just do it. That's all."

"Ain't no place to hide him—in the henhouse," Delphina said.

Ignoring her protest, Goosehead took the old man's arm and motioned her round to the other side. Together they led him down to the henhouse. While Goosehead opened the narrow door, Amen stood by, impassive, and when Goosehead pushed him inside, he offered no resistance and, squatting on the litter of corncobs, stared out at them with the patient look of a hound dog.

"He look mighty crowded," Delphina said dubiously.

Goosehead closed the door and fastened the hasp with a whittled plug. The rooster strutted over from the garden with the two hens ambling behind him, cocked an eye at Goosehead, and pecked one of his blue toenails. Goosehead kicked at the rooster and he backed off, ruffled his feathers, and stood in spraddle-legged defiance.

"You ain't going to cotton none to that hen we just put in your henhouse," Goosehead said.

Delphina giggled.

"You reckon Amen lay us an egg in there?" she said.

She followed Goosehead up to the shanty. Inside, there were two beds with a sheet hung between them, a table, a chair, a three-legged stool, and a woodstove. A fire burned in the stove, and the air in the room was stifling.

"I fix you some breakfast," Delphina said.

Goosehead sat on the edge of a bed and began to put on his shoes.

"Whereabouts you aiming to go?" Delphina said. "Ain't church for three-four hours yet." Then she remembered Morgan. "Goosehead!"

Goosehead said quietly, "I see you disremembered that letter."

Delphina's hand went automatically to her bosom. A corner of an envelope protruded from under the drawstring above it. Goosehead had forgotten to give the letter to the mayor on Saturday when he brought the mail up from the post office to the City Hall and he had told her to put it beside the mayor's plate at breakfast. "It look like it from Mister Jack maybe," he had said. In her flight from the house on Audubon Street she had forgotten all about it.

"You got no call to leave me here alone for no little old letter!" she cried.

Goosehead stood up and extracted the letter from her bosom.

"Goosehead, you ain't leaving me, I tell you!"

"Delphina," he said, his face solemn. "I ever receives me a letter and Mayor Clayburn he got it, he give it to me. Mayor Clayburn, he receives him a letter and I got it, I give it to him. That's all."

Delphina knew that Goosehead was using the letter as an excuse. Sometimes letters for the men at the City Hall lay round the cabin for a whole week before he remembered to deliver them, and some of those letters were for Mayor Clayburn, just like anybody else. Goosehead's going had something to do with his man's way of acting, which Delphina did not understand. She felt the same way about Mayor Clayburn as Goosehead did, but she saw no reason to get mixed up in white folks' business on a day like this one.

"You got no call to leave me, Goosehead Taylor! You staying right here!"

Goosehead backed off and stood in spraddle-legged defiance, like the rooster in the yard.

"You better get out of my way, Delphina. I going."

She stood her ground for a moment; then a crafty look came into her eyes.

"Go on then! Git!" she said. "You be safe enough with white men round you, I reckon. But when you come back and find Amen stole and me with my th'oat cut, don't you come dragging your wings around me saying I ain't told you."

Goosehead wilted under this unexpected attack.

"If you going, git!" Delphina said. She did not like to see him that way, after all. She pushed him out the door and down the steps. She could not stand the foolish helpless look in his face, and when he turned about, indignant and like his natural self again, she felt better.

"Who you pushing?" he said. Then he turned and loped off round the corner of the house, and she wished she had not pushed him quite so hard.

"Ain't me scared!" she called after him, although she was trembling all over.

She waited till he had time to reach the railroad trestle. Then, sure that he was not coming back, she flew down through the high weeds of the yard to the henhouse. When she opened the door, Amen stared out at her dumbly, still squatting in the litter just as he was when they left him. She reached in and grasped his skinny arm.

"Ain't no place to hide him—in the henhouse," she said.

She drew the old man out gently and led him up to the cabin. As he shuffled along beside her, his bearded chin wobbled as if he were talking, but no sound came from his throat.

"Beats all what a man can think up sometimes," she said. "Hiding him in the henhouse."

By the time they reached the cabin, her trembling had quieted a little.

"Ain't me scared," she said again; and inside the house with the old man, she began to feel better.

The captain of the gunboat greeted me at the top of the ladder to his pilot house. A squat bandy-legged man with a full black beard, he stood solidly on the deck, as fixed and permanent as a binnacle. Although he was officially a commander in the United States Navy as a consequence of the war, he was still more riverman than anything else and spoke at close conversational range in the same voice that he used to command roustabouts on the boiler deck.

"You're out early, Mayor. Had your breakfast yet?"

I shook my head.

"I'll have the boy bring you something. Ham and eggs? Steak? Pork chops?"

"Don't trouble, thanks. I haven't time."

"Nonsense! You've got something to tell me or you wouldn't be here so early. A man can't talk on an empty belly. You can

eat while you talk. Sam—! Hey, you, Sam—!" A Negro appeared
at the top of the ladder. "Bring the gentleman some breakfast.
Ham and eggs. That's the quickest. How do you like 'em,
Mayor?" After I told him, he motioned to the bench that ran
along the after-side of the pilot house and sat down beside me.
"Now, what's on your mind, Mr. Mayor?"

I told him what I had seen that morning upriver, and while
I talked the captain sat with his enormous hands splayed on his
knees, listening attentively.

"About six hundred, you say?" he said, when I finished.

"Yes. They had Parrott guns, and that seems like pretty heavy
artillery for so small a force. So there may be more somewhere,
maybe crossing at another point."

Captain Price nodded. The Negro boy brought the breakfast
at that moment, and the captain leaned over and inspected it
carefully before he would let me eat it. His black beard almost
dipped into the yolks of the eggs. When the Negro was gone, he
returned to the subject of the raiders. "They usually carry howitzers," he said. "Call 'em bull pups. Small and tough and easy
to handle. You're right. Parrotts look like big business. You're
calling up the Home Guards, I reckon."

"Yes. There aren't any Regulars, except the squad that's attached to your gunboat."

The captain chuckled.

"I'd hardly call them Regulars," he said. "Three months ago,
they were hopping clods over in Kentucky." He got up and
stood under the high arch of the steering wheel, smoothing out
his long beard thoughtfully. "I don't understand why the government don't garrison our cities behind the lines. Now, you
take Indianapolis. They tell me there's more Confed prisoners
up there than Union soldiers. If a troop of Rebel raiders ever
reached a place like that—or even Offitt, say—!" He broke off,
his eyes narrowing. "Maybe I shouldn't talk to you like this,
Mayor, but you ask me, I'd say a little less of this Provost Marshal business, like this Burnside over in Cincinnati, a little less
of this —— snooping around to find out who thinks what and
how you're going to vote in 1864 and a little more real honest-to-
God fighting and this —— war would get along a whole lot
faster. Sometimes I wonder what the — they think they're doing
in Washington."

I wonder that sometimes myself. So many new purposes had been grafted onto the original reason for the war, and so many unconstitutional measures had been adopted by the Administration that it was little wonder there was growing disaffection everywhere. The Radicals seemed more interested in winning elections than in winning the war.

"If it is a large force," I said, "the situation in the whole state will be serious. But the immediate problem is to break up this crossing at the Draper place. If we act at once—"

The captain smiled, as if he recognized that I was saying, "If *you* act at once," but he remained relaxed and casual and asked what seemed at first an idle question. "You didn't recognize the boat they were using?"

"I couldn't see anything but the top of its stacks," I said. "It looked like a small packet."

"I was just wondering if they captured the *Matilda*," Captain Price said.

I was startled. I glanced out a window of the pilot house and saw that the *Matilda* was missing from the nest of steamboats at the waterfront. I had not noticed the absence of the boat when I came aboard. The *Matilda* was owned by Ben Marvin and was scheduled to depart on Monday with supplies for Grant's army.

"The *Matilda* was supposed to go downriver tomorrow," I said.

Captain Price nodded.

"But she didn't. She went upriver last night. I supposed you knew. Mr. Marvin came down himself to clear her last night. He had papers made out for her to run up to Brandenburg and take on a drove of mules before she started South. I'd have got in touch with you about it, only it was late and Mr. Marvin came down to the wharf himself, and him being a city official and all, I figured everything was in order."

I too hoped everything was in order, and I saw no reason for voicing my misgivings to Captain Price.

"The order probably came in after I left the office yesterday evening," I said.

The captain shrugged.

"Well, if it's the *Matilda* they've captured, they've got all the provisions she had aboard her for Grant."

"But they'll have to unload them before they can ferry their men and horses across."

"That's what I've been thinking," the captain said. "I'm sure it's the *Matilda* because the timing sounds just right. And the unloading gives us all the more time. Fact is, Mayor, except for the loss of the *Matilda,* I think we're in a pretty good position. I think it would be a mistake to be in too much of a hurry. I'd rather not appear at Draper's Bend till they're split in half, half of them on one side of the river and half on the other. Think how Morgan would feel in that predicament, two hundred miles or more from friendly country with a mile of river water separating his forces and me in between!" He rubbed his hands gleefully.

"It may not be Morgan himself, of course," I said.

"I've got a hunch, kind of, that maybe it ain't. Morgan would not try to take his whole forces across at a place like Draper's Bend. Too risky. He'd go to Brandenburg or someplace like that, where there'd at least be a levee. This is probebly just a diversion, although six hundred men is plenty to worry about."

"Brandenburg," I said. That was where Ben Marvin had got the *Matilda* cleared for.

The captain lighted a cigar.

"Even men as smart as Morgan make mistakes sometimes," he said, looking out at the wharf boat. "What's that word I heard young Rodney Marvin use the other day when he was down here at the wharf boat? Logistics, is it? Well, Morgan is not as good at logistics as he is at manoeuvering and fighting. His men could very well capture his own supply boat before it reached him." He turned and looked at me. "———! Mayor Clayburn, what am I saying? I've got no right to think a thing like that!"

Nor had I, I thought. But I did. I could not help it.

I stood up.

"If you can break up the crossing while it's in progress," I said, "that would be best. You understand the timing better than I do. Start when you think best. Meantime, I'm going over to the station to telegraph Offitt for help—and, of course, the governor. I hope Charlie Gosport is there by now."

"I saw him over there just before you came aboard," Captain Price said. "Had somebody with him. I couldn't tell who it was." He stood at the top of the ladder as I descended it. "We'll take care of the Rebs upriver for you. Don't worry. But you'd better get Regulars into the town, just the same."

As I crossed the gangplank to the wharf boat, a jangle of bells had already begun behind me and men were swarming out on the boiler deck.

"Looks like you brung us some business, Mr. Mayor," the sentry said, as I passed him.

But I did not answer. I was thinking about Ben Marvin and the *Matilda* and there was no room in my mind for the boy's bright new world.

When Bradford heard Doc Pendleton ride Secesh out of his stable across the street after they had both come home from Lucy Torr's house the night before, his conjecture had been right; the doctor was going out on a call to a farmhouse upriver. Doc Pendleton had been in bed and asleep about an hour when Old Man Syke's Negro boy rapped on his bedroom window sill and said, "Mist' Sykes he say come right away, Doctor. Mizz Sykes she 'most dead!"

Mrs. Sykes was already dead when Doc and the Negro boy, riding a mule behind him, reached the farm in the bottoms; but after Mrs. Sykes, there had been Mr. Sykes to care for, because Mr. Sykes had gone into a state of shock; and by the time he got Mr. Sykes sufficiently revived, the Negro boy had vanished and there was no one to help him carry the old man to his bed, because young Estol Sykes's vacant-faced wife, who was staying at the house while her husband was in the army, became as fluttery as a bird and seemed eager to vanish too. So when it was all over, Doc felt entitled to a little refreshment and, knowing the Sykeses made the best corn liquor in the county, he went out into the kitchen and found a supply of it and helped himself; and, as usual, he helped himself to too much. The reason was always the same: his dead wife, whose stern admonishing Quaker face still hovered over all his acts and thoughts as relentlessly as it had hovered over them when she was alive. That very evening it had thwarted him and made him do all the wrong things in his courtship of Lucy Torr. At least, that is the reason Doc gave to himself and would give to me afterward.

But by the time Bradford overtook the doctor on the River Road, it was not Sykes whisky altogether that made him half crazy with heat and anger and so coarse in his language that he knew and regretted, even as he spoke, that he was shocking the

boy beyond forgiveness and thus destroying a hero-worship that
had been apparent to him for a long time and was a solace to his
chronically aching vanity; it was the fact that, a half-hour before
the boy came along the River Road, the doctor had lost his
dearest possession to the stranger with the little black beard and
the raccoon eyes.

Riding up out of the corn bottoms on the wagon trail that
connected the Sykes farmhouse with the River Road, Dr. Pendleton had come upon the stranger unexpectedly. The stranger
was dismounted at the roadside examining his mount's right
forefoot, and when the doctor saw him, he pulled up and asked
if he could be of any help.

"Thrush," the stranger said disgustedly, looking up at the
doctor and making a wry face. "He's gone quite lame."

Dr. Pendleton blinked to clear his vision and then took note
of the lather on the horse's flanks.

"You've been riding him hard," he said.

The stranger laughed.

"It's thrush, just the same," he said.

He held up the forefoot for the doctor to see, and the doctor
leaned forward in the saddle. A watery discharge was flowing
from the frog. The sight sobered him a little and he spoke
professionally, pronouncing the word with great care. "Suppu-
ration." Then he relaxed. "Does it stink?"

The stranger wrinkled his nose above the black beard.

"Stinks like —!"

"You've been riding him hard," the doctor said again.

"Haven't I?" The stranger smiled with a kind of pride. "I
crossed the ferry at Brandenburg only four hours ago. He went
lame all of a sudden, just before you came along."

"Happens that way with thrush," the doctor said gravely.
Then, as an afterthought, he said, "Brandenburg—? That's opposite Mauckport. I didn't know that ferry ran at night."

"It don't," the stranger said, "unless you have the where-
withal."

The doctor was on the verge of offering the stranger a lift into
town when he saw what the stranger had meant by "the where-
withal." It was the double-barreled revolver. The stranger had
pivoted about on his heels and, still squatting at the roadside,
was pointing the revolver up at a sharp angle between his legs.

"You have a gun," the doctor said, as if he expected the information to surprise the stranger as much as it had surprised himself.

The stranger nodded.

"I'll have to ask you for your mount," he said politely.

"I was just going to offer to carry you into town," Dr. Pendleton said; and as he spoke, the revolver went out of focus before his eyes and he began to wonder whether he had actually seen it.

"Much obliged, sir," the stranger said, "but I don't want company."

He rose beside his lame horse, and the revolver in his hand came back into focus. The doctor glanced up and down the road. His vision was almost supernaturally clear of a sudden, and he could see the road stretch away empty in both directions, empty and yellow in the sun. A buzzard wheeled against the bright sky. Its motion was the only motion in the still hot morning.

"I don't see any need—" Dr. Pendleton began. "If you want money, I'll give you what I have. But the bay?"

"I know," the stranger said sympathetically. "She's a beauty, and I don't blame you. A saddler, ain't she? But I'm in a hurry, Mister—"

"I'm a doctor."

"Doctor," the stranger amended. "I'm behind schedule now."

"I have only a dollar or two with me, but we could stop at my house. I will give you my word—"

"Just the mare," the stranger said.

The doctor finally dismounted. But as soon as the stranger swung his leg over Secesh's back, the full sense of his loss overcame the doctor's discretion and, disregarding the revolver, he grabbed for the bridle.

But the stranger was too quick for him.

"Easy, Doc," he said, laughing. As soon as he was settled in the saddle, he glanced over the doctor's head and spoke to the lame horse. "Terry—! Off—!"

The horse leaped across the road and then, remembering its lameness, limped off into the weeds.

"You'll have trouble catching him, even with that foot," the stranger said. "If I was you, Doc, I wouldn't even try. It's too — hot to be chasing a thoroughbred that's got his orders." He slipped the revolver inside his coat and touched his hat in a salute. "Thanks for the bay," he said, and galloped away toward town, leaving the doctor standing in the sun at the side of the road.

The stranger's horse, which had begun to graze at the edge of the road, was a beautiful small black thoroughbred, no more than fifteen hands high, shorter in the saddle space than Secesh but properly long from brisket to whirlbone. It had some saddler blood, the doctor was sure. The deep girth and straight back suggested strength; the arched back rib and clean firm legs were charged with speed. Between the streaks of drying dust-caked lather, the horse's black coat shimmered in the sun like satin.

"Terry," the doctor said gently.

The horse lifted its muzzle from the grass and eyed him inquisitively. The doctor began to move across the road at a pace that was almost steady.

"Easy, boy—"

The horse waited until the doctor was at its side, showing no signs of restiveness; then, as he reached for the bridle, it tossed its head and, leaping sidewise, limped off a few yards out of his reach.

"Terry—"

For a half-hour the doctor stalked the thoroughbred, staggering only slightly, up and down the road between the Bug Slough bridge and the entrance to Old Man Sykes's wagon trail, scheming, coaxing, speaking always softly; but when he finally caught the horse and in almost the same moment Bradford appeared in the River Road, the liquor, which seemed to have drained almost entirely out of his blood, poured back into it with a rush. Then the anger that he had suppressed for half an hour got out of control.

Dr. Pendleton was knocked down in the road but not injured by Bradford's rearing pony. After Bradford and the pony were gone, he picked himself up, waited until the lame horse, free again, had quieted; and then, sobered once more, he began the exercise of stalking the horse again.

The task was easier the second time. The thoroughbred made only two half-hearted attempts to elude him and gave up docilely on the doctor's third try. Thereafter, Dr. Pendleton set out once more for Crescent City, keeping to the weeds of the ditch, as before, to spare the animal's diseased foot as much as possible.

As I climbed the cobblestone levee toward the railroad station on my way to talk with the telegrapher, I continued to ponder the problem of the *Matilda*. Asa Ross had warned me repeatedly about Ben Marvin, my city comptroller, the owner of that steamboat. But Asa Ross was hardly an unbiased judge of Ben Marvin's character. Ben had got in on the ground floor with the new railroad when Asa had not, and years ago Asa had courted Matilda Whiting unsuccessfully before Ben married her. Furthermore, Asa Ross was so embittered by his defeat in the race for mayor three years ago that nothing would please him more than to turn up a scandal in my administration, and certainly Ben Marvin's office was the most likely place for such a scandal to occur.

Asa Ross and I had been friends once and ostensibly we were friends still, but since that election in 1860 it had been a difficult friendship. Asa had never been gracious about his defeat. "I think the people of this town have made a grave mistake," Asa had said when he conceded the election in the columns of the Crescent City *Gazette*. "If we have to have a Democrat as mayor, I am glad it is to be a man like Henry Clayburn, but a great many chancey Copperheads will ride into the City Hall on Mr. Clayburn's coat-tails."

That was the first time I had ever seen the word Copperhead used so in print. When Helen asked me what Asa Ross meant, I told her, as lightly as I could that Asa was only speaking out of his unhappiness. "It sounds," I said, "as if he means that anyone who disagrees with him is, by definition, treacherous and venomous, a snake that prefers dark to daylight. But I don't think he really goes that far. He'll reconsider his words when he cools off." Helen was so furious that she wanted to march down Audubon Street to the Rosses' house at once and give Belle Ross a piece of her mind, and I had a hard time dissuading her. As for myself, I was at first more saddened than angered by Asa's attitude, but ever since the election, Asa's accumulating innuendoes and accusations had festered in my mind.

As for Ben Marvin, I myself did not like him or altogether

trust him, and I suspected that very few people in Crescent City liked him. He had got himself elected comptroller only by riding in on the tail of the Democratic landslide of 1860, the weakest man on our ticket. But I was determined not to condemn him until I had proof. I would believe that orders for the *Matilda* to go upriver for a drove of mules had indeed come in by telegraph and that Ben Marvin had made out her papers to spare me the trouble. That was what I would believe until I had proof to the contrary. It would be easy enough to check on the message with Charlie Gosport at the railroad station.

But when I arrived at the railroad station, Charlie Gosport was not on duty.

Standing in the doorway of the ticket office, I pondered the situation for several minutes. Captain Price said he had seen Charlie earlier in the morning. Charlie ought to be there now, for a train was due from Offitt in about an hour. It was possible that Charlie had had to return home for something after he had come to work, but it was unlike him to leave the office door open in his absence. Charlie could not be said to embody all the virtues by any means, but carelessness was not one of his vices.

Finally, it struck my notice that the telegraph instrument was silent. I did not understand the operation of that instrument, but I remembered that it was usually chattering away even when Charlie was paying no attention to it. I did know, however, that the telegraph was cantakerous and unreliable, and I concluded that it had broken down and Charlie was outside somewhere repairing it.

Through the window, I could see no one on the river side of the building, and I was sure there had been no one on the town side when I entered; but I believed that if I went out and looked round a bit, I would come across Charlie somewhere. Turning, I re-crossed the waiting room and stepped out on the platform. And there, instead of Charlie Gosport, I saw Goosehead.

Goosehead was standing motionless beside the tracks halfway between the station and the Dove Creek trestle, and when I called to him, he seemed not to hear, remaining motionless, like a signal post, beside the tracks. He was peering over the edge of the high road bed and did not look up when I called to him. When I called a second time, he indicated that he had heard by beckoning silently with an angular semaphore of arm, and I started down the track toward him.

"I want you to run over to Mr. Gosport's house for me—" I was saying when I reached Goosehead's side; but he raised his hand peremptorily for silence and pointed, without speaking, over the edge of the cinder embankment.

In the weeds at the bottom of the embankment was a man's body, feet and hands bound with wire, fat legs doubled and pinned to his torso. It looked like a plump turkey dressed for roasting.

"Looks daid, don't it, Mayor Clayburn?" Goosehead said at last.

I leaped down the embankment then, speaking Charlie Gosport's name, and rolled the trussed body over. He was not dead.

When the young man with the double-barreled revolver interrupted Charlie Gosport in the telegraph office, Charlie was chatting over the Sardis wire with his friend Frank Callahan, the Sardis operator. I learned later that Charlie was what is known in the telegrapher's trade as a "plugger," a man who presses the key heavily and deliberately, as a slow-witted man speaks; but Frank Callahan was a "chatterer." Frank skipped along as merrily as a cricket and could make the instrument sing, Charlie told me.

When the young man spoke to Charlie Gosport from the doorway, Charlie said he must have risen straight up in the air two feet above the stool on which he had been sitting, and when he came down again and, turning, saw the young man, he was at first more amazed by the presence of the stranger in the little room than he was frightened by the two black muzzles of the revolver in the young man's hand.

"Take it easy, Charlie," the stranger said.

"Who are you?" Then the menacing black-eyed stare of the revolver became the most important thing in the room and Charlie raised his arm before his face defensively. "Don't point that thing at me, mister!" he said.

The stranger motioned Charlie off the stool, transferred the revolver to his left hand and, with his right hand, began pressing the key calmly.

Hold it, Frank. Back in a minute.

Charlie noticed that the stranger had a plugging style at the key exactly like his own, and he was not surprised when Frank's unsuspecting answer came back.

Take one for me, Charlie. I got a customer at the window. Back in a minute.

The stranger waved the revolver toward a chair by the door and said affably, "Sit down, Charie. And if anyone knocks on the door, get up and open it a little and talk to them. If they see me, tell them I'm a friend of yours who rode down on the cars from Chicago yesterday. I'm an operator, too, like you, tell them. I'm in the depot up there. If you have to introduce me, my name is John Smith. I'm just passing through town on my vacation."

Charlie Gosport gulped and wiped his forehead with his sleeve. He could feel the sweat running in rivulets all over his fat body. He did not believe a word the stranger said. In the first place, there was no John Smith on the depot telegraph in Chicago. He had never heard of an operator anywhere by that name. In the second place, there was a double-barreled revolver staring at him. He remembered the money in the till by the ticket window and couldn't decide which would be smarter: to hand over the key to the till at once or to stall in the hope that someone would come to the door. He chose stalling to begin with.

"Crescent City's a — of a place to spend a vacation this time of year," he said.

The stranger smiled.

"Isn't it?" he said. "If anyone asks, you can tell them I'm on my way to Kentucky to see whether the Bluebellies have left anything standing on my folks' old homeplace."

A Kentuckian, Charlie thought. But that didn't mean anything. Then his mind echoed the word, "Bluebellies." That was a Secesh word. But that didn't mean much, either. You didn't have to look far to find a Secessionist these days, what with bounty-jumpers as common as horseflies and President Lincoln's war getting nowhere. Sometimes Charlie himself wondered if it wouldn't be a good idea for the Northwest to pull out of the Union, like the South, and let the East fight it out alone, the way men like Doc Pendleton and Ben Marvin said sometimes in the Pepper House Bar, although he reckoned that so long as Democrats like the mayor stuck it out, saying the Union came first, he'd stick too.

But all that wasn't any skin off his tail right now, either way. Right now his job was to keep the stranger from shooting him, Secesh or no Secesh, and to save the money in the till if he could.

"Now, this friend of yours," the stranger continued, "this Frank who thinks you've gone to the latrine—what station does he operate in?"

Charlie wanted to say, "None of your — business," but the muzzle of the revolver's lower barrel was beginning to look as big as the entrance to the new railroad tunnel north of town and the stranger's interest in the telegraph was beginning to puzzle him. If the man intended to rob the ticket office, why didn't he go to the till right off, demand the key, and take the money, instead of asking him about Frank Callahan, who was two hundred miles away in Sardis?

"St. Louis," Charlie said finally, not sure why he thought it wise to lie.

A frown flicked across the stranger's face, but he continued to speak softly and politely.

"And the next train—when is it due here?"

At once everything became clear to Charlie. The man was a train robber. The thirty dollars in the till would be nothing but chickenfeed to him. He was planning to hold up Number Seven when it came in on the Straight Line.

"There's nothing on Sundays till evening," Charlie said.

A sorrowful look came into the stranger's eyes, and at first Charlie was sure he had thwarted him. Then he realized the stranger was only looking sorrowful because he recognized the lie for what it was.

"My information," the stranger said, "is that Number Seven comes in on the Straight Line from Offitt Sundays as well as weekdays. Two cars and a caboose, with mail from the South." He glanced thoughtfully at the weapon in his hand; and then he looked up at Charlie, smiling again. "Ever see one of these before?" he said. "It's a nine-shot Le Mat. Made in New Orleans. The lower barrel is loaded wth a charge of grapeshot. Makes a mess out of a man when it's fired at close range."

Charlie stared at the sixty-calibre barrel and licked his lips. He had stopped sweating suddenly and felt cold all over.

The stranger waited a moment and then said, with a note of finality, "Now, let's start all over again, Charlie. This Frank is an operator in Sardis, isn't he? *Not* St. Louis. There isn't any St. Louis line from Crescent City. Just Sardis and Offitt. And you've got the Sardis line open. Isn't that right?" Charlie swallowed and could not speak for a moment. Finally he said, in a voice so low that he could hardly hear himself, "Yes—Sardis."

"Good."

Without looking at the telegraph instrument but keeping his eyes on Charlie, the stranger began to press the key.

Frank. Frank. Charlie back. . . .

Feeling better now, Charlie?

Stay on, Frank. I have an important message. . . .

Charlie Gosport was dumbfounded. Listening to the stranger operate was like hearing his own voice or reading his own handwriting produced by someone else. The muscles in his forearms twitched a little each time the stranger pressed the key, as though he himself were sending the message; and up in Sardis, Frank Callahan, who boasted he could recognize any operator on the circuit by his style, was being completely taken in.

Shoot, Charlie old boy.

Mayor of Crescent City has urgent official message for the governor of the state.

Charlie's eyes bulged. He knew everybody in Crescent City, by sight at least, and this man wasn't anybody he had ever seen around City Hall. But the man was so convincing that for a moment Charlie was taken in as completely as Frank Callahan himself.

Don't kid me, Charlie.

Urgent, Frank. Get this. You ready?

Go ahead.

General John Hunt Morgan crossed Ohio River in night five miles below Crescent City with estimated five thousand men Stop Passed around city without attack and full force is now headed northwest in direction of Sardis Stop Situation here quiet Stop No troops needed Stop Suggest concentration all forces Sardis area and immediate pursuit from Camp Offitt up Dark River Valley Stop More reports to follow if and when available Stop End of message Stop Repeat.

The instrument was silent for several seconds. Then the message came back to the sender. At the end of it, Frank Callahan rattled off: *Holy Mary.*

The stranger smiled.

"Now, open the line to Offitt for me, Charlie," he said. "We might as well have a little fun with the Bluebellies there before we quit."

As Doc Pendleton trudged homeward, leading the lame horse, he tried to make a reasonable appraisal of my son Bradford's news about Morgan's raiders. He knew that the youngster was over-imaginative and guessed that he was acting upon a rumor he had heard among his playmates and was following up his wish that it was true. Or maybe he had invented the story and, after daydreaming over it for a while, had come to believe it. Doc himself did that sometimes, after a few drinks. On the other hand, Doc reasoned, the boy could have been telling the truth. His encounter with the stranger at the roadside fitted into the boy's story. Although the stranger was not in uniform, he had a military look. And his horse was wearing a McClellan saddle, which was not likely to be the choice of a civilian so fastidious as he seemed to be. Furthermore, he had said something about being behind schedule. When Doc finally convinced himself that a Rebel raid was not only possible but even probable, the way home seemed suddenly twice as long and the morning sun twice as hot.

Although Doc had named his horse Secesh, he really did not believe in Secession. He had chosen the name only to needle his Radical Republican acquaintances, for whom he felt a profound contempt; and when he argued boldly in the Pepper House Bar for the secession of the Northwest from the East and said, "Let the — Yankees do their own fighting," it was to needle the agents of the new Federal Secret Service, who were mostly Easterners who had been swarming all over Crescent City in the past few months. Actually Doc desired the restoration of the Union as fervently as any of these men desired it. He was not a Copperhead. But, like me and like many other loyal Democrats, he desired also the preservation of the Constitution, for which the Radical Republicans seemed to have but little respect. Doc was convinced that the South was already defeated and could be persuaded to rejoin the Union if the Federal government would only act magnanimously. But now, he told himself, as he staggered along the ditch beside the River Road—but now, if the Confederacy sent bands of irresponsible raiders across the Ohio in reprisal for the havoc the Federals had wrought in the South, the peace movement in the North would never make any progress.

"Of all the —— stupid things to do!" he muttered, as he walked along leading the lame horse.

Along with his concern over the stupidity of the Confederates Doc was suffering indignation over the loss of his mare; and in the end the concern and the indignation grew together in his sluggish mind until there was nothing left in it but a conviction that the whole country, North and South, had been riding to hell on a split rail ever since the election of Abe Lincoln. He was still drunk by the time he reached his home on Audubon Street, just drunk enough to believe that he was the last sane man in the United States when he led the stranger's horse up the front steps and hitched it to the porch rail. He had lost his mare. Without a horse, he could not practice his profession. Beside his mare and his daughter Laura and perhaps myself, his profession was the only other object of permanent affection in his life.

After he tied the horse, he went into the house and began to remove the furniture from the front parlor, setting it in the back hall. Afterward, he rolled back the flowered carpet, baring the wide poplar boards of the floor. Then he returned to the porch and led the horse through the front door and the hall and into the empty room. Shutting the door into the hall, he stood for a moment admiring the accommodations he had made for the horse.

"Now, Terry," he said, "let's have a look at that foot."

From his office he fetched a jar of blue vitriol and some cotton and lint bandaging; and kneeling at the horse's forefeet, he packed the suppurating frog with the powder quickly and skillfully.

"You'll be all right in a day or so," he said, when he finished bandaging the foot.

Thus reassuring the horse, he stood up and was immediately afterward startled by his daughter's voice behind him.

"What is the matter with the horse, Father?"

He turned about expecting a rebuke, but Laura was smiling at him from the doorway. He knew by the look in her eyes that she thought he was drunk.

"I'm not drunk," he said. "It's the best place to hide him."

"Of course," she said. "It's a wonderful place to hide a horse. Nobody would ever think of looking for a horse in a Sunday parlor."

She advanced into the room, the hem of her skirt gliding smoothly across the bare floor; and watching her, grateful as he always was that her beauty was light and gentle and nothing like her mother's, which had once tormented him and tormented him still sometimes, he felt suddenly sober and weary and weak and longed to lay his head on her breast and weep.

She seemed to recognize the possibility of such a scene and stopped a few feet from him, and her outstretched hand, instead of touching him, began to stroke the horse's neck.

"He's a beautiful horse," she said. "What is wrong with his foot?"

"Thrush," Doc said. "He'll be all right soon—tomorrow maybe. I packed the frog with vitriol."

Laura nodded, as if she understood all about thrush.

"And Secesh—?"

"I met a stranger in the road—" Doc began.

And afterward he told her about Bradford and the raiders.

The stranger had done an expert job of binding Charlie Gosport. He had twisted the ends of wire into long spirals and bent them back upon themselves, so that Goosehead and I, working over Charlie in the weeds below the railroad tracks, were unable to loosen them with our bare hands. But the stranger had done Charlie no serious harm, and as soon as the gag was out of his mouth he was able to direct Goosehead to the tool cabinet in the station where he would find a pair of pliers.

While Goosehead was gone, Charlie explained to me what had happened. After using the telegraph for false messages to the governor and to Offitt, the stranger had wrecked the outfit. He not only cut the wires in a dozen places, he also destroyed the coils and the armatures. Charlie was not sure how long it would take to repair the damage, if he could repair it at all.

As soon as Goosehead returned with the pliers and Charlie was freed, I sent the Negro off to Major Hefflinger's house with instructions to call up the Home Guards and afterwards to meet me in my office in the City Hall. Then, returning with Charlie to the telegraph office, I asked the question that had been in my mind when I was climbing the levee from the steamboat to the station.

"Did you receive any instructions for me last night about the *Matilda*?"

"From Offitt," Charlie said, nodding. "I've got a copy of it here somewhere."

"From Offitt?" I said.

That was downriver.

"Well, it was from Brandenburg, by rights," Charlie said. "You see, there ain't no line from Brandenburg to here and whatever comes from up around there has to be sent down the river to Offitt and then relayed back up here to me. The message come from Brandenburg originally. Here it is. It's signed by General Hobson himself, says—" He handed over the sheet of paper and began to read it painfully over my shoulder. "Says, send the *Matilda* upriver for a drove of mules."

"When did it come?"

"Time's on there somewheres. Seven o'clock. I sent my boy Dave up to City Hall with it as soon as it come in, told him to take it up to your house if you'd gone home. But when he came back, he said Mr. Marvin was there and took it."

Since there was a telegram, I was thinking, Ben Marvin had not lied; and since the telegram concerned a boat that Ben Marvin owned, he was certainly justified in handling the order himself. It was good to have the matter settled.

"Do you have any idea which way the stranger went?" I asked Charlie.

"I thought I heard him run up Division Street, but from where I was in the weeds I couldn't rightly tell. Then I thought I heard a horse galloping, but I ain't sure."

"Well, he has got away. There's no doubt about that," I said.

I was thinking again about Secesh racking past my house earlier in the morning, and I made a mental note to check on Doc Pendleton as soon as I could.

"Start trying to fix the telegraph, Charlie," I said. "I'll write out some messages for the governor and the colonel at Offitt and leave them here on your desk."

Charlie went out on the station platform, and I wrote the messages, asking for aid for the city, without any certainty that they could be sent; then I left the station and headed for my office.

The City Hall, halfway up Main Street from the river, was not a separate building but only the third floor of the Liggum County Courthouse, a temporary arrangement while the new city hall was being constructed on the site of the one that had burned in the first year of the war. As I crossed the courthouse lawn, I could hear the bugles and drums of the Home Guard patrols that were already marching through the streets of the town summoning the rest of the men to arms, but Main Street was still deserted and I had to use a key to enter the building.

I was not in my office long, however, when both Goosehead and Major Hefflinger arrived, the major a pompous elderly man in whom I had small confidence but whose army would be the city's sole defense for a while if the raiders got past Captain Price's gunboat in sufficient numbers to attack. After a conference with the major, who was obviously more eager to get out on the courthouse lawn and make a show of himself on his white horse than he was to deliberate over reasonable plans for defense, I dispatched Goosehead to the homes of the city councilmen to summon them to a meeting in the City Hall at noon; and then, shutting my door against the possibility of intrusion, I drew up the proclamation that I intended to present to the City Council for its approval.

I had just finished the proclamation when Goosehead returned from his mission, and it was only then that the Negro remembered the letter he had snatched from Delphina's bosom early that morning. But Goosehead did not tell me at that time that the letter had come the day before, and I assumed that he had picked it up at the post office that morning, where the postmaster kept the window open for an hour before church-time each Sunday for the anxious parents of sons in uniform. I saw at once that the letter was from Jack. I sent Goosehead down to the station to check on Charlie Gosport's repairs, and then, standing beside the desk in my office, I tore the letter open eagerly.

There were Knights of the Golden Circle in Crescent City. I was well aware of this fact. They numbered about three hundred, and I was pretty sure that I could name the leaders of the Copperhead society. There was Kyd Warren, the attorney; there was Blaston Merrill, the locksmith; there was Roy Peters, the cotton-mill foreman; and there were a few others. If among them there had been a single first-class man, either a genuine Southerner presumably sent North as an agent or a citizen of Crescent City of substance and standing, I would have believed that there was cause to worry; but the leaders were all second- and third-rate men, disgruntled men who had never quite succeeded at anything and yet had never quite failed, who were drawn together, I was sure, not by a common well-defined conviction but by a common vague dissatisfaction. I was confident that in a crisis they would not rise to any organized support of the cause they professed to believe in, and for that reason it seemed to me that the society's fanciful rituals and little escapades, so long as they were kept under surveillance, were a safe outlet for the simmering of its members' discontent.

As for the rank and file of the Knights of the Golden Circle, if anyone had asked me whether I thought Estol Sykes was one, I would have answered promptly *yes*; and I would have been right. Estol was just the type.

"But Estol drew the first number in the conscription lottery last May," I would have added, delving into the dossiers in my mind of almost all the citizens of the town, "and he is in the army now, somewhere down in Mississippi." And in that assumption I would have been wrong.

At the very moment that I was tearing open the letter from my son in the office in the City Hall, Estol Sykes was only a few miles away waking to the sound of cannon fire in a half-faced camp that he had built in the river bottoms when he was a boy. In the City Hall, I heard the cannon fire too and knew whence it came, from the river where Captain Price was engaging the Confederate raiders. But Estol, just awakening and much nearer the scene than I, believed he was back in Mississippi again, where he was supposed to be.

Estol had joined the Knights of the Golden Circle in the autumn of 1862. He was living in town then with his new wife, Nellie. He signed up with the Knights, just as I would have

guessed, not because of any convictions about the war but because the secret meetings of the Crescent City Castle appealed
to him as mysterious and exciting. They also offered a frequent
escape from Nellie, whose company was beginning to pall.

At that time, Estol was a hackman for the Pepper House
Hotel. He met all packets at the wharf and all trains at the
station. In summer, his hack was a long yellow open-air convey-
ance with bright red awnings; in winter, it was a long enclosed
many-windowed carriage painted the same brilliant yellow.
Both hacks bore the name PEPPER HOUSE along their sides in
large red Roman capitals that could be read by the most myopic
of travelers, and one glance at Estol's seedy competitors was
enough to convince the most skeptical that the Pepper House
was first-class, at least by contrast. However, Estol shouted at all
comers a truculent spiel about the merits of the Pepper House,
for he had never before in his life had an opportunity to assert
any kind of social supremacy.

Between these performances, there were long intermissions
of idleness for Estol, and it was then that the agents of the
Knights of the Golden Circle worked on him. On the levee,
along Water Street, in saloons and sporting houses, at the railroad station, in the stables of the Pepper House, at the hitching-
racks of the streets of Crescent City, he was constantly approached with enticements to become a member of the local
Castle. "Just take the vestibule degree," the agents urged, with
a unanimity and monotony that would have convinced a more
discerning man than Estol that they, too, had memorized a spiel,
"just take the vestibule, and when you're in, we'll show you the
elephant."

After Estol paid his fee and joined, he never saw an elephant.
Indeed he was never quite sure what the elephant was and, after
six months, still half-believed that it was an actual beast with
flapping ears and a dangling trunk which would be brought out
of hiding for the parade on The Appointed Day. He was bored
by the interminable speeches and the ritual, and it was only the
prospect of The Appointed Day and the weekly evening of
escape from Nellie that kept his interest in the Knights alive
through that fall and winter.

The Appointed Day was, of course, the day when Confederate armies would invade the North. Each member was told to

have ready for that day a five-pointed red star to hang in his window as identification for the invading Confederates, and Nellie Sykes devised such a symbol from the skirt of a dress she had once worn as a waitress in the Pepper House Bar. After she cut out the star, she hemmed it and embroidered the letters K.G.C. across it with pink thread. Then she framed the star in the steel hoop of the skirt she had cut up. It was too large for any of the windows in their log cabin on the white people's side of Dove Creek, so Estol planned to hang it from the cabin eaves on The Appointed Day.

In late May, when the Conscription Act was put into effect, it was the bad luck of Estol Sykes to see his number come up on the very first turn of the big lottery wheel in front of the post office. He went at once to his father to borrow the necessary three hundred dollars for commutation of his drafting, but Old Man Sykes refused to help him. Estol's mother would have helped him, but she had no money of her own. Since Estol himself never saved a penny in his life and his credit in Crescent City was worthless, he could neither buy commutation nor offer bounty for a substitute. In due course, therefore, he was enrolled in a company and shipped off to Grant's army.

In Mississippi, however, Estol's luck changed. A week after he arrived, he ate some cornmeal mush that was made by grinding dried corn in a coffee-mill and immediately developed a severe case of Mississippi quick-step. The colonel of his regiment took pity on him and granted him a furlough, and he was back in Crescent City within three weeks after his departure for the front.

Estol was determined not to return to duty. Arriving in the city at night, he went directly to his father's farm, prowled around till he found the room Nellie had moved into with all their possessions in his absence, whispered to her his plan to hide from the draft officials, and set himself up before sunrise in the half-faced camp by the river.

Every night for a week before the raiders appeared on the Kentucky shore, Nellie Sykes had been slipping out of the farmhouse after bedtime and carrying to Estol the food that she and Estol's mother had conspiratorially cooked for him during the day. On the morning of the raid and of Mrs. Sykes's sudden death, Nellie had retured to the farmhouse only a few minutes ahead of Dr. Pendleton's arrival. Meantime, Estol was sleeping soundly in his camp by the river, unaware of his mother's death and his father's subsequent collapse, and he did not open his eyes until mid-morning when he was awakened by the Confederates and Captain Price's gunboat.

The first thing Estol saw that Sunday morning was Nellie, who had just returned to the camp and was standing outside it with her back to him looking out across the river.

"What's all that shooting?" Estol said, as soon as he was awake enough to realize where he was.

Nellie did not answer but only pointed at the river.

What Estol saw first when he rolled out of his bed of brush and leaves and went to Nellie's side was Captain Price's snub-nosed gunboat, paddles turning slowly to hold her steady in the river and headed upstream. A converted packet, the boat was boarded up with tiers of heavy planking, and through embrasures on her port and starboard bows bluish-white funnel-shaped clouds were spouting alternately. After each puff of smoke came a hollow boom from the twelve-pound howitzers with which the captain was shelling both shores of the river at once. Estol recognized the gunboat, but he was too slow-witted to realize immediately that the only target a Federal gunboat would be shooting at on a Sunday morning was Confederate soldiers. Even when a cloud of smoke floated off the top of the clay bank of the Kentucky shore and a few seconds later a solid shot from one of the raiders' Parrotts plunged into the river off the gunboat's bow, raising a plume of white water, Estol did not fully comprehend.

"What they up to?" he said.

Then there was a burst of musket fire from the side of the river on which he and Nellie stood, and the rattle of balls against the planking of the gunboat told him that men were fighting in dead earnest.

"Let's git the — out of here!" he cried then and, bending low, started running along the riverbank downstream, with Nellie after him.

A hundred yards from their starting point, Estol stopped for breath and pulled his wife into the shelter of a tangle of tree roots under an overhanging bluff; and at that moment, in an interlude of silence, there came from somewhere on the ridge above them a succession of inhuman yelps.

Estol had heard the Rebel Yell once before, in Mississippi, and as he heard it now the blood charged again through his body as it had done the first time, his scalp tingled, and the loose flesh on his belly felt as if a swarm of ants were crawling over it. When finally he recovered, a look of discovery came into his heavy face.

"It's The Day!" he whispered to his still-shivering wife. "It's The Day they been talking about! It's come! They're here! Come on!"

He led Nellie down the river bank. When they came to the mouth of Bug Slough, they crossed on a fallen tree and plunged into the corn field on the other side, cutting diagonally across the rows till they came to the foot of the Indian mound on which the Sykes farmhouse stood. Only then did Estol remember that his Unionist father would have no sympathy with the invading Confederates, and he stopped by the rail fence, perplexed.

In the same moment, Nellie Sykes remembered her reason for returning to the half-faced camp in mid-morning. She clutched her husband's arm and looked up at him, her face distorted by fear more than grief or sympathy.

"Estol, your ma died this morning," she said abruptly.

Estol stared at her.

"I plumb forgot to tell you. That's why I come back to the camp. To tell you."

"Ma—?" Estol said finally. Then his face twisted from shock to grief to anger and he struck at Nellie.

"—— you!"

"I come right away," Nellie whined. "Honest to God, Estol! I come straight from the house!"

Estol struck at her again, and this time the blow reached her, slanting across her face, and she screamed.

"Shut up" he said. "You want them to hear you?" Then he said, "How come you never told me?"

"I forgot," she whimpered, cringing by the fence. "All that shooting and hollering—"

"I mean before," Estol said, stepping toward her.

Puzzled, Nellie did not know what to answer. "Don't hit me!" she whimpered. "For God's sake, honey, don't hit me no more!"

"How come you never told me she was ailing. I been sitting out there in that camp while she was dying and you never told me."

Understanding came to Nellie then.

"Oh, she never ailed none," she said. "She just up and died all at once. She was dead when I got back to the house about sunup, and that was the first I ever knowed about it. Your pa sent a nigger for Dr. Pendleton and was wondering where I was at. Honest, Estol! That's the God's truth! She never ailed none at all, and then your pa he took awful bad and the doctor was there and I couldn't get away, right off, to tell you, because I had to help him. He got drunk in the kitchen, after."

"Ma," Estol said to himself. "My ma's dead."

"Your pa's awful bad, Estol. Doc said he might be bedrid."

"That old shitepoke!" Estol said, and spat into the weeds by the fence.

Nellie moved closer to him.

"I can't tell you how sorry I am, honey. You got my sympathy."

Estol uttered a vulgar word spiritlessly.

She studied him for a moment; then she moved toward him. "Honey . . ."

He pushed her away.

She remembered the Knights of the Golden Circle.

"I'll look after everything here," she said. "You just go ahead and do what you got to do for the Castle and all, and I'll look after everything here."

"To — with that!" Estol said.

He started to climb over the fence, and Nellie grabbed his arm.

"You ain't aiming to go up to the house, are you?"

He looked at her contemptuously over his shoulder.

"My ma's dead, ain't she?"

"But your pa, Estol. He thinks you're in Mississippi."

"I said to — with it, didn't I?"

"You mean—?"

"I don't mean nothing."

Nellie climbed the fence after him and followed him up the slope to the house. The cannonading shook the earth under their feet. Estol did not look back at her until he reached the front door.

"Where you got her at?"

Nellie pointed up the stairs.

"But your pa's up there too."

Estol used the vulgar word again and started up the stairs, but when he was halfway up the steps he stopped and turned about.

"You still got that star you made last winter?"

Nellie nodded.

"Get it out and set it on the porch. If the Confeds come and there ain't no star, they'll take everything we're going to heir."

"But your pa ain't dead, Estol."

An ugly look came into Estol's face.

"Doc said he would be bedrid, didn't he?"

Nellie nodded.

"Well, he's as good as dead then, and I'm the boss here now. Get your tail moving."

There was good news in the letter from Jack. His company had elected him second lieutenant. "Now that I've got my pumpkin rinds," he wrote, using the soldier's name for an officer's yellow shoulder-straps, "you can expect Vicksburg to fall almost any day."

Sitting at the big mahogany desk alone in my office after reading the letter, I experienced a curious sense of isolation from the events of the morning that were beginning at last to take a definite course around me. I was like an axle at the center of a turning wheel, necessary, I supposed, but seeming in my stationary function to make no progress. But I was resigned to the fact that until the Council assembled there was nothing more that I could do about the raiders. I could not march off with the Home Guards to Bug Slough, much as I would have liked to be with them when, if ever, the raiders moved toward the city. I could not join Captain Price upriver in his operation at Draper's Bend. Nor could I expedite the labors of Charlie Gosport in the repair of his coils and wires in the telegraph office and so speed the arrival of aid from Offitt, their mystery being one that only Charlie himself understood.

Years before, at the front in Mexico, my comrades and I had been contemptuous and at the same time envious of men assigned to headquarters behind the lines, regarding such assignments as sinecures. Now, being a kind of headquarters myself, I would gladly exchange, if I could, my frustrating immobile position of authority for Jack's pumpkin rinds down in Mississippi with all their hazards.

I took my son's letter out of its envelope and, leaning back in my chair, read it again; and after I finished I sat motionless at the desk for a while, thinking of the hours the boy and I had spent together hunting and fishing on the river and in the bottoms along Dove Creek, reading and talking beside the fire on winter nights when Nancy and I still lived with her father in the old house on the ridge, traveling with the boy at my side in the blacktopped buggy in which I used to ride the circuit from one county seat to another. After Nancy died, the boy had been closer to me than most sons were to their fathers, I supposed. Certainly I had never had the same kind of companionship with Bradford, although that may have been because I was much older and more preoccupied with the world's affairs when Bradford came along.

If Nancy had lived . . . I wondered what my life would have been like if she had lived. She and I had dreamed of a more ambitious political career than the mayorship of a little Ohio river town. But of course we had not foreseen the disastrous effect of a war on all private ambitions, even though we had grown up in the shadow of the war's coming. Had old Supply Clayburn in New Hampshire dreamed of being something more than a selectman in the town of Dunbar? I wondered. Had he too felt himself thwarted by the divisiveness of that War of 1812, which had brought some of his fellow New Englanders, more hotheaded than himself, to the point of speaking for secession? Even so, had he, like me, envied his son, my father, who had run away to be a drummer boy in that war? Those brief years with Nancy had been good years, and I was not sure that more recent years, with their modest successes and affluence, had been as good. I knew that I had changed since my marriage to Helen, although I could not be sure what the change was and whether it had come about as a result of my new prosperity or the different quality of my love for her or simply the sag of middle age.

"But I am not old," I protested aloud, thinking again of Jack in Mississippi. "Not too old."

And then I smiled at myself. I had spoken as if I were arguing vehemently with someone in the room. Too old or not, I told myself, my duty at this moment was to sit in this office on my unheroic tail and wait for the town fathers to come down to the City Hall and, by democratic process, ratify the autocratic measures I had outlined for meeting the danger of the raid.

For a moment the irony of my situation amused me. My program for the emergency violated all my principles, included everything that I disapproved of in the policies of the Federal Administration: martial law, conscription, seizure of private property, and all. I proposed to become a little Abe Lincoln myself—and a Thad Stevens and a Charles Sumner too, combined in one self-righteous small-town mayor.

But with a difference, I amended immediately. The city was cut off, isolated, had no resources but its own with which to save itself. It was not a federation, like the states, but a single compact unit, with no constitution to respect and no traditions to violate. And it was the invaded, not the invader. Whatever I did in this emergency I would quickly undo as soon as the emergency was past. I was not establishing a precedent for tyranny that could grow and become irrevocable in the future. I was a little Abe Lincoln maybe, but no Stevens or Sumner.

As I contemplated my situation, I became aware of an increasing number of shadows moving back and forth across the opaque glass of my office door, and finally one of them stopped and there was a loud rap on the pane. I started to get up but leaned back in the chair again when I recognized the shadow of Arnie Lutz. Wakened that morning in the cellar of the courthouse, where he was allowed to sleep, Arnie, the halfwit newsboy, had assumed from the commotion of the Home Guards on the lawn that it was a weekday and, gathering up his hoard of unsold back copies of the Crescent City *Gazette*, had begun to hawk them before the closed doors of the empty offices, in spite of Goosehead's gentle efforts to dissuade him.

"Paypah-hum-m-m . . ." Arnie's voice moaned outside the door.

I did not have to disturb myself for poor Arnie. I did not have to disturb myself for anyone until the Council began to gather in the chamber adjoining my office. Whatever the right and wrong of my course of action, I told myself, I had an undeniable right to these few minutes of solitude now without distraction. I supposed that some men would not have remained in their offices on their unheroic tails on an occasion such as this. They would have sought to lose their anxieties in an appearance of busy-ness. Perhaps it was a weakness in me that I preferred to sit and brood till the time for action came.

Thereafter, I took a small delight in trying to identify each shadow as it passed on the doorpane—Ben Marvin, Goosehead, Asa Ross. Only once, when I recognized Cupid Hollar, the justice of the peace, was I tempted to get up and go to the door. With Cupid Hollar, of all the men who had offices in the courthouse, I should have liked to share my news of Jack's promotion.

Cupid's eyrie under the cupola of the courthouse, where pigeons cooed and winds from the river hummed like the harps of angels in appropriate accompaniment to the marriage ceremonies he performed there as justice of the peace, had been a favorite haunt of Jack's in his boyhood days between my two marriages, when I used to bring him downtown to roam the building while I argued cases in the courtrooms or pored over records in the county offices. In those days, Cupid had hovered over the boy like a nursemaid, restraining him from climbing too far up into the dome of the cupola, preventing him from riding down the dumb-waiter that carried ledgers from the clerk's office to the Circuit Courtroom, and standing patiently in the rotunda of the first floor to catch the ball the boy dropped from the third-floor balcony. Cupid Hollar had little else to do when there were no marriages to be performed, and although he was a man of sixty, his mind was not far advanced beyond the interests that absorbed Jack, who was only ten or eleven then.

After Jack went off to war, Cupid inquired about him almost every day. "I tell you, Mayor, if they was enough young men like that one wearing the Blue, we'd be through with this war in no time!"

But I restrained myself from going to the door and sharing my good news with Cupid, because Cupid, once engaged, was not easily dismissed.

Finally, Goosehead's lean shadow stopped on the other side of the door's glass, and I heard him say, "Miss Laura's out here to see you, Mayor Clayburn."

I came immediately to life then. Laura Pendleton was the one person in Crescent City to whom Jack's promotion would mean even more than it meant to me.

I got up and, crossing the room, unlocked the door.

Earlier in the morning, standing on the bluff almost directly above Estol Sykes's half-faced camp, my son Bradford had watched the fight between Captain Price's gunboat and the Confederate raiders, unaware of the presence of Estol and Nellie Sykes below him. After he fled from Dr. Pendleton on the River Road and found the ruins of the Draper house not yet occupied by the raiders, Bradford had wandered for some time among the ravines and ridges along the winding river in a vain effort to discover the point of their crossing. When he heard the first shots on the river, he returned to the high backbone of the River Road at the spot where I had paused to rest earlier in the morning. There he wheeled Dancer into a horsepath through the woods and, descending into a ravine and climbing the next ridge, reached the point of vantage on the bluff.

There, in the silences between gun blasts, Bradford might have heard Estol's and Nellie's voices below him if his ears had not been deafened by the noise. Certainly he could have seen the Sykeses fleeing along the river bank, but just as they set out a wild shell from the gunboat's port howitzer toppled a tree on the bluff close to the spot where Bradford sat astride his Welsh pony. The pony reared and Bradford clung to its neck, and in the ensuing minutes, while the Sykeses were fleeing, he was too preoccupied with his terror and the pony's to be aware of anything but his own predicament.

When Captain Price reached the scene of the Rebels' crossing that morning, some of the troops had already been put over the river and the *Matilda* was in midstream on her way back to the Kentucky shore to load the men's mounts. It was exactly the situation Captain Price had hoped for when he was talking to me at the Crescent City wharf: the Confederates divided and their ferry boat caught between them. He began to throw shells from his bow gun, but he failed to hit the *Matilda* and she was able to turn about and scuttle back to the northern shore. There she nosed under the bluff bank, leaving only her paddles visible. They made such a poor target that, after a few more shots, Captain Price gave up trying to disable her.

If he could have advanced to closer range, he could have sunk the *Matilda*, but he dared not do that because, in the meantime, the Confederates remaining on the Kentucky shore had got their Parrotts into position and were sinking shots dangerously close to his bow, while the men on the north shore were firing muskets from the bluff above the *Matilda*. At the distance that the captain kept between his gunboat and the shore, the musket balls only bounced off the boat's thick planking like hail, but at a shortened range they would have become a serious hazard. Standing staunchly then in the middle of the river, his snub bow pointed upstream, Captain Price began to lob shells at both shores at once with the two twelve-pounders in his port and starboard embrasures.

By that time, Captain Price knew the disposition of the enemy's forces. The majority of them were still on the Kentucky side, and those who had crossed the river were without heavy artillery. If he could have known that those on the north shore were without horses also, he would have concentrated all his fire on the Parrotts on the south shore, for he had seen enough fighting in his day to know that no soldiers were more pathetically ineffectual than a troop of horseless cavalrymen. There was little danger that the men who had already crossed the river would attack Crescent City afoot. But Captain Price had no way of knowing the plight of the men on the north shore and consequently he kept one howitzer trained on them to keep them immobilized.

After the wild shell from the captain's howitzer struck the tree near Bradford, it took the boy several minutes to get himself and Dancer under control. When this was finally accomplished, another sound more dreadful than the cannonading filled him with fresh terror. It was the Rebel Yell that made Estol Sykes's scalp tingle, a ventriloquial sound that seemed to Bradford to come from all directions at once. The pony shied, and once more the boy clung to its neck, completely unnerved. Suffering a common ague of fear, they trembled together like a single animal, each casting wild glances all about. There was no clear view in any direction, however, except riverward. At the edge of the bluff, the horsepath turned sharply south, skirting the river, and vanished after about fifty feet or so into a sassafras brake. Behind the boy and the horse, where the path came up from the ravine, the range of visibility was not much more extended. The rest of their surroundings was a thick screen of foliage.

The yell came again, and this time it was accompanied by a clattering of stones in the path behind Bradford. Holding the pony in check with all his strength, the boy glanced fearfully over his shoulder and, to his great amazement, saw Dr. Pendleton's mare Secesh laboring up from the ravine. He was on the verge of calling out the doctor's name when he saw that the rider was not Dr. Pendleton but a black-bearded stranger in what looked like a black uniform.

When the stranger reached the top of the bluff, his bright quick eyes took in the situation on the river, glanced about at the surrounding bushes and trees, and settled on Bradford. The boy straightened in the saddle.

"Hi, son," the stranger said, in a quiet voice. "Got yourself a gallery seat, haven't you?"

Bradford tried to speak, but his tongue stuck to the roof of his mouth. Two guns blasted almost simultaneously from Captain Price's boat at that moment and spared him the embarrassment of sobbing audibly in the stranger's presence. When the guns' rumbling echoes had died away in the Kentucky hills, Bradford came out with a breathless, "Was that you?"

"What?" the stranger said inattentively. He had watched the trajectory of the port howitzer's shell, and as he spoke he was peering over the edge of the bluff, scanning the water's edge below them.

Secesh snorted, and Bradford reached out and stroked her, as much to comfort himself as to quiet her.

"Who gave the yell," he explained, still breathless.

"Oh," the stranger said, straightening in the saddle and grinning at the boy, white teeth flashing in his black beard, "you mean this?" He threw back his head and, without seeming to take a breath, gave the Rebel Yell again.

It was a series of explosive, heart-bursting yelps from the back of his throat, followed by a long blood-curdling wail. As Bradford watched the stranger's adam's apple rise and fall among the short black whiskers on his neck and saw it finally quiver in the throes of the ultimate wail, it seemed to him the sound was the sound a man might make in his final agony if his throat were cut. The shivers that began at the top of the boy's scalp poured down over his body into the toes of his boots like a shower of icy water. When the cry was finished, the stranger looked at him, grinning again, and the boy let the air out of his lungs in a long "O-o-oh" of admiration.

The last echo of the yell had hardly died away when an answer came from the point on the bluff where the muskets had been firing a few minutes before, but the reply had none of the agony of the stranger's call. It was a sharp yipping, fiendish and gleeful, and without the blood-curdling finale.

"So that's where it is," the stranger said. "They told me it was on the road."

"What?" Bradford asked.

The stranger gave a little start, as if he had forgotten the boy's presence, and afterward, turning in his saddle, looked Bradford over carefully.

"Ruins of an old brick house," he answered finally.

"That must be the Draper place, my grandfather's old place," the boy said.

The stranger nodded.

"Which way were you going on the road?"

The stranger hesitated and then said, "From town."

"You've been to town and back since you stole the horse?"

"Stole?"

"Took."

"Borrowed," the stranger said.

"Borrowed," the boy said. "You didn't go far enough along the road. The house is just beyond the highest point on the ridge."

"I thought I had passed it maybe."

"It's an old brick house—"

At that moment, muskets rattled on the bluff, the gunboat replied, and the man and the boy were silenced. Bradford felt no longer frightened in the stranger's company, and Dancer too had quieted. The acrid scent of gunpowder floated up to the bluff where they were and Bradford ran his tongue along his lips and tasted it.

"You look like a city boy, son. What you doing out here?"

It was Bradford's turn to hestitate.

"I came to join General Morgan's army," he said after a while, boldly; and the stranger laughed and bared his white teeth again.

"So you're a Copperhead!"

"Oh, no, sir!" Bradford replied emphatically, without thinking.

The stranger stuck out his lower lip, and it gleamed in the nest of his beard like a bubble of blood.

"Spy? Yankee or Confederate?"

"Oh, no, sir!" Bradford protested gain.

"If you're not a Copperhead, you must be a Yankee."

"I mean—" the boy said, confused, "—no one wants to be called Copperhead—not respectable people, even if they do sympathize with the South—what I mean is, my father says—"

"Who is your father?"

"He's the mayor of Crescent City."

"I see," the stranger said gravely. "And this Draper place we're talking about is your granddaddy's old place."

A bright hope dawned suddenly in Bradford.

"I say!" he said. "You aren't my mother's Cousin Stacey, are you?"

The stranger shook his head.

"No, boy, I am not your mother's Cousin Stacey." The red bubble reappeared in his beard. "Come along," he said. "You can show me the way."

"Can't we stay to see how the fight comes out?" Bradford asked.

The stranger glanced without interest toward the gunboat, which was now almost invisible in a cloud of smoke.

"I'll tell you how it's going to come out," he said. "Either the Feds will run out of ammunition and hightail it back where they came from, or Colonel Morey will get in a lucky shot and blow their boat to Kingdom Come. But in either event, your Bluebellies will have put us way behind schedule, and that's not good."

"Colonel Morey!" Bradford cried excitedly. "That's his name! Stacey Morey! I couldn't think of it." The stranger frowned. "He's my mother's cousin. I couldn't remember his last name. My mother said he would be with General Morgan."

"He may be your mother's cousin, for all I know," the stranger said. "But he's not here with Morgan for the simple reason that Morgan isn't here himself—though, God knows, I wish he was!"

Bradford's face fell.

"Where is General Morgan then?"

"In Indianapolis maybe by now—or Sardis—or Chicago maybe—God only knows! But wherever he is, he's sure wondering where *we* are!" The stranger wheeled Secesh round to the edge of the cliff between Bradford and the river and made her throw her flank against Dancer. "Let's get going," he said. "You go first. And no monkey-business, boy! Understand?"

Only then did the boy realize that he was a prisoner.

As he trotted Dancer back to the River Road and then along the River Road ahead of the stranger, his legs seemed to dangle weakly like a marionette's; and although he controlled the sobs in his throat and kept stoically silent, his heart screamed in rebellion against the injustice that was being done to him. He tried to console himself by imagining what would happen to the stranger as soon as he laid his case before Colonel Stacey Morey. The stranger would be court-martialed, he was sure. But it was cold consolation.

When they turned in at the old Draper place among a group of officers who had established headquarters there in the rubble that had once been Rueben Draper's parlor, no one paid any attention to him. The men, who appeared to have been lolling about in disconsolate idleness, came suddenly to life at the sight of the stranger and gathered round him to shake his hand, calling him "Lightning" and asking for news of "the General."

"Best spirits I've seen him in for a year," the stranger said. "He was going to cross at Brandenburg a few hours after I did, and so far as I know everything went all right. He's probably in Indianapolis or Sardis by now."

"Maybe this time he'll forget the little lady long enough to finish what he's started," one of the officers remarked sharply; and the stranger gave him a quick angry look. The officer was a slight elegant young man in a beautiful gray uniform with a scarlet sash, and he wore a scarlet plume in his hat, which was pushed back high on his forehead. Above his blond cavalryman's beard and long whiskers, his cheeks were as rosy as a girl's and his blue-gray eyes, clouded by long lashes, were large and melting. His uniform blouse, with gold and scarlet embroidery on the collar and sleeves, was buttoned only at the top, exposing an immaculate white shirt and a pointed end of black silk neckcloth above the loosened sash. He had not risen from the fallen beam where he sat with one black-booted leg thrust forward, and as he spoke, he tapped the boot with the scabbard of a cavalry sword. "In any event, you're late, Lightning," he said.

"Yes, I'm late, Major Tolliver, but I see I'm not the only one behind schedule this morning," Bradford's captor said, smiling his white-toothed smile and speaking respectufully, but with a taunting note of independence in his voice, as if he regarded himself subordinate only to General Morgan; and as he spoke, he cast a quick glance about at the other men, as if to remind them all of this fact. "It looks like I still had a few hours to spare," he said.

Major Tolliver began to sing softly, tapping his boot in the rhythm of the song.

> *"Who passes by this road so late?*
> *Compagnon de la Majolaine!*
> *Who passes by this road so late?*
> *Always gay . . . !"*

When he finished, he sighed and stared for a while at the toe of his extended boot; finally, he said, "You had more than a few hours to spare, I fear. More than just a few, alas." He sighed again. "You could have taken the rest of the day if you had wanted to. But did you bring us anything from Crescent City, Lightning? Wine, food, pretty maidens—?"

Bradford's captor laughed.

"Only this," he said, gesturing over his shoulder; and for a moment Bradford thought his captor was indicating himself, until he heard him add, "Beauty, isn't she? I took her away from a tipsy fellow on the road when my horse went lame."

Major Tolliver looked the mare over with admiration.

"Actually, I was speaking of information—not wine, women, or horses either," he said after a while, turning his gaze back to Lightning. "Did you learn anything of value in Crescent City?"

Lightning shrugged.

"The town was asleep. I sent a message to the governor but didn't wait for an answer. Had a chat with the Feds at Offitt, but they didn't have time to be sociable after I told them we'd gone around Crescent City and were headed north." He laughed. "They are probably riding ——-for-leather now straight into the ambush the General planned to set for them on the Dark River.

There won't be a Bluebelly within a hundred miles when we go into Crescent City, if we ever do."

"If we ever do," Major Tolliver echoed, with another sigh. He glanced ruefully in the direction of the river, and everyone listened for a minute or two to the sound of the firing. Now, muted by the intervening ridge, it sounded more like thunder than gunfire. "I left a squad on the ridge to draw the steamboat's fire so we could enjoy a little peace and comfort here while we waited." He took in the surrounding ruins with a wave of his ungloved white hand. "Charming spot. Great place for Copperheads, I should imagine."

The word Copperhead must have reminded Lightning of his prisoner, for he jerked his thumb over his shoulder and said, "I found this youngun up on the bluff watching the fight. He says he is the mayor's son."

Major Tolliver turned slowly and gazed up at the boy, as if he had not noticed him until that moment.

"Clayburn?"

Bradford nodded.

"Bradford Clayburn, sir. I came to join the Confederate army. My mother is from Tennessee."

"So is Mr. Lincoln's military governor, Andy Johnson, my boy," the major said. "So are a lot of disloyal people—from Tennessee."

"He says Colonel Morey is his cousin, sir," Lightning said. "I believe that's true. I remember the General told me something of the sort yesterday in Brandenburg. He said if I got into trouble in Crescent City I should appeal to the mayor's wife."

Bradford found himself suffering from a strange loneliness among the men. Nothing was at all as he had expected it to be.

"If you will take me to Colonel Morey, sir—"

The men all laughed.

"Why, I'd be delighted to do that, my boy!" the major said. "We'll go over on the next boat. Find out when the next boat leaves, one of you, will you? Get tickets for all of us. We'll take fried chicken and have a picnic. Or perhaps we ought to bring the colonel over to this side—that is, if he's not too busy." The men laughed again, until the major frowned and said, turning his back on the boy and looking at Lightning again, "Turn him over to Black, Lightning. He's over there in the orchard. Tell Black to be gentle with him. He'll be useful as a hostage."

Lightning told Bradford to dismount and, taking his arm, led him across the weedy yard into the orchard, where a group of soldiers were building an abatis of logs facing the road. Bradford's eyes were hot with tears and he only half-saw the soldiers looking at him speculatively.

"Howdy, Lightning," they said. "How's the General?"

"What you got there, Lightning? Abe Lincoln?"

"Git him an ax an' we'll put him to work."

Lightning handed the boy over to a burly red-bearded sergeant, who was directing the chopping down of trees in the old orchard.

"Been cradle-snatching, ain't you, Lightning?"

"Better tie him up," Lightning said. "But go easy. He's the colonel's kin."

In the excitement of learning about Jack's promotion, Laura Pendleton remembered only to tell me about her father's loss of his horse to the stranger who had later tied up Charlie Gosport and wrecked the telegraph. She completely forgot to tell me that her father had seen Bradford on the River Road headed toward the point of the raiders' crossing. She did not think of her news of the boy's flight from home until she reached her house on Audubon Street; and by the time she returned to the City Hall to tell me about it, the Council had already convened and I was inaccessible at the far end of the noisy Council Chamber.

She stood at the door looking into the room for several minutes, but no one in the constant milling about in the hall and the room itself noticed her. Ben Marvin sat on the far side of the room, but she was reluctant to beckon him when she finally caught his eye. She did not like Ben Marvin any more than she liked his son, Rodney, who had been trying to court her during his furlough in Crescent City, although he knew she was engaged to my son Jack. Finally, Goosehead stood at her elbow, saying, "Can I help you, Miss Laura?"

She told him then about Bradford, while Goosehead frowned and gazed down at her with his habitual look of indignation.

"Where the boy at now, Miss Laura?"

"He said he was going to join General Morgan. Go in and tell the mayor for me, will you, Goosehead?"

Goosehead looked doubtful.

"The meeting has done started, ma'am."

"But he ought to know."

"Your papa seen the boy on the River Road, you say?"

Laura nodded.

"He was headed out toward the Draper place?"

She noded again.

Goosehead had got between her and the door into the Council Chamber and began to guide her toward the stairs.

"Don't you worry none. I'll take care of it, ma'am," he said.

As she went down the stairs, she heard the rapping of a gavel in the Council Chamber above a loud confusion of voices, and over her shoulder she saw Goosehead standing at the top of the stairs, his long head thrust forward, watching her.

"Don't you worry none," he said again, when he saw her hesitate. "You just git on back to your house now, Miss Laura. They ain't holding no church this morning, and the police is running folks off the streets. I just now took Delphina and a friend up to the Clayburn house. Ain't nobody safe by theirselves. You git on home, Miss Laura. I'll look after it."

He was still standing there when she reached the foot of the stairs.

Goosehead waited until Laura Pendleton went out the door of the courthouse; and then, instead of delivering her message to me, he descended to the bull's-eye window on the landing of the stairs and watched until he saw her yellow crinoline float across the sunlit courthouse lawn and down Main Street toward Audubon. When she had disappeared, he lingered a moment longer at the window, glanced back up the stairs toward the Council Chamber and finally made up his mind.

"Folks always troubling him about something," he said. "Ain't no sense in it. A man do just so much. That's all. Even him."

Then he, too, descended to the street floor, crossed the lawn, and loped up Main Street toward Audubon. There he took to the alley behind the houses on the river side of Audubon, instead of following the street itself. When he came to the crape-myrtle bushes that edged the orchard behind the Clayburn house and the Marvin house next door, he was very careful that he could not be seen from the kitchen windows.

"That fool gal see me," he thought. "She see me, she start yelling, 'Goosehead, where you going at?' " He had mimicked Delphina so well in his thoughts that he grinned and shook his head, as if he had actually heard her. "That gal!" he said, with a note in his voice that was both disdainful and admiring. "Hide old Amen under the bed, after all. Lucky I found him."

When he emerged from the alley at the sawmill and entered the River Road, Goosehead broke into the long smooth loping trot that had made him famous as the fastest man on Dove Creek; but within a quarter of a mile of Bug Slough, where he knew Major Hefflinger's men were stationed, he turned off the road and strode more laboriously through the bottoms toward the Sykes place. The corn was beginning to fire, and pausing once to get his wind, he turned his face up to the rolling thunderclouds and scolded them, "You can't do nothing but just set up there and grumble 'thout doing nothing, you no help at all." As if in answer, there was a rumble of thunder louder than the distant cannonading on the river, and he nodded. "But you got to try harder than that," he said.

When he came to the clearing round the Sykes farmhouse, he saw Estol Sykes and his wife in the family burying ground, and he skirted round the place, through the corn field behind the barn and down among the horseweeds that grew rank in the waterless drainage ditch. When he was past the couple in the graveyard, he looked back to make sure it was Estol, remembering that Estol was supposed to be in the conscripted company that had been sent South in the spring. It was Estol, all right. He was digging a grave under a hemlock tree, and his wife stood beside him, arms folded, bare elbows cupped in her palms, in that peculiar way that all women stand when they watch a man work.

"He don't hanker to see me no more'n I hanker to see him, I reckon," Goosehead said to himself. "All the same, I ain't taking no chances getting mixed up with that gun-toting white trash."

Safely beyond the Sykes place, Goosehead took a deep breath and broke into his loping pace again. He followed irregular paths along the river for a while but finally climbed the first ridge until he came out on the bluff where Bradford had stopped in the morning to watch the fight between the gunboat and the raiders.

The fight had come to a conclusion. Just before he reached the top of the bluff, Goosehead heard the earthshaking blast that ended it as a shot from the Confederate Parrotts struck the gunboat's boilers and what he saw on the river was a tall spool of steam that rose a hundred feet into the air and swelled out at the top into a white cloud against the leaden sky, like the cloud, he thought, from which the Lord appeared to Moses and his people on Mount Sinai.

As he watched, the steam thinned out at the base of the spool and floated away in shreds, and seeing the spot where the gunboat had been, he shivered as if a cold wind had struck him. There were only a few scattered fragments of wreckage on the frothing water, and among them dark heads bobbed about like fishtrap buoys.

He sucked in his breath.

"God A'mighty!" he said reverently.

For several minutes there was nothing in him but awe, as if he were witnessing the end of the world. Then it came to him that he ought to return to Crescent City at once and report what he had seen. But in the end he decided to push on.

"Ain't no sense bothering him about this neither," he said. "He find out soon enough. Everybody going to find out about *this*!" It seemed to him more urgent than ever that he find Bradford.

A few minutes later he was shouldering a path through the brake and brush into the ravine, elbowing aside the branches of small trees, his eyes half-covered with his hand to protect them against unpredictable darts and jabs of twigs and brambles.

So far he had traveled only by instinct, without a plan, simply following, like a dog, the least obstructed path between himself and the spot where he was sure the boy would be. He had not thought beyond the moment of encounter, and as the moment drew near he still could make no plans. His only resolve was to keep himself invisible and see what he could see before he acted.

What he saw first, after he had made a wide circle round the ruined Draper house and come in upon the rear of it, was a group of officers in the rubble of the old parlor where Mr. Reuben Draper had given him, years before, his first lessons in reading and writing and had taught him to be a houseboy instead of a field hand. "Port and sherry in the little glasses;

whisky in the big ones, unless they want it neat," he could hear
the old man calling to him from that room into the next, where
he had hovered fearfully over a gleaming array of bottles and
glassware on the sideboard. "Never ask a gentleman if he wants
a second; just take his empty glass when he sets it down and pour
it for him." Now, where Mr. Reuben used to sit with Mr. Henry
and their friends, three or four men in gray uniforms were
gathered in a little knot and two others were just leaving it to
cross the road to the ravine opposite.

What Goosehead saw next was the breastworks of felled trees
and piled-up brush between the road and the orchard where he
and Mr. Jack once played a game that Mr. Jack called "Tippy
Canoe," although there was never a canoe among its properties,
just as there was no profit in it, either—for Goosehead, at least
—although Mr. Jack always called him "The Profit." Mr. Jack
invariably ended the game by taking Goosehead's scalp with the
hatchet from the woodpile. Now, where Goosehead used to lie,
apprehensive, under the upraised hatchet while Mr. Jack said he
was his "grapewhite father," a company of soldiers were tres-
passing, roasting corn; and, for a moment, as he watched them
and recalled the games with Mr. Jack when Mr. Jack was only
six or seven and he was himself ten years the boy's senior, he felt
a superior contempt for the white men from the South, a contempt that was enhanced by the knowledge that the corn they
were going to eat was too green to eat and would give them all
the botts, for sure.

Finally, Goosehead saw the boy Bradford and at first he was
puzzled by the disconsolate look on the boy's face as he sat on
the ground a few yards away from the men with his back against
a tree, until he saw that the boy was bound to the tree with a
rope around his waist.

As he lay in the weeds at the edge of the orchard, surveying
the situation and trying to decide what his next move should be,
what he failed to see was the Confederate picket who was creeping up behind him; and he failed also to hear the picket until the
picket said, "Get on your feet, nigger!" and pricked his buttocks
with a bayonet.

Goosehead, who up to that moment had felt no fear, was
unnerved by surprise and hardly able to obey the command. His
legs were like willow wands, and the picket cursed him and

prodded him forward. But by the time they reached the orchard he had recovered.

The picket prodded him up to a burly man with a flaming beard, who cursed him as the picket had done; but when the boy Bradford told the bearded man Goosehead was his father's servant, the bearded man gave the picket a nod and the bayonet stopped pricking his buttocks. Afterward, when a gentleman with a red feather in his hat and a red sash around his waist came across the orchard and asked, "What you got there, Black?" and the bearded man told him, the gentleman with the feather said, "Tie him up with the boy." "Yes, sir," the bearded man said and saluted. "When are we moving, Major?" The gentleman with the feather sighed and said, "As soon as they fish all the Yankees out of the water." "I'd let 'em drown, I would, sir!" the bearded man said; and the gentleman with the feather sighed again and said, "So would I, Black. But we're not the colonel. Anyhow, there are two more boatloads to bring over the river. It will be three or four hours at the least, maybe more."

The bearded man tied Goosehead and Bradford together to the tree; and when he was gone, Goosehead whispered, "Was that old Robber John?"

"Who?" the boy asked.

"That fancy-Dan gentleman with the feather. Is he General Morgan?"

"That's only Major Tolliver," the boy said. "He's not much!"

"Ain't none of 'em much, you ask me," Goosehead said, and spat on the ground beyond his feet.

The Council wrangled most of the afternoon but in the end gave its consent to my proclamation of martial law and my municipal conscription act. Because it was dark when the meeting finally broke up and nothing could be done until the next morning, my victory was something of an anti-climax. I could only hope that Charlie Gosport would repair the telegraph in time to get in touch with the Offitt Regulars, who were presumably off somewhere in a wild-goose chase up the Dark River, or that Number Seven would finally come in, so that I could send it back to Offitt for help. Major Hefflinger had dispatched couriers to Offitt but there had been no word from them and it was beginning to look as if they had been intercepted. Meantime, the firing upriver had ceased, but no reports had come from Major Hefflinger in that vicinity.

I failed to notice that Asa Ross had remained in the Council Chamber after the meeting, until, glancing up from the papers I was assembling on the table, I saw Asa seated at the far end of the room. Asa's shaggy head was supported on the fingertips of his right hand, which pushed up crescents of loose flesh from his forehead into his scalp. A grotesque little man with a long torso and short legs, when he was seated Asa looked taller than he actually was and bore a startling resemblance to Abraham Lincoln. During our campaign for the mayorship, I had teased him once by saying I suspected he was a follower of the Rail-Splitter only because he looked like him; but Asa was not amused. Lincoln was not radical enough for his tastes. "That compromiser!" he exclaimed. "I'd almost prefer to look like John C. Calhoun!"

Reminding myself that Asa and I were now allies of sorts, since it was the unanimous support of the Republicans in the Council that had carried my measures against the misgivings of my fellow-Democrats, I spoke to him more warmly than I felt.

"Well, Asa, it's a rare occasion these days when you and I find ourselves on the same side of the fence. I appreciate the support you gave me."

Asa made no reply. He remained motionless with his head resting on his fingertips, his eyes fixed on me intently. I waited a moment, laid the papers in their folder, stood up, and then waited another moment. Still Asa did not speak. With a shrug, I finally turned my back on him and went into my office. Sometimes Asa Ross made me uneasy, and this time was one of them.

The office was so dark that I had to light the gas before I could put my desk in order. I glanced at my watch and saw that it was not as late as I thought, however. It was the thunderclouds that caused the premature darkness. I told myself I had better hurry and get home before the rain. Opening the top drawer of my desk I began to sweep things into it from the top of my desk.

When nothing was left on the desk but Jack's letter and the pistol holster, which had lain there ever since I had taken it off early in the morning, I heard a noise behind me and, glancing round, saw Asa again. He had stopped in the doorway that

opened into the Council Chamber and stood looking at me with
the same intent gaze that had made me uneasy a few minutes
earlier.

I was annoyed. I wanted to be alone for a few minutes. I
wanted to go home and see Helen and Bradford briefly before
I went out to Bug Slough to check on Major Hefflinger and his
Home Guards and then returned to the City Hall, where I had
already spent at least ten hours of that day. I was in no mood
for a post-mortem with Asa over the Council meeting, which
was what I supposed Asa had in mind. Whatever Asa had in
mind, I had no desire to have a conversation with him at that
moment. It had been years since I had heard Asa utter a cheerful
or optimistic thought.

But when I spoke to Asa, I again spoke cordially and waved
him toward a chair, reminding myself that I was the mayor of
a city in danger and Asa was one of my supporters.

"I was just cleaning up here," I said.

Asa closed the door behind him and came across the office.
Like a halo, the word MAYOR in clear glass on the frosted pane
of the door shone ironically in reverse above his head, and I
thought, "Here, but for the grace of a few votes, comes the
mayor." It seemed to me that the halo fitted him better than it
fitted me. To Asa Ross everything was either black or white;
whereas, I was always conscious of an endless variety of shad-
ings. I had done that day what I thought was right. But I had
only *thought* it. Asa would have *known* he was right.

"I went to the post office this morning," Asa said, as he sat
down in the armchair at the other side of my desk. He spoke
according to his habit, with a seeming irrelevance but ponder-
ously, as if anything that passed at random through his mind
was a matter of great importance.

I had buckled the holster about my waist and was about to
pick up Jack's letter and tell Asa about the boy's promotion
when Asa added, "I got some bad news."

"It's not about Tom, I hope," I said.

Asa's son Tom was in Jack's company in the South.

"No, it's not about Tom," Asa said.

For a moment, I wondered whether Joe Johnston had broken
through Grant's lines and raised the siege of Vicksburg. But that
was unlikely, and I would have heard such news as soon as Asa.

Asa's bad news, I told myself, was probably some unauthenticated scrap of information from a remote and inconsequential corner of the war where Asa had a friend, or a rumor such as the one he had come into the office with only a few days before, that Stonewall Jackson had not been killed at Chancellorsville after all but had escaped with his army from Virginia and reassembled it in Canada and was planning to invade the United States from the north.

"It's not very bad news, I hope," I said.

"Yes, very bad," Asa replied, in a tone so lugubrious that I could hardly keep from laughing at him.

"Now, Asa," I said, cajolingly, "you're always getting upset unnecessarily. Don't mistake mole hills for mountains, the way I did this morning." To divert him, I told him then about the *Matilda* and how I had suspected Ben Marvin of treachery and how, later, Charlie Gosport had confirmed Ben's statement that an order had come over the wires from Brandenburg in the night. "In the light of what happened at the telegraph office this morning," I said, "I suspect the message from Brandenburg was a hoax by that fellow with the double-barreled pistol, so that the raiders could pounce on the *Matilda* as it passed Draper's Bend. But just the same, Ben Marvin is exonerated. If I had hastily clapped him into jail on my original suspicion, I'd have lost his ultimate support at the meeting this afternoon. He behaved very handsomely there at the end, I thought, didn't you?"

When I finished, Asa was staring at me open-mouthed; but when he spoke at last, he spoke quietly.

"No, Henry," he said, "I don't think any Democrat behaved handsomely this afternoon except yourself, and I'm not sure you would have acted as you did if—" He stopped and averted his gaze, seeming to choke on the word *if*, and afterward, closing his jaws tightly, he worked them back and forth as if he were trying to crush a raspberry seed between the edges of his front teeth.

My irritation with him got suddenly out of hand.

"All right!" I said sharply. "What is your bad news then? Is Grant drunk again?"

He turned a slow reproving look upon me for a moment, as if I had been blasphemous. Grant was his hero. But all he said at the end was that he had got a letter from his son Tom. "He's coming home soon on furlough," he added.

"Well, that's certainly not bad news," I said.

"No, I don't mean that of course. Not the furlough. It's something else."

I could not imagine young Tom Ross writing a letter; but even if he was not illiterate and knew how to put words on paper, it was hard to imagine him in correspondence with his dour father. Tom was a likable boy, but oafish, like an oversized dog that was not very bright and always breaking something whenever it wagged its tail. I was sure that Asa knew nothing about Tom's escapades in the army, his misdeeds. In the letter that was at that moment lying on my desk between Asa and me, Jack had written: "Tom Ross in action is one of the most valuable men in the company. I think he doesn't know the meaning of fear. But between battles he gets bored and is a troublemaker. He shares my tent with me, you know, and now that I'm an officer I'm entitled to a tent by myself and I'd like to have one. But I'm almost afraid to move out on Tom. He needs looking after. Sometimes I wonder why I put up with him. He's more trouble than his friendship is worth. But there's the bond of old times between us, and I always end up feeling fond of him. Do you have friends like that, too, Papa?"

Recalling Jack's question, I smiled at Asa, who was, after all, in spite of our differences, my old friend.

"Tom's bad news is probably not half so bad as the boy makes out, Asa," I said. "I got a letter this morning, too—from Jack—and he didn't mention any trouble Tom was in. They're pretty close, you know, and I think he would have if it was serious." I started then to mention Jack's promotion, but said instead, knowing that poor Tom Ross would never be promoted, "The letters must have come in together last night, since there wasn't any train this morning."

"I'm afraid your boy's letter wasn't written later than my boy's, Henry," Asa interrupted me. "In fact, it couldn't have been."

For a moment, Jack's letter, lying on the desk before me, was as good as Jack himself in the dim gas-lighted room. But only for a moment. Then Asa's words seemed to repeat themselves in my ears and, with my arm still poised over the desk, my fingers only a few inches above the blue envelope, I stared at Asa.

"Go on," I heard myself saying at last; and when Asa did not speak, I heard myself say again, louder, "Go on."

Still silent, Asa got up and came stiffly round the desk to my side, and I felt his hand on my shoulder.

"Go *on!*"

"Maybe you'd better read Tom's letter for yourself, Henry," Asa said, and he laid something on the desk before me.

Looking down, I saw the coarse blue-lined yellow pages on which Tom Ross had written, and I snatched Jack's letter from beneath them, as if there might be contamination in them; and for a long time thereafter I could only stare at Tom Ross's clumsy scrawl without reading it, until finally the lines came into focus and I had to read.

Yesterday we was caught in the Johnnys crossfire on the Bayou Pierre. Por Jack Claybun was kilt and we had to leave him behind. . . .

I closed my eyes; then, opening them, I read the words again.

. . . we was caught in the Johnnys crossfire . . .

The words had meaning but no import. I felt nothing. I was empty, my head as well as my heart. I closed my eyes again, and when at last a small annoyance came to life in me, I welcomed it almost exultantly into the vacuum of my mind and my heart. It was something, at least. Then I realized that it was more than something. It was what I needed. It would become a dam, temporary, but proof for the necessary time against the grief that was surely somewhere in me, still outside my mind and my heart, still unseen and unfelt, like a mounting wave below a horizon, but soon to rush over me and overwhelm me.

I opened my eyes.

. . . Por Jack Claybun was kilt . . .

Asa Ross's oafish son had been able to spell the unfamiliar name *Bayou Pierre* but he could not spell the name of the friend who had loved him for old time's sake, who had saved him from dishonor and perhaps from the firing squad when he was absent without leave just before Shiloh. It was a trivial annoyance, but I allowed it to grow, encouraged it. I had to. It became the dam that I needed.

. . . Por Jack Claybun was kilt . . .

And Asa Ross's son was still alive and whole, looking forward to his furlough.

. . . and we had to leave him behind . . .

The annoyance became anger, grew to rage, loomed profanely

larger than the onrushing grief that was both visible and palpable now, beating at last against my heart and mind, still outside them but not long to remain there, clamoring to be admitted, to wash over them, over me, to dissolve me, annihilate me.

I stood up, grasping the edge of the desk.

"You've known this since morning," I said. My voice was hardly more than a whisper, and I peered at Asa Ross as if I had just then descried him from a great distance.

"I was afraid if you knew, Henry—"

My grasp tightened on the edge of the desk. When I spoke again, my voice was stronger but still controlled, a cold, remote and quiet voice that seemed not to be my own.

"You were afraid that, if I knew, I would not take the stand I took this afternoon at the meeting."

Asa Ross's face faded, vanished for a moment, then reappeared; the face of my one-time friend, hateful; the face of the times in which we lived, of suspicion and intolerance and tyranny; Abraham Lincoln's face, but without the suffering and the humanity that sometimes made Lincoln's the face of a man and not a faction; the face of our past friendship long since mutilated but now broken and never to be restored; an ugly face, staring at me from the depths of the rising inexorable wave of grief and pain.

"You did not tell me that my son was dead because you did not trust me," I cried out at the face before me. "Well, —— you then! —— you and your needless bloody war! —— you all, both North and South!"

Without looking at the face again, I walked carefully round the desk and across the office and, taking my hat from the row of pegs beside the door, went out.

Estol Sykes heard a sudden drumming of hoofs under the trees in the yard and, ordering Nellie to stay out of sight, he lighted a lantern and went out on the porch.

The first Rebel he saw in the wavering circle of light was Major Tolliver, and recognizing in the plume and sash nothing that any Home Guard wore—or any Union Regular, either, in his brief experience of the war—he guessed at once who his visitors were.

"We're K.G.C., here!" he announced, and swung the lantern toward the big red star that Nellie had set up between the two front doors.

"We want something to eat," the major said.

Estol shook his head.

"We got sickness in the house," he said. "My pa's ailing and I ain't got no woman handy."

The major rode up to the porch steps, and Estol saw the pointed blond beard and the whiskers.

"Whatever you have," the major said. "Bread. And water for the men and the horses. Where's your well?"

"Round back."

"And some bread?"

Estol hesitated. Should he give him the bread from his mother's Saturday baking? It was the last bread she would ever bake. The labor of its baking was probably what had killed her. He felt a squeamish reluctance. But he was thinking also of the three hundred dollars he had found in a spool box under the bed in his parents' upstairs bedroom that afternoon.

More men emerged from the shadows under the trees, and he said again, "We're K.G.C., here."

As he spoke he waved the lantern once more toward the star.

"You're *what?*" the major said.

"K.G.C.—Knights."

The major looked puzzled.

"What's that thing?"

"A star," Estol said.

"I see it's a star, man. But what does it mean?"

"K.G.C.," Estol repeated. "We're on your side."

The major laughed and spoke over his shoulder to the men in the darkness behind him.

"He says he's on our side, boys."

One of the men, invisible under the trees, responded, "The — he is! Where's his Johnny suit?"

"Sign him up, Major," another said. "Give him a gun."

"He don't look like no Reb to me," still another shouted from the depths of the darkness. "Looks like a —— niggerhead!"

"How about some bread?" the major asked, turning back to Estol.

"You all come round back," Estol said.

As he passed through the house, he sent Nellie up to the attic with the spool box. "You stay up there, too, you hear?" he whispered. Then he lighted a lamp in the kitchen and opened the back door.

The red-haired sergeant named Black came up to the stoop. His big truculent frame filled the doorway, blotting out the others, some of whom had dismounted and were gathered round the stoop.

"Where's your woman at?" the sergeant said.

Estol was bending over the tin safe, taking out the bread, and he did not turn round.

"I ain't got none," he said.

"Took a woman to bake that bread," the sergeant said. "You didn't bake it."

"It was my ma baked it," Estol said, as he loaded the sergeant's outstretched arms with loaves of his mother's bread.

"Well, where's she at?" the sergeant demanded. "Tell her to come out here and make us some coffee."

"I can't," Estol said.

The sergeant stared at him over the loaves.

"How come? She ain't dead, is she?"

"Yes," Estol said. "She's dead."

The sergeant almost dropped the bread. He stood in the doorway peering suspiciously at Estol. Finally, he turned and went out into the night.

"I ain't sure we ought to eat this stuff," Estol heard him say to someone outside. "You don't reckon that star out front means smallpox or something, do you?"

"Maybe it's a — house," a voice replied. "Maybe that star means there's women inside. Maybe we ought to go in and have a look. Maybe it's for them the bread was baked."

Then Estol heard the voice of the officer with the plume.

"Hurry! Eat the bread. Then we'll take their horses and move on."

Estol moved to the door and peered out into the darkness. His old man used mules for labor and the one buggy horse was worthless, but there was a good saddle horse in the barn, a roan stallion. The old man had paid eight hundred dollars cash money for it last winter. If the old man died, the stallion was one of the most valuable pieces of property Estol would inherit.

"General Morgan!" Estol cried out into the darkness. "Wait!"

He went out the door and ran down into the yard amongst the men, calling the name.

A burst of laughter rose round him in the darkness, and someone stuck out a foot and tripped him. He was kicked in the ribs, and a voice said, "Get up, niggerhead!" All around him the men were mimicking his cry, "General Morgan! General Morgan!"

Estol struggled to his feet, and out of the babble round him he finally distinguished the major's voice.

"*What's in a name* . . . ?" the major said; and afterward his soft voice went on and on for a long time in gibberish about smelling roses that sounded like English but made no sense at all to Estol Sykes.

"Don't take the stallion, General!" Estol begged, as soon as the strange speech ended. "Don't take the stallion! I'm on your side! I told you!"

"Like — he is!" someone said. "Let's truss him up on a fence-rail!"

"If you're on our side," the major said, "you ought to be glad to give us your stallion."

"I need it," Estol said. "I come home from the army and I don't aim to go back and if they come after me—" He stopped. Catching his breath, he became aware of a plan slowly forming in his mind. "You see, I aim to ride South and join the Confeds, soon as I get cleared away here. It's only because my ma died and my pa—"

The major cut him short.

"So you're a deserter. My men like to shoot deserters."

Estol began to shake all over.

"From the Union army, General," he said. "I'm K.G.C."

"A polecat by any name smells just as bad," the major said. "Shall we shoot him before we take his stallion, men?"

An affirmative roar went up from the men and someone laid a hand on Estol's shoulder in the dark.

"I've got three hundred dollars I'll give you ruther than you shoot me and take my horse, General!" he whimpered.

"*My kingdom for a horse!*" the major said. "Three hundred dollars? Where is it?"

"I'll fetch it," Estol said, "if you promise."

"Fetch it," the major said.

Estol returned to the house and climbed the stairs to the attic, where he found Nellie watching the men through the slatted window at the back.

"There's millions of them out there, Estol!" she cried, throwing herself upon him.

He pushed her off.

"Where's that box at?"

"You ain't aiming to give it to them, are you?"

"They're going to kill me if I don't, and steal the stallion."

"Estol, I'm scared!"

He slapped her hard across the face. Fumbling under her skirt, she drew the spool box out from amongst her petticoats and handed it to him.

When he returned to the yard, one of the soldiers came with a lantern while the major examined the box.

"You made a mistake," he said. "You have three hundred and five dollars here."

"You can have it all," Estol said.

"No," the major said. "We agreed on three hundred, and three hundred it is." He handed over a five-dollar note. Then Estol heard the clink of his saber-chain as he stuffed the remainder of the money in his pocket.

"Much obliged," Estol said.

"Don't mention it."

At that moment, Estol heard the scroop of the barn door and, looking across the barn lot, saw the big sergeant come out with a lantern, leading the roan stallion.

"Nothing else in there but mules and a sway-backed plug, Major," the sergeant called out. "You want them, too?"

"No. Turn them out. All we want is the stallion."

For a moment Estol could not find his voice. He could not believe that a man so meticulous about giving him back five dollars would not keep his word about the stallion.

"But I paid you!" he cried finally.

The major laughed.

"You paid me not to shoot you," he said. "I did not say I would not take the stallion."

For several minutes Estol was unable to move from the spot where he stood; and while he stood there, he heard the men's footsteps falling away in the dark and it was as if the earth itself

were falling away beneath him. At last, enraged, he ran as fast
as he could back to the house.

In the kitchen, he snatched his hunting rifle from behind a
door. His fingers felt thick and clumsy and his hands shook so
that it took several minutes for him to ram the wadded ball home
in the barrel and sprinkle powder in the pan; and by the time
the gun was loaded and he went to the back door, there was no
longer any sound in the yard but the chatter of insects. Off in
the bottoms below the knoll, he could hear the faint pounding
of hoofbeats.

For a long time he stood slack and frustrated in the doorway.
Finally, with a slow, dreamlike, despairing gesture, he raised the
gun halfway to his shoulder and fired it futilely into the night.

Almost at the same moment, as if the report of the rifle had
produced it, a ponderous thump, like the dropping of a moun-
tainous grain sack on the earth's floor, shook the doorsill where
he stood; and in the next instant a red balloon of flame soared
up through the roof of the barn and a blast of needling sawdust
struck him in the face. He dropped the gun and raised his hands
to his eyes, but before they were covered he saw a dark figure
fly across the red light of the barn lot, and afterward he heard
horseshoes clang against the stone slab in the lane under the
walnut tree. After that, the roar of burning timbers deafened
him.

As soon as I reached the hallway outside my office, with the
door slammed shut between me and the hateful face of Asa Ross,
the dam of trivial annoyance that I had purposefully compounded into rage collapsed and the wave of grief surged in and
over me at last.

. . . Jack Claybun was kilt . . .

I braced myself against the roughly varnished wall under the
gasjet and stood still, panting, as if the carefully walked distance
of twenty feet from my desk to the door had been a mile that
I had run headlong. It must have been several minutes before I
was able, eyes wide open and still dry but seeing nothing, to
grope along the wall to the top of the stairs and down them,
stumbling, to the second floor and then through another hall
and down the next flight to the windowed door that admitted

the lighter darkness of the street, where, pushing it open, I went through and out, past a guard who was stationed there by my own order earlier that day.

The guard's heavy shoes scraped behind me on the stone flagging outside the door, and there was a voice: *Good evening, Mayor.* I heard but could not answer and went on, walked stiffly across the dry grass of the courthouse lawn in the violet darkness, passed under the darker trees that edged the street, left the courthouse square behind me, and entered then the tunnel under the awnings and galleries that hung above the sidewalk of Main Street.

In that intensified darkness, in the dark center of the wave of my grief now also, I moved more easily, like a man swimming under water, buoyant but not afloat, past all the familiar places that I could not see but knew were there as markers of my progress, past Grumby's Store and Blackburn and Emmart's, past Holsapple's Livery Stable and the post office and the iron stairway of the *Gazette,* through the Sunday ghosts of familiar weekday smells—shoes and harness leather, peanuts, stale beer, rotting vegetables, horse droppings, street dust—through the Sunday silence that was more than Sunday silence in the police-enforced desertion of the street and a sharper silence still after the rapping of my heels on the wooden banquette broke it into fragments and, repaired, it closed again behind me, walking easily, miraculously, until under my feet I felt the falling away of Main Street toward the levee. There, in the opening darkness of the widening street and of the wide river, but still sealed within my own darkness, I turned left on Audubon.

I marched then, still miraculously, over the uneven planks of the walk, along the first sycamore-and-maple-darkened block and then the next, past the silent shadow of the church, past the Whitings' house and Asa Ross's and Doc Pendleton's, dimly lighted, and, at the entrance to Doc's drive, across the street, where my own house rose tall above Ben Marvin's. But as soon as I was inside it, under the gas-lit splendor of the front-hall chandelier, and Helen called from upstairs at the sound of my entering, *Is that you, Bradford?* and I heard her light running footsteps in the upstairs hall, I knew that my new home where Nance had never lived was not the place I sought and I turned quickly and, without answering Helen, fled.

Through the door and down the steps, down the short front walk and into the night once more I went, recognizing, as I re-crossed the street, but ignoring the shadowy figures of a man and a boy approaching side by side. *E'nin', Mayor Clayburn, e'nin', suh. I fotched Master Bradford for you.* . . . Again I heard but could not answer and went on, turning sharply, commencing once more to march, miraculously sure-footed in the darkness, retracing my path down Audubon to Main. *You go in an' see your mama now.* . . . And after that I was not alone. Footsteps followed mine, and the voice: *Mayor Clayburn, suh.* . . .

At the top of the sharp steep slope of Main, I entered the tunnel under the awnings again, as dark as before, as familiar, but the silence fragmented by my heels on the banquette not healing this time behind me because the soft Negro voice persisted and the other footsteps, an echo of my own. Still I walked without turning round till I came to Willow, where I bore left, heeding neither the voice nor the footsteps, until I reached a place in the darkness that I knew well.

Mayor Clayburn, suh. . . . The voice was at my shoulder.

Without answering, I took a key from my pocket and climbed a familiar rickety flight of wooden stairs that hung from a familiar rickety gallery; and when I stopped at last before a familiar battered door at the top, I opened it and entered the sanctuary of my old law office, a place long unused and musty, but a place that neither my wife Helen nor my son Bradford would dare to invade and my servant and friend Goosehead would not enter uninvited, though he had dogged my steps all the way from the house on Audubon Street, proffering with every other breath his hopeful, diffident, half-whispered *Mayor Clayburn, suh.* . . . like a man reaching out in the dark for something that he feared might not be there, had followed me at the last up the rickety stairs, too, and stood murmuring at my shoulder on the narrow wooden platform above the street while I unlocked the door, and even after I closed the door, shutting him outside, had sunk with a sigh and an uneasy thump, like a tired dog, to the floor of the gallery and continued to speak for a time through the cracked thin slat of the doorpanel, softly, *You want me, I be right here, suh. I be right here all the time. That's right.* . . .

When I finished weeping the first time, I got up from the desk where I had dropped my head on my arms and paced the thin-carpeted floor as if I were a sentinel on the banks of the Bayou Pierre itself, and sometimes the Negro on the gallery outside heard me and sometimes not. That pacing did not cease until I dropped from exhaustion on the horsehair sofa, as Jack himself must have dropped behind a heap of driftwood when he heard the rattle and whine of the Johnnies' crossfire on the Bayou Pierre, and lay there, as Jack and I together once had lain in our blinds on the river, watching for the mallards to come over from Kentucky, as I knew Jack alone, a small boy, had sprawled many times on Dove Creek's banks and the banks of the river and the slough, waiting for the mud cat to tug at his drifting line.

When I finished weeping the second time, I got up from the sofa and went to the window and stood looking out at the night, unseeing at first, but ultimately seeing in the sky a faint fast-fading glow that I knew, because I knew that countryside as I knew the back of my own hand, was a fire on Old Man Sykes's place, either his house or his barn or maybe both. I spoke the word *fire* aloud then, wonderingly, and afterward heard hoof-beats in the streets. But I allowed the sight and the sounds to call to my mind only the night that Reuben Draper's house had burned and Jack had ridden Helen's carriage horse out the River Road—*my grandpa's place*—and after that I turned my back upon the window and all that the fire and the hoofbeats meant and began to pace the floor again.

Outside the door, Goosehead coughed, and I heard him say, *They coming now, Mayor Clayburn. They riding through the streets. They here. . . .* But I did not answer. I continued to pace the floor, unheeding, until once more I was exhausted and flung myself back upon the sofa, this time not to weep, for I was no longer capable of weeping, but to live, over and over through the rest of the night, a lifetime that I cherished more than my own, a span of years that seemed to me, pitifully, not so long as the night itself. . . .

My son Bradford could have told me about the incident at the Sykes farm if I had stopped and spoken to him that night when we met in the dark before my house on Audubon Street; and Goosehead, too, if I had heeded his presence, could have told me about the fire and the Rebel feint toward the Bug Slough bridge and the plan they had devised for capturing the city, for Bradford and Goosehead had been with the raiders at the Sykes farm.

Before that, bound together to the tree in the Draper orchard, Bradford and Goosehead had shared a full view of all that happened on the River Road in the few remaining hours before the night fell. First, there was a steady increase of the Confederate numbers along the road past the orchard, as groups of men kept coming up out of the woods from the river where they were disembarking. After the men, horses were led up, to the men's cheering; and after the mounts, more animals dragged up the Parrotts that had sunk the gunboat from the Kentucky shore. Finally, a new officer appeared among the men on the road. A tall, straight, fair-haired man with a sharp, towcolored beard and a stern face, he obviously superseded Major Tolliver in command, and Bradford guessed that the officer was his cousin Stacey Morey. From where he sat, tied to the tree, he called out to the new officer, but he was too far from the road to be heard.

Soon after the colonel appeared, he led the majority of the men off up the road in a direction away from the city. Then followed a quarter of an hour or more in which Bradford and Goosehead were sure that they were going to be left behind, forgotten, alone in the orchard, tied fast and helpless in the dark. But finally the red-bearded sergeant returned to the orchard and, untying them, ordered them to precede him down the road. Not far away, Dancer was waiting, and the sergeant made them mount, Bradford in the saddle and Goosehead on the pony's rump; and then he roped them together again. Trotting past toward the head of the column they were in, Major Tolliver saw them and, laughing, shouted, "How now, Cassio! Does the Moor offend thee?"

Where the major's remaining small unit of raiders was going proved to be the Sykes farm although, from the conversations Bradford and Goosehead heard along the way, it was obvious that the men did not know of the farm's existence. Their intention was to flank the Home Guards and either drive them across the slough and north along the River Road away from Crescent City or to draw them off into the corn bottoms, keeping them occupied while Colonel Morey, with the main body of the troops, circled the city in the hills and ultimately entered it at the north through the railroad tunnel. To deceive any Home Guard vedettes that might be watching them, Major Tolliver's men left the River Road and followed the river itself; but they obviously did not know that the Sykes farm lay in their path, and Bradford and Goosehead saw no reason for enlightening them.

The men started off gaily, the major himself leading the vanguard in singing:

> "*We are the sons of old Aunt Dinah,*
> *And we go where we've a mind to,*
> *And we stay where we're inclined to,*
> *And we don't care a damn cent. . . .*"

But off the road and in the woods they quieted, and only a few persisted in song, carrying softly then the dreamy melody of "Lorena" instead, while the others rode in silence or talked in low voices:

> "*The years creep slowly by, Lorena,*
> *The snow is on the grass again,*
> *The sun's low down the sky, Lorena. . . .*"

"I got me a Yankee dollar says the General is in the capital by now."

"Eating in the governor's mansion."

"Could be, boy! Could be! But what I say is I wish I was back home in Jessamine County right now with my feet under my daddy's table. . . ."

> " *. . . A hundred months have passed, Lorena,*
> *Since last I held that hand. . . .*"

"Well, I heard the major say . . ."

"Sure, you heard the major say. But just you remember, the major ain't the colonel!"

"And the colonel ain't the General . . ."

> " *. . . We loved each other then, Lorena,*
> *More than we ever dared to tell:*

And what we might have been, Lorena,
Had but our loving prospered well. . . ."

"Let's let the nigger settle it. Boy, you ever hear of a dog eat
a possum?"

"No, suh, I ain't. That's right."

"See! What did I tell you? They won't touch 'em."

"They kill 'em."

"Sure, but they won't touch 'em, after. I don't care how hungry he is, a dog won't eat a possum. . . ."

" *. . . these were words of thine, Lorena,*
They burn within my memory yet. . . ."

"It's like a hog won't eat a pawpaw. You know that . . . ?"

So they rode through the woods along the ridges and the
knolls by the river, up and down and finally down through the
corn bottoms, first in the cloudy rain-threatening twilight while
flashes of lightning made the men's faces bloom briefly like
moonflowers in the night and, later, in the night itself, with no
lightning and a faint moon floating in and out among the clouds,
and always the beat of hoofs and the clink and rattle of harness
mingling with the hum of voices and the song, and all around,
so steady and insistent that sometimes it was no sound at all, the
incessant chant of insects.

" *. . . It matters little now, Lorena. . . ."*

And all the way, as they rode, Bradford felt Goosehead's
fingers working at the rope that bound them together. "No, suh,
I ain't. That's right," Goosehead said, when the soldier asked
him if he had ever seen a dog eat a possum; but his fingers never
stopped working as he spoke; and by the time they reached the
Sykes farm, he had the coils so loose that Bradford had to keep
one arm pressed against his belly to prevent them from falling
off altogether; but by that time it was so dark and the men were
so busy eating Mrs. Sykes's bread and taking Estol's money and
the stallion and burning his barn that no one would have noticed anyhow.

When Estol Sykes ran back into his house for his gun, Goosehead finally whispered, "All right! Let's go!" and then Bradford,
who had edged the pony sidewise into the wagon road beside the

barn lot, threw off the rope, wheeled Dancer about, and kicked him in the flanks; and Dancer's hoofs scrambled and rang loud on the stone slab in the road for a few terrifying seconds before he leaped into the darkness and galloped away with them into the forest of corn, Bradford clinging to his neck and Goosehead clinging to Bradford, until they heard a shout and, afterward, a concerted pounding of hoofs in the wagon road.

"Pull up!" Goosehead yelled hoarsely into Bradford's ear then; and Bradford obeyed at once, but before Dancer came to a full halt, Goosehead was off his rump and pulling Bradford down after him.

"Come on!" Goosehead shouted, grabbing the boy's wrist and dragging him through the corn.

They were several hundred feet from the wagon road when the Confederates overtook Dancer and at once fanned out and began to thrash around in the corn, shouting. Goosehead pushed Bradford down to the warm earth between the corn rows and whispered, "Ain't no good us running no more. They hear us and find us." And Bradford squatted beside Goosehead, trying to hold his breath, listening to the men's voices and, close at hand, the dry rattling dance of grasshoppers in the corn, or crickets maybe, he did not know which, until finally the raiders gave up the search and rode away and there was only Goosehead's sharp breathing at his side.

"Let's go," Bradford said then.

But Goosehead laid a hand on his arm and said they must wait; and soon he was glad they had waited, for the raider who had stayed to fire the Sykes barn galloped past in pursuit of his comrades.

After he was gone, they rose and fled, running down the corn rows in the dark, endlessly, it seemed to Bradford, with the corn blades lashing their hands and faces. They came out of the corn at last, however, and entered the River Road at the sawmill, and because they were well behind the Home Guards' line and knew the raiders would cut off a Home Guard retreat toward the city, they felt safe enough to slow to a walk. They rounded the jog in the road and entered the broad unlighted reach of Audubon Street, and in a few more minutes they were in front of our house.

When Bradford saw me coming down the steps, he told me

later, he realized all at once for the first time the enormity of what he had done that day. What had been an adventure became suddenly treason—treason thwarted but treason nonetheless. He kept on walking toward me thereafter as a man must walk to his execution, with legs working involuntarily but mind and body rebelling against the motion.

Then Goosehead spoke to me with a casual innocence in his voice—"E'nin', Mayor Clayburn, e'nin', suh. I fotched Master Bradford for you"—and Bradford's fright left him as abruptly as it had come.

At the same time, he said, he made a startling discovery about himself. The treason was treason in his own eyes, too. He had been a boy when he fled that morning to join the Confederate raiders, and now he was a man and thought as a man should, as his father thought. But the change did not absolve him. He must be punished, he told himself; he *wanted* to be punished; so that he could prove his new manhood; so that afterward he would wholly merit a place at his father's side.

But Bradford's new sense of maturity and well-being lasted only a moment; for I turned sharply and walked away down Audubon Street without acknowledging Goosehead's greeting, without acknowledging the presence of either of them on the sidewalk in front of the house; and as Bradford watched me disappear into the shadows of the night, the old gulf widened between us once more and he ceased to be a man. He became a small boy again, frightened by his own guilt; and breaking away from Goosehead, he ran toward the house, in full retreat toward the soft safe shelter of outstretched arms that his mother held ready for him at the front door.

The next morning, I was awakened by Goosehead's voice on the gallery outside the door of my old law office.

"Ain't none you gentlemen coming up them stairs. You waiting till the mayor he's notified."

For what seemed a long time, I lay on the sofa, neither sure where I was nor able to disentangle from my waking senses the dream I had been having. I had been lying among cat-tails with a boy and a gun beside me, and I had been trying to tell the boy something. I could not remember exactly what, except that it was of great importance to the boy's future and it was urgent. It concerned evil and violence and what the boy must do when they confronted him. "One must not hide like this," I had been saying; and as I spoke, I parted the cat-tails and pointed at black clouds that lowered above the opposite shore of a river. But each time that I raised my hand to point at the clouds so that the boy would always recognize their kind thereafter, men's faces floated above the aperture in the cat-tails like white moons and obscured the clouds, and then there was a burst of flame, and the boy would cry out, "But it's my grandpa's place, Papa!" After that, it seemed to be Goosehead who was pushing the faces aside, and I heard him say, "You waiting till the mayor he's notified."

Finally, I sat up on the sofa, speaking the boy's name. But the boy had vanished. Then I remembered where I was.

"I'm warning you gentlemen," Goosehead was saying outside the door.

At first it was no more than a fact.

Jack Claybun was kilt. . . .

"You ain't coming up them stairs. . . ."

And where, in the evening and the night just past, there had been flaming anger and molten grief, there were now only ashes and an aching dryness.

Goosehead whispered through the thin panel of the door, "Mist' Clayburn, you woke up yet?"

Yesterday, in the moment of discovery that Asa Ross had withheld the news from me till I had taken my loyal stand and won in the Council meeting, I had hated Asa. Now, in the aftermath of my anger and grief, I felt nothing and wondered whether I would ever feel anything again.

"Mist' Clayburn. . . ."

I sat with my elbows on my knees and my head between my hands.

"Mist' Henry. . . ."

I got up wearily and unlocked the door, and Goosehead slithered into the office in one quick lizard-like motion, shot the bolt into its socket, and stood with his back to the door, both hands pressing against it, as if the bolt alone were not enough to hold it shut.

"It's Mist' Ross and them," he whispered.

I must have looked puzzled, for he seemed to feel the need to elaborate.

"They was another gentleman, too, a while back, a soldierman in a fancy-Dan suit, had him a feather in his hat."

"Morgan?"

"Mister Bradford say no. I seen him out to the farm yesterday, sashaying around. Us rode up with him last night. Then this morning he come the first time with Mist' Ross and them, but they went away. Now Mist' Ross and them come back. I told them anybody come up them stairs, I cut they th'oats. But you ask me, Mist' Henry, I reckon it was them stairs scared them much as anything else. You ask me, you don't fix them stairs soon, somebody's going to bust right th'ough one of these days."

Goosehead's immediateness in the room, but, more than that, his concern about the rickety stairs, his singleness of intent upon the present that moved him safely from one moment to the next, were a restorative. They drew me gradually out of the wasteland of my despair, until it seemed to me that I was only then at last awake. At the same time, the situation in which I found myself had a new quality of unreality. Jack was dead; the Rebel raiders were in the streets; the town was lost; yet everything was exactly as it had always been. The old stairs needed repair; Asa Ross was at my doorstep; and Goosehead was protecting me from intrusion. My paraphrase of the day before came back to me: *I think it; therefore, it is.* So I was cogitative once more. And then another axiom came; this one unparaphrased. *A man is never so happy nor so unhappy as he thinks he is.* I had quoted that maxim of La Rochefoucauld's to Bradford once when he was a little boy, and Bradford had startled me by answering precociously, "But being happy is only thinking!" I supposed someday he would be a lawyer, a judge, if there were no more wars, no more Bayou Pierres, to cut his life short, like Jack's.

So I was thinking again! I marveled, incredulous and slightly dizzy, like a man walking from his bed to a chair for the first time after a long illness from which he had not expected to recover.

"Let them in, Goosehead," I said.

"Don't you want I shave you first. You a sight, Mist' Henry."

I rubbed a hand over the stubble on my face. The hand trembled a little. I shook my head.

"You can run down to the Pepper House and fetch me some breakfast while I talk to Mr. Ross and these men. You can bring a pitcher of hot water back with you and shave me after they go."

Goosehead stared down at his feet.

"You reckon them Rebs let me pass?" he said. "They had me and Master Bradford tied up out at the farm yesterday. You don't reckon they stop me?"

"You said that before. You were out at the farm yesterday?" I had still been half-dreaming when Goosehead spoke the first time about seeing the plumed officer at the Draper place. "You went out there by yourself? You say the boy was there?"

Goosehead nodded.

"How did you know he was there?"

"Miss Laura. She told me."

It all seemed very long ago. And now I had something I had to tell Laura Pendleton. But I would do that in my own time.

"And so you went out there on your own, to rescue him if you could," I said.

Goosehead hung his head.

"You was busy, Mist' Henry, and it seemed like a shame to burden you."

"I'm not scolding you," I said. "I—" I broke off, knowing by Goosehead's face that he understood I was blaming myself. "I think if you were brave enough to do that," I said finally, "you needn't be afraid now."

The indignation came back into Goosehead's face.

"Ain't me scared!" he said. "I only thinking about getting you back some breakfast 'thout no Reb messing it up."

"Of course," I said. "But I guess they're all well-fed now. They won't pay any attention to you. You aren't worth as much to them today as you were yesterday."

"Yes, suh. That's right."

"Let the men in now."

When Goosehead unlocked and opened the door, Asa Ross and "them" had already climbed the stairs and were waiting on the gallery outside. To my amazement, "them" proved to be only one other man, and that man was Ben Marvin.

"That nigger of yours!" Asa Ross fumed, as he pushed past Goosehead and came, stiff-legged, into the room, looking, I thought, like one of Volck's ugly caricatures of Abraham Lincoln. "That nigger of yours drew a knife on us!"

Above Asa's head, Ben Marvin appeared more affable. Softer and vaguer, his big round face, which I recognized as one of the moonfaces I had seen in my dream, was impassive; but his eyes were alert.

"We're sorry to disturb you at a time like this . . ." he said.

I turned upon Asa Ross.

"You told him about Jack?"

Asa scowled and nibbled at something behind tightly closed lips.

"Yes. But only just now, Henry. I thought I should, to explain . . ."

For a moment, there was something of the old bond between us. Asa was not altogether insensitive; he was only inept.

"You haven't told anyone else, have you?"

"No. Of course not."

"Because it will be hard for Helen if she hears it from anybody but me. And I want to be the one to tell Laura Pendleton, too."

"I'm sorry I told Ben. I only thought . . ."

"It's all right."

Asa's contrition vanished then, and in the next breath he said belligerently and indignantly, "The Rebels are all over town. They've burned the railroad bridge and torn up the tracks in the tunnel and planted cannons on the levee to stop all commerce."

He spoke the word *commerce* with a kind of reverence, as he might have used the name of the divinity. He owned a steamboat-chandler's warehouse, and I supposed that whenever he looked at the river he never saw anything but commerce. What had he seen, I wondered, when he first looked upon Belle Forman? Her money only? What did a spring morning mean to a man like Asa? Music—? Painting—? History even—? Did my ancestors fight at Dunbar and Bunker Hill for commerce only? Was that why Jack had died at Bayou Pierre? I felt a momentary compassion for Asa, as if he were blind.

"And they've rounded up all the horses in town and have got them in the stockpens down on the levee," Asa went on. "And they've fixed the telegraph and got it working again and that fellow they call Lightning is sending messages all over the state, confusing the authorities."

"You seem to have been around," I said. "Have you seen John Hunt Morgan yet?"

"It isn't Morgan."

"I had guessed it wasn't."

"It's a cousin of yours, a Colonel Morey. Your wife's cousin, rather. Same thing."

"No, it is not the same thing, Asa," I said. "You always have trouble making distinctions."

"Well, that's why we've come to you, anyhow. Helen has put him up at your house, and that could be a good thing in the end. It all depends on you."

So Helen had her Cousin Stacey from Tennessee as a house guest, after all, I thought. I remembered how I laughed at her only yesterday morning. I supposed I should be angered by the news that a Confederate officer was being entertained in my home while my son lay dead in Mississippi, killed by Confederates; but in my mind I was able to see Stacey Morey only as a man like myself, or Asa, or even Ben Marvin, another actor in a little drama that none of us had written. It did not matter.

"We want to know what you intend to do," Asa finished.

"Do?"

"Yes, *do!*"

"Why, whatever there was to do should have been done last night apparently," I said, "and it wasn't. We failed to do it. *I* failed to do it, rather, if you like. I take the blame. The little that I did was the wrong thing."

"If they begin to steal and destroy our property—"

"Oh, property," I said.

"I think you are taking this much too lightly, Henry!"

"No," I said; "I was only thinking that yesterday in the Council meeting you were all for arresting people, Asa, without warrants, searching their homes without warrants, taking away their rights, putting them in jail. But those were only persons. Now property is different. It is a value we must not lose."

While I spoke, Asa drew his mouth as thin and white as a string above his fringe of chin whiskers; and when I finished, he said, "This is no time to be vindictive, Henry Clayburn."

"No, of course not, Asa Ross. The time for intolerance and suspicion has passed, because we're all in the same boat now and our property is in danger."

At that point, Ben Marvin spoke, repeating what Asa had said earlier.

"They've already burned the railroad bridge and torn up the tracks in the tunnel."

Ben held a large interest in the new railroad.

"And yesterday," I said to Ben, "while Asa was for depriving our citizens of all their rights, you were for doing nothing, for letting the Rebels have their way."

"I am still," Ben Marvin said, "up to a point."

I turned to Asa.

"The railroad bridge and the tunnel are lines of communication," I said. "I suppose you could call them military targets. Destroying them, therefore, isn't reckless vandalism. They haven't touched any strictly private property yet, have they?"

"Those horses in the stockpens on the levee."

"But they, too, are lines of communication, in a sense. And they will probably leave their own in exchange. I am speaking of looting and vandalism."

"Not yet," Asa said. "But they may. That's the point." He paused and swallowed, his sharp little Adam's apple rising and falling beneath the whiskers on his throat; and his lips tightened again and he snapped viciously at whatever it was that seemed always caught between his front teeth. "Your cousin—" he said, "this Colonel Morey—he is in command, and he seems to be a reasonable man, from all we've heard. But there's another, the second in command, a young major. Tolliver. He's over at the hotel now, has set himself up like a king with everybody running around waiting on him. Ben and I went over to see him this morning, because Helen wouldn't let us disturb the colonel, who was still asleep, and he—this major—began to talk about ransom first thing, said if he had his way he'd burn the city to the ground if we didn't pay. He walked over here with us a while ago, wanted to see you, talked all the way, reciting poetry, Shakespeare and stuff like that. I tell you, Henry, Ben and I—"

Ben and I. I remembered Asa's former suspicions and innuendoes. *You'd better keep a close watch on that Ben Marvin, Henry.* . . . Self-interest made strange bedfellows. Now they were calling on a Confederate officer together. Next year they might be running together on the same ticket. I felt suddenly very tired.

"Did the Knights of the Golden Circle help them?" I asked, thinking of Asa's innuendoes about Ben.

Ben Marvin laughed, somewhat bitterly, I thought.

"Nobody has seen hide nor hair of the K.G.C.," he said.

"But this cousin of yours is apparently a reasonable man," Asa Ross persisted, refusing to be diverted from his theme, "and Ben and I thought—"

"Helen's cousin," I corrected him.

"So if you'll just let him stay on at your house and cooperate with him—"

"*Cooperate,*" I said. "So that's it!"

"Cooperation," Asa said. "After all, that was the line you Democrats took only yesterday. It's the line you've taken all along."

"*Some* Democrats," I corrected him again. "Not all of us. You're distorting facts again, Asa. I will cooperate with Colonel Morey so long as he conducts himself with military propriety, but I have no intention of knuckling under to our conquerors. I will insist that everything be legal and correct."

"What I'm trying to say is—"

Asa was interrupted at that point by Goosehead's return. He came in balancing a tray covered with a white napkin.

"I must ask you to excuse me now," I said to Asa and Ben.

"Well, it does seem to me that, being a Democrat—" Asa began; but I did not allow him to finish.

"I never gave you a licking when we were boys together, Asa," I said, "because you were a runt, but now that we are middle-aged men, I'm not sure that old boyhood code of honor still holds."

"Now, Henry—" Ben Marvin interceded; but whatever else he wanted to say I did not allow him to say; for I was holding the door open for both of them.

As soon as the men were out on the gallery, I shut the door and bolted it and, returning to the desk, sat down before the tray that Goosehead had brought in. The window was open and I could hear the men's voices as they descended the stairs, but I could not hear what they were saying.

"Pusillanimous renegades!" I muttered.

Then I caught Goosehead's eye. He was still standing solemnly in a corner of the room where he had stood during the men's exit; but now, hearing the words I muttered and catching my eye, he suddenly lost control of himself and the glee that had been bottled up in him over my expulsion of my guests exploded.

"That's right!" he shouted, and began to laugh.

Then I, too, found myself suddenly seized with laughter.

"Man, oh, man!" Goosehead shouted, slapping his knees and bobbing his head up and down. "Listen to that white man talk! Yes*suh*!

He spoke in the exhortatory chant of the camp meeting, and I laughed louder.

"Yes*suh*! You talking just like you used to in the court, Mist' Henry! All them big words! Man, oh, man!"

We laughed together, each of us incited by the other. I got control of myself first, but even after that, little waves of receding laughter jolted me from time to time, like sobs, and my shoulders shook. When I finally lifted the napkin from the tray, Goosehead quieted too and peered admiringly at the food.

"They sure cook you up a powerful breakfast over at the Pepper House," he said; and somehow the remark struck us both as funny and we laughed again.

"You had any?" I said finally.

Goosehead made a deprecating face, with the laughter still bubbling on his lips.

"Nossuh. I mean, yessuh. Cook give me a little something while I was waiting."

"Have some of this."

Goosehead grew solemn and shook his head.

"Here," I said. "I can't eat all of it. Those men spoiled my appetite."

"*Them!*" Goosehead said. "But they got theyself told, all right! What that big word you say, again now, Mist' Henry?"

"Pusillanimous. It's from *pusillus,* meaning tiny, and *animus,* meaning mind."

Goosehead shook his head with awe.

"Man!" he said.

I scraped half the scrambled eggs and some of the fried apples off my plate into the platter that still held two pork chops, set three biscuits on top, and handed the platter to Goosehead.

"You ain't saving none for youself," he said.

"I have plenty."

Taking the platter, Goosehead stepped back several paces from the desk and began to eat standing up.

"Sit down," I said. "Pull up a chair."

The look of indignation came into his face.

"Mist' Henry!" he said. "You know better'n that!"

"I mean it. You've been a better man than I've been these past twenty-four hours."

Goosehead shook his head solemnly and remained standing, and I let it go at that. When we finished eating, he took a razor out of his pocket and shaved me. We were both silent, as we always were during that ceremony, but afterward, while he was cleaning up at a basin in a corner of the room, I told him about Jack.

"It happened three weeks ago," I explained, "but I didn't learn about it until last night, from Mr. Ross."

While I was speaking, Goosehead stopped wiping the razor on the towel, and for a long time after I had finished he stood motionless with his back half-turned to me, his lank body bent sharply from the hips, the bone handle of the razor lying flat on the yellow palm of his hand. Finally, he said, in a low flat voice, "Seemed like I knowed it last night when I first saw you in front of your house. I knowed last night it was something like that made you act like you was when you walked over here without speaking to me. Only other time I ever see you act like that was when Miss Nancy passed on." That was all; but in the awkward position of his body, in the flat emotionless voice and the words he spoke, I recognized a profound and ultimate expression of his own grief and his sympathy.

I was silent for a long time; then, clearing my throat, I said, "But you were just a child when Miss Nancy died."

Goosehead gave me a quick look.

"Black folks ain't never children very long, Mist' Henry. White folks only ones ever got time to be a child."

I stood up, embarrassed, and paid him the customary five cents for the shave and thanked him; and when my eyes met his, I knew it was unnecessary to explain that only the money was for the shave; the thanks were for something else.

He put the five-cent piece in his pocket with a "much obliged," and then stood silent and thoughtful for a few seconds.

Finally, he said, "Mist' Henry, you talking about me being scared a while back. I been thinking. Yesterday, before the Rebs come, they was times I was scared. Out at the farm I thought I was done for, sure enough. Looking after the boy was all that hold me together. But now I've seen 'em and they're here, I ain't scared at all no more. They ain't so much. They just folks, like everybody else, and bye-m-bye they going to git tired of hanging round Crescent City, like everybody else, like you and me sometimes, and they going to pack up and git. Meantime, I reckon it ain't nothing to be scared of at all, like Mist' Ross and them, is it?"

"That's about the way I look at it, Goosehead," I said.

I sent Goosehead on ahead to Doc Pendleton's house with a request that Doc meet me at the City Hall by mid-morning; and as soon as Goosehead was gone, I descended the gallery stairs to Willow Street and walked slowly homeward. It troubled me that I had no plan, that I could think of nothing to do now that the raiders had captured the town. I did not expect Doc to be of any help; but Doc, with all his faults, seemed at that moment like my one true friend in Crescent City, and I needed his company while I found my way.

It was a beautiful morning. Although the dust was still dry and deep in the streets and the maples and sycamores were olive-gray with the dust on their leaves, I found it hard to believe there had been no rain in the night, for the sky was one of those morning-after-rain skies, washed as clean and blue as a china saucer, and the air smelled freshly of the river. It was more like a morning in late August than a morning in early July; it was a squirrel-hunting morning, and I wished Jack were at home to spend the day with me rambling among the hills behind the river.

As I caught myself wishing for Jack, as if Jack were still alive, I remembered Bayou Pierre again with a sharp returning pang of my first grief of the night before; and for a moment the magic of the morning vanished. But in the next moment I was pleased to find myself already thinking of Jack in that manner. I knew it would be a long time before I ceased having such thoughts about the boy, if indeed I ever ceased having them. For a long time after Nancy died, I had caught myself thinking that I must not forget to tell her about something that had happened during the day. I still talked to her in my thoughts sometimes, and I supposed I would be talking so to Jack the rest of my life. I had never much believed in any other kind of immortality; for this kind—the survival of the dead in the minds of the living—was as comforting to me as any that I could imagine. I would be uneasy with Jack and Nancy in the resplendent paradise that the Reverend Mr. MacLeod described in his sermons; and in such a reunion there would be Helen to consider, too. I could not imagine her and Nance making much of a go of it together, especially with me around, even with the heavenly atmosphere to aid them and their own newly acquired angelic attributes. Perhaps, I thought, seeing as I did so the toss of Nance's head as I teased her in my mind, perhaps that was why Mohammedans denied the existence of souls in women: to keep peace in heaven.

"So," I said, half-aloud, addressing Jack again, "we'll do a little fishing and hunting yet, you and I, before I join you and your mother; and then, I hope, we'll all have a good long restful sleep. Whatever the Lord plans thereafter will be all right with me. . . ."

When I reached Main, I abandoned my thoughts of the hereafter and looked about at the strange men in the street: men on horseback, some of them leading strings of confiscated horses toward the river, others either on patrol or sightseeing, it was hard to tell which from their casual manner and the way they nodded friendly greetings without curiosity or suspicion, as if I were one of them; men on foot, strolling singly and in groups, peering into shop windows, some greedy-eyed, others already satiated, with half-eaten pieces of fried chicken, chunks of ham, pork chops, bags of candy, and ripe plums in their hands; all of them armed men, with Colt pistols in their belts or medium Enfields over their shoulders, but only a few wearing anything that resembled uniforms and none of them looking very warlike; young men mostly, boys even, like any group gathered up in Liggum County to be sent South to fight them and kill their kind, more hardened and lean of face and limb than the Liggum County boys were when they departed, but that was all, the only difference; young men not much different from Jack—and yet enough different that one of their kind had shot and killed Jack three weeks ago on the Bayou Pierre, I reminded myself. *We was caught in the Johnnys crossfire . . .* and here they were on Main Street. I supposed I should feel vengeful, but I could not.

As I walked among them, I pondered this fact and the reason for it came to me gradually. I could not feel vengeful toward these men, because there was no difference between them and Jack, between them and myself. Not only were they the same as Jack and myself, but so was that comrade of theirs on the Bayou Pierre in Mississippi, that Confederate soldier, dead now himself perhaps, who had fired the bullet that killed my son. That man himself I believed I could forgive if ever I should meet him; for it was not a man who had killed Jack but a force. Violence. Evil. "Satan," the Reverend Malcolm MacLeod would call it, if he could forget his wartime zeal long enough to remember his religion. Whatever its name, it was an all-pervading force that worked not so much in men individually and alone but, more powerfully and destructively, through them, united against each other. It was the force only that I hated, or should hate, and upon which I should seek vengeance if I could learn what it was and where it ultimately resided, in myself as well as others.

Crossing Audubon Street where it became Lower First, I descended the last steep block of Main to the waterfront, and there, on the levee, I saw more soldiers. They were gathered in larger numbers and looked more businesslike than their comrades on Main Street. Most of them were concentrated round the stockpens and at the wharf; but at the top of the levee, a group of them perched on the unlimbered caissons of the three guns that now commanded the sweep of the river's bend.

"Nobody allowed on the levee, mister," a guard said in a friendly drawl; and I nodded and turned left into Water Street, seeing, as I did so, the smoke from the railroad bridge downstream and recognizing then the odor of burning tar and creosote that I had begun to smell in the fresh morning air.

A young man was talking earnestly with the soldiers on the caissons, and failing to recognize him at first, I realized only after I had passed the guns that it was Ben Marvin's boy, Rodney. Lieutenant Rodney Lycurgus Marvin. Was not Lycurgus a Spartan, I asked myself, trying to remember my Ancient History, and an idealist of some sort? Rodney Lycurgus Marvin was not wearing his Federal blue uniform this morning, and in civilian clothes he looked neither Spartan nor idealistic. Indeed, he was a liar. "I'm a Canadian," I heard him say to the Confederates, after I passed. "I was in town on business, and if you will allow my boat to leave—"

—*I can return to General Burnside's headquarters in Cincinnati,* I finished for him acidly in my thoughts, as I moved on down Water Street out of earshot, *to General Burnside's headquarters where there is no enemy except the civilians we choose to designate as such.* ... But let Rodney Lycurgus Marvin flee to safety if he can, I thought; for I saw in my contempt for him an incipient danger. If I was not going to hate Confederates, now that Jack was dead, neither must I spitefully despise every young Union soldier who succeeded in remaining alive, not even the cravens like Rodney L. Marvin. Perhaps, I told myself, young Marvin had matters in his mind other than his own safety. I must give him the benefit of the doubt. Perhaps he had a plan, which was more than I, the mayor, had yet devised. Escaping to Cincinnati seemed like a poor way of going about saving Crescent City, for Cincinnati was two hundred miles away and General Burnside was a frail reed to lean upon in such an emergency; but if Rodney L. Marvin could talk his way out of town, whatever his motives, I wished him success.

In Audubon Street, I saw two strange horses tied to the hitching-posts in front of my house. A uniformed soldier was standing by, and when the soldier challenged me as I turned in at my front walk, I assumed that he was Colonel Morey's orderly and the extra mount at the edge of the plank sidewalk was the colonel's.

The soldier looked me over skeptically, and I realized that in my soiled and rumpled clothes I hardly looked like the town's mayor. For a moment I was afraid that the soldier might want to search me and would find the pistol in the holster beneath my coat. Since it had been of no use to me so far, I supposed it would be no great loss if he took it; and yet the pistol became suddenly a matter of serious importance to me and I found it difficult to meet the soldier's gaze for fear of revealing the secret that I was armed. Finally, the soldier decided to let me pass, and I went up the steps as slowly and deliberately as I could.

On the porch, I began unexpectedly to dread seeing Helen again, and I paused before the door. I did not know how I was going to tell her about Jack. For some reason that was not clear to me, I wished that I did not have to tell her, ever. I wished that I did not have to speak of Jack's death again to anyone. But, in the end, Helen opened the door before I could take the key out of my pocket and began talking at once, before I myself could speak.

"Stacey is here, Henry. We've just had breakfast. He's in command. He's a colonel. General Morgan is in Indianapolis or someplace. I don't know. Stacey was always vague about things. But where have you been, darling? You're a mess! Bradford said he saw you last night, so it *was* you who came to the house. I called down the stairs. Didn't you hear? But where have you been all night? They haven't hurt you, have they?" She kissed me and began to smooth the wrinkles of my coat. "Oh, darling, is everything all right?"

I could not help smiling at her prattle, wondering for a moment why I loved her. And yet, in the same moment, I knew. Even this morning, with the weariness and the sadness deep in my heart and her childlike babble making the world seem more topsy-turvy than it was, I felt the inevitable tremor of desire as I looked down at her, fresh and lovely as a flower, in the doorway. But it was not that only. There were strength and courage in her deceptively fragile loveliness, and in her heart a devotion as sturdy, in its own way, as Nance's had been; and those I needed. I knew that in that moment Helen was as deeply troubled as I was, as Nance would have been, and far more frightened than either of us could ever be, and so braver, in the end. Talking was her way of being brave.

"I love you, Mrs. Clayburn," I said; and I saw her tremble and she leaned lightly against me and said, "Oh, darling!" Then she straightened and looked up at me. "Is everything all right, Henry?"

"I wouldn't say everything is all right," I said. "But I'm all right, if that is what you mean. Where is he?"

"Who?"

I was sure then that I had been right about her. While she was prattling about her cousin Stacey Morey, she had not been thinking about him at all. She had only been covering her fear.

"The colonel."

"Oh, Stacey—he's in there."

She pointed toward the parlor door, which was closed.

"I've never met him, you know."

"Now, please, darling," she began, resuming her former manner, "do try to be civil to him. After all, he is my cousin and—"

I put my arm about her as we crossed the hall.

"I can't afford to do anything else, Mrs. Clayburn," I said.

"I gave him breakfast, after he'd had a little sleep. I had to get it myself. Delphina and that old darky—Goosehead brought them both up from their cabin yesterday noontime—well, they've disappeared. They always know when something is going to happen."

"I should say something has already happened."

"But I mean—"

We were beside the closed door to the parlor, and before I opened it I took her in my arms and kissed her.

"You're crazy, Mr. Clayburn!" she whispered.

"Now let's have a look at Cousin Stacey," I said.

Colonel Stacey Morey wore a plain gray uniform with no ornament but the insignia of his rank on the high collar and two rows of polished brass buttons down the front of his blouse. Soft, black riding boots covered his breeches halfway up his thighs. He had removed his swordbelt, and it lay beside his holstered Colt and scabbarded cavalryman's sword on a table by the window. As he came across the parlor with his hand outstretched, there was nothing of the soldier's stiffness nor the cavalryman's awkwardness in his movements, although he had the straight back and sharply squared shoulders of a West Pointer and he walked with the slightly rolling, sailorlike gait of a man accustomed to the saddle.

As I shook his hand, it seemed to me at first that the colonel's face was humorless as well as stern. The wide blue eyes were fixed upon me in an unwavering gaze that was almost rudely staring, and the mouth was set in a firm unequivocal line above the sharp-pointed beard. But as soon as he spoke, a latent merriment came alive in his eyes; and I liked him at once.

"I don't expect you to say you are glad to see me, Henry

Clayburn," he said, in a voice so loud that it filled the room. "Considering the unpleasant circumstances, I can't ask that. But I hope you are as pleased as I am that we are meeting at last."

In spite of the too sonorous voice and the somewhat stilted words, there was a warmth in what he said and in the firm grasp of his hand; and studying him, I surmised that he was a man idealistically in love with his career of soldiering and so not brutalized by it or blinded to the rest of life about him, as so many professional soldiers were. I had known a few such officers in Mexico. They were the best kind, but like the best of anything, they were rare. With such a man in command of the raiders, there would be no cause for anxiety about persons or property in Crescent City. Whatever he did, I was sure, would be not only correct but also just and humane.

Beyond my surmise about the colonel's soldiering, I thought I saw a man who, without the West Point indoctrination, would have been a man very much like myself; and I could not help smiling at my vanity in taking such an immediate liking to him.

"No," I replied; and I was further amused to hear myself speaking in something of the colonel's own stilted manner, "these aren't the circumstances I would have chosen for our meeting, Colonel. But I am glad to make your acquaintance. Helen has been singing your praises for a long time. If you were not her cousin, I think I should be jealous."

The colonel laughed, and it was the kind of laugh I expected, sudden, loud, and abruptly ended. As soon as he stopped laughing, his face was stern again, and I wondered whether it was capable of any intermediate expression between gravity and laughter. Then I noticed the deep, live eyes again and knew better. It was odd, I thought, that he too wore a mask, like Ben Marvin. But it was a mask of military steadfastness and purpose, not soft and balloonlike, like Ben's, a mask that engaged confidence, not deceitful. I reminded myself that all men wore masks of one sort or another and wondered momentarily what my own was like.

"That was only Helen's strong sense of family loyalty," the colonel said. Then, with the same abruptness with which he had ended his laugh, he reverted to his original subject. "I shan't impose on your hospitality long. We'll be on our way by noon."

I wondered whether my surprise and pleasure showed

through my own mask. From the looks of things downtown, I had assumed that the city was in for a prolonged occupation. Now Colonel Morey's announcement changed my problem considerably, removing at once both the need and the possibility of making plans for resistance and for seeking aid. If the raiders were to be in town only a few hours longer, there was nothing I could do. It amused me to discover that, after all, I had no choice but to follow Asa Ross's advice and cooperate.

"I shan't urge you to stay," I said. "Indeed, I can't help wondering why you came at all."

"For several reasons," Colonel Morey said; and this time he only smiled, indicating that he had no intention of revealing all of them. "One is horses. In the last five days, we've ridden and fought all the way across Kentucky from the Cumberland River. Our horses are exhausted."

And soon, I was thinking, you are going to have to ride and fight all the way back across Kentucky. But I only motioned the colonel back to his chair and myself sat down near the window beside the stand that held the Clayburn family bible-box, leaning my elbow upon it and wondering, momentarily, what my ancestors, whose names were written in the book therein, would have done had they found themselves in my present circumstances. Only Supply, I supposed, who had fought in the Revolution, would have understood what it was to face as an enemy his own kin. By the time his son, my father, stood in battle against the English, they were another race.

I had already guessed some of the colonel's other reasons for occupying Crescent City. His next objective was undoubtedly Offitt. Drained of troops by the Rebel telegrapher's false messages, Offitt would be an easy prey if the colonel struck soon, before the Union cavalry returned from their wild-goose chase up the Dark River, if indeed they did return. The main body of Morgan's troops had probably already ambushed and destroyed them somewhere along the river's shores. If only there were some way of getting word to them, or to Offitt, such a disaster might be averted. But that was another reason why the colonel had so thoroughly invested Crescent City; he wanted no bold citizen riding out to spread the alarm.

"Are you swapping horses with us?" I asked. "Or do you intend to buy ours outright?"

He laughed his abrupt laugh.

"You'd rather have our horses than our money, wouldn't you?" he said. "Good Tennessee horseflesh is worth more than Confederate money."

"Your men have herded the town horses on the levee," I said, "but I notice they are still riding their own."

The colonel nodded.

"That's something I want to work out with you—a method of distributing our horses, after we leave."

"Why not before you leave?" I asked him slyly, thinking again of the bold citizen who might spread the alarm; but he saw what was in my mind and said, smiling, "Would you do it that way, if you were me?"

I admitted that if I were in his place, I would not.

"It pleases me," I added, "that you don't assume I'm a Copperhead just because I am a Democrat. You show more understanding of Northern politics than some of my fellow-citizens here in Crescent City."

"I can see what goes on in the North only from a distance," the colonel answered gravely, "but it does seem to me that most of your Vallandighams up here are the creation of your Stevenses and your Burnsides. Without their persecution, your Vallandighams might remain as loyal, if not as stable, in their opposition as your Seymours." Looking at Helen then, he continued, "Helen was telling me at breakfast about some of your views. I think they puzzle her a little."

I looked across the room at my wife. She was sitting on the sofa under the portrait that had been painted of her in her wedding gown fourteen years before. She looked no older than the portrait, I thought.

"I don't understand either of you," Helen said. "At breakfast, Stacey was trying to tell me that he is a Unionist, too."

"I'm even something of an Abolitionist, Helen," the colonel said. "I freed all my slaves in Tennessee several years before the war began. I'm opposed to slavery on moral and economic grounds both. And, yes, I am a Unionist. In Tennessee, I worked against Secession to the very last." He paused and studied the pattern of the carpet between the toes of his boots, which were set squarely side by side on the floor before his chair. "But when Tennessee left the Union, it seemed to me I had no choice." He looked up at me suddenly, an appeal in his blue eyes, as if he wanted confirmation of what he was about to say. "You know, Henry Clayburn, I suspect there are a lot of us on the same middle ground—men like you and me with much the same convictions, stubbornly taking opposite sides only because of opposite geographical loyalties. We're reasonable men. It's a pity we can't get together."

"Instead of increasing our mutual bitterness by stupid and futile invasions such as the one you're engaged in now," I said sharply—and much too sententiously, I thought, as soon as I had spoken.

He gave me a long slow look and, to my surprise, nodded in frank agreement.

"Futile maybe. But not stupid; foolhardy. If we stayed home and let the dissatisfaction with the war in the North take its course— But there is Grant down there in Mississippi. It seems to me all men are innately decent—or most of them—and can work out a decent and just way of life for themselves ultimately —or ought to be able to—without violence."

"But a few thrive on violence and adventure," I suggested; and the colonel nodded again.

"Morgan is a brilliant officer," he said. "A genius. But he fights for the wrong reasons, unprofessional reasons—for the love of fighting. And usually in the wrong places—from the professional point of view. He ignores all plans, even orders. I'm afraid this time he has made a serious mistake. You are right. This raid can come to nothing in the end."

He stopped short and stood up, changing his manner abruptly. It was obvious that he thought he had already said too much.

"If Helen will excuse us now, we might go down to your office and arrange for the exchange. We are not robbers, and in the end, you know, you will profit by having some very fine blood introduced into your local stock. I can assure you there will be no violence while we are here, so long as there is no trickery or resistance, of course. I regret the barn-burning by Major Tolliver's men last night. But so far there have been no casualties. Your Home Guards at the bridge dissolved into thin air last night before Major Tolliver got there."

"But you sank the gunboat at Draper's Bend," I reminded him.

The colonel shook his head.

"It's unbelievable," he said, "but no lives were lost on either side in that engagement. I'm always amazed how few men are hurt at the expense of so much powder and shot, but I guess it's because the Lord cherishes men more than materials in spite of man's foolishness. We saved all the gunboat crew from the river. They are prisoners now on the *Matilda,* and we'll have to parole them of course when we leave."

At that point, Helen began to protest against our leaving the house.

"Stacey hasn't told me anything about the family yet. He hasn't even seen Bradford."

"Where is Bradford?" I asked; and a guarded look came into Helen's eyes. She did not know that I knew about the boy's escapade the day before.

"Asleep," she said.

I turned to the colonel.

"He ran away yesterday and tried to join your army, but I understand he had a change of heart when you made him a prisoner."

"That was Major Tolliver," the colonel explained.

"Bradford doesn't like your Major Tolliver," Helen said; and the colonel, his eyes dancing with malice, replied, "The major recites and sings beautifully, Helen, and he's very fond of the ladies."

He had buckled his swordbelt round his waist, fastening the holstered Colt to it, and the three of us were moving out into the hall, the colonel with his hand affectionately on Helen's shoulder, Helen protesting again against our leaving, while I followed; and I heard the mantle clock behind me strike ten and my mind automatically calculated that in two hours the raiders would be gone.

In the hall, Stacey Morey took his hat from the rack and bowed.

"I hope I can come back for a peaceful visit someday," he said to Helen.

I turned to kiss Helen goodbye; and it was for that reason that my back was toward the front door and I only heard and did not see what happened in the next instant.

In quick succession, there was a deafening shot from the doorway; then two more, like reverberations, from the yard. The first was so close that I hardly heard the other two. Then Helen screamed.

Turning about, I saw the colonel lying in the open doorway, one leg thrust across the sill onto the porch. His pistol, still smoking, was clutched in his right hand. A thin line of blood, ruby red in the sunlight, trickled down through his hair and his blond beard and was already forming a small round puddle on the polished floor.

"Henry! Look out!"

When Helen cried out that second time, I was stooping at the colonel's side. Looking up, I saw what I supposed had frightened her. In the yard, the man who had shot Stacey Morey was also dead—or dying, at least. He lay beside the althea bush at the corner of the house, his legs kicking grotesquely in the air like a baby's. On the grass beside him was a long rifle.

But I was mistaken about what had frightened Helen. It was not the dying man but the colonel's orderly, whom I then saw standing a few feet from the dying man. He had just finished reloading his pistol and was raising it and pointing it at me with both hands wrapped around it halfway down the barrel. The hands loomed startlingly large and white before the orderly's face.

Helen had shrunk back to the foot of the stairs and was clinging to the newel.

"Henry!"

I had no time to spring away from the door, although it seemed to me that I waited hours while the orderly aimed the pistol at me and finally fired.

The bullet struck the thick doorjamb behind me with a sharp noise that seemed louder than the pistol's discharge, and a little shower of splinters fell on the floor at my feet.

The enormous white hands in the yard parted, shrank to normal size and fell to the orderly's sides, dropping the pistol, and the orderly stood looking at me foolishly, as if he were asking himself why he had done what he had done, while near him, beside the althea bush, the assassin's kicking slowed, like a wind-up toy running down, and eventually ceased and the long legs stretched out on the grass at rest. Finally, the orderly began to talk in a loud voice, as if he had been accused of something, although I had not spoken and Helen, at the foot of the stairs, was strangely still.

"It was the colonel got him," the orderly said, the hands gesticulating now. "It was the colonel got the draw on him. I was out there with the horses and I was watching the colonel come out of the house and the ———— must have been there behind the bush all the time, because I saw the colonel draw and fire, and then I saw the ———— and I fired at him too. But I missed him because he'd already fell. It was the colonel got the ———— after he was shot himself. I was out here with the horses and—"

The orderly went on and on, repeating, but I heard then another voice and, turning my head, I saw Doc Pendleton running up the walk.

"You all right, Henry?" Doc was saying. "You all right?"

". . . and the ———— was there behind the bush all the time. . . ."

"I'm all right," I said. "He missed me."

It was only then that I clearly understood what had happened. It was only then, too, that I remembered the pistol I had been carrying strapped about my waist off and on for more than twenty-four hours, the pistol that it had seemed so important to conceal from the orderly when I entered the house a half hour before. I had not even reached for it.

"It's that Sykes boy," Doc Pendleton said, pointing at the dead body by the althea bush. "Old man Sykes's son. Estol Sykes."

"I think Helen has fainted, Doc," I said.

We carried Helen into the parlor and laid her on the sofa under her portrait.

"She'll be all right," Doc Pendleton said. "Get some smelling salts or ammonia and cold water. I'll have to look after the officer. He's dead, though. And then that Sykes boy out on the lawn." Afterward, I heard him calling to the colonel's orderly, "Here, you, give me a hand."

Bradford had run down the stairs at the sound of the shooting, and I was proud of the efficiency with which he obeyed orders in spite of his obvious fright, running back upstairs to look for smelling salts, fetching water from the kitchen pump, wringing out cloths over the basin he had set on a table in the parlor.

By the time Helen was revived, Major Tolliver had appeared

at the front door and, with a dozen soldiers, had taken over the house.He moved languidly from room to room, picking up objects here and there and admiring them, a small victorious smile playing at the corners of his mouth, so that he looked not so much like a sightseer as a man who, having made an unexpected purchase, was for the first time examining what he had bought.

"We'd better take her upstairs and put her to bed," Doc Pendleton was saying when Helen opened her eyes. He and Bradford and I were standing beside the sofa, and the major had just come to the door to inquire for the second or third time after her welfare. "She's all right," Doc said, "but she'll be better off in bed. Maybe I can get Laura to come over—"

Helen sat up on the edge of the sofa. She looked past us at the major in the doorway.

"Who is he?"

"Major Tolliver," I told her.

"The man who tied my son to a tree?"

"Only to keep him out of danger, ma'am," the major said, bowing, the gold and scarlet embroidery of his uniform flashing in the sunlight that poured in through the windows. "Only to protect him."

"Why is he here?" she asked, still addressing me.

"He's in command now."

"Stacey . . ?"

Doc spoke then. "Now, Helen, I'll have Laura come over—"

"Stacey?" Helen said again.

I told her bluntly that he was dead. She closed her eyes and sat on the edge of the sofa swaying a little. When she opened them, she stood up, pushing Doc aside, and smoothed out her crinoline.

"And you?" she said, looking past us again at the major. "You are going to be here now?"

"It will be a pleasure, ma'am," the major replied, bowing once more, speaking as if her question had been an invitation.

"But you'll be gone by noon, Colonel Morey said."

The major only smiled.

"I'll see about Laura," Doc said, plucking at my sleeve and drawing me toward the door. "She'll be all right, but maybe I should send Laura over."

"Where have you got the colonel?" Helen asked.

"In the parlor, ma'am."

He had entered the room, passing Doc and me, and she began to talk to him, scolding him for his treatment of Bradford at the Draper place. It was obvious that he was enjoying her scolding.

"I had only just told Laura a few minutes before I heard the shots," Doc was saying to me at the front door. "She was taking it pretty hard, poor girl, and then I ran over here."

"Laura?" I said.

"Laura. Yes. She didn't cry. She just stood still for a minute and then she ran up to her room. I was halfway up the stairs after her, when I heard the shooting."

"Told her what?" I asked.

"About Jack," Doc said. "Goosehead told me when he came with your message to meet you at the City Hall. Henry, I—"

I shook my head, and he broke off and laid his hand on my arm.

"Don't disturb her," I said. "I'm glad you told her. I won't have to now. I've been dreading it. But don't send her over here. We'll get along, and anyhow—I'd rather not have Helen learn about Jack until I can tell her, till things are squared away here and we can be alone."

Doc nodded.

"Of course," he said.

When I turned to re-enter the parlor, I discovered that Doc and I had not been talking privately. The sentry who was stationed in the front hall, a big red-bearded sergeant, had followed us out on the porch and stood directly behind me. When I started indoors I almost bumped into him. He remained rudely where he was, blocking my way, and I had to step around him to go inside.

In the parlor, I found the major sitting on the sofa beside Helen. Bradford stood before them. The major was addressing the boy but all the while obviously putting on a show for Helen. "So you thought you'd like to be a soldier, eh? I believe you'd make a good one. But you must wait until you're a little older...." Bradford stood awkwardly in the middle of the room, his face red, his arms straight at his sides. Helen gave me a quick look, and then her face became a mask.

"Colonel Morey and I were about to go down to my office to

arrange for the exchange of horses," I said. "We might do that now, major."

The major did not look at me.

"No hurry now," he said, dismissing me. "I have a nephew about your age at the Citadel," he said to the boy.

Helen stood up.

"Come, Bradford. I'll fix you some breakfast."

Bradford followed her to the door, but before they reached it, the major was on his feet, too.

"I'll come along," he said. "I could do with a cup of coffee, ma'am." As he passed me, he glanced up into my face, his soft blue-gray eyes insolent under their long lashes. "You are perfectly free to go down to your office, if you like," he said.

I watched him go down the hall after Helen and the boy, his body swaying, his arms swinging gracefully—too gracefully, I thought—his fingers drumming lightly on the polished top of a mahogany table as he passed it. I knew then that I dared not go anywhere, that I was a prisoner in my own house, more securely incarcerated there than I would have been if the red-bearded sergeant had been told to stand over me with a gun.

The morning was endless. The clock on the mantle ticked, but the hands seemed not to move. Outside, however, there were signs of time's progress. The raiders, informed of Colonel Morey's murder, began to grow restless, although at first their reactions were little more than skylarking, a kind of celebration of Major Tolliver's succession to the command. The major never left the house, seemed to give no orders, and the consequence was a relaxing of discipline. There was more riding through the streets than there had been earlier. There were occasional pistol shots and Rebel Yells, and once, just before noon, a cannon boomed on the waterfront.

These were the audible signs of change. The first visible sign —and somehow more ominous than any sound—was the dust that rose in the air and failed to settle. Stirred by the raiders' increased galloping through the streets, long before noon it became an ugly saffron cloud above the housetops, coloring the sky like the herald of a summer storm; by noon, there were other signs, both audible and visible, indicating that the spirit of the

town's captors had changed. They galloped past the house with
bolts of colored cloth flying out in long streamers from their
saddles and with women's bonnets on their heads. One carried
a pair of ice skates slung round his neck; another held a bird cage
beforc him like a lantern; still another flung bright bone buttons
into the sunlight, making showers of colored raindrops. Finally,
I saw the first to come past the house with a girl up, her flounces
fluttering over the saddle, her eyes bright with fear and ardor.
After that, there were others.

"Your men are looting, Major."

As I heard my own frustrated and silly words, I remembered
Asa Ross announcing earlier that morning that the raiders had
captured the city, as if the mere announcement might somehow
ameliorate the fact; and impotence defiled my blood and un-
strung my sinews in the presence of my wife and son and the
dapper little officer. There were guards at every door of the
house, inside and out; on the lawn before the window where I
stood, a half-dozen Rebs were wrestling like boys after school is
out; and nearby, on the bible-box by another window, where I
had leaned my elbow earlier that morning, my pistol and its
holster were at arm's length from me, yet infinitely out of my
reach, placed there by the major himself to tantalize me after the
red-bearded sergeant had searched me and found the weapon
under my coat. "You are at liberty, you know," the major had
said to me a dozen times during the morning; and to Bradford,
"A boy your age should be outdoors, playing." But both of us
had stayed stubbornly in the house with him and Helen. Yet all
I could say to him was, "Your men are looting, Major. . . ." I
thought for a moment I was going to be sick.

Major Tolliver smiled. He was having a little lunch in the
parlor, on the sofa beside Helen; and when I spoke, he had been
praising the smoked ham, wiping the grease of it from his pink
lips with one of Helen's damask napkins, all the while caressing
her with the light of his clouded blue-gray eyes.

"They have so little, sir," he said to me. "You have so much."

I tried speaking to him then as a soldier.

"If you don't stop it, you will never get them into any kind
of order for the road."

The major smiled again and picked up the knife and fork he
had laid on the plate that was balanced on his knees.

"Your fellow from the country changed our plans," he said, nodding in the direction of the front door where Colonel Morey had fallen; and once more he turned his gaze upon Helen. "That and other considerations," he added significantly.

I wanted to leap upon him then. I thought of snatching up my pistol and shooting him in cold blood. But I knew that if I did I would be overpowered by his red-bearded sergeant and the other men stationed about the house; and then Helen would be completely at their mercy.

"I am pleased that Colonel Morey is to be buried in your family plot in the cemetery," the major said to Helen, as if I were not in the room. "Since he is your cousin . . ."

Looking out the window again, I was startled to see Laura Pendleton coming across the street. At first I was annoyed, assuming that Doc Pendleton had ignored my request; but in the next moment, I was thinking that, ironically, another woman in the house would be a better protection for Helen than myself, and I was pleased. Without turning from the window, I said, "Helen . . ." and she rose and came to my side, the major instantly following her.

"It's the doctor's daughter," Helen explained to the major. "She is engaged to my husband's son."

Major Tolliver glanced at Bradford, puzzled.

"By his first wife," Helen explained. "He's with Grant in Mississippi." There was a note of pride in her voice.

"She is lovely," the major said; and when the soldiers on the lawn broke off their wrestling and swarmed about Laura Pendleton as she came in through the gate, he left the room quickly to disperse them.

"He has been at the brandy in the sideboard all morning, Henry," Helen whispered, as soon as the major appeared outside the window, offering Laura Pendleton his arm.

"That may be to our advantage in the end," was all I had time to say before they came into the house.

Laura Pendleton came across the parlor without speaking and kissed me without a word. There was a strange look in her eyes: grief, which I had expected, but something else that I failed to recognize. She stood nervously in our midst without speaking, until finally her voice cut sharply across the major's prattle like a wind snapping off the heads of flowers.

"I'd like to be alone with Helen."

The major was pleased to have an opportunity to be ingratiating.

"But of course, dear lady," he said.

Helen took Laura up to her room, and they were closeted there for a half-hour. Meanwhile, in the parlor, the major finished the ham while I stood at the window, silent, with my back turned squarely upon him. When the women came downstairs, the major insisted on escorting Laura across the street to her house, and I was alone briefly with Helen and Bradford for the second time that morning.

"You have a rival," I said, as we stood by the window watching the two cross the street. I spoke so, inanely, because I did not want Helen to speak of Jack. I assumed that Laura had told her.

Helen took my hand.

"Laura insisted that we go to the funeral this afternoon, all of us," she said.

I looked down at her, puzzled.

"Was that all she talked with you about?"

Helen nodded.

"She wouldn't say why she wanted us to go. She just kept insisting."

A wave of relief passed over me, but I was more puzzled than ever.

"All three of us," Helen said again. "She insisted."

"I doubt whether he will let me go," I said.

"Laura said I must *make* him let you go."

"Why?"

"She didn't say why—she wouldn't. She seemed to have some kind of plan, she and her father. There was something on her mind. But she wouldn't tell me. Henry, I think she did not trust me." She pressed my hand hard. "Henry—"

"Yes," I said.

"He's coming back now," Helen said. "Let me say this quickly, and believe me. *You* can trust me, Henry. You can trust me."

I bent over and kissed her.

"I know that," I said. "I've known that all along, my darling."

"Your gun . . ."

I saw then that she had taken the holster from the bible-box and was concealing it in the folds of her skirt. She held it out to me gingerly.

I shook my head.

"He will notice that it is gone," I said, "and the second time they take it away from me, he won't leave it lying round so handy."

I laid the holster back on the bible-box; and Helen clutched my arm for one brief moment before the major came back into the room. "Darling!" she whispered at my ear; and then she spoke lightly to Bradford as the major entered, "Run out and play in the yard now, darling. Go talk to the soldiers. The major is right. It's too nice a day for you to stay indoors." I wondered for a moment whether she would send me away too. That would have been too obvious, although I noticed that the major swayed slightly as he crossed the room. The brandy was still having its effect, in spite of the smoked ham he had just eaten. The brandy and Helen and now Laura. We were dealing with a fool. But in his own way a fool could be more dangerous than a wise man.

"You have been very kind to us, Major," I heard Helen say, as she joined him on the sofa.

Turning back to the window, I could not have said whether the disorder outside worsened or improved, although I tried to keep my gaze fixed stonily on the street and not listen to what went on behind my back: the laughter, Helen's lilting voice, the rustle of her crinoline, the major's little speeches. I wondered how a man could be so easily deceived. But he was a fool.

To distract myself, I recalled an old theory of my youth, invented when I was in college and derived perhaps from Berkeley: that women exist only in men's imaginations. Looked at squarely, if that were possible, without desire, illusions, ideals, they would vanish. To become what—? my classmates used to ask. I had never got that far. Fecundity in the abstract maybe. It was like the tree falling in the forest and making no sound because no one was at hand to hear. Once, when Helen was in a fit of jealousy, I had expounded the youthful theory to her, arguing that because of it I could love both her and Nance without comparisons or contradictions. Helen was not impressed; she only held out her arms to me; and afterward, lying in the bed at my side, said victoriously, "And did you think *that* was a figment of your imagination, Mr. Clayburn?" I am sure she had never heard of Dr. Johnson stamping his foot to confute Berkeley.

Behind me, the major had been singing "Lorena" softly. "You have a beautiful voice," I heard Helen murmur. It was true. I concentrated upon the window again. The men on the lawn were tumbling about like puppies. The dustcloud above the rooftops had thickened. A cannon boomed on the levee. Behind me the clock on the mantle chimed the half-hour. Half past one, or half past two? I wondered. In any event, they were no longer firing the Parrott only on the hour. It had become a celebration. In the street, two horsemen rode past in a race, and I recognized Ben Marvin's blood bay. The other horse, a black mare, was trailing by half a length. Their dust momentarily obliterated the Pendleton house across the street. I wondered again about Doc's plan. Why did he want me to go to the funeral? I wondered whether Laura would ever marry now, how she had managed to keep her grief a secret from Helen. *I think it; therefore, it is.* Except in men's imaginations. . . . Maybe the theory applied to enemies, too, as well as women, to dapper little majors come up from the South where they had nephews at the Citadel. . . .

"Henry . . ."

Without turning, I said, "Yes?"

Helen's voice was a blend of coaxing and command.

"Major Tolliver wants us to go to the funeral this afternoon."

I looked at them over my shoulder. They sat very close on the sofa under Helen's portrait. The major's face was pink. Helen was self-possessed, but her eyes betrayed a triumph not unlike the triumph that lighted the picture above her in her wedding gown. There was triumph in the major's face, too, where it should be. He was an ass.

"All of us," Helen said. "You, too."

The major nodded his confirmation. He was beaming, tipsy, but not drunk. He was an ass. Looking at Helen, I was sure that if I were the major, I would believe, as he obviously believed, that the idea of going to the funeral was entirely my own. I would be an ass, too. My God, how beautiful she was!

"If the major insists . . ." I said.

The funeral procession left the house in mid-afternoon and moved slowly through the heat to the beating of muffled drums; down Audubon Street toward Main; then out Main to the cemetery. Major Tolliver rode smartly at the head of a small troop of uniformed men. Behind the flag-draped coffin, which was mounted on the carriage of a Parrott gun, Helen and Bradford and I followed in the family buggy. No one came into the street to watch us, and only a few soldiers loitered on the wooden banquettes. As the cortege moved past, they stood at attention, but immediately afterward they sloped into idleness and indifference as if already sated by the freedom the colonel's death allowed them.

The cemetery was an oak-studded knoll high above the Negro settlement on Dove Creek, and as the procession crawled along its dusty serpentine lane, the air was hot and bright and empty and very still. When at last the volley of Confederate guns crashed through the silence over the grave, I thought the noise was a vulgar intrusion, less appropriate to the occasion than the subsequent muted thunder of birdwings above the motionless trees and the faraway cry of a flicker that came loudly at first across the knoll, like an alarm, hovered in a falling cadence on the hot, still, summer air, and finally lost itself before its promise of song could be fulfilled. After that, the heat and the bright empty stillness closed in again, more oppressive than before.

When the obsequies were over, Major Tolliver walked with us to the buggy, telling me to meet him at the City Hall as soon as I had taken my wife and son home. He spoke softly, molding his words into the shape of a polite request; but there was no mistaking the command in them and the threat also, for all the while he was speaking he was looking at Helen.

I glanced at the troop of soldiers down the lane and then at the two Negro grave-diggers, who had already begun to tumble yellow earth into the hole. The thumping of clods on the coffin top was a hollow rumbling, like the muffled beat of the drums a little while before. Noticing my quick glance, the major smiled and said, "You have worried all day about my apparent lack of discipline. Let me assure you that all exits from the city are carefully guarded."

Then he mounted his horse, saluted Helen gallantly, and rode away toward his men, leaving us alone beside the buggy, the

Negroes watching us above their work with slantwise, white-eyed caution.

I touched Helen's elbow to help her into the buggy but held her back when I saw Doc Pendleton loitering among the tombstones in the distance and knew at once, somehow, that the Negroes had actually been looking at him, not at us, that they had indeed been expecting him to appear, although I could not have said why. By the little start that Helen gave, I knew that she had just seen the doctor herself. When Bradford raised a hand to point, I whispered, "No!"

Doc Pendleton approached warily, keeping the largest tombstones between himself and the departing major. Finally, he was with us beside the buggy.

"You must not go home, Henry," he said. He was short of breath and sweat stood out on his forehead.

"I am not going home," I said. "The major told me to meet him at the City Hall after I took Helen and Bradford home. But I am not taking them home. I am taking them to the City Hall with me. I shan't let them out of my sight."

"No, not that either."

A little man with a big nose and a beet-red face and coarse black hair, Doc spoke hoarsely, as if he were angry or drunk or both; but along with the fever of choler and dissipation in his bloodshot eyes I saw also the fever of devotion. Whatever the instability of his character, I knew there was no instability in his attachment to those he loved.

"Why not?" I said.

"I was at the inquest," he said, "—or what they called an inquest. They already have Ross and Marvin in jail, and there will be others. You will be next. The thing has got out of hand, Henry. They've sacked Grumby's store." I saw the bolts of cloth and the bright bone buttons and the bonnets in Audubon Street. "There've been several shootings in the saloons along the waterfront. And now they're stacking bales of cotton along Main Street."

"Cotton on Main Street?"

"To burn."

"So—?"

"They'll put you in jail, too, Henry."

"We couldn't get far in this buggy," I said, "if that's what you're suggesting. He has all the exits to the city guarded. He likes his game of cat-and-mouse. That's why he left us."

Doc glanced at Helen. She was leaning against a wheel of the buggy, clutching one of the red spokes with a black-glove hand. I knew what he was thinking.

In the next moment—irrelevantly, I thought—he was telling me about the telegrapher's horse in his parlor on Audubon Street. With Laura's connivance, he had kept the animal concealed in the house for two days, and now it was cured. "I am going to ride it to Offitt tonight," he announced at the end.

I was startled, but I concealed my amazement, as I had concealed my mirth a moment before when he was telling about the horse.

"You can't, Doc," I said. "They'll have guards and patrols everywhere."

"Everywhere," he agreed. "I know." Then he told me his plan. He was going to wear Colonel Morey's uniform as a disguise. He tilted his head in the direction of the two grave-diggers. "They're going to fill in only a foot or so. I've paid them." I glanced at the grave-diggers again and saw that they were not actually working but in that state of levitation that Negroes often practiced to simulate work, that miracle of illusion which, like the Indian rope trick, was the exclusive secret of a race. "And tonight Goosehead will come back with one of them, a neighbor of his, and they'll dig it up."

I laughed then. The plot was too fantastic.

Doc's face darkened.

"It's our only hope, Henry. In the uniform I may be able to ride past them on that horse I've got, fool them if I'm challenged. In my own clothes, that would be impossible."

I glanced above Doc's head at Helen. She was still leaning against the buggy wheel. I could not tell by her expression whether she had been listening or not. In her attitude of waiting, she had the look of a child excluded from the conversation of its parents. Beside me, Bradford stood wth his mouth open. Doc's plot, I thought, was an adolescent fancy, the kind that would appeal to a boy.

"Not you, Doc," I said, solemnly. "If you'll let me have the horse, I'll go. But that idea about the uniform is crazy. I'll go in my own clothes."

"No," he said. "You're the mayor."

"All the more reason," I said.

"You can't leave Helen."

He was right about that.

"Let *me* go, Papa!" Bradford spoke up then. "*I'll* go!"

" 'It's my grandpa's place, —— it, sir!' " I thought proudly; but I shook my head, and the doctor, putting a hand on the boy's shoulder, said, "I thought of that, boy. But the uniform wouldn't fit you."

"It won't fit you either, sir."

"No; that's right. It won't. But I'll be on horseback, and I'm an old codger and—well, I guess I'll look more like a colonel."

It was a fool's errand, a comic-opera masquerade.

"What abut Laura?" I said. "You can't leave her."

"That's what I was going to tell you," Doc said. "She's already at Goosehead's cabin. She's there now, waiting. And you're to go. You three. Now. They're used to looking for runaway niggers in white men's houses, but no Southerner would expect white people to hide in a nigger's."

Like the masquerade, it was a romantic notion; but for that very reason I thought it might work.

Delphina and Amen were in the cabin too, Doc said; and Goosehead was waiting at that very moment among the tombstones beyond the open grave to guide Helen and Bradford and me down to Dove Creek by a hidden path.

"No," I said. "Helen and Bradford, all right. It's not a bad idea. But not me. I'm going to the City Hall."

"And what good will you be to Crescent City in jail with Asa Ross and Ben Marvin?" Doc asked. His voice became urgent. "Henry, we can trust Goosehead to get the uniform tonight and bring it to me at my house. I'd fetch it myself, but I think I'd better keep myself in sight all evening. In the public eye. Drunk, you know. At the Pepper House. With the major. He'll try to get something out of me. I can put him off the scent." His face became suddenly redder. "But I won't be drunk, Henry. You can count on that. I'll be at my house when Goosehead comes with the uniform. I'll be in the orchard behind the house, with the horse, ready."

A silence fell between us. I was still debating but already knowing what I was going to do. I was going to make the desperate, romantic, foolhardy venture myself. I would have Goosehead bring the colonel's uniform back to the cabin and, donning it myself, would go to the rendez-vous with Doc in his orchard in Goosehead's place. If I appeared wearing the uniform, Doc would have no choice about letting me have the horse.

Doc's choleric eyes were searching my face. Between the buggy shafts the horse shifted its weight, and the wheels creaked. I could hear Helen's quick breathing and knew that she had been listening, after all. Across the knoll, the flicker sent up its brief plaintive alarm once again.

"It's a wild idea," I said.

"It's a chance, though, Henry. Hurry! Make up your mind. We've taken too long already. He's not going to wait for you very long at the City Hall before he starts wondering where you are, starts looking for you."

"Helen—?"

She nodded her agreement. I wondered what she would do when she learned that I intended to make the dash out of the city on Doc's horse.

When Goosehead finally came in with the bundle, the moon had risen and blue-white phantoms had begun to emerge from the blue-black night outside the cabin on Dove Creek. The bundle was long and cylindrical, somewhat bent in the middle, a roll of carpet to anyone who might only glance at it and, failing to heft it, remain unaware of the stiff spine within it; and by the manner in which Goosehead dropped it on the bed beside me —gently, as if it were alive, and yet hastily, as if he were anxious to get rid of it—and moved away from it quickly with a sigh that expressed both repugnance and relief, and went at once to the water bucket by the door to wash his hands before he uttered a word, I assayed the price in fear and horror that he had paid for it. Although Goosehead had been accompanied by his neighbor, Quarter Brown, the presence of Quarter must have made the performance of the task possible only; it had mitigated for Goosehead none of the terrors.

"Quarter home now?" Mrs. Quarter Brown asked softly in the darkness of the little room; and Goosehead, still sloshing his hands about in the water bucket, grunted an affirmative. "I reckon I git on home my ownself then," Mrs. Quarter Brown said; and the springs of the other bed rang a little gong and in the next moment her woman's shape was darkening the doorway. " 'Bye, you all," she whispered. " 'Bye, Mist' Mizz Clayburn, Miss Laura, Mist' Bradford"; and Delphina said, " 'Bye, Mizz Quarter"; and there was a murmur from the others in the room; then Mrs. Quarter Brown vanished.

I began to unroll the bundle on the end of the bed where Helen and Laura Pendleton and I were sitting, with Bradford lying asleep behind us, and the smell of damp earth came up from it. In the darkness, I felt Helen slide squeamishly away.

"Ain't no pants," Goosehead muttered from the waterbucket, where he was still splashing. "We couldn't git his boots off." There was a note of defiance in his voice, and I laughed, with more nervousness than I had realized I was feeling.

"We don't need the pants," I said.

"Aint' no hat neither," Goosehead added.

He stopped washing his hands and shook them out over the bucket, splattering drops noisily against the tin sheeting on the wall. "Git you a towel, Goosehead?" Delphina offered; and he said, "Ne'mind." I heard him rub his hands dry, on his shirtfront probably; and after that his voice was more natural than it had been.

"How come they don't never bury folks with they hats on, Mist' Henry?"

"That would be no way to meet the Lord, I suppose," I said. I had the bundle unrolled across my knees now, the end of the carpet falling over my legs like a buggy robe. With groping hands, I was checking over the bundle's contents. "The hat is still at the house," I said. "On the rack in the hall. I can pick it up on my way."

I heard Goosehead suck air through his teeth with a sharp hiss. Behind me, Bradford stirred in his sleep; and at the same time, I felt Helen's hand move across the counterpane toward me, and, letting go of the bundle on my knees, I reached out and put my own hand on it accurately in the dark. She had made no protest when I altered Doc's plan and announced that I was going to ride out of the city in his place.

Something dropped to the floor with a clatter, and Helen's hand jerked away.

"What was that?" Goosehead whispered.

"The sword," I said.

Helen leaned toward me again. Her hair brushed my face, and I felt her breath on my cheek, cool and light.

"Oh, God!" she said softly; and across the room, Delphina moaned.

I raised my hand and touched Helen's face.

"The worst is over," I said.

We had been huddled in the cabin since late afternoon, seven of us; Helen, Bradford, myself, Laura, Delphina, Amen, and Goosehead, Goosehead going out at midnight and coming back finally, but Mrs. Quarter Brown in his place while he was gone. Now it was my turn to go, and for the rest of them the vigil of inaction and waiting must continue. For them, the worst was not over. What I had said to Helen was not true; but I could think of nothing else to say; so I said it again.

"The worst is over."

All that late-afternoon and into the evening, there had been nothing to do but wait in Goosehead's cabin. There had been occasional shots in the distance outside, the smell of smoke—woodsmoke, not gunsmoke—a shout or two, dust seeping through the wide cracks in the siding, and once, in the lane above Dove Creek, hoofbeats so loud that they threatened to thunder directly into the tiny room; but these passed, receded, died away, and did not come again. Doc had been right; it never occurred to them to search the Negro cabins. Mostly, however, that afternoon and into the evening, there had been the whites of Delphina's eyes in the shadows, Amen's asthmatic breathing, Bradford's restlessness, Goosehead's indignant profile at the crack of white light in one of the draped windows, Laura's grieving silence, and Helen's questions—"Do you think . . . Will they . . . Do you suppose . . . ?"—to which I could only answer that I did not think so, although there were times when I did think so. And constantly there had been the heat—we kept the door closed all but a narrow crack, ready to bolt, and the windows were covered wih gunnysacks—and the confinement—there was no room to move about in and nothing to sit on but a hard chair, a hard stool, and the two beds—and the endless hours.

At dusk, Delphina passed around cold cornbread and mo-
lasses apologetically. "I can cook you up a mess of something,"
she offered; and I said no, explaining that the raiders might see
the smoke rising from the chimney and wonder why there was
a fire in a closed-up cabin on such a hot night, but thinking also
of the additional heat from the stove in the tiny room and the
intensified smell of bodies, black and white. "The cornbread is
delicious, Delphina," Helen said. After we had eaten, we waited
a while, and then Goosehead went out on his mission and a few
minutes later Mrs. Quarter Brown crept in, afraid to stay in her
cabin next door alone. We waited then together, and now
Goosehead had returned with the bundle, and for me at last, the
worst—the waiting—was over. But for the rest of them it was
not.

I rolled the uniform and the sword back into the carpet and
stood up. I kissed Helen and Laura and touched the sleeping boy
lightly. "No, don't wake him," I said, when Helen leaned over
the bed and spoke the boy's name. "But, Henry—" I found her
mouth and kissed her again, cutting off her protest. "There's
nothing to worry about," I said. Then I moved into the light of
the door.

"You ain't putting on the uniform?" Goosehead said.

"I'll put it on at the house. It wouldn't be right without the
hat."

I heard the quick sibilant intake of Goosehead's breath again.
It was the same sound he had made the first time we had talked
of the hat, and I realized then that there was some significance
in the sound that I had not recognized before.

"Ain't no need for no hat," Goosehead said. He was talking
faster than was natural to him. "I see lots of them Confeds riding
round town 'thout no hats on they heads. Seems like Confeds do
it more than Yankees."

"Not colonels, Goosehead," I said.

He moved out of the darkness and stood close to me, a shadow
suddenly as well as a voice.

"You go straight for the doctor's house now, Mist' Henry.
You hear? Don't you waste no time. You put on that uniform
here and go straight for the doctor's house. You got no call to
go poking around in your house for no fool hat. You hear? You
just leave the gentleman's fool hat be."

"I'd be easily recognized without the hat," I said.

Goosehead was quiet for a moment, absorbing the truth of the argument. "I guess that's right," he said. Then he sucked in his breath again. "Then I go in your place, Mist' Henry," he said. "We going back to the doctor's first plan, for me to take the soldier suit to him and him to ride. You staying here, Mist' Henry. I can run faster than you, and the doctor he waiting in his orchard right now. Give me that bundle."

"You went into town, didn't you, Goosehead?" I said quietly; and Goosehead, caught off his guard, said, "Yessuh."

"You might have been caught."

"I was just noseying around, Mist' Henry. I reckoned maybe I ought to check up a little."

I knew a sudden sharp anxiety. Part of Goosehead's motive for "noseying" might have been postponement of the dreaded ghoulish mission to the cemetery; but Goosehead knew the doctor's weakness and he had a strong sense of responsibility.

"Where did you go?"

"Well, I traveled round to the Pepper House first and looked in on a boy I know in the kitchen."

"Was the doctor at the Pepper House?"

"He had been there, but the boy say he was gone."

"So you went out to his house."

"Yessuh, that's right."

I hesitated, framing the next question.

"Was the doctor all right?"

"Oh, yessuh. He was standing out in his orchard with the horse. I seen him, but he didn't see me."

I released a sigh of relief and stepped out on the stoop. Then, of a sudden, I felt a shock of discovery and stopped and said, "And after you saw the doctor, you went across the street to my house. Why didn't you bring the hat?"

"I didn't rightly notice it," Goosehead said, and afterward began talking fast again. "That's what I mean, Mist' Henry. Maybe that old hat ain't there. Maybe you just wasting your time going to look for it. You go straight to the doctor's orchard now, you hear. Or maybe it better if you let me go and we go back to the doctor's first plan. I can run faster'n you and—"

"Goodbye, Helen," I said over my shoulder, ignoring Goosehead.

"Now, you leave the gentleman's old fool hat be, Mist' Henry!

You hear?" Goosehead called after me, his voice louder and more troubled than Helen's "Goodbye"; and as I moved off into the shadows of the yard, I knew, as certainly as if I had already seen it, what I was going to see in the house on Audubon Street.

With the bundle under my arm, I followed in reverse virtually the same route that Delphina had taken in the early morning of the previous day when she fled from the house on Audubon Street to Dove Creek. I could not cross the creek on the railroad trestle, however, as Delphina had done; the raiders had burned it. Beyond that point they had destroyed the Straight Line too. Deep into the swampy jungle behind the Negro settlement, piles of burning crossties gleamed like a vanishing row of sentinel fires in the night. Close at hand, before I slid down the creek bank, I saw that the raiders had torn up the tracks and thrown them across the fires. Beneath the black tangles of twisted rails, the flames blinked ruddily, like grated coals.

I waded through the drought-shallowed stream and, after climbing the opposite bank, found my way through the alders to the ditch where Goosehead had discovered Charlie Gosport bound and gagged. As I expected, there were soldiers in the railroad station, but there were no sentries in evidence outside. In the waiting room, a cluster of men huddled under the gaslight near the door to the telegraph office. Their distorted shadows yawed and stretched gigantically on the far wall above the benches. I was tempted to creep up to one of the windows, but I remained where I had emerged from the ditch, in the tall weeds beside the track.

One of the men was cursing in an endless monotone, and I guessed that he was drunk. Another said, "Get Sardis, Lightning. Get Sardis again"; and after he spoke, I recognized the voice as Major Tolliver's. "Tell them . . ." But the drunken monotone drowned the rest of his words. The name of the Federal general, Hobson, emerged several times from the clamor in the room, and the man who was drunk took it up and composed a chant, adding obscenities. "Shut that —— up, somebody!" a man shouted from inside the telegraph room; but nobody obeyed. The drunk's voice continued. "Where's Black?" It was the major speaking again. "Go find Black!" A segment of the dark clot under the gaslight detached itself and moved toward the door, and I ran.

Across Water Street, I darted under an awning, paused, then fled down an alley. As I entered it, a small troop on horseback galloped by, and I heard a voice from the station platform cry out, "Black! Is Black with you? Where's Black?" Before that, I had caught a glimpse of bonfires and dark shadows in motion on the levee, and as I ran, I became aware of the smell of burning cotton. Remembering the bales Doc Pendleton said they had stacked along Main Street, I wondered what I would find in the center of the town. But there was no glow in the sky, and after the blaze-dotted levee, the alley was a blackness that was shafted only here and there by moonlight; and a few minutes later, Main Street itself was like the alley, dark and still.

I crossed the street cautiously, keeping in the long shadow of Grumby's store, picking my way, with an incipient horror, a foreboding, through the debris of merchandise scattered at my feet. Buttons and bonnets and bolts of calico. I wondered what else. But on the south side of the street, I stopped thinking and flattened myself against a wall under a gallery, all my senses alert. I had heard voices and could not locate them. There was a silence when I stopped; then came a murmur, a little moan, a kind of keening. When I recognized the meaning of the sound, I let the air out of my lungs and began walking again. A man and woman were on the gallery directly above me and what they were doing would make them deaf as well as blind. Nevertheless, I set my feet down carefully on the uneven banquette and held my free hand out before me to keep from bumping into anything in the dark; but in the end, in spite of all my precautions, I kicked something made of metal and it clattered into the cobbled street.

The keening on the gallery stopped. After a breathless silence, the woman whispered hoarsely, "What was that?"

I did not wait for the man to give an answer. Entering the alley, I fled again.

It was my own alley, the one that ran behind my house on Audubon Street, and there was only one more street to cross. I drew up in the shadow of Ben Marvin's carriage house, scanned the street in both directions, and bolted for the dark mouth of the alley on the opposite side. There I paused again to catch my breath and, afterward, walked instead of running.

By the time I arrived at the back yard of my own house, I was no longer fearful of pursuit or capture. Abandoning caution, I broke through the border of crape-myrtle bushes, ran boldly across the orchard, and entered the latticed summer kitchen without a glance in any direction to determine whether the house was guarded; but when I saw at last what I expected to see, I was stopped by a final and unforeseen stupefaction and stood motionless in the back entrance of the house, staring.

It was an entrance only. There was no longer a door. What had been a door was a scattering of splinters mixed with a chaos of other wreckage across the doorsill at my feet. At the far end of the moonlit central hall, the front door had vanished too. Beyond the litter of smashed furniture and pictures in the hall and through a segment of balusters that dangled from the staircase like a wind-ravaged shutter, a framed view of Audubon Street shone, pale blue in moonlight, composed and still, as if it were a painting that the vandals had spared.

After a long while, I took a step into the house. Glass crunched under my feet like crusted ice, and I stopped again. I had felt nothing at first and, afterward, experienced only a foreboding and impersonal horror, such as I had felt momentarily in Main Street among the rubbish from Grumby's store. It was a large horror, as if the house were not my own and I was appalled only that men could do what they had done and not that they had done it to me. But, once inside the house, I felt suddenly small and weak, alone, and it seemed as if the walls sagged inward, heavily, above my head.

Trembling, I took another crunching step; then another, diffidently now, as if I were intruding; reverently, like a thoughtful man entering the ruined sanctuary of a faith that was dead; then another; and another; until at last, having moved with care beneath the pendent balusters and round two broken chairs, I arrived at the door into the parlor.

Moonlight flooded through the naked windows and washed the wreckage on the floor as white as bones; curtain rods and legs of chair and tables; china, glassware, gewgaws; a flush of letters from the ax-split desk; a rocker upside down and back broken; firedogs; lampstands; the marble bust of Blackstone; the ancestral bible-box; and, dragged in from the street to be used

no doubt as a bludgeon, a white-painted hitching-post alone
erect among the crazy planes and angles.

Finally, above the sofa where Helen and the major had sat that
morning, I saw the silver rectangle that had held the portrait of
her in her wedding gown; and at that moment my impersonal
and half-reverent horror vanished and rage took its place. The
picture had been slashed half out of its frame. Below it, a wire
spring spiraled upward from the sofa, pointing with a zany,
inanimate glee at the ripped and drooping canvas.

My rage became greedy for the worst that the raiders could
have done in the house, and I turned, crossed the hall, and
climbed the ruined stairs. Long before I reached Helen's bedroom, I was sure I had imagined everything they could have
done to it—the sword-slashed curtains, the smashed armoire,
her ravished clothes, our stripped and trampled bed, the obscenities I knew they could commit but which I dared not name
in my thoughts. But when I arrived at the bedroom doorway,
I was stopped for the second time by a final and unforeseen
stupefaction and stood staring.

The room was undisturbed.

I stood in silence at the door for several minutes before I
laughed, the sound of my voice then a ghostly clamor in the
stillness of the house; and finally, when my laughter stopped as
abruptly as it had begun, I stood silent again and a strange
composure began to enter my spirit, like the order in the moonlit room before me, ultimate and still; and as I continued to look
in at the door, it seemed to me that my own composure and the
room's were spreading throughout the house, restoring it, as if
Helen herself had come in, while I stood there, and was setting
everything aright. It seemed to me that Nance was with her; and
Jack, too; and old Reuben Draper and Bradford and Doc Pendleton and Goosehead. I believed that if I listened closely, I would
hear their voices.

I think it, I said to myself; *therefore, it is.*

But that was not it. Not altogether. At least, not this time. It
was not only that I thought it, I corrected myself; it indeed *was.*
Not only Helen and Nance and the others were with me in the
ruined house, but all men and women of conscience and good
will of all time. They had been with me all along these past two
days: when I first saw the raiders through the rising morning

mists on the river; in the bright hot streets of Crescent City; in the City Hall, at the meeting and later, when I read Tom Ross's letter about Jack on the Bayou Pierre; and still later, in my old law office; and again this morning, when I was a prisoner in my own house; and afterward, in Goosehead's cabin on Dove Creek. That was what I had failed to see these past few days in the face of my overwhelming responsibility for the town. I had thought that I was alone. I had failed to believe that anyone besides myself could be counted upon to do what had to be done in the presence of evil. I was indeed my brother's keeper, but I had forgotten that in turn my brother was mine. I thought again of Jack and young Tom Ross down in Mississippi and remembered the question in Jack's last letter: "Do you have friends like that too, Papa?" I wished then that I had been able to answer the question before Jack was killed, to assure him that no man was ever alone and that such a friend felt a responsibility for him, too. I unrolled the bundle then, where I stood, in the doorway of Helen's bedroom, and put on her cousin's military blouse and sword.

The blouse fitted me well enough and the sword hung correctly at my side. I wished for a moment that Jack and young Tom Ross could see me. A Confederate uniform, I would tell them, was as good as any other for a man to wear if he was doing what he had to do.

I turned about and descended the stairs, and before I reached the bottom step, I saw the colonel's hat hanging on the rack by the front door, the only object in its proper place amidst the wreckage on the first floor. I had failed to notice it before I went upstairs, for I had forgotten that the hat was what I had come for. It was as if Colonel Morey, like Helen and the others, had come in while I was in the upper hall and had left the hat for me. But of course the hat had been there all along; and if that was so, I reasoned, the colonel himself had been there all along. No doubt it was the colonel's lingering presence in the house that had saved the upper rooms from devastation. The fantasy pleased me more than ever, now that I knew it was not altogether fantasy.

At the foot of the stairs, I fixed my gaze on the blue blur of the doorway and walked toward it, no longer mindful of the sound of glass and splinters underfoot. As I passed the rack, I took the colonel's hat and put it on my head. I marched down the front steps then and across the street with Colonel Morey's sword clinking lightly at my side, and it seemed no longer like a masquerade. I was the colonel, as well as myself. Only once, when I turned to close the Pendleton's gate behind me, did I glance back. Across the street, the moon-washed brick of my house shone briefly through the trees, like marble.

I heard Doc Pendleton's voice at my side and swung about.

"You came yourself, Henry!"

"Yes."

"In the uniform."

"Yes."

"I won't let you go. I won't let you have the horse."

"And I won't let you have the uniform, Doc," I said, and went past him into the orchard behind his house where Goosehead had told me the horse was tethered.

As I guided the horse down through Doc's orchard and galloped away through his alley, five Federal cavalrymen a mile or two outside Crescent City were riding toward the town along a moonlit road. One of them was Asa Ross's son, Tom.

"We'd better leave the road here," he said to his companions.

He wheeled his horse to the right, leaped a ditch, and, riding out of the moonlight, vanished under the shadow of a row of trees along the hillside, his companions following him.

"How far is it to the city now?" the lieutenant asked, riding up beside him.

"Mile maybe," Tom Ross said, "mile and a half."

"We're that close?"

Tom did not like the sound of the lieutenant's voice. There was fright in it.

"Sure. May meet Johnnies anywhere now. There's houses in that hollow beyond the turn." He pointed down the road, forgetting that the lieutenant could probably not see the gesture in the shadow. "That's why I thought we'd better turn off. From that ridge up there, we could see the city."

He pulled up, and the five men rested their horses for several minutes in silence. They were vedettes. They had been riding ahead of the Offitt regiment for more than an hour. They were at the northwest edge of Crescent City now, on the last long slope of the ridge that curved semi-circularly behind the town. Tom remembered it as a region known as The Barrens, sparsely wooded and bleak.

"Why is the regiment coming this way, I wonder," the lieutenant said, as if he were speaking to himself. He had seemed confused and faint-hearted about their mission of scouting from the start.

"No other way to come," Tom said, "unless you wanted to take your chances in the railroad tunnel or go clear round to the River Road. The Rebs are sure to have the tunnel mined, and the River Road is 'way-to- — -and-gone too far."

"You used to live here."

"Yes, sir. I told you."

Below them, the road through The Barrens was without cover in the moonlight. On the opposite side, another hill rose, almost treeless, a few bushes and gullies etched in black across its face. To the south, above the hollow, a faint ruddiness rimmed the sky. Tom had led the vedettes into the only shelter available. He did not know that actually there was no need of shelter. He had no way of knowing that an hour or two before Major Tolliver had withdrawn his pickets and patrols and there were no Rebs between them and the city's riverfront.

"Looks like a fire," one of the men said; and the lieutenant said, "Maybe we ought to go up on the ridge and have a look."

"It's too exposed for all of us," Tom said. "I'll go. You all stay here and watch the road."

Without waiting for the lieutenant's approval, he spurred his mount and it began a laborious ascent of the slope. The lieutenant had tacitly yielded the command to him shortly after they rode out ahead of the Offitt regiment, which Tom guessed was now several miles down the road behind them. "You used to live in Crescent City," the lieutenant had said a dozen times, making apologies to himself for yielding his command. He had no confidence or experience. As soon as Tom had realized this, he had taken over, hoping the other men would not discover that the lieutenant was afraid. It was something he would not have done in Mississippi. The realization that this was so puzzled him a little. "Let the pumpkin-rinders hang themselves by their mistakes if they want to," he had always said, before. He had thought only of saving his own skin.

Just under the brow of the ridge, where he was still invisible from the road, Tom drew rein and looked down. Below him, the rooftops of Crescent City glimmered under the moon, a pale cluster of blue and white dots, like mussel shells. Beyond the roofs, at the river, was the source of the red glow in the sky, and Tom guessed that the raiders had set fire to the stacked-up steamboat cargoes that always cluttered the levee.

His pulse quickened at the prospect of encountering some of Morgan's men within the next hour, although he already knew that Morgan himself was not among them. That afternoon, word had come to the Offitt regiment from the town of Vernon that Morgan was fleeing into Ohio with General Hobson at his heels and, if any flesh-and-blood Johnnies were left in the region, they must be in Crescent City. No one had suspected this fact until Morgan had turned tail at Vernon. Then the confusing reports continued to come into Offitt over the Crescent City wire, and the colonel of the Offitt regiment finally guessed that it was Rebels who had been sending the reports all along. At once, the regiment swung south from its wild-goose chase along the Dark River Valley and headed for Crescent City, where it should have gone in the first place. Tom Ross, on the hillside, expected the regiment to come down the road very soon, catching up with the vedettes that had been sent ahead.

"I'd like to get just one Reb for myself before they come," he said to himself.

He had arrived at Offitt by boat early Sunday morning, coming home from Mississippi on his furlough. From Offitt he had intended to take the train to Crescent City, but the Straight Line was not running and, anyhow, the town of Offitt was a-buzz with the news of Morgan's raid. So he had volunteered to serve as a scout with the Offitt regiment, since he knew the country, and he had spent the last two days with the regiment scouring the Dark River Valley in vain.

"Just one —— Reb!" he said.

He told me later that he could not help thinking of it as revenge for Jack's death and as atonement for his own escape from the Johnnies' crossfire on the Bayou Pierre; and that, too, puzzled him a little. He was incapable of much introspection and could not put his thoughts into words with any precision, but I gathered that he had always regarded Jack with a kind of amused and affectionate contempt, thinking Jack took life too seriously and made everything more difficult than it needed to be. Even when they were small boys together in Crescent City, he remembered, Jack had been like that, always reading books and inventing games that were too complicated to be any fun. "There was one called 'Tippecanoe,'" he told me, "about that battle Jack said his grandpa fought in. At the end of it, we were supposed to scalp Goosehead, but, —, Mr. Clayburn, we couldn't really scalp him, so what was the fun of it?" Tom remembered how I had taught them to shoot when they were six or seven years old and not yet strong enough to lift the long Kentucky rifles to the targets, so that they had to rest them on a rail, and how the recoil threw them back, head over heels. He said he could still see Jack's solemn face as they practiced at the old Draper place. Tom was a natural shot and soon got bored after a few rounds and became impatient for the day when they would be big enough to go off into the woods and hunt real game; but Jack practiced conscientiously every day; and when the time for real hunting came, it annoyed Tom that Jack was the one who always returned with the most squirrels. In the army, Tom said, in Tennessee and Mississippi, it had been the same; and when Jack chose to sit by the campfire at night writing letters or talking about the war in big words that made it hard to tell just what he was driving at, Tom sometimes laughed at him outright and walked away to find a sutler who could sell him a jug of tanglefoot to get drunk on.

But since Bayou Pierre, apparently, Tom had been feeling differently about Jack. By staying behind on the banks of the stream and getting himself killed, Tom told me, Jack had drawn the Johnnies' crossfire long enough to save the whole company. It was something he would have done himself, Tom said, if he had thought of it. But he had not thought of it. He was too busy saving his own skin. And anyhow Jack had the authority of his pumpkin rinds to make the rest of the men obey him and retreat. Since Bayou Pierre, Tom had caught himself several times trying to model his actions on his memory of Jack, like on this reconnoitering venture with the vedettes, he said, when he had quietly taken over the command

to save the men from the hazards of the lieutenant's inexperi-
ence and fear.

On the ridge, when Tom finally turned his horse about to
rejoin his companions, he heard hoofbeats in the road below and
stiffened suddenly and sat still in the saddle. Soon he saw a
horseman riding up out of the hollow at a gallop; and in the same
instant, there was a pistol shot from the vedettes hidden among
the trees where he had left them.

"That —— lieutenant!" he said.

The lieutenant had the advantage of darkness and should have
made sure the rider was alone before he gave away his own
position by firing. A whole company of Confeds might come
galloping out of the hollow behind the horseman. Then where
would they be?

But no horseman appeared on the road. The solitary rider
drew rein and, peering into the darkness where the lieutenant's
pistol had flared, called out, "Yanks or Rebs?"

One of the men below Tom answered, "What do *you* think?"
and Tom ground his teeth. He could see from where he sat
astride his horse just below the ridge that the man wore a
Confederate uniform. He waited for a time that seemed to him
long enough, and then, pulling his carbine out of its holster,
raised it to take aim. But as he did so, an idea came to him. A
prisoner, he told himself, would be more valuable than a dead
man. His comrades below him could have emerged from the
darkness onto the road and surrounded the Reb, for they were
closer than he was and they outnumbered the Reb four-to-one.
But, instead, they fired again, a scattering of shots, and the rider
in the road spurred his horse and it leaped into a gallop.

"Head him off!" Tom shouted. "Stop him!"

But there was only another volley of wild shots from the
shadows, and the horseman by that time had ridden safely past.

"I'll get him!" Tom shouted then. "Hold your fire!"

In an instant, he calculated distances and believed he had a
chance, riding down the hill at an angle, to catch up with the
horseman at a point a hundred yards up the road.

"I've got him!" he shouted above the pounding of his horse's
hoofs, as he rode past the vedettes and into their range where
any further shots from them might hit him instead of the Reb
in the road. "Hold it! I've got him!"

The vedettes held their fire, but he had miscalculated the speed of which the horse in the road was capable. In response to the rider's urging, it stretched its legs and flew. Before Tom was halfway down the slope, it was obvious that the pursuit was hopeless. In sudden anger and frustration then, he pulled in his mount and raised his carbine, cursing.

For one brief beautiful instant, he had a perfect bead on the rider's back between his shoulders; but again the new Tom Ross within himself that puzzled him took over. A prisoner could give them information about the town. A dead man would be of no use to them. He hesitated, lost his aim, and then, lowering it, fired at the horse instead.

The wasted moment saved both the rider and the horse. The rider threw up his arm and his hat flew off into the road, but he kept his seat and the flying horse, unharmed, carried him on over the next hill and out of sight.

Tom cursed again, not sure this time whether he was cursing himself or the Reb. Loosening his grip on the bridle, he let his horse lope slowly down the rest of the hillside and come to a halt in the road. He started to call to his companions. But instead, he turned and stared down the empty moonlit road, beginning to realize that, in the brief glimpse of the rider's hatless head, there had been something familiar; and slowly it came to him who the rider was.

"You missed him."

It was the lieutenant's voice. The vedettes were riding down the hillside toward him, the lieutenant in the lead. "It was a Reb," the lieutenant said, coming up beside him. "An officer."

At the roadside, one of the men was dismounting, calling out, "Here's his hat!"

"It was a Reb," the lieutenant said again, a kind of wonder in his voice, revealing that it was the first Reb he had ever seen. "But you missed him," he added, reproachfully.

"It was his old man, his father," Tom Ross said at last; and all the men turned toward him.

"What?" the lieutenant said. "Whose father?"

"A friend's. Clayburn . . ." Tom said. "He's the mayor."

"The Reb?"

Tom nodded.

"Mayor Clayburn," he said.

"It was a Confederate officer," the lieutenant said.

"I don't understand it," Tom said.

The men were silent for several minutes, one of them, re-mounted, holding the Confederate officer's hat in his hand, the lieutenant still breathing hard, the others shifting their weight in their creaking saddles.

"He'll run smack into the regiment," Tom said, finally. "They'll be here soon. We'll know then."

When the vanguard of the Federal regiment finally appeared on the road in The Barrens, I was with them, riding beside their colonel. I was still wearing the Confederate blouse and sword, but Tom Ross told me later that it was obvious to him at once that I was not a prisoner.

The lieutenant of the vedettes, however, was not so discerning. Riding out to meet his commanding officer with a smart salute, he said, "He outrode us, sir. We tried our best to get him. In fact, we almost got him."

The colonel, a squat man, sat his horse with short legs sticking almost straight out before him in the stirrups. Above the saddle, he was mostly beard, broad, black and bristling.

"You — near did, Lieutenant," he said.

The lieutenant looked puzzled.

I recognized Tom Ross in the group then.

"Aren't you Tom Ross?"

"Yes, sir."

"He's my son's friend," I said to the colonel. "They were with Grant together."

"He joined us at Offitt," the colonel said. "Ross, was it you who tried to shoot the mayor?"

Before Tom could answer, the lieutenant of vedettes leaned forward, eager not to be left out of the conversation, and said, "We all took a try, Colonel."

"I thought I aimed at the horse, sir." Tom said.

I laughed then.

"I wish I had taught you to shoot better than I did when you were boys," I said.

Tom said later that he noticed then for the first time that my right arm hung straight and limp at my side and there was a bulge of bandages under the shoulder of the Confederate coat.

"I'm sorry, Mr. Clayburn," he said. "I aimed at the horse too late, I guess."

"Well, come along!" the colonel said gruffly to the lieutenant, jerking his fat short legs in a vain effort to dig his heels into his horse's belly. "The mayor says the Rebs have drawn in their pickets. You boys were the only ones who tried to stop him on his way out of town. Let's go!"

A half-hour later, when Tom Ross and I rode together with the Offitt regiment down Main Street toward the levee, the Confederate raiders had vanished from the town; but in the long black shadows the cobbled street and the walls of the buildings that flanked it glowed red from the fires that still burned along the river, and I knew the angry red glow would continue in Crescent City for a long time after the fires on the levee were extinguished.

Part Four

THOMAS BRADFORD
CLAYBURN III

1934–

Matilda was dead. Otherwise, I would not have gone back to Crescent City. She was killed in a plane crash in the Rocky Mountains on October 31, 1961, just ten years to the day before I returned. When I saw her name in the published list of passengers—it was in the Washington *Star*, I think—I made my own private investigation of the report, and I must confess that the ultimate certainty that she was dead gave me a guilty sense of deliverance. It was almost as if I had murdered her.

By that time, my father had been dead several years, also killed in an accident. One night, in the summer after my junior year in college, he took our ancient Packard out of the garage in Crescent City and drove out into the country and struck a tree. I was in Arizona when it happened. Aunt broke the news to me on the telephone with one of her standard euphemisms: "Your poor father has gone to his rest." My father was never a hard drinker, except for a brief period after his return from Europe at the beginning of the Second World War; but I like to think that he put away a bottle or two of wine before he went out and hit that tree. A good Pouilly-Fuissé maybe, or even a Château Lafite 1924. But of course by that time he no longer had access to Matilda Herrick's cellar.

Not everyone from those old days had met a violent death, of course. Aunt had not and was not likely to in the nursing home where I saw her on that trip to Crescent City in the autumn of 1971. The afternoon I arrived, I hired a cab as soon as I checked in at the New Century Hotel and went out to visit her. The nursing home, a new one, was on Eisenhower Boulevard, which in my time had been a pleasant country road known as Outer Audubon Street, or the River Road, but had become a suburban artery clotted with shopping centers. In the nursing home, at the end of a long corridor littered with old people adrift in wheelchairs or caught, like blown scraps of yellow paper, in trembling immobility against the rails of walkers, I found Aunt in a white bed. She had the look of an angry wounded hawk and bore no resemblance to the woman I remembered, except in her sunken eyes, which were still beautiful and frightening. I had never known how old she was.

"It's Tom, Aunt!" I shouted at her from the bedside. "Do you remember me? Tom . . ! Tersh . . ! Tersh Clayburn . . !"

The sheet was drawn up tight at her chin, and she kept picking at it with her fingers, gathering it into a ruffle and smoothing it out, as if she were sewing. There seemed to be no body beneath the sheet; there were only those fleshless claws at its edge and, above them, the shriveled hawkish head.

"Tom . . !" I said. "Tersh . . !"

Each time I shouted at her, she responded by pointing into the vacant air and saying imperiously, "Hand that down to me, will you! Hurry!" Finally, to quiet her, I gave her a box of Kleenex from the bedside table, and she took the tissues out, one by one, and methodically tore them into shreds. After I gave up telling her who I was, she complained over and over, beckoning to me to bend close and listen in confidence, "I'm doing the best I can. . . ."

I am sure she did not recognize me. Perhaps I should have said something to her in French. That used to annoy her, and it might have shocked the fragments of her shattered mind back into a momentary order. "*Tu n'est pas ma tante! Je m'en fiche!*"

But Matilda Herrick was the only one who mattered. And Matilda was dead. So it would be all right, I had told myself, if I returned.

I did not realize how much I had looked forward to seeing Matilda's daughter Deedee until I began my lecture that night in the brand-new auditorium of the town's college, which had grown up to be a "university" since my time. As I talked, I found myself searching the audience for Deedee. Because the auditorium was darkened and the lectern's light shone in my eyes, I could not see very well. I had been told that there would be as many townspeople as students and faculty at the lecture, and so I hoped that Deedee would be one of them.

About halfway through the lecture, I noticed an attractive woman who could have been Deedee. She was blond and appeared about the right age and sat, as I imagined Deedee would sit, discreetly, in the ninth or tenth row, and she seemed to be looking at me with more interest than was merited by what I was saying about France's role in Europe. Thereafter, I concentrated on her.

But in the end the woman I believed was Deedee proved not to be. After I finished the lecture, she came up to the platform and identified herself. "I'm Eileen Trautwein," she said, "I used to be Eileen Betz." Her eyes searched mine defensively. "Do you remember Eileen Betz?" When she saw that I remembered, her lips curled in a triumphant little smile and, with a mincing disdain, she went away. I had not allowed myself to think of Eileen Betz for years.

From the auditorium I was escorted to a reception at the home of the university's president, an old house on Audubon Street in the neighborhood where I had once lived. "It used to be the John Ross home," the president's wife explained. "Mrs. Ross gave it to the university." John Ross the indefatigable tennis player, I thought. The house where the mockingbird sang. The house that Asa Ross had once lived in and had probably built. In its parlor I stood for a long time with my host and hostess before a marble fireplace, shaking hands, smiling, making banal remarks, remembering old family names—Ross, Whiting, Marvin, Dreisch, Hefflinger—and believing I recognized some of the faces, yet all the while looking over heads and shoulders for Deedee and Cooper Cox, for Deedee Cox especially.

When at last Cooper Cox came up to me, he had to tell me who he was. He was not at all the kind of man I had been looking for; not sinister or supercilious, as I had imagined he would be, neither brute nor clown, but mild, pink, plump, and more middle-aged than I had expected, wearing gold-rimmed spectacles below a stubble of graying hair. I wondered then whether I would fail to recognize Deedee too when she joined us; after all, I had already been mistaken once that evening about Deedee.

The president of the university and his wife, yielding to the priority of what they mistook for an old friendship, left Cooper alone with me, and we sat down together on a stiff settee by the fireplace.

"How long has it been since you were here last, Clayburn?" Cooper asked; and when I told him, he said, "That was the summer before we graduated. It won't be long now till our twenty-fifth, will it? I suppose you will go."

"Our twenty-fifth what?" I said.

"Reunion," he said. "Everybody says it's the best one."

Our twenty-fifth class reunion was all of nine years away! I wondered what Cooper Cox was going to do in the meantime. Strike the days off his calendar one by one? I did not tell him that I would not attend our twenty-fifth reunion, that I had never returned to Cambridge since our graduation and had no desire to see Harvard College ever again. Instead, I said blandly, "I've heard they make quite an occasion of the twenty-fifth."

"They do indeed!" Cooper exclaimed. "I went with my father to his twenty-fifth when I was a boy."

In the Rolls Royce? I wanted to ask him, picturing little Cooper Cox and maybe his twin brother with Uncle Jack and Aunt Beulah in that ill-fated automobile careening drunkenly across Ohio, New York, and Massachusetts—and back again.

There followed an awkward silence between us, while Cooper drummed plump fingers on plump knees and I wondered impatiently where Deedee was. I saw no one in the crowded room who looked as I thought she ought to look at thirty-four or thirty-five. Not even Eileen Trautwein, née Betz. But there were other crowded rooms behind the crowded room we were in. I could hear them.

"You went on to law school, didn't you?" I said to Cooper, finally.

"Yes. I have my father's old practice now." Silence again. Then Cooper said, having as difficult a time as I apparently, "You won a scholarship or something to Europe after college, didn't you, Tersh?"

Tersh—! It was the second time that day. "*Tom!*" I used to correct Deedee; and she would say, "I mean Tom. . . ."

"France," I said.

After that year in France, my life had been newspaper work and several books—one of them, I always reminded myself proudly, a novel, even if it was a flop—and traveling about and a rather late marriage to Laura and then two small daughters. Laura and the two daughters were the best thing that had ever happened to me, and I was quite ready to talk about them, even to Cooper Cox, if he asked. But Cooper did not ask. He was interested only in Harvard and football games. After he discussed the 1970 Yale game, he launched into pro football. He watched the pro games on TV. But he had also gone to Pasadena to see Indiana play California in the Rose Bowl, and he told me about that. He did not mention Deedee.

As he talked, I wondered what Deedee's life had been like with such a man. My cousin! If they had children, they would be my cousins, once-removed! The best that could be said about Cooper Cox, I decided was that he had not inherited his father's weakness for alcohol. At least, when a black man in a white jacket approached us with a tray of drinks, Cooper waved him away before I had a chance to snatch a Scotch and soda for myself. But maybe Cooper was a member of A.A. Surely Uncle Jack himself had tried the wagon once or twice before he finally drove that old Rolls into the river. Aunt was always predicting that Aunt Beulah would have to "put Uncle Jack away."

Wondering about Deedee's marriage, I found myself remembering my telephone call to Laura in Washington the night before. Where had I been the night before? In Louisville—? After a few weeks on a lecture circuit, every town begins to resemble all the others, although that did not apply to Crescent City, of course. "I am taking the girls to the ballet tomorrow night," Laura had said. "So don't try to call me from Crescent City. I'll call you. If it's late we may stay in town. Anyhow, I suppose you'll be out with that old girl of yours, won't you, darling?" Laura's intuition amazed me. I was sure I had never told her about Deedee, but she even knew what Deedee was like. "That rich, beautiful, little blond girl you used to be in love with," she called her. I was sure, however, that she had never guessed about Matilda.

"Is Deedee here tonight?"

I asked Cooper Cox the question finally with a blunt irrelevance, interrupting the Rose Bowl game in the third quarter just after California recovered an Indiana fumble, and for a while Cooper stared at me as if I had talked out loud in church.

"Deedee!" I wanted to repeat irritably. "You know! Deedee

Herrick! The girl I used to be in love with and you married and took to all those goddamn football games!" But I did not say that, of course. Aloud, I said, "Didn't Deedee come with you tonight? I was hoping I would see her again."

Cooper was a long time recovering.

"I guess you didn't know," he said finally. "Deedee and I are divorced. She was at your lecture. I saw her there. But I guess she went home afterward. I haven't seen her here. As I was saying, after California picked off that fumble—"

At that moment, a young woman came between us and, ignoring Cooper Cox, dropped to the floor at my feet. "Mr. Clayburn," she began at once, "tell me what you think of the anti-novel in France—like, you know, I mean Robbe-Grillet and Natalie Sarraute and Michel Butor." She reeled off the names with the confidence of a recent French major. "I have just been reading *L'emploi du temps,* and I mean do you agree that—you know—reality is seen only when you strip away—you know— the personal point of view?"

She had long hair that fell straight to her shoulders and long, unpainted fingernails the color of fish scales, and neither the hair nor the nails were very clean, and a long neck and a long sharp face that had the glazed pallor of too many cigarettes and too many cups of coffee and probably pot, and her knees were drawn up under a sharp chin so that the naked undersides of her long shanks were exposed, white and luminescent in the shadow of her skirt, like two lean fish bellies. She was inordinately pleased with herself.

"I am not a literary man," I said. I was sure she had never heard of my novel. "I'm only a newspaperman who happens to have written a few books."

My curt reply was motivated not so much by annoyance with the girl for her rude interruption—after all, if Cooper and Deedee were divorced, what more was there for me to learn from him?—as by my resentment at Deedee's failure to come to the reception. I was sure she had been invited. However scandalous her divorce might have been, although I could not imagine Deedee doing anything scandalous, she was, after all, a Marvin, a descendant of Rodney Lycurgus Marvin. No university president could afford to overlook her.

The pale-shanked girl did not linger after my rebuff, but

when she was gone I discovered that Cooper Cox had disappeared. I did not see him the rest of the evening.

The party broke up early, and I declined all offers of rides to the hotel. I said I wanted a little exercise before I went to bed, but what I really wanted was to have a look at the houses on Audubon Street where Matilda and Deedee and Cooper and I had lived when I was a boy.

It was a windy night and very dark. As I walked a half-dozen blocks out Audubon Street and then back to the New Century, jack-o-lanterns grinned at me from the windows of some of the houses, reminding me that it was Halloween. No children were abroad, however; Audubon Street was empty and still. The smell of dead leaves and the dampness from the river filled me with memories of my boyhood, but as a sentimental journey my nocturnal stroll was otherwise a failure; Matilda's and Deedee's house had been torn down to create a parking lot for my own, which was next door and which had become a mortuary with aluminum awnings and neon signs in place of the two galleries laced with iron grillwork that had once ornamented it. After my family had moved out of the house, it had been Cooper Cox's home for a time; but I had always thought of it as my own. "The Clayburn house" Crescent City people called it.

In the lobby of the New Century I bought a *New York Times,* only to discover, as I rode up to my room on the elevator, that it was a day old and I had already read it in Louisville. *"Plus ça change . . ."* I thought and chucked it into a wastebasket in the corridor. In Crescent City one still obviously made do with the *Gazette.*

In my room, I went to the window without turning on a light and stood there for several minutes looking out while I filled my pipe. Below me, new tall streetlamps marched along the riverside, the kind that are supposed to produce the effect of daylight but succeed only in washing the night in a cold lunar radiance. The room was overheated, and I opened the window an inch or two and breathed the damp fragrance of the river before I struck a match and put it to my pipe. A string of barges had appeared around the bend downriver, and the towboat sounded its bullhorn in what I imagined was a brash and hollow mockery of more melodious steamboat days that I had never known. From time to time a car whispered past on the levee below me.

As I stood mesmerized by the reflection of white lights on black water, I remembered that when I was in high school a boy had drowned in an attempt to swim across to Kentucky in front of the hotel. I could not remember the boy's name. He had sat next to me in a history class and came to school in a bus from the country and he had large teeth like grains of field corn and his hair was burnt-orange red; but I could not remember his name. While the Coast Guard searched in vain for the boy's body, a crowd had stood all day on the levee. People often drowned in the river in those days, but now, I supposed, with pollution in everyone's thoughts and more swimming pools available, the river was not the challenge that it had once been. I tried and tried, but I could not remember the boy's name.

After a while, I laid my pipe on an ashtray and, crossing the room, turned on the bedside lamp and slipped the telephone directory out of its slot in the table.

Both names were there, Cooper's twice: *Cox, Cooper, atty*; *Cox, Cooper, res*; and *Cox, Mrs. Dorothy H.* Neither of them lived on Audubon Street any longer; Cooper's address was Valley Road, Deedee's was River Hill Drive. The addresses meant nothing to me, but I pictured large, rambling, modern houses set back from winding lanes newly laid out among tall old trees in the country. Reading *Cox, Mrs. Dorothy H.*, I was vaguely pleased that Deedee had not remarried.

Finally, I dialed her number; but as soon as I heard the first ring I hung up, slid the directory back into its shelf, switched off the light, and returned to the window, mildly amused at myself because I was skittering across the room as if the telephone could pursue me.

"At least, she came to my lecture," I said aloud.

Taking up my pipe, I relighted it and sat down before the window to await Laura's call from Washington. The barges on the river had come abreast of the boat landing below the levee, and when the towboat horn blasted this time, the window rattled. I still could not remember the name of the boy who had drowned. I wondered then whether Matilda too would have come to my lecture if she had been alive. I doubted it. But of course, I reminded myself, if Matilda had still been alive, there would have been no lecture. I still could not remember the name of the boy who had drowned.

The woman I saw in the nursing home that day was not my aunt. I knew that from the beginning, from the day, long ago, when the Pullman porter delivered me to her off the train from Boston. She had said to me at once, "We're kin of course, except 'way back. But that's no matter. Call me Auntie, will you"; but because I was going to be seven years old that summer and calling anyone Auntie sounded infantile to me, I said promptly, "I'll call you Aunt"; and that was what I always called her thereafter.

I remember how she stopped in the middle of the station platform that day, blocking everyone's passage.

"*Aunt*—?" she repeated after me, mocking my speech. "We say *ant*."

"That's a bug," I told her.

Afterward, trailed by a porter with my heavy European suit-cases, we marched together down the platform and through the rows of oaken pewlike benches of the waiting room to the street, Aunt a tall woman, big-boned, plain-of-face, but with beautiful dark eyes that seemed always haunted by a morose passion, a contradictory creature whose smartly tailored suit and stylishly flowered hat belied the countrywoman's wariness with which she held me close to her; and I a contradiction too, I can imagine, a city-bred boy obviously, with a city boy's sureness in the way I strode at her side, but clinging all the while to her hand as if Crescent City were the first city I had ever seen.

Certainly, if old photographs of that period in my life do not lie, Crescent City had never seen anything like me before. No Crescent City boy in that year 1941 would have worn those gray flannel trousers and that blue blazer with the red-and-gold emblem or that blue cap with the big cloth-covered red button on top. But it was not my dress alone that gave me singularity. Nor my speech either, which I am sure was more precise than was common in Crescent City: "Shall we see the river . . ? Can one see it from Grandpa's house . . ? How wide is it . . ? When is Papa coming home . . ?" At least, no boy in Crescent City in those days pronounced papa with the accent on the second syllable, as I did.

No, not dress alone; nor speech either; myself it was that was singular that day long ago, with something foreign, all but exotic, in that thin white face—too thin and white—in those black curls fringing the blue cap, in the wide mouth that was too mature and firm for my age, in the straight and already high-bridged Gallic nose, and in the eyes that were at once innocent and wise behind thick lashes. Boston, where I had come from on that train, might have dressed a child thus, outlandishly, or trained one to speak thus, painstakingly; but Boston could never have bred such a boy as I was on that day.

In the taxi she hailed for us, the woman I had decided to call Aunt told me that her name was Maude Ewbank and she had been taking care of my grandfather for almost a year in the old family house on Audubon Street.

"I've done the best I can," she said. "There was no one else. Your Aunt Beulah could not come from Tacoma—or would not. She has a problem of her own, I guess, in that man she married. And now I'm going to take care of you too, till your papa comes home from Paris, France. Your grandpa is dying."

"I am not dying," I said.

Afterward, that is what she quoted me as saying when at last my father came home and what she repeated in my presence to her friends with never-diminishing astonishment: " 'I am not dying,' he said to me! Imagine!"

Like my Cousin Claudia in Boston, Aunt was an old maid. "Not married yet" was the way she put it that day in the taxi. Although I thought she was homely, I supposed she wasn't because she looked like a picture in Cousin Claudia's house and surely, I thought, no one would take the trouble to paint a picture of a lady who was homely. Her face and the face of the lady in the picture were both long and dark and slanted oddly sidewise and her eyes and the lady's were dark and deep-socketed, like plum tarts. Most remarkable of all, her first name and the first name of the man who had painted the picture of the lady were the same. Or so I believed. I thought it was a funny name for a man, but Cousin Claudia had told me that the painter used to live in Paris before I was born, and I knew that foreigners had funny names sometimes. My mother's name had been Alberte.

"Maude . . ." I mused, as I sat beside Aunt in the taxi. "Maude Ewbank . . . Modigliani . . ." I mused; until finally I said it aloud, and Aunt said, "What?" and I told her about Cousin Claudia's painting. "Maude Ewbank," I said. "Modigliani."

"Delaney—?" Aunt said, frowning. "There are Delaneys in Crescent City, but I never heard of one named Maude." She twisted about and looked down at me suspiciously. "You say your father painted a picture of this woman before you were born?"

"No, it was a man. In Paris. That was his name."

"Well, I never!" she said.

At that moment, the cab stopped in Audubon Street, and I did not have to talk about the painting anymore. I was seeing the old house, "the Clayburn house," for the first time. It was built of brick, of the same rose color as the bricks that paved the street, and it still had the galleries across the front with the iron grill-work, and there was an iron fence around the front yard.

"Where is the river?" I asked.

Aunt pointed across the street.

I saw only houses.

"Beyond them," she said. "The houses behind them face the river. In the flood of thirty-seven it was ten feet deep right here at this gate."

"The river was?"

"Yes."

"Will there be another one?"

"Another what?"

"Flood—like you said."

"I hope not! With that new levee there shouldn't be."

I was disappointed.

"What's a levee?"

But I got no answer. By that time we were at the front door and someone was waiting for us behind the screen.

"Well, here we are," Aunt said to the person behind the screen. "Thank you for staying with the Judge. I'm sorry I had to ask you, but I couldn't get anyone else, like I said." As she spoke, she was searching in her purse for money for the cab-driver, as if that were more important than her thanks or the person she was speaking to.

After the cabman was gone, the person behind the screen door

opened it and, stepping out on the porch, held it wide while
Aunt carried the heavy suitcases into the house, one by one, and
I saw that the person was a young woman, much younger than
Aunt, and much prettier. In fact, she was beautiful. She had
very blue eyes and golden hair that shimmered, and her smile
was not like the smiles that grownups usually bestow upon
children; it made me feel grownup myself, like a man.

"Well, thank you," Aunt said again, when she came out on the
porch for the last suitcase.

"He looks like his father," the beautiful lady said.

She had taken me by the shoulders and, bending over, was
looking into my face as she spoke, still smiling, but now, somehow, as if the smile were for herself as well as for me. In her
enveloping nearness, I thought she smelled nicer than any lady
I had ever smelled. Finally, she kissed me on the mouth, and her
lips were cool and soft and tasted like the candied violets that
Cousin Claudia served sometimes at tea.

After that, she straightened up and, without another word,
skirt aswirl, went down the steps and down the short brick path
to the gate, swaying with a grace that enchanted me. In the sun,
her pale green dress, her golden sandals, and the white skin of
her arms and neck shimmered like her hair; and outside the gate,
in the softer light that filtered through the trees that marched
along Audubon Street, she became a floating cloud of green and
gold for a moment before she disappeared behind a clump of
bushes at the corner of the yard.

"Now you'll have to wash your face," Aunt said, when she
was gone.

"Who is she?" I asked, as soon as we were inside the house,
which was cool and dark and smelled of medicine.

"Who?"

"That lady who was here?"

She looked as if it pained her to have to tell me.

"Matilda Herrick," she said. "She lives next door."

I ran to a window and peered out in the direction Matilda
Herrick had taken, but I could not see her house through the
bushes that separated the two yards.

Soon after I came to live in the house on Audubon Street, my grandfather died, and for a long time Aunt would not let me play outside, not even in the back yard among the apple trees, where there were rabbits and where I could see Matilda Herrick's house. "What would the neighbors think?" Aunt said. So I moped about indoors, indifferently wandering from one high-ceilinged room to another with no toys to play with, and every afternoon I had to take a bath in the high claw-footed tub and dress up in my gray flannel trousers and the blue blazer because women came to call, and I had to stay in the parlor with them, sweating and itching, while they talked about my grandfather. When I protested, Aunt said, "You're the man of the family now, till your papa comes home from Paris, France."

The women smelled like the flowers at my grandfather's funeral in the First Presbyterian Church, but none of them so nice as Matilda Herrick had smelled. Matilda did not appear among the callers, but one day her grandmother came. "Mrs. Rodney L. Marvin." Aunt called her. She was taller than Aunt and very thin and wore a stiff black dress that rustled when she walked through the hall and into the parlor. She stood aristocratically erect and Aunt was obviously intimidated by her. What interested me most about her was the black button pinned to her shoulder from which hung a pince-nez. To put the glasses on she pulled a thread of spring-wound gold chain out of the button and pinched them on the bridge of her bluish nose. This she did perhaps a dozen times during her call, giving little yanks at the chain to make it go in or out of the button, while I stood behind a chair, fascinated. "She lives next door with her granddaughter," Aunt told me, after she was gone, "and it's a good thing, too, although they're three of a kind at bottom." By that time I knew that the third female in the house next door was Matilda's daughter, Deedee. I could not imagine Mrs. Rodney L. Marvin's bottom or Matilda's either, for that matter, but I had already seen Deedee's the day she had come over to play with me before my grandfather died and we sat on the front porch opposite each other, playing jacks. I wondered how their bottoms differed from other people's. "They are three of a kind at bottom," I repeated to myself over and over, and wondered.

All the women who came to call said the same thing in one way or another: "Of course it's for the best, considering the condition he was in, but it always comes as a shock, just the same. Tom Clayburn will be grateful to you for what you've done, Maude Ewbank." Then Aunt would say, "Well, there wasn't anyone else, and we are kin, you know, but 'way back of course and not blood-kin, at that. One of my great aunts married a Bradford." The women nodded and said they supposed Tom would be coming home from Europe soon; and Aunt said yes, she hoped so, she guessed Tom was lucky to be alive; and at the end the women invariably said, "So this is the little boy—Tom Junior, is it?" and Aunt never failed to correct them: "The Third. Thomas Bradford Clayburn the Third. He's called Tersh, for Tertius."

"*Tom!*" I always protested from behind my chair; but no one ever heard me.

"He looks like his father, doesn't he?" the women said; and each time they said it Aunt would study me as if she had never seen me before, tilting her head even more to one side and squinting, as if she were peeking at me through a hole. "Why, yes, I believe he does, a little—around the mouth maybe. They get their mouth from the Mayor's wife, you know." For proof, she would nod at the portrait above the mantel. I myself thought my great-great-grandmother's mouth looked nothing like my own. There was a crack across it in the canvas that made it look like a doll's broken mouth that had been mended. In fact, everything about her looked more like a doll than a great-great-grandmother, I thought. In the portrait she wore a wide skirt and her bare arms and shoulders gleamed like painted porcelain. Reddish curls hung stiffly over her temples, and her eyes were wide and staring. "She was a Bradford," Aunt always explained. "That's where the middle name comes from. Of course he has all those saints' names too that the Catholics give them, but he only uses the Thomas Bradford. One of my great-aunts married a Bradford, you know. So we're not blood-kin at all, the Clayburns and me. She came from Tennessee, like the boy's great-great-grandmother." She always said *Ten*nessee when she spoke of the Bradfords, as if she came from there too. At other times, she said Tennes*see*, like everyone else.

The women never failed to ask how I liked Crescent City, and I had to say I liked it, because Aunt scolded me the one time I said I didn't like it.

"He has an accent, hasn't he?" the women said. "But it doesn't sound French. It sounds more English than French. He does have a foreign look, though."

"It's from living in Boston," Aunt would explain. "He can speak French. Say something in French, Tersh." I could never think of anything to say, and after a while, despairing of me, Aunt would continue. "His father sent him over to Boston as soon as the war started, and he has been staying there with a relative—a cousin twice-removed. Sometimes I can hardly understand him, the way he talks. Say something in English, Tersh." But I could never think of anything to say in English either; and after another despairing wait, Aunt would continue once more. "He even has different words for things, like he calls soft drinks tonic—or did, till I corrected him. *Tonic*! Imagine! Spoils the taste of it for me! And when I say uh-huh or huh-uh —you know, the way you do sometimes when you aren't thinking—he can't tell whether I mean yes or no. What does huh-uh mean, Tersh?"

Once, toward the end of the season of afternoon callers, when she asked me what huh-uh meant, I said, "Rest in peace," and she became angry. "Don't be impudent, young man!" she said. "That's blasphemy!"

I had no idea what blasphemy was, but obviously it was something bad. Still, I wondered, if it was bad, why had she put it on my grandfather's tombstone?

THOMAS BRADFORD CLAYBURN
1870–1941
Son of Bradford and Mary Torr Clayburn
JUDGE
Liggum County Circuit Court
Democrat
REST IN PEACE

That was what she had put on the tombstone. I had memorized it.

The first day after the stone was set in place, Aunt had taken me out to the cemetery to see it. For the trip she hired a Negro to drive the ancient Packard that stood idle in the garage behind the apples trees. The trip was delayed for three days after she hired him, because he had to repair "slow leaks" in the tires, get the battery recharged, and put in new spark plugs. "I still don't think a taxicab would have been appropriate," Aunt said.

At the cemetery, as I spelled out my grandfather's name on the tombstone, his name and my own became suddenly one and the same, in spite of all those saints' names in my own. We shared the name in a way that we had never shared it while my grandfather was still the sick and mumbling old man I had been required to visit every day in the downstairs back bedroom when I first came to live in the house on Audubon Street. That day in the cemetery, my grandfather and I and my father as well owned the name together for the first time. At least, I had never thought of it that way before.

"*Nous sommes tous les mêmes!*" I exclaimed aloud.

"What does that mean?" Aunt asked.

It was an intimacy I would not share with her.

"Nothing," I said.

"Well, stop talking French. It makes me nervous." She studied the stone for several minutes, plucking her chin. "I hope he likes it," she said finally.

"Who?"

"Your papa. I know I've been criticized for taking things upon myself this way, and maybe I should have waited for him to come home and choose for himself. But it's not right to leave a grave unmarked, and if I know him, he never would have got around to it himself, unless he's changed a lot, which I doubt."

"It's pretty," I said.

But that was not what I was thinking. I was thinking that something had just happened to me that had not happened to me all that summer: not when I got off the train from Boston or when I saw for the first time the house my great-great-grandfather had built, where, after him, my great-grandfather and my grandfather and my father had all lived as boys. I had known about the house and about my family before I came to Crescent City, because Cousin Claudia had told me about them the day the letter arrived from my father saying she should send me "out there" to live in the old house. But hearing about the house and my family was not the same as seeing my own name on the tombstone, if only because Cousin Claudia, when she showed me on the map where "out there" was, had to run her fingers back and forth along the Ohio River several times before she found it. I began to lose faith in Cousin Claudia's infallibility on that day, and although I knew she was smart, smarter than Aunt probably, because she could speak French—*un peu mal, quand même*—and Aunt couldn't, I had learned since that there were a lot of things Cousin Claudia did not know that Aunt knew, such as how you had to say Paris, France, or people might think you meant Paris, Kentucky,' or Paris, Illinois. Cousin Claudia had probably never heard of Paris, Kentucky, or Paris, Illinois, and wouldn't know how to find them on a map. But no matter. What mattered that day in the cemetery was that my grandfather, who had lived in Crescent City all his life, had always been Thomas Bradford Clayburn, just like me and my father, and "out there" was "here" now because it was where I was. It almost made up for being called Tersh.

"What did you say?"

"I said it's pretty."

For a while after that, I followed Aunt about over the parched grass, and she explained the other tombstones. One was my Grandmother Clayburn's. It said: *Born in Boston, 1872.* Another was for my great-great-grandfather, Henry Clayburn. Aunt always called him "the Mayor." Two others were for his two wives, Nancy Draper Clayburn and Helen Bradford Clayburn. The second one was the doll-lady with the porcelain shoulders in the mended picture over the mantel on Audubon Street. There were more. But none of them interested me until we stood before a stone that did not bear the Clayburn name.

COLONEL STACEY MOREY, C. S. A.

"What does that mean?"

"What?"

I spelled out to her the letters after the name.

"He was in command of Morgan's Raiders the time they captured Crescent City—when Henry Clayburn was the mayor."

"But what do the letters mean?"

"They mean he was a Rebel."

I had no idea what a Rebel was.

"He was a cousin of the mayor's wife," Aunt said. "That's why they buried him out here. They shot him while he was going out the door. You can still see the bullet hole."

I lost interest in learning what the letters meant and said, "How can you tell, if he is buried?"

"How can I tell if *who* is buried?"

"No," I said. "I mean the bullet hole. How do you know you can still see the bullet hole with him all covered up with dirt?"

"You can't see the bullet hole in *him*, silly!" Aunt said. "He's all dust and ashes now. I mean over the front door."

"On Audubon Street?"

"Of course! That's where they shot him."

"*C'est trop bête!*" I exclaimed.

"Stop talking French!" she shouted at me. "I've told you a thousand times it makes me nervous!"

"Pardon," I said.

I was unable to ask any more questions about the bullet hole, because Aunt started off again at that moment across the dry grass among the graves. I ran after her, and when I caught up with her I discovered that this time there was a pattern in her marching, zigzag, across the grass, three long strides in one direction, counting, "One, two, three . . ." half-aloud; then two at a right angle, "One, two . . ."; then three again, "One, two, three. . . ."

Throwing back my head, I marched behind her in stealthy mockery, stretching my legs to match her steps and myself counting, "*Un, deux . . . Un, deux, trois . . .*" under my breath. "*Un, deux . . . Un, deux, trois . . .*" I counted, until finally, remembering some nonsense that my father must have taught me in Paris, I began to chant, "*Un, deux . . . Voilà les flics . . . !*"

Aunt finally stopped, short of breath, and said, "I guess we can just about squeeze in three more."

"Three more what?" I asked.

"Bodies."

She was looking down at me speculatively as she spoke, and I shivered in the hot sun, picturing three dead bodies, my own among them, squeezed upright into a hole in the ground, like the cucumber pickles she had been packing in jars all that week in the kitchen on Audubon Street.

"You'll be the last one," she said. "That's for sure."

I shivered again.

When we returned to Audubon Street and Aunt had paid the Negro for driving us out to the cemetery in the old Packard, she showed me the bullet hole.

It was not over the door, where she had said it was, but beside the door, in the doorframe, where I could reach it and put my finger in it. Because it was such a satisfactory bullet hole, I forgave her for not telling me until that day that it was there.

Soon after we visited the cemetery, Aunt said it would be all right for me to go out and sit on the steps of the front porch if I was quiet, and I went out hoping the little girl named Deedee would come over from next door and play with me as she had done earlier in the summer; and after a while Deedee did appear, wearing a yellow dress and a yellow ribbon in her hair.

She skipped along in the mottled sunlight outside the iron fence, but as soon as she saw me she stopped skipping, and after that she pretended not to see me and was not at all like the little girl I had played jacks with the previous time. She walked straight past the gate without speaking, and when I called out to her she tossed her head and kept on walking.

"My grandfather's stone is up," I said to her, "and I don't have to stay in the house anymore."

But she kept on walking.

At every step, her little bottom flounced, and I wondered if that was the family distinction Aunt had spoken of, but I could not imagine her mother or Mrs. Rodney L. Marvin walking like that.

"I know a secret," I said.

I had no secret to share with her, unless it was the bullethole, which I had no intention of sharing with anyone, least of all a girl. But I could invent a secret.

She paid no attention.

"Aunt says I can play now."

She stopped then. She had reached her own gate and she stopped before she opened it and, turning, froze me with a stare.

"*Aunt—*!" she said, mimicking my pronunciation. "My mother says your aunt is a bitch."

"*Elle n'est pas ma tante!*" I cried out, as if Deedee had struck me.

"Aunt Bitch!" she said.

"She is not my aunt! I just call her that!"

Deedee opened the gate and marched up the walk to her door and into her house, bottom flouncing. The screen door slammed behind her.

I stood up and yelled after her, "She is not my aunt! She is not, she is not, she is *not* . . . !"

"Tersh!"

It was Aunt's voice calling from inside the house behind me.

"Yes, ma'am."

"Stop that racket this minute!"

"Yes, ma'am."

"What will the neighbors think?"

"*Je m'en fiche!*"

I went out to the lawn and, sitting by the fence, began to pull up handsful of grass as fast as I could and tossed them wildly into the air. I hated Deedee Herrick. I hated Aunt. I hated Crescent City. I hated everything.

As I sat on the earth, hating, I did not at first see the man who was standing on the sidewalk outside the fence, but when I saw him at last I knew somehow that he had been there a long time, watching me.

"Having woman trouble?" the man said.

I did not know what that meant; so I said nothing. Anyhow, the man was a stranger, and Aunt had said I must not talk to strangers. The man was thin and sad-looking and he had a black moustache with sweat sparkling in it. He smiled, but the smile made his face look even sadder than when he was not smiling. He came over to the fence, and when he took hold of one of the spearheads that capped the iron pickets, I saw his right sleeve for the first time. It was empty. The end of it was tucked inside the pocket of his dark blue jacket.

"*On n'est jamais si heureux ni si malheureux qu'on s'imagine,*" he said.

At that time in my life, I still thought in one language as much as in the other, and consequently I was not startled when the man spoke French. But again I did not know what he meant, so again I said nothing.

"That must have been Matilda Herrick's little girl," the man said in English.

"They call her Deedee," I said.

"Deedee, eh? Well, she called your aunt worse than that."

"*Elle n'est pas ma tante!*" I yelled at him.

"*Du calme, du calme,*" he said gently. "*C'est entendu.*"

"I just call her that," I said, looking at the man's sleeve in spite of myself. "I just call her that because she told me I had to." I looked at the sleeve a long time, until finally, although I knew I shouldn't, I asked, "Where is your arm?"

"In France," the man said.

"My papa is in France."

The man laughed, and the laugh was even sadder than the smile.

"No, he isn't," he said. "He's right here on Audubon Street, talking to you."

At first, my father's return changed life very little in the old house on Audubon Street. Aunt stayed on, continuing to sleep in the upstairs bedroom that was beside my own, while my father established himself in the large front room that Aunt called "the master's bedroom." He slept late and came down-stairs about noon to have breakfast while Aunt and I had lunch, and after the meal he returned to his room and remained there till suppertime. After supper, he went promptly back to his room again. He must have smoked cigarettes constantly, day and night, for the house became saturated with their dry sweet smell.

When he came to the table, noon and evening, Aunt plied him with questions at first about his experiences in France and in London, where he had been recuperating from the loss of his arm; but he was reluctant to talk about them. The little I know about what happened to him I learned from others—from Aunt and, later, from Matilda. After the start of the war he stayed on in France in order to help remove works of art from the Paris museums to hiding places in the country, until finally the Nazis, occupying the city before the task was finished, caught him. I had supposed that he was a soldier, gloriously wounded in combat, and I remember that when I finally learned that he had lost his arm as a result of Nazi tortures in Paris, I was disappointed. When I was a few years older and read accounts of the Nuremberg Trials in the newspapers, I understood better the nature of his heroism; but that new understanding gave me such bad dreams, in which I saw the Nazis chopping off his arm an inch at a time from his fingertips to his shoulder, that I could take no pleasure from his reinstatement as a hero in my thoughts. It was a dream that haunted me for years.

What actually happened, I suppose, was that my father developed blood-poisoning from whatever it was the Gestapo did to him in Paris, and his arm had to be amputated. But who amputated it and how he escaped to England I have never known. The rest of his life he seldom mentioned the war, at least not his own part in it. I remember that whenever Germans came into a conversation, he never spoke of them as Germans but said "They" or "*Ils,*" as if the anonymity might prevent contamination of the air he was breathing. I suppose there was no word in his vocabulary, English or French, hateful enough for them.

Often in those first days after he came home, he spoke French to me at table, and then Aunt would put on a pained, aloof expression and tap her fingers impatiently on the tablecloth as if she were humoring children. Oftener in those first weeks, he ignored us both and ate his meals in silence. When he did talk with Aunt, it seemed to me his chief purpose was to torment her.

"I can't stay in this house any longer, Tom Clayburn. What will the neighbors think?"

"To hell with them!"

"That's easy enough for you to say, but what about me?"

"What *about* you?"

"You know what I mean! You know it doesn't look right."

"Oh—that? Then why don't you try to find someone to take your place? I can't do it. I wouldn't know where to start looking."

"Do you think one of those Taylors would be all right? They've worked for your family ever since your great-grandfather's time. I suppose they're all getting rich working in the war plants, but there might be one of them who could come. Still, I don't know whether a Negro—"

"Black or white. I don't care. Anybody."

"But the boy needs somebody to teach him his manners, Tom."

"He's learned enough manners from his Cousin Claudia to last him a lifetime. Eh, Coco? *Tu n'as plus besoin des dames officieuses dans ta vie, n'est-ce pas?*"

Reluctance then to be drawn into the debate at my side of the table, and at Aunt's side the aloof, pained expression and the tapping of fingers on the tablecloth.

"You can't just let your son grow up like a savage, Tom Clayburn!"

"The Taylors aren't savages, Maude. Their people have been in this country as long as the Clayburns probably. Longer, maybe. The first slaves were brought here in 1619. The first Clayburn didn't come till 1650."

"You never did have the proper respect for your ancestors!"

"Well, John Clayburn was a slave too, of sorts, an indentured servant. The English brought him over here from Scotland against his will.

"You're impossible!"

"All right, all right! Why don't you stay then, Maude? Hire somebody to come in and do the housework and you stay on and teach Coco and me manners. Get a woman to come in and live in that back room where Dad was and you stay on. That way, the neighbors won't know which one of you I'm sleeping with."

"Tom!"

Eventually, that was what she did. She hired Florence Taylor to come and live in the back bedroom downstairs, and she remained in the room upstairs next to mine. After the decision was made, she explained to me a thousand times that, after all, she had no family of her own except some cousins in the town of Amity twenty miles away and, anyhow, she and my father were kin in a way, "though not blood-kin actually."

The arrangement pleased me enormously, for Florence Taylor brought life and laughter into the old house. She was full of warmth and love and I thought she was beautiful. Her skin was the same rich color as the walnut woodwork in the house, and every sentence she spoke was a melody. She was the first Negro I ever knew.

Florence Taylor quickly entered into a conspiracy with me against Aunt. She covered for me in my wrongdoings, doctored my cuts and bruises, surreptitiously baked little treats for me, told me horrific tales that would have thrown Aunt into a faint if she had heard them, and even defied Aunt's prohibition against the French language by encouraging me to entertain her with the strange sounds of that language when we were alone. Sometimes, under my tutelage, she ventured into the language herself.

"*Mussoo,*" she called me, when Aunt was not around. "*Bomjoo, mussoo,*" she greeted me, when I came downstairs first in the morning and joined her in the kitchen; and when I replied, "*Bonjour, Florence,*" she rocked with laughter. "Now ain't that something!" she would say. "You calling my name Floor-ants! I bet you making that up, *mussoo!*"

I loved her.

One afternoon shortly after my father's return from Europe, Matilda Herrick appeared at the front door with a package wrapped in striped green-and-gold paper tied with a gold ribbon to which was attached an envelope bearing my father's name in a large square handwriting. The package had the unmistakable shape of a bottle. I was at Aunt's side when she answered the doorbell's ring, and I felt her stiffen when she recognized Matilda on the porch. Matilda had to open the screen door herself to hand the package in.

"It's wine," she said. "It will be good for him."

Aunt took the package dubiously, as if it contained explosives.

"How is he?"

"All he needs is to be let alone," Aunt said.

A few days later, Matilda was back with another package. Like the first one, it was bottle-shaped and wrapped in green-and-gold paper. Aunt had set the first package on a marble-topped table in the hall, and it still stood there when Matilda came the second time. When I offered to take the first package up to my father, who always used the back stairs and had not yet seen it on the table, Aunt had said, "Let him find it for himself." Now, with Matilda at the door looking on, she set the second bottle on the table beside the first.

"I'll bring another in a few days," I heard Matilda say from the other side of the screen. "If you don't give them to him soon, your front hall is going to look like a bistro."

Afterward, Aunt asked me if bistro was a French word, and I said I thought so.

"Well, what does it mean?" she said.

I did not know; so I said, "It's blasphemy."

"I'm not surprised," Aunt said.

Three bottles accumulated thus on the table before my father discovered them and took them, still unwrapped, to his room. After that, he always used the front stairs and took Matilda's offerings to his room one at a time, as they were delivered. Soon empty French wine bottles began to appear regularly on the kitchen sink with the cans and wrapped garbage that Florence collected for me to carry out to the hopper by the alley fence. If Aunt was not present when I performed this chore, Florence let me drain the last drops of wine from the bottles. "Only, don't let her smell your breath," she warned. "Don't you go hugging and kissing her, *mussoo.*" I was not likely to.

One afternoon, the doorbell rang when neither Aunt nor Florence was in the house, and I, sure that it was Matilda, ran breathlessly through the long dark hallway from the kitchen, where I had been playing. Maybe she would kiss me again, I thought. By the time I reached the door, the taste of candied violets was already on my lips.

But she did not kiss me. She appeared not even to see me. When I said, "Hello, Mrs. Herrick," she stood staring over my head, beyond me, as if she had not heard. Even when I opened the door to take the package that she held in the crook of her bare arm, she remained motionless and unseeing. She wore the same pale green dress she had worn the first time I ever saw her, and she stood aglow in a shaft of sunlight on the porch like a young tree in spring.

"Hello, Mrs. Herrick," I said again, this time with embarrassment, as I might have spoken to an adult whom I had been told to waken from sleep.

Still she did not hear me.

There was a sound behind me then, and I turned and saw my father coming down the carpeted stairs. He wore no jacket, and the left sleeve of his white shirt was rolled up to the elbow loosely, baring a forearm that was white and bony. The right sleeve was pinned to the shirt and ballooned a little as he descended the stairs. In his face was something that frightened me. He was smiling, but the smile did not make him look sad; he looked angry. His head was thrown back and his eyes were narrow and the smile bared his white teeth cruelly beneath the black moustache.

I stepped back to make way for him, and he passed me and stood in front of me as if I were not there.

"Oh, Thomas! You look awful!" I heard Matilda say.

My father laughed through his nose.

"Naturally," he said. "Come in."

He opened the door, but Matilda remained where she was.

"Is it all right?"

He laughed again.

"No," he said. "But she is not here—if that's what you mean."

Matilda cried out as if he had hurt her.

"Oh, Thomas!"

He reached toward her and took her arm just below the shoulder and tried to draw her into the house, and I was afraid that he was really going to hurt her then.

"Don't," I said.

He let go of her and looked down at me.

"What's that?"

"Nothing," I said.

His fingers had left red marks on her bare shoulder, like chevrons, and I hated him in that instant.

"He looks like you," Matilda said. "So much! Oh, Thomas!"

"He looks like Alberte," my father said angrily.

After that, they were both silent for a time, my father still holding the screen door half-open between them, the eyes of both of them fixed on me. I squirmed. I had a strange feeling of not really being there with them, as if what they were seeing was not myself but someone or something beyond my knowledge.

Finally, Matilda handed my father the green-and-gold package and, without speaking, turned and went down the porch steps. When she was outside the gate, on the sidewalk under the trees, she almost ran.

After she was gone, my father remained at the door a long time, staring after her, the package forgotten in his hand. He seemed to be talking to himself; his lips were moving under his moustache. I listened closely but I could not hear what he was saying. At last, he turned about and strode down the hall toward the kitchen carrying the wine bottle by the neck at his side, and at a discreet distance I trotted after him.

When I reached the kitchen, he had yanked out a drawer by the sink and was rummaging about the knives and forks and spatulas noisily. After he found a corkscrew, he unwrapped the package, looked at the label on the bottle, seemed to hesitate, and then, setting the bottle resolutely on the floor and holding it between his feet, pulled the cork out. I expected him to drink the wine in one long draught, because he seemed angry and determined, but instead, without hesitation, he poured it out into the sink.

The wine came out of the bottle in spurts, like gushes of blood, splattering the porcelain sink and filling the kitchen with a sweet-sour odor. As he poured the wine, holding the bottle by the neck, I read the label below his hand: *Château Lafite.* I had read a book from the library about a pirate named Lafitte, and I pretended the sink was a ship's deck running with gore. It was very exciting. When the bottle was empty, my father turned on the hot water and let it run into the sink until most of the red stains were gone.

All the while, watching him, I had believed he did not know I was in the room; but as soon as he shut off the faucet, he swung about and said to me, "Have you ever seen a ball game?"

I was so startled that I could not answer, and he repeated the question.

"Cousin Claudia took me to the tennis once," I said.

"She would!" he said. "Get your cap!"

Riding to the ball park in a bus beside my father was a brand new adventure for me. He told me I had ridden on a bus in Paris, but I could not remember it. The windows were open and many kinds of smells came in, good and bad, and I loved them all: exhaust fumes and street dust and factory smoke and food smells. At a stop on Water Street, there was a carnival atmosphere of bars and hamburger joints and pool rooms. The scorched fragrance of roasted peanuts stung my nostrils, and I saw a man in a peanut-shaped suit wearing a top hat walking up and down the street. I waved to him and he waved back and came over and handed me a peanut through the window.

Leaving Water Street, the bus mounted to the top of the levee and skirted the river for a while, and there a warm, wet, musky smell, like lilacs past full bloom, filled the air. Across the river, a stubby boat was pushing a string of barges loaded with coal. The long flotilla hugged the shore, a mile away, but I could see men on the boat. Along the river bank behind them a fringe of trees rose like feathers on an Indian bonnet.

"Regarde les bateaux qui marchent à la queue leu leu!" I said excitedly to my father. *"Il y en a douze!"*

But he paid no attention to me; he had begun to explain the rules of baseball.

When the bus turned away from the river, it entered Main Street, where I had been several times with Aunt, but always on foot. Being there on a bus was much better. High above the people in the street, I felt like God and pretended I was God and could make the people do anything I wanted them to do. "That man will go into that store," I would say to myself, and he would go in. My power amazed me, although I was not always honestly sure whether the man had entered the store because I had willed him to do so or whether I had waited till I saw him turn to enter the store before I gave my command. When the bus stopped and passengers got on, I watched closely to make sure they paid their fares. I felt very sorry for one old woman with many bundles who I believed had not paid, because, being God, I had to send her to hell. All the while, at my side, my father continued to explain the rules of baseball.

I should have listened to him. The baseball game was not nearly the fun the bus ride had been. Because I did not understand what the men on the grassy field were doing, I soon became bored. What is more, my father bought me too many hot dogs and soft drinks and my stomach began to ache before the game was half over. At the seventh-inning stretch, I was ready to go home. But I dared not suggest leaving the game, because my father was having too good a time, drinking beer and arguing with a man at his other side next to his empty sleeve.

"What do you expect?" he kept saying to the man. "They're all 4F's. The draft has got the best ones."

The game finally came to an end. By that time, my father's sleeve had come unpinned from his shirt, and it flapped wildly as he lurched at my side down the ramp to the exit. When he bumped against people, he said, *"Pardon,"* in the French way, and that made them turn and stare at him. Once, a man spoke to him angrily. "Watch it, Jack!" he said. On the bus going home, my father fell asleep and slumped over to one side, pushing me against the windowsill, and that ride was a misery for me because he snored and people stared again and my stomach ached worse than ever.

Aunt was waiting for us at the front door when we got home. She said she had worried about us all afternoon. "I worried myself sick," she said. "I had no idea where you were."

We told her we had been to the ball game, but that did not quiet her.

"You're not well enough for that sort of thing, Tom Clayburn," she said. "You ought to know better. And just look at the boy's clothes!"

Catsup and mustard stains, which I had not noticed until that moment, spotted my white shirt, and in my frantic haste to pee in the men's room at the ball park, after four cherry sodas, I had torn a button from the fly of my Boston-bought gray flannel pants.

"You're a mess!" Aunt said. "Both of you!"

But as soon as my father, refusing supper, went up to his room, her tone changed, became conciliatory, cajoling, as if all she had said before was only an act.

"Now, Tersh," she said, "tell me all about this afternoon."

"Crescent City lost," I said.

"No. I mean earlier. Was she here?"

"Who?"

In the excitement of the bus ride to the park, the disappointment of the game, and the misery of the trip home, I had forgotten about Matilda Herrick's call.

"Matilda Herrick," Aunt said.

"She brought Papa another present."

"I knew it!" Aunt said.

If she already knew it, I wondered, why had she asked me?

"And then—?" Aunt said.

"We went to the ball game."

"I know that! I mean, when she came, what happened?"

"She gave him the present."

"I mean, did she come into the house? Did they drink the wine?"

"No."

"It smells like a saloon out there in the kitchen. Florence says she can't smell anything and she says that empty wine bottle on the sink was there this morning when she left for her day off, but I don't believe her. She's lying for him. But you tell me the truth, Tersh. What happened? Did she come in the house?"

"No."

"No, ma'am."

"No, ma'am," I said.

She studied me skeptically for a time and finally, with a note of despair in her voice, said, "I guess you're two of a kind. Well, come on back to the dining room and eat your supper."

"I don't want any supper."

"You have to eat something. You've got to have some sensible food in you after all that junk you ate."

Soon after that day, my father began going next door every evening after supper to call on Matilda Herrick. Trailing cigarette smoke across our lawn and breaking through the crape-myrtle hedge that separated the two houses, he went up to Matilda's door and appeared to enter without knocking.

Matilda's house—"the Marvin home," as it was called by people who knew Crescent City's past—was one of those Tuscan villas that came into fashion in the early 1870s. There were several of them on Audubon Street. It sat farther back from the sidewalk than our house, which was older, and it had no front porch. Its heavily corniced door opened directly upon the brick path that led out to the street. This doorway was at the base of an Italianate tower that was square and four-storied and flat-topped. At the top of the tower, arched windows marched around under elaborate cornices like a guard of ornamental soldiers.

When I was a boy, I longed to see the interior of the tower, but I was never invited to do so, and by the time I finally had free run of the Marvin home its architecture was no longer its main attraction for me. Yet even in that year after my father came home from Europe, when I begged to be allowed to go next door with him in the evening, my primary interest was not to visit the tower but to share Matilda with him. I said I wanted to play with Deedee, but what I really wanted was to be with Matilda. Aunt never allowed me to go, and my father never intervened in my behalf.

Sometimes he and Matilda came out of the house and sat together in a latticed pergola in her back yard. Sometimes she took her car out of the brick carriage house, which was also towered and Tuscan, and they went off together for the evening. But that was not often, because gas rationing had begun. When it rained and after the autumn weather turned cold, they stayed indoors.

The evenings they sat in the pergola I watched them from the kitchen window, and Aunt watched too. I stood tiptoe, leaning against the sink, and thought how beautiful Matilda was, sitting beside my father with her blond head tilted toward him, while Aunt breathed heavily on my neck and clucked her tongue and muttered.

"Hussy!" she hissed one evening; and when I turned about and asked her what a hussy was, she said it was not nice and I must not tell my father she had said it.

"Is it like a bitch?" I asked.

"Tertius!" she exclaimed, and slapped me. But only lightly, almost affectionately; and afterward she laughed. "Where on earth did you learn that word?" she asked.

I was tempted to tell her that a bitch was what Matilda called her, but I said nothing.

"I guess they do mean the same thing, sort of," Aunt said. "But you must not use words like that. I shouldn't have, myself, except I was thinking he is going to catch his death of cold out there in the night air. He hasn't got his strength back yet."

I could not see how Matilda's being a hussy had anything to do with my father's catching his death of cold.

On the nights when Matilda and my father stayed indoors, Aunt was even more disapproving than when they were in the pergola. "At least, old Mrs. Marvin is in the house," she said; and that too puzzled me. I could see no relationship between Mrs. Marvin's presence in the house and my father's health. "But they're all the same at bottom," Aunt always added; and I couldn't see how their all having the same kind of bottoms had anything to do with it either.

That fall, Deedee Herrick became my friend again. We weren't in the same grade, because she was younger than I was, but we walked to school and home again together every day. After school we often played together, usually at my house, because Aunt could think of a thousand reasons for not allowing me to go next door. Deedee told me many things that she heard my father and her mother say to each other; but I never told her anything that happened or was said in my house, how I stayed awake sometimes and listened for my father to come home from next door, how occasionally I heard him climb the stairs and tiptoe across the creaking floor of the upper hallway to his room, and how, in spite of his stealth, he stumbled and bumped into things and swore in a harsh whisper, or how, usually, Aunt got out of bed and went to her bedroom door and scolded him in a low voice.

"You're trying to kill yourself, Tom Clayburn."

I wanted to get out of bed too then and and run to him and beg him not to kill himself.

One afternoon at school, after we returned from lunch, which we ate at our homes, Deedee told me in the school yard her mother wanted my father to learn to paint with his left hand. "She was telling Grandmother Marvin about it at lunch, and do you know what she said your father said?"

"What?"

"She said he said, 'To h— with it!' "

She giggled and put her hand over her mouth. She was blond like her mother and pretty, too, with a pouting upper lip that looked bee-stung. When she was older her mouth was very enticing, but in those days I did not like it. I expecially did not want to look at her when she giggled, because spittle gathered at the corners of her mouth and her eyes screwed up into tight puckers as if she were about to cry. Her face was never so fine as her mother's.

"To hell with it!" I said, boldly pronouncing the whole word. "My father says worse things than that when he wants to. He says 'goddamn!' "

"Oh, Tersh, that's awful!"

"*Tom!* "

"I mean Tom, that's awful! He won't go to heaven for saying things like that. And you won't either."

"He says *merde* too."

I had heard him say *merde* for the first time only that day, at our breakfast-lunch on Audubon Street.

"What does that mean?"

I did not know; so I said it again, *"Merde!"* Then I ran away from Deedee and her bee-stung mouth, sprinted across the school yard, shouting at the top of my lungs, *"Merde, merde, merde . . . !"*

My father had said *"Merde!"* that day because of what happened in the night. What had happened was that, instead of going into his own room when he came home from next door, he went into Aunt's room and they made sounds there that frightened me at first. I thought they were fighting. There was a thumping against the wall that separated Aunt's bedroom from mine and Aunt uttered little cries as if my father were hurting her. But at the end I decided they had not been fighting, because after the thumping stopped I heard Aunt say, "You're a man, Tom! You're a real man!" with a kind of joy in her voice that I had never heard before.

When we had breakfast together that morning, Aunt and I alone, she found nothing to scold me about and I thought she looked different, almost pretty, her eyes dark and lustrous. I would have thought there were tears in them if she had not been smiling all the time. I was more confused that ever about what had happened in the night.

At noon, at our breakfast-lunch, when my father came to the table, she reached over and touched his hand as he unfolded his napkin. "I feel like I was seventeen again," she said; and that was when he said, *"Merde!"* Afterward, he said, "I'm sorry, Maude. I'm a beast," and got up from the table and, leaving his breakfast untouched, went back up to his room. I did not understand it.

I did not tell Deedee about that night or the next morning or our breakfast-lunch at noon, because it was already a rule with me to tell her nothing. Moreover, I knew that whatever had happened that night was like the day I saw my name carved on my grandfather's tombstone, a private matter, a family matter, *entre nous*, an intimacy I should not share with anyone. I did not know why, but I was sure. So I did not tell Deedee about the strange things I heard Aunt and my father say to each other, dialogues that always ended as monologues delivered by my father.

My eavesdropping started one day quite by accident. After leaving for the afternoon session of school I came back into the house for something I had forgotten and I overheard Aunt and my father talking in the dining room and I lingered, listening, in the hall. Often thereafter, when I finished my lunch I walked noisily down the hall to the front door, opened it and slammed it shut behind me, and waited on the porch till Deedee came by for me. "I forgot something," I would say to her then. "You go on. I'll try to catch up, but I may be late." I knew she thought I had to go to the bathroom, but I did not care. After she was gone, I would open the door very quietly and tiptoe back down the hall and take up my post outside the dining room door.

It was very wicked of me. Florence said so. "Eavesdroppers hear no good of themselves," she said. But I knew she would not betray me. Anyhow, I was not expecting to hear anything about myself; I wanted to learn all I could about my father. Sometimes, when I asked him, he talked to me about Mayor Clayburn and Morgan's raid and the bullet hole, things like that, but he never talked about himself the way he did at the dining room table after he thought I was gone from the house. So I had to listen, even though I did not understand all that he said.

When Aunt was convinced that I was out of the house, she began the dialogue obliquely, with remarks that were to me, lurking in the hall, mostly repetitious and without much interest.

"Yesterday, when Mr. Goodrich came to collect for the milk, he said, 'I see Mr. Clayburn now and then coming home from next door about sunrise.' That's exactly what he said, 'About sunrise.'"

"Is that right? About sunrise—eh? Milkmen have to get up early, don't they, Maude?"

"And John Ross—I saw him on the street the other day—and he said, 'I hear Tom and Matilda are getting together again.' I could have slapped his face, the way he said it!"

"Why didn't you?"

"And last week, that Miss Whiting that works in the bank, she said, 'Tom was in the bank yesterday, and I thought he looked tuckered.' "

"Tuckered—eh? Now, what do you suppose she meant by that, Maude? There's a French word—*pompé*. But she couldn't have meant that. I'm sure Miss Whiting has never seen a man *pompé*."

"And the mailman—"

"The mailman too? Has the F.B.I. said anything about me, Maude? Have you consulted the Board of Health?"

"It's not your health I'm thinking about, Tom Clayburn, and you know it!"

"So—? What is it?"

"It's your reputation. And mine!"

"Yours—?"

"Staying in this house with you while all this is going on."

"Why, Maude, I thought we settled that. I thought you decided that with Florence here it would be all right for you to stay. I'm sure there's no need for you to worry about your reputation. If the milkman is telling everybody on his route that I don't come home till sunrise, they'll know I'm not tuckered because of you."

"Tom!"

"Little Tommy Tucker, he tucks for—"

"Tom, stop that!"

"So don't worry about your reputation, Maude. And don't worry about Little Tommy Tucker's either. He hasn't any. They buried his reputation when they buried his painting arm. I guess that's what they do with them, bury them."

"You're disgusting! Sometimes I wish you had stayed in Paris, France."

"Yes, it would have been better all around if I had stayed in Paris, France, Maude. They smuggled the wrong part of me over to London, England. They should have sent my arm over to London, England, and buried the rest of me in Paris, France. Then they could have shipped my arm over here and you could have buried it in the family plot and put a stone over it. 'This is the arm that painted the pictures that hang in the house the mayor built. . . .' "

"Stop it, I say!"

"Only, the pictures don't hang here of course. They don't hang anywhere. They burned them in Paris, France. They had an *auto-da-fé* one day in the Tuileries Gardens. So maybe, instead of burying my painting arm, you could have had it stuffed and mounted and hung on the wall in the parlor beside that god-awful portrait of my great-grandmother. You know. Like a fish. *Le maquereau qui s'est échappé.*"

"You're disgusting!"

"I'm sorry, Maude. I forgot myself, mourning for my paintings."

"Well, I wasn't talking about your paintings. I was talking about your morals."

"Oh—morals! So you think fornication is immoral. I didn't know that. You think Matilda and I are fornicating every night till sunrise and that is immoral. Right? Well, we're not."

"Tom Clayburn, stop using foul language! Do you hear? I won't listen to such talk. What I was saying is that everybody in this town knows about you and Matilda Herrick, how you went off to France and married that French girl and how Matilda went over there after you and tried to break up your marriage, and then your wife died and—"

"Everybody—?"

"Everybody. You know it all got back to Crescent City. Even your poor father knew. He talked about it all the time at the end, when he was out of his mind, poor thing. I was afraid he would say something in front of the boy. He never forgave you for going to France in the first place, and marrying a foreigner and painting pictures of women without any clothes on."

"Nudes, we call them, Maude. It doesn't sound quite so naked."

"And then getting mixed up with Matilda over there. He never forgave you for that either. You really can't blame him for what he did in his will. I get awfully mad when I think about it, this old house going out of the family, but you really can't blame him, with you sending that poor child over to Boston and not coming home yourself, as you should have. The war wasn't any of our business till we got into it."

"Beulah is in the family. She's my sister. She's a Clayburn."

"But her name is Cox now, and that Jack Cox she's married to—oh, Tom, I know how you love this old place! Don't you give me credit for any sense at all?"

"I do, Maude Ewbank. I do indeed. You do the best you can. Everybody does, one way or another, although what I do isn't very much, I must say. Certainly not next door. Next door, it's nothing. So if that's what is worrying you, Maude, let me assure you that I would if I could, but she won't let me."

"I don't believe you."

"No I am nothing. I am a Dadaist. That's what I am. Nothing in painting, nothing in life. *Fini.* You've never heard of Dada, I suppose. Well, neither has Matilda. When it comes to art, you are two of a kind, you and Matilda. She thinks I ought to learn to paint with my left hand. Did I tell you?"

"Well, why don't you?"

"Matilda is like you. She thinks painting is just pictures, all Norman Rockwell and those pretty girls on billboards that advertise our local beer, all moonlight and roses. 'Why don't you start with the Ohio River, Thomas?' she says. 'Something familiar. Something you know.' "

"Well, that makes sense."

"C'est trop con!"

"Whatever that means."

"It means intensely, and means good. But not with Matilda and me, it doesn't. I can tell you that. I am nothing. I might as well be dead—like art. Did you know that art is dying? Nothing will ever be the same again after the war is over, no matter who wins. Everything we have always lived by is dying, large and small, love, things like this old house and being a Clayburn, even enmity, all the old crap about pride and honor and integrity, all the abstractions. Only guilt will be left. You'll see. And man cannot live by guilt alone. . . ."

"I don't know what you're talking about."

"'Why, it's simple, Maude. Man cannot live by guilt alone, especially if there is nothing to feel guilty about but guilt itself. Don't you see? Even style will go. After Roosevelt and Churchill die, men will no longer do things with style, even the wrong things. If De Gaulle survives them, he will become an anachronism. *La Gloire* will be just a lot of horseshit—"

"Tom!"

"—and only old men will wear their medals. And in this country—you'll see—Lexington and Concord, Gettysburg—all those poor bastards will have died for nothing—kids will be taught to despise George Washington, men will call him a fascist, the Revolution a commercial gamble, Lincoln a demagogue, the Civil War a parochial, irrelevant, political affair that accomplished nothing, and all those poor bastards who died to create and save the Union will have died for nothing, and those of us who have roots in America will see them torn up and will be left with nothing but the guilt. You'll see."

"Stop talking nonsense!"

"That's just the point, Maude. They'll say it's all nonsense. Everything will be nonsense. Love, honor, history, America, and all that goes with it. . . . Art. . . . But none of it will affect people like you and Matilda. People like you and Matilda never believed in the abstractions, anyhow, except as slogans. You don't know what I mean when I say art. You would call it art if I painted the goddamned Ohio River so it looked the way it sounds in the song. How does it go? Bee-yoo-tee-ful O-hi-o— ta-ta—moon-lit stream. . . ."

"Tom, the neighbors will hear you!"

"All right, I'll tell you about Dada, then. They called it Dada because of the baby's cry. To a baby, every man it sees is Dada. So the word is meaningless, you see, and thus denies the validity, the identity, the very existence of art—and of the artist as well. Yessir, that's my Dada; nossir, don't mean Nada. . . . Hey, that's not bad! Our Dada who art in Nada. . . . That's how Hemingway should have written it. . . ."

"Tom, you've had enough! Don't . . . !"

"*Comme La Rochefoucauld nous dit, 'On n'est jamais si heureux ni si—'*"

"Stop it, Tom! You're drunk!"

"Ah, Maude, if only I were! I wish I were! I do, I do! I'm only doing the best I can. Why don't we have wine with our meals in this house every day, like civilized people? A good Pouilly-Fuissé with my breakfast, a Champagne at dinner. . . . I tell you what! I'll swipe some of Matilda's. She has a whole cellarful. Château Margaux . . . Grands Échézeaux. . . . It was her grandfather's, Rodney L. Marvin, *bavard et bon vivant*, horse's ass par excellence—"

"Tom!"

"—mortal enemy óf Clan Clayburn. Put the Mayor in the clink, he did! It's priceless stuff, and Matilda has no idea of its worth, much less its merit. Confidentially, Maude, she's not

very bright, that Matilda. Château Lafite 1924! Imagine! Even
you could learn to like that, Maude. . . . But I forgot about Dada.
I was hoping if I told you about Dada you would understand
what has happened to the world and to me. But you don't even
try to understand. . . ."

"There is one thing I do understand, Tom Clayburn. That
Herrick woman and her liquor are doing you no good."

"Wine, Maude; not liquor. But Matilda Herrick is not a
woman; she's only a girl, a child. She's just a babe in arms. In
arms—! Ha! That's good . . . !"

"She's all wrong for you, Tom."

"So you're talking about my arm at last, aren't you? That's
what I've been talking about all along. My arm. Yes, you're
right. This time, for a change, you are right about Matilda. She's
all wrong for me. Or I'm all wrong for her. My red-white-and-
blue stump is too much for her. It makes her sick just to think
about it. She can't let me go, but she can't face up to my patriotic
red-white-and-blue stump either."

"I hate her! Your arm wouldn't bother a woman who really
loves you, Tom. It doesn't bother me, darling. It didn't. Oh,
Tom, darling . . . !"

"Now, Maude, for Christ's sake, don't start that again!"

All that winter, I had a bad record for tardiness at the afternoon sessions of school.

Meantime, Deedee continued to report on the progress of our
parents' courtship; and one rainy morning in the early spring
she had incredible news for me.

"Guess what's going to happen to your father."

I could not guess.

"His arm is going to grow back on."

I stared at her.

"It can't," I said.

"Yes, it can. My mother said so."

"They don't."

"My mother said so. I heard her. They were in the parlor and
I went downstairs for a drink of water and I heard her. Your
father was crying."

"My father does not cry."

"And he kept saying, over and over, 'It's my arm, isn't it? It's my arm!' and my mother said, 'Be patient, Thomas. It will come back again and be the way it used to be. But it will take time.' That's exactly what she said. I heard her."

"It couldn't," I said.

All that day, as I watched raindrops streak the panes of the tall arched windows of my schoolroom, I kept saying to myself, over and over, "It couldn't . . . they don't. . . ." But I half-believed what Deedee had said.

In the end, my father did not marry Deedee Herrick's mother. Late that spring, leaving old Mrs. Marvin to live alone in the house next door, Matilda departed suddenly with Deedee for California; and my father married Aunt.

Neither of them ever told me in so many words that they were married. All I knew was that soon after Matilda and Deedee went off to live in California Aunt moved into the front room with my father, the room she called "the master's bedroom," and people began calling her Mrs. Clayburn instead of Miss Ewbank, but I was unaware of any particular day when the ceremony took place. Aunt never suggested that I call her mother, and for that I was grateful.

For several years I accepted the situation without question, but a period came in my boyhood when I was deeply concerned about morality, especially the morality of others. Looking back upon that time, I think that for a while I must have been an insufferable prig. At any rate, one day I went downtown to the county clerk's office in the courthouse to make sure that Aunt and my father were not living in sin.

I had been in the courthouse only once before, when Aunt took me there the first summer I lived in Crescent City to show me the courtroom where my grandfather had presided as Judge of the Circuit Court. All I remember of that first visit was that the building smelled of whisky and tobacco, like the room in the house on Audubon Street that my grandfather occupied, and men stood about in the corridors in a manner that seemed to say that something very important was about to happen and it could not happen unless they were standing exactly where they were. On my second visit, the smell remained the same, and the men were still there, where they had been before, waiting for something to happen. They looked like the same men. I am sure that if I had gone back to the courthouse on my visit twenty-five years later, when I gave the lecture at the college, they would still have been there, unchanged.

"It's something I have to do for school," I told the county clerk.

It was a plausible lie. My teacher was constantly sending her students out on such assignments, to ask people about their jobs, why they chose them and whether they liked their work, or to attend public meetings or search records in public offices. Along with thirty or forty other children in her class, I was well trained that year as a public nuisance.

At first, the clerk, a ruddy-faced fat man with an American Legion button in his lapel, eyed me narrowly. On the counter that separated his office from the small lobby where I stood, his moist white hands lay inert, like two plump dressed chickens on a grocery counter. When he learned that I was "Tom Clayburn's boy," he lost his belligerence.

"There's nothing short of the Ten Commandments I wouldn't do for Tom Clayburn," he said." We went to school together. Did he tell you? Central High School. He was a pistol. How is your dad, anyhow?"

"He's all right, I guess."

I really did not know how my father was. At that time, I was unaware of everything but my own virtues.

"Well, tell him Vergil Waters asked about him."

"Yes, sir, I will."

"He had tough luck, your dad did. I guess he made quite a thing of those hand-painted pictures of his before the war. I remember they hung some of them on the walls here in the courthouse once, before he went to live in France and started painting those naked women. I think his old man must have arranged it. He was Judge of the Circuit Court then. But now your dad can't paint pictures anymore, they tell me, because of his arm."

"No, sir."

"Well, that's too bad. Being a Clayburn, he don't hurt for money, and, just between you and me, I never did think much of those pictures, although it said in the paper they were first-rate; but I always say a man ought to be allowed to do his own kind of work, just the same, whatever it is, so long as it don't hurt anybody. Of course he shouldn't have gone over there and lived in France. It was un-American of him, a lot of people thought. I always said he should have come home when the war started over there; then, after Pearl Harbor, he could have joined the American armed services, like the rest of us, and he wouldn't have lost his arm, except maybe fighting for the U.S.A. But I always liked your dad and, like I said, it's a shame when a man can't do his own kind of work. He was a pistol in high school, always up to something. You're part French, aren't you, son?"

"Yes, sir."

"I suppose you parlez-vous."

"Yes, sir—a little."

"Copper-goosie-wee-wee," he said and, winking at me, laughed. I had no idea what he meant, but I laughed too, politely. "Well, there've been some fine Frenchmen of course," he said. "You take Lafayette, for instance. But right now there don't seem to be anybody over there who knows how to run their country. They talk about this De Gaulle, but I never thought much of him myself. Stuffed shirt, kind of. And there's that other fellow they've got—the one that wants everybody to drink milk—what's his name? A Jew, they tell me. Not that I have anything against the Jews. Now, what was it you wanted, son?"

I explained again, and he unlatched a wooden gate in the counter and let me into the inner office and led me back to a big dusty room with steel shelves stacked high with ledgers.

"Make yourself at home," he said, "and if you need any help, call me. And, like I said, be sure to tell your dad Vergil Waters asked about him."

"Yes, sir. Thank you."

"Tell him I said not to do anything I wouldn't do."

I laughed nervously.

"Yes, sir, I will," I said.

He left me alone in the big room, and I spent a long time pulling down ledgers and running my fingers over red-and-blue-lined pages, getting dust in my nose, until I found what I was looking for.

June 29, 1942: Thomas Bradford Clayburn, Jr., 35; Maude Ewbank, 18+.

I was perversely disappointed.

On the way out, I asked Mr. Waters what "18+" meant, and he said, "That's when they're over eighteen and it's legal but they don't want to tell their age. It's usually when the woman is older than the man."

By the time I made that excursion to the courthouse we were no longer living on Audubon Street. After my grandfather's will was probated, we had to move because he bequeathed the old house to his daughter Beulah, leaving my father the income from a trust fund that would eventually become mine.

"He never forgave you for going to live in France and marrying a foreigner," Aunt said. She seemed much more aggrieved by the will than my father was. "Beulah will put the place up for sale," she prophesied, "and it will become the Elks or the American Legion or a funeral parlor. That's what is happening to a lot of those big old houses down near Main Street."

To quiet her, my father agreed to buy the house from his sister; but Aunt Beulah wrote back from Tacoma, where she lived, that the place was not for sale. She and Uncle Jack were going to move back to Crescent City and live in it themselves, she said.

The letter from Tacoma robbed Aunt of some of her grounds for complaining, but not all of them. "Of course it's better than if she sold the place," she conceded. "After all, she is your sister. She's a Clayburn, like you say. But that Jack Cox, now! Nobody ever heard of him till he married her! He may be somebody out there, but he's a nobody so far as Crescent City is concerned." She was as vague about "out there," where Tacoma was, as Cousin Claudia had been about Crescent City.

Through it all my father appeared to remain unperturbed. "It's a double therapy," he said to Aunt. "Beulah will get Jack away from his drinking pals in Tacoma, and I'll be forced to break with this Audubon Street crowd." Recluse though he was, he spoke as if his days and nights since his return from Europe had been a constant exhausting round of social involvement with his neighbors. I think he had never been inside a house on Audubon Street except Matilda's and our own.

That was the first time I remember hearing him refer to the kind of people who lived in the neighborhood as "the Audubon Street crowd." Thereafter, it became his stock label of contempt for the first families of Crescent City, the rich and the near-rich whose ancestors, like our own, had settled the region. Before he died he broadened the term to include everybody in Crescent City who had a lot of money, no matter what part of town they lived in. Like Dada, the term of contempt became part of the vocabulary of his nihilism, which cynically cheered at the same time that it deplored the passing of the America his forbears had created.

Apparently Aunt reminded herself that Matilda was the strongest bond he had with the Audubon Street crowd, for his remark silenced her at last. "Maybe if we move it will be good for your father, after all," she said to me.

He bought a comfortable frame house on Willow Street in Crescent City's developing East Side, and we moved out there. Originally a farmhouse, built in the 1880s, it had a big yard with plum and pear trees in the back, an obsolete cistern and outdoor privy, and a dangerously dilapidated fruit cellar. The fruit cellar soon became headquarters for the friends of my own sex that I found at last in the new neighborhood, and the privy, in spite of Aunt's prohibition, was our greatest convenience. Because the war had stopped construction of houses in the development, there were still many vacant lots roundabout with large trees not yet bulldozed out of them, and thus the new world of my boyhood had an ambience of bucolic delights. The change was good for me.

It was also good for my father, as Aunt had predicted. Shortly after we moved, he bought an easel and canvases and paints and, for a while, tried to recapture with his left hand some of the skill he had lost as an artist. The attempt was a failure, although I think it was the wound in his heart and his mind and not his physical maiming that blocked him; but by the time he acknowledged defeat, he was beginning to make posters for the war effort. "I'll end up painting beer ads, after all," he said contemptuously. But the work filled his days, and his presence in the house was less abrasive than it had been in the old house on

Audubon Street, although he remained as sardonic and taciturn as ever.

In spite of the pleasures of my new life on Willow Street, I was not altogether reconciled to the move. I had never been happy in the big gloomy house on Audubon Street with only one little girl and no boys to play with, but after we left it I became perversely homesick for it. Perhaps I suffered from envy more than any genuine yearning to return, for it turned out that Aunt Beulah and Uncle Jack had twin sons my age, Cooper and Clayburn Cox, whom I regarded as wholly unworthy of the birthright they had taken from me. They were a noisy, undisciplined pair, given to bragging about their previous life in the Northwest and disdain for their new life in Crescent City. In their boisterous presence, I always felt inadequate if only because, together, they outnumbered me. Most of all, I think, I resented their ownership of the bullet hole in the doorframe of the old house. They did not know of its existence and I certainly had no intention of pointing it out to them, but its being in their possession, even though they did not know it, gave them a kind of title to the Clayburn family history.

In those days, I cherished a foolish notion that we Clayburns had a romantic, pariah-like status in Crescent City, that everyone in town knew our story as well as I did, and that whenever the Clayburn name was spoken a shudder of mild horror ran down people's spines. This misapprehension rose from the fact that my great-great-grandfather, Henry Clayburn, was sent to prison for treason after the Civil War. I myself knew that he was not a traitor, that he was not even a Copperhead, that his principal concern at the time of Morgan's raid was to prevent a bloody disaster in Crescent City, and that he was sent to prison because of the machinations of his political enemies; but it meant something to me that, until the Cox twins came along, I was the only boy in Crescent City with an ancestor who had served a term in prison. Or so I assumed. At least, no other boy in Crescent City had an ancestor who endured such a glorious injustice as the sentence that was meted out to mine.

The villain in our family's drama was Matilda's grandfather, Rodney L. Marvin. "*Him* . . !" I remember my father saying one day as we sat on a bench on the library lawn beneath Rodney L. Marvin's equestrian statue. In a rare fit of conscience about his fatherhood, like the one that had seized him the day he took me to the ball game, my father had just introduced me to the Rodney L. Marvin Free Public Library, which rose on the grassy knoll behind us, turreted and ugly. I am sure he had no intention of indoctrinating me in an old family feud and spoke so only because the statue reminded him of Matilda and bile stirred in his throat. "*Him* on a horse . . !" he said. "Never had his ass in a saddle, I bet!"

He told me then how Rodney L. Marvin returned from Cincinnati after the war and charged my great-great-grandfather with treason.

"When I was a boy," my father said "Rodney Marvin was still living, in the house next door. That Audubon Street crowd used to call him 'The Patriarch.' 'Savior of Crescent City,' it says up there on the pedestal. *Merde*! All he ever saved was his own skin. My grandfather told me that when Morgan's men came Rodney Marvin high-tailed it back to Cincinnati, where he had a desk in the Provost Marshal's office and didn't come home again till the danger was over. *Him* . . !"

Gazing up at the statue, I repeated after my father, "*Him* . . !" and under my breath, "Never had his ass in a saddle, I bet!"

"The point of it all is, son," my father said, "never have anything to do with people like the Marvins. They'll make trouble for you every time. They're the kind that think only of themselves. They're the same the world over. It was people like Rodney Marvin who castrated France at the beginning of the war."

How he must have been hating Matilda in that moment!

Above us, the bronze cavalry officer on the rearing bronze horse pointed a bronze sword toward the river and Kentucky whence Colonel Stacey Morey and Morgan's men had come in the summer of 1863. Below the statue, on its stone pedestal, I read:

RODNEY LYCURGUS MARVIN
MAJOR U. S. A.
SAVIOR OF CRESCENT CITY
1863
Mens Sibi Conscia Recti

When I asked my father what *Mens Sibi Conscia Recti* meant, he said, "A silly man conscious of his rectum, probably. I don't know."

By the time I was able to translate the Latin for myself, I had read the whole story in the Rodney L. Marvin Free Public Library, where it was preserved in the attic in old newspapers, court records, and half a dozen diaries, and in a mildewed book by my great-great-grandfather, a kind of novel, entitled *The Fires of Anger*. This book I stole, without conscience, and took home, only to discover later that we had a copy of the book ourselves, stored in our own attic in a battered box that contained also the Clayburn family Bible.

When I brought the box downstairs and asked about it, Aunt looked accusingly at my father.

"I thought you took that down to the bank when we moved. It oughtn't to be here in the house. It's probably the most valuable thing you own. What if the house burned down?"

Sheepishly, my father took the box and its contents down to the bank and I never saw them again until I inherited them when he died; but at the time none of my ancestors interested me except Henry Clayburn, and I had the library copy of Henry Clayburn's *The Fires of Anger* hidden in my room. From it and from the old newspapers and court records I had learned that in the Civil War Major Marvin was a lieutenant, not a major, that his majority was a rank bestowed upon him by the G.A.R. afterward, that he was indeed safe in the Provost Marshal's office in Cincinnati during the raid and occupation, having fled there from a furlough in his hometown as soon as the Confederates appeared. Henry Clayburn, I had learned, wrote his book while he was in prison and published it when he was finally "pardoned" by a governor of his own political party.

Thus, by the time the Tacoma Coxes came to town and took over the Clayburn family home on Audubon Street, I was fully indoctrinated and informed and prepared to scorn them as uninitiated intruders and outlanders.

At that time, my former home on Audubon Street was one of the finest houses in Crescent City, as it probably still would be if today's mortuary neon and aluminum were stripped from its facade and the old grillwork replaced. A conglomerate of Greek Revival of the 1850s with a French Mansard third-story added later, it stood a few feet back from the spear-picketed fence that glistened with fresh black paint along the edge of the sidewalk, and because of its closer proximity to the street it seemed to soar above its neighbors. Its rosy bricks had been made rosier by the sand-blasting and the pointing the Coxes had given them as soon as the war ended and such luxuries could be indulged in. Aunt Beulah and Uncle Jack had also repaired the broken iron grill-work that ornamented the two galleries running the full width of the face of the house, and this grillwork, also lustrous with fresh black paint, etched lacy shadows on the bricks behind it. Five tall windows reached from the floor to the ceiling of the lower gallery and from the floor of the upper gallery, which was roofless, to the corniced eaves. Above the eaves, two dormer windows jutted out of the mansard.

If I felt exiled from the house, it was only because I had exiled myself, for every Saturday when I appeared at the front door to collect for my paper route, Aunt Beulah invited me inside.

"No, ma'am, thank you, I'm late," I always said.

She was a mild-looking woman, obese, with brown eyes like a cow's set in a round placid face. A cascade of pretty bracelets always jangled on her plump wrists, and in tune with them she laughed a great deal—giggled, actually—as if she were apologizing for anything she might say. I refused her invitations mainly, I think, because of her smothering sweetness, because in her presence I lost my breath and felt a desperate need to escape. Aunt attributed Aunt Beulah's manner to "Christian humility," which my father said was probably what had driven Uncle Jack Cox to drink in the first place.

"No, thank you, I'm late, Aunt Beulah. . . ."

"The twins are around somewhere," Aunt Beulah would say then. "I know they'd love to see you."

What she seemed never to know was that Cooper and Clayburn had already seen me as I came up the walk to the house, that Cooper and Clayburn were at that moment on the gallery above us, waiting for me to leave the shelter of the porch and ready to pelt me with horse turds or whatever other ammunition they had gathered for that weekly ceremony.

After she disappeared into the obscurity of the house, it was

my custom to loiter at the door, ostensibly recording her pay-
ment for the *Gazette* in my notebook but actually watching until
she was gone and I could put my finger in the bullet hole in the
doorjamb unobserved.

That hole was a shrine at which I worshipped my ancestry
every Saturday morning, reaffirming each time my secret title
to the temple from which I had been excommunicated by my
grandfather's will. In that moment of ritual I became Mayor
Henry Clayburn himself, flattened against the doorjamb, as I
remembered him in his book, with Colonel Stacey Morey,
C.S.A., lying dead at my feet and another dead man stretched
on the lawn while the Colonel's panicked orderly took aim at me
with both hands wrapped around his pistol. Standing straight
and tall, I waited until the orderly fired and missed and I heard
the thud of the bullet in the doorjamb beside me. "I am all right,
Doctor," I said then, "but I think my wife has fainted." Thereafter, with the mantle of ancestral dignity still cloaking me and
my title to the old house reaffirmed, I marched down the steps
of the porch, prepared to ignore the barrage of horse turds from
above.

One summer morning, after I had been delivering newspapers on Audubon Street for several years, the Cox twins failed
to fire their obscene missiles at me as I descended the porch
steps. Disappointed, I discarded my mantle of ancestral dignity
long enough that day to glance upward and see why they were
neglecting me.

Cooper and Clayburn were not on the upper gallery that day,
but above it, on the cornice below the mansard. Clayburn had
walked out along the cornice about ten feet from the nearest
dormer window and appeared to be searching for something in
the gutter. Cooper was halfway between the window and the
spot where his brother stood. Apparently neither of them had
seen me come down the steps.

"I wish they'd fall and break their neck!" I said to myself
when I saw them; but in the next moment I called out a warning, "Hey, you guys, you'd better be careful! You'll fall and
break your neck!"

Clayburn Cox turned and looked down. He had just taken

a croquet ball out of the gutter and stood with it in his hand.

"It's old One-Arm Papa!" Cooper shouted. "Sock him, Clay! Sock him with the ball!"

Clayburn promptly drew back his arm and let fly at me with the ball, but it missed me and rolled harmlessly into the street. I ran out into the street and retrieved it, and when I came back into the yard, I raised my arm and pretended I was going to throw it back at them. In the scramble for safety that followed on the cornice, Cooper reached the open window first and climbed through it, but instead of pulling Clayburn in after him, he turned quickly and shut it in his brother's face.

Outside, Clayburn began to pound on the windowpane and yell, "Let me in, you bastard!"

From the walk below, I jeered, "If he's a bastard, that makes you one too, Clay! Hey, Clay, if your brother is a bastard, you're one too!"

But Clay Cox took no interest in my lesson in genetics. He continued to pound on the window and yell.

I began to feel sorry for him, betrayed thus by his own brother, and I called to him then, "I won't throw it at you, Clay!"

But Clay kept on clamoring at the window. Behind the glass, Cooper thumbed his nose.

Finally, I noticed that the downspout at the corner of the house had begun to buckle and the whole length of the gutter and cornice was sagging under Clay's weight, and I cried, "Look out! The gutter's coming down!"

Clay paid no attention. Horrified and helpless on the walk below, I watched him jump up and down outside the window and saw the cornice sag lower and lower, until, not knowing what else to do, I ran up on the porch and yanked at the brass bell pull beside the door, calling out for Aunt Beulah.

There was no answer. I continued to jerk at the bell and call for Aunt Beulah, until at last something fell with a heavy thump on the floor of the gallery above me and a rain of dust came down upon my head. I stopped calling then and held my breath. For a long time after the thump overhead there was not a sound. Audubon Street was empty and still.

I stood frozen, waiting, while an endless time elapsed, and then I heard a man's voice inside the house and running footsteps in the upstairs hall and then the man's voice again, above me: "You ... Clayburn ... ! Oh, my God! Beulah ... Beulah ... !" The voice became a womanish scream. For a long time the high scream pierced my ears until I heard Aunt Beulah's voice overcoming it: "Now, Jack, now—there now, Jack—that's enough—don't try to lift him—no, Jack—wait here while I call the doctor —Jack. . . ." I was unable to move until I heard her inside the house talking on the telephone: "Come right away. . . ." Then I turned and ran down the steps.

I did not stop running until I reached Willow Street.

Without knowing why, I did not tell Aunt about the accident that afternoon; nor could I tell my father, later, when we were all at supper. There was nothing in the evening paper about it, but the next morning I read the story in the Sunday *Gazette* while I was on my paper route. The *Gazette* said Clayburn Cox was in the hospital, in a coma. In Sunday School, after I finished my route, everyone was talking about the accident; but again, without knowing why, I did not tell anyone I was there.

Aunt, who never looked at the paper before she went to church, did not know about the accident until someone told her after the service. By the time she got home, my father had read the paper and knew all about Clay Cox; but that did not prevent her from going over all the details in the *Gazette*. She talked of nothing else at dinner.

We were halfway through the meal when she turned upon me suddenly with a gleam of discovery in her dark eyes and said, "Why, you were there yesterday, Tersh, collecting for the paper! Didn't you hear anything about it?"

"About what?" I said.

"Why, about Clayburn Cox's fall of course!"

To delay answering I filled my mouth with food.

"Tertius . . . ?"

"M-m-m. . . ."

"Did you know about it yesterday?"

I had to say then that I did.

"Why on earth didn't you tell us?"

"I forgot to," I said.

Her mouth fell open.

"You *forgot?* A person doesn't forget a thing like that! Tertius, look at me!" I raised my eyes and found myself looking at her breasts. I was at a time in life when women's breasts fascinated but embarrassed me, so I lifted my gaze to the wallpaper above her head. "Why didn't you tell us?"

"I don't know."

I really didn't.

She turned to my father. "Did you hear what he said? He doesn't *know* why he didn't tell us!"

"A boy always has a lot on his mind," my father said.

"Nonsense!" Aunt said. "Well, you just tell us now, young man! Do you hear?"

"Tell you what?"

"About the accident."

"But it's in the paper," I said. "You already know about it."

At that point, my father came to my rescue.

"Let the boy alone, Maude," he said. "I've heard enough about those Tacoma Coxes for one day."

I cast a grateful look at him, and he turned, pivoting stiffly at the waist because of his missing arm, and smiled.

"What's a coma?" I said.

"It's the state half the human race is in most of the time," my father said.

"A state," I said. "Like Indiana. Tacoma, Coma."

He laughed and countered, "Paris, Trance."

"Madrid, Pain," I said.

"Washington, D.T.'s."

I knew what D.T.'s were. Aunt had prophesied that Uncle Jack would have them someday and Aunt Beulah would have to "put him away."

"Crescent City," I said; but all I could think of was "Crescent City, Shitty," and I did not say the rest of it.

"A coma is when you're real sick and don't know anything," Aunt said.

"That's what I said," my father said. "Real sick and don't know anything—the state the human race is in most of the time."

I started to laugh, but of a sudden I was crying. I dropped my head into my arms beside my plate and shook with sobs.

"What on earth has got into that boy?" I heard Aunt say; and then I heard my father tell her to leave the room.

After she was gone, I heard him get up and drag his chair around the table to my side, and then I felt his arm drop across my shoulders. It lay there like a stick.

"What happened, son?" he asked.

I told him then, between sobs, about the wish I had made when I saw the Cox twins on the cornice, how I had wished they would fall and break their necks. I explained about the croquet ball, how Clay had thrown it at me, and how I had threatened to throw it back. "I didn't say the wish aloud," I sobbed. "I only thought it. I didn't say it aloud. I didn't mean it. . . ." When I finished, my father was silent for a long time.

"If you weren't up on the roof with those boys yesterday," he said finally, "and if you didn't throw the ball back at them and you told them you weren't going to do it, it wasn't your fault. You ran up on the porch and tried to get help."

"But the wish . . ."

"If you wished they would fall and break their necks, that's too bad. But you didn't really wish it. Everybody thinks things unintentionally now and then without really meaning them. You must try not to make mountains out of mole hills, son. This Presbyterianism she has filled you with—you mustn't take it so hard. What we've all got to learn is . . . I don't know. . . . Take me, for example. Sometimes when I remember Paris, I. . . ." He stopped, and his fingers clutched my shoulder painfully; then his arm slid stiffly off it. "Oh, for Christ's sake! What am I talking about?" he said.

I felt sorry for him, without knowing exactly why, and I said comfortingly, "I won't think about it anymore, Papa."

"See that you don't," he said, and got up and left me alone in the room.

And I did not think about it again, until several days later when I was delivering papers on Audubon Street and saw Cooper Cox alone on the upper gallery of the house.

It was the first time I had seen him since his brother's fall, and he did not look the same. He was dressed in his best clothes, the blue suit that he wore to Sunday School, a white shirt, a tie, and he was standing by the iron railing of the upper porch, idle, all the aggression and the malice gone from his round face. He looked white and doughy. He did not seem like a boy of my own age, but much older, a man in boy's clothes, a little ancient wizened man, a homunculus.

"Hi Coop!" I said, and threw a *Gazette* up on the lower porch.

"H'lo," he said.

"How's Clay?" I asked.

"He's dead," he said.

When I came to Crescent City I had already been christened in Paris in the Church of Saint-Sulpice with the statues of four great Christian orators—Bossuet, Fénelon, Fléchier, and Massillon—looking on from the fountain in the square outside. Aunt, however, was not impressed by this precaution against the eternal damnation of my soul. In fact, she regarded as only slightly less than idolatrous "all those Catholic names" the Church had given me, and soon after she married my father she began a campaign to undo the pagan ceremony of my infancy in France. He objected, but in theology he was no match for her. Attrition, if nothing else, eventually won the day against him, and at the age of twelve I was properly anointed in the faith of my ancestors in the First Presbyterian Church of Crescent City. It was to this second baptism that my father alluded when he spoke of "this Presbyterianism she has filled you with."

He used the word "filled" with some justice. For a time after the event in the First Presbyterian Church, my newly acquired godliness not only filled me, it overflowed. Twice saved, I spilled self-righteousness on everyone like rain from a lowering cloud. I am sure I dampened the spirits of all who came within my range. I may even have aggravated the chronic mildew that afflicted my Sunday School teacher, the Miss Whiting who worked in the bank and who, several years before, had expressed concern for my father because he looked "tuckered."

It was in this state that I had gone to the county clerk's office to check on the legality of my father's and Aunt's cohabitation; and it was this piety and excess of conscience, in part at least, that accounted for my confession about the wish after Clay Cox's fall from the roof on Audubon Street. My father's brief, stammered lecture on that occasion, however, did not wholly cure me of my piety. I needed stronger medicine than he gave me that day. It was not until the next winter that I got it.

One evening in January, when I came home from a meeting of Christian Endeavor and announced that I had taken a pledge never to drink alcoholic beverages, Father looked up from his drawing board and said, "Jesus Christ, Coco, when are you going to stop being such a sanctimonious boob?" That night in my room I cried like a girl before I went to sleep, hating at first my father but in the end, salubriously, myself; and the next morning when I woke I felt better than I had felt for months. I was cured.

Perhaps what I had been suffering from was not so much piety as late puberty and early adolescence. No longer a boy but not yet a man, I had discovered that the earth I trod was as insubstantial as the cloud of self-righteousness on which I tried to live and have my being—and far more hazardous. Exiled from the true company of angels but not adjusted to the habits of adult mortals, I suspected that I was destined to be a pariah all my life.

Discovery of my image in mirrors had reinforced this suspicion. At that period of my life I observed a hundred times daily that my face, always too white, had taken on a sickly look as well; that pimples, for which I had heard a horrendous explanation from my peers at school, adorned my forehead like lights on a theatre marquee; that my hair, always embarrassingly curly, had grown into an uncontrollable lustreless mop; and that my nose, which reminded me of the Breton Peninsula where my mother's family came from, was larger than ever and as red as Brittany appeared on the map.

That summer and in the winter that followed, my truce with Aunt ended and I quarreled with her sullenly when she ordered me to stand up straight, to stop glowering, to tuck my shirt-tail in, to go take a bath, not to pick at my pimples, to take my feet off the furniture. Florence ceased to be the refuge she had been and had no patience with my unpredictable fits of sulking and outbursts of temper. As for my father, his empty sleeve embarrassed me in a way that it had not done before; I could no longer look straight at him; it was as if his fly were open.

At school, in spite of a carefully cultivated pose as a hard-boiled man-of-the-world, I was constantly suffering injured feelings and shocks to my modesty. In the fashion of my contemporaries, my "wit" was gross insult and horseplay, but when my friends turned such attacks upon me, I cringed. I guffawed as raucously as anyone at dirty jokes, most raucously when I least understood them, but the common indelicacies of daily life revolted me. The indecent exposure of the shower room after gym classes, for example, made me miserable, and the expert and widely admired and applauded belching of one of my classmates in the lunchroom filled me with disgust.

I blushed easily and lost my voice unexpectedly. One day, I remember, when Eileen Betz and I had to read from Shakespeare together before our English class, I felt my face begin to burn as she spoke Lady Macbeth's lines, "I have given suck and know how tender 'tis to love the babe that milks me. . . ." Eileen Betz had the most famous pair of "boobs" in our class! And when I saw that her next line after Macbeth's rejoinder was, "Screw your courage to the sticking place," I was struck dumb and could not go on with our performance.

Finally, in that fateful year I exhausted all the sources of information in the Rodney L. Marvin Free Public Library about my great-great-grandfather and thus lost my happy retreat into the past from the harsh realities of the world in which I had to live. To compensate, I invented dreams of a glorious future for myself. I would run away; I would go to Boston, to France; I would head for the West and find uranium; I would become a millionaire, President of the United States, a famous poet, a movie star—but all the while I knew that I would do none of these things, and I continued to idle away my days, slouch, sprawl, lean against things, gorge on candy bars and Cokes between meals, and accept chronic indigestion and boredom as my everlasting fate.

Spring brought some relief. My complexion cleared, my hair came under control at last. I grew to be the tallest boy in my high-school class. With the maturing of my body, the immodesty of the shower room became less painful. Although in public I was still awkward and without confidence, before mirrors in the privacy of bathrooms I developed a remarkable poise and self-assurance. But by that time my studies at school had suffered almost irreparably from the disastrous year behind me. I may indeed have become the biggest and manliest in appearance of all the boys in my class, but of a sudden I found myself regarded as one of the "dumbest."

In May, one Friday afternoon, after I had failed three weekly quizzes in a row, my Latin teacher, Miss Treen, kept me after school.

"You began so well last year, Thomas," she said. "I thought you were going to be one of the best students I ever had. You could have been, if you had tried. I think you still could be."

Miss Treen was probably in her early forties, a gentle, fragile little woman with a warm affection for her students and a trusting manner that made her especially popular among the boys, in spite of the subject she taught. I suppose, like most of them, I was in love with her. I found it pleasant to be close to her, and that afternoon I stood silent and contrite beside her desk, admiring her long-fingered hands, which lay characteristically folded and relaxed on her desk, and trying to keep my gaze from straying down to the mystery of the soft silken valley where her gray skirt fell between her thighs.

"When I call on you in class, you look startled, Thomas, as if I had wakened you from a dream. And sometimes you are sullen to the point of rudeness. I am sure you don't intend to be, but you are. Your father was a star in Latin when he was in high school. You didn't know that, I bet. He was, though. And you could be too. You have inherited his fine mind."

I had seen a picture of Miss Treen in my father's old high-school album. In fact, I had covertly cut it out and kept it in my bureau drawer under my socks. In a long-waisted dress and with her dark hair done in absurd puffs over her ears in the fashion of the 1920s, she looked more quaint than pretty, but below the short skirt, her legs were beautiful, and she had fine breasts. The snapshot was taken at a school picnic, the caption under the picture said. Miss Treen was leaning against a high rail fence with my father and, of all people, Vergil Waters, the county clerk. Vergil Waters, rotund and vacuous, could have stepped from the photograph into his county clerk's office of a quarter of a century later with hardly a change in his figure and face; but I saw almost no resemblance between the other young man in the picture and the man who was my father. He wore tight-fitting pants that ended high above his ankles, cuffless and revealing striped socks. His flowered necktie, ridiculously wide and wound over and over in a long knot, was askew, and his shirt sleeves were rolled up in clumsy lopsided folds above sharp elbows. The right arm, the one that he was to leave in France years later, was laid boldly across Miss Treen's shoulders. There was a mockery in his narrow face even then, but he looked happy.

As I stood beside Miss Treen's desk thinking of the picture in my bureau drawer at home, I remembered that Vergil Waters had said my father was "always up to something" in high school —"a pistol" Mr. Waters had called him—and all of a sudden, without expecting to, without wanting to, I found myself wondering whether my father had ever screwed Miss Treen.

As soon as the thought came to me, I blushed; and although I said nothing and Miss Treen was not looking at me, in almost the same instant she seemed as embarrassed as I was.

"You may go now, Thomas," she said abruptly, without looking up. "It is late and they will be closing the building soon. Try to do better from now on. Please."

A few minutes later, in the dark and deserted corridor outside Miss Treen's room, while I was bending over my locker taking out books for the weekend's homework, two bare white arms encircled me from behind and held me in a tight hug. Incredulous, I could not move. I had seen no one in the hall. I was sure the only other person in the building besides myself and possibly the janitor was Miss Treen. Finally, trembling, I straightened up; the arms withdrew from around my waist; and I turned about. It was Eileen Betz.

"Boo!" she said.

She was standing so close that I could feel her warm breath on my face. A big girl, almost as tall as I was, blond, blue-eyed, she was wearing a white blouse with a deep V-neck that, even in the dim light of the corridor, gave me a disturbing view of the cleft between the famous "boobs" that had given that mortifying "suck" in Lady Macbeth's lines. In contrast with gentle, fragile Miss Treen, whose presence was still haunting me, Eileen Betz was coarse and full-blown, like a gaudy summer flower substituted for a delicate spring blossom. I stepped back, bumping into the door of my locker, and it shut with a clang.

"Scared you, didn't I?" Eileen said.

I could not trust my voice. It sometimes rose to an uncontrollable falsetto when I was excited. I shook my head.

Eileen smiled and nodded her head. Whether she had frightened me or not, she knew the effect she was having upon me.

"You going home? I live near you."

I cleared my throat and came out with a weak "No."

She pouted.

I cleared my throat again and said, "I have to stop downtown and buy some things."

It was a lie and its unpremeditated invention startled me so much that I was sure she recognized it as a lie. She continued to smile and nod her head. She had a curious way of nodding, as if she were reading your mind and knew what you meant no matter what you said.

"What things?" she asked.

For the life of me, in that moment, I could not think of a single purchasable item in all of Crescent City.

"What things are you going to buy?" Eileen asked again, as if she were speaking to a child.

"Things," I said.

She smiled and nodded more knowingly than ever.

"Oh," she said. "Excuse me."

She made it sound as if the "things" I intended to buy were very intimate, wicked perhaps; and I blushed violently.

We remained facing each other in silence for several seconds. Her breath was scented with spearmint. Her "boobs" were still excitingly close. I tried to think of Miss Treen in her room down the hall.

"You're sweet," Eileen said finally. "You know it?"

I did not know how to answer.

"Some other time maybe—huh?" she said.

Then she left me, sauntered off without looking back, her long bobbed hair dancing at her shoulders in rhythm with the sway-ing of her hips, and ultimately vanished into the blaze of sun-light that filled the doorway at the end of the corridor.

For a long time I was unable to move from where I stood by my locker. Now that Eileen Betz was out of sight I felt a stiffness developing in my tight Levis, and I dared not go into the reveal-ing light of the out-of-doors. At the same time, my situation was complicated by a fear that Miss Treen might come out of her room and see me standing, inexplicably idle, in the dark corri-dor. But I dared not move until the embarrassing stiffness sub-sided.

Fortunately Miss Treen did not appear, and after a while it was safe for me to gather up my books and go home.

The next day, a Saturday, I saw Charlie Dart downtown. Charlie Dart was currently my "best friend." His father was a barber on the west side of town, and Charlie had the first "crew cut" I ever saw.

I told Charlie about my encounter with Eileen.

"She sneaked up behind me and put her arms around me," I told him. "I didn't know she was anywhere around. I thought everyone had gone home."

"Man!" Charlie said.

"I had to wrestle with her to get loose."

"Man!" Charlie said. "You should have screwed her right then and there!"

"I would have," I said, "except Miss Treen was still in her room, and anyhow it was late and I had to buy some things downtown."

"Man!" Charlie said, and cracked his knuckles. He had enormous hands and always cracked his knuckles when he was excited. They were more eloquent than his speech.

"She wanted me to go home with her," I said. "But I had these errands to do and anyhow it was late. So I told her, 'Some other time, Eileen.'"

"You've got it made," Charlie said. "That's fine pussy."

"Yeah," I said. "But it just so happened it was late, and anyhow I wasn't really in the mood yesterday. You know how it is. So I told her, 'Some other time, Eileen.'"

After my lunch period the next Monday, the assistant principal of the high school called me to his office and without explanation ordered me to go down to the boys' toilet in the Old Building and "scrub those initials off the wall."

I was dumbfounded. I never wrote my initials on walls, not because of Aunt's admonitory rhyme about fools' names and fools' faces but simply because graffito was not among my adolescent vices. What was more, I never used the boys' toilet in the Old Building; it smelled too bad.

The assistant principal was a man who could not endure a conversational vacuum. Although I had not uttered a word, he said, "Don't argue with me, young man! There is only one 'T.B.C.' in this whole school. I have checked the rolls."

The assistant principal's name was Haddon, but the students called him Ichabod Crane. His skin was the color of a dead oakleaf. One of his characteristic gestures was to point a bony forefinger, like a pistol, at his temple, and whenever he did this you half-expected his face to crumple like a leaf under the suicidal finger. He wore a black leather bowtie that rose and fell below a splinter of Adam's apple as he spoke.

"I must say I am surprised that you would be guilty of such an obscene defacement of public property, Thomas Bradford Clayburn. A young man of your supposed fine breeding! I guess it is your French blood. I was a Doughboy in the First World War and I have seen what the French do to their own beautiful churches. Even the altar screen of Notre Dame is defaced. But writing a girl's initials with your own in such a foul place as the boys' toilet is beyond my comprehension!"

"A girl's initials—?" I said, finding my voice at last.

Mr. Haddon replied by reaching for a pad of paper on his desk. He wrote something on it, tore off the sheet, and pushed it across his desk toward me.

"Don't tell me you don't recognize that," he said.

He had drawn a heart on the paper, with the initials "T.B.C." and "E.B." inside it.

When I looked up from the drawing, Mr. Haddon leered an acknowledgment of male understanding between us, and the bond he tried thus to establish was more offensive than his animosity.

"I don't think I need to ask you who 'E.B.' is," he said.

He did not need to ask me. I am sure that my face had revealed that I recognized the initials as Eileen Betz's. But I was thinking of Charlie Dart in that moment. Charlie was the only person to whom I had spoken about my encounter with Eileen Betz.

"I did not write this on the wall, Mr. Haddon," I said stiffly.

Mr. Haddon's jaw dropped. When he closed his mouth finally, his false teeth clicked.

"Oh, you didn't, didn't you?" he said. "Well, I say you did, Thomas Bradford Clayburn. And you will go downstairs at once and clean that wall. The janitor is waiting for you with a bucket and a scrub brush."

"But I did not write these initials on the wall, Mr. Haddon."

Leering again, he leaned across the desk toward me.

"Are you trying to infer that it was the young lady in question who wrote them—in the *boys'* toilet, Thomas Bradford Clayburn?"

"I am not trying to imply anything," I said.

Mr. Haddon taught English, in addition to his duties as assistant principal, and my correction of his misuse of the word infer was a mistake. If I had kept my mouth shut, he might, in the end, have talked himself out of his determination to punish me. Now he felt no such compulsion. His face turned crimson and his hands began to shake.

"Go and scrub that wall this minute!" he commanded.

"I will not," I said.

And so he suspended me from school for three days and that was the end of my friendship with Charlie Dart.

But it was not to be the last of Eileen Betz.

"You did not do it?"

My father was pacing back and forth across the living room of the house on Willow Street, rubbing his moustache with his forefinger. By the fireplace Aunt sat in a rocker, silent for once, a pile of sewing in her lap. I stood in the doorway. I had just come in. It was past suppertime and I was hungry. The fragrance of burning applewood in the fireplace whetted my appetite.

"No, sir."

"You're sure?"

"Yes, sir."

Since my interview with Mr. Haddon, I had spent the afternoon wandering aimlessly about the city, full of apprehension, and had gravitated eventually toward the river, to a path along the waterside below the levee where it was unlikely that I would encounter anyone I knew. In April spring had come with a rush that year, but in May it had gone away for a little while. The sky was gray. The dogwood and redbud and flowering quince had all lost their blossoms, and the mock orange and magnolias had not yet come into bloom. Aunt called this time of year "blackberry winter." She had seasonal names for every spell of unseasonable weather round the calendar. To keep warm, I threw stones into the river while I tried to rehearse for the report of my suspension from school when I got home. I was not guilty, but I was not sure that Aunt and my father would believe me. Adults were irrational and unpredictable.

At one point, I seriously considered not telling them at all. Maybe I could get away with it. I would get up at the usual schoolday hour each morning and leave the house with my books under my arm, and after a day of idling—in the library, at a movie, or wandering about aimlessly as I was doing now—I would reappear on Willow Street at the expected time. Evenings, I could catch up on neglected homework, especially for Miss Treen. The plan seemed feasible until it occurred to me that a notice of my suspension would be mailed to my home or telephoned from Mr. Haddon's office. I could think of no way to intercept it.

To escape the sharp wind from the river, I finally went into the museum that the city had built that year in a park by the riverside, and I spent the rest of the afternoon there. The paintings did not interest me, but the basement of the building was filled with curiosities that the museum had inherited from its predecessor, the Liggum County Historical Society, and there I found enough to occupy my time: arrowheads, tomahawks, shards, stuffed birds and animals, a hearse to which two mounted black horses were hitched, hides glistening, legs prancing, black plumes cocked between their ears, replicas of pioneer cabins, interiors and exteriors, a doctor's office of the 1870s, political posters promoting Benjamin Harrison and William McKinley for President and Rodney L. Marvin for governor, a two-headed calf, muskets, rifles, pistols, and military uniforms of every war since 1812, the 1812 exhibit being the drummer boy's outfit and drum that had belonged to my own ancestor, Samuel Clayburn. Although I had seen it all before, I lingered over each item as if this were my first visit to the museum.

"You had no part in it?"

"No, sir."

"You're sure?"

"Yes, sir."

My father stopped pacing at last, reached for his hip pocket, awkwardly extracted a five-dollar bill from his wallet, and handed it to me.

"Then you might as well enjoy your vacation," he said.

Behind him, in her rocker by the fireplace, Aunt nodded and broke her silence.

"I never did like that Willis Haddon. His family come from upstate. And he has made us all late for supper."

I was dumbfounded for the second time that day.

An hour later, in my room where I was trying to review my neglected Latin lessons, I was dumbfounded a third time when my father came into the room abruptly and, without any preface, told me bluntly, gruffly, and in relentless detail what I had already known for some time: how men and women made babies.

I suppose he believed that our united front against Mr. Haddon had created an opportune camaraderie between us, and a sense of guilt for his prolonged neglect of my sex education, similar to the remorse that had inspired him to take me to a ball game and to the library years before, had propelled him impulsively into my room. Whatever the cause, the result was as disastrous as the ball game had been. He spoke nervously, standing before my desk like a lecturer and fixing his gaze upon me ruthlessly, making me feel that somehow I was responsible for nature's reprehensible plan for preserving mammals. I cannot remember ever being more embarrassed in my life than I was that night.

Father's description of the sexual act was painfully graphic, but after I survived that ordeal he began to talk about wet dreams and morning erections, and I was more shocked than before. I supposed grownups never mentioned such matters. Indeed I found it difficult to believe that they even knew about them. Perhaps because he saw how he was embarrassing me, he tried to introduce a note of levity, and that only made matters worse. The English, he said with a harsh laugh, called the condition I found myself in when I awoke each day "a morning-glory." I tried to laugh, but that only made me angry with myself as well as him. When he moved on to his next topic, masturbation, it was all I could do not to get up and stalk indignantly out of the room, as if, like Aunt, "I never heard of such a thing!"

The conclusion of the lecture was an anti-climax. Father was thoughtful for a while and said, with a note of consolation and hope in his voice, that if I took a lot of exercise and did not worry about myself I would soon be feeling better.

I supposed then that it was my turn to speak; and in the end, without looking at him, I muttered defiantly, "I feel okay."

He stood before me for a long time rubbing his moustache with the back of his forefinger. The moustache had turned gray in the previous year, and the finger, as always, was heavily ink-stained. Finally, he exclaimed, *"Mais c'est trop con!"* and bolted out of the room.

A few minutes later, I heard him banging about in the kitchen, and when Aunt called out from the living room and asked what on earth he was doing, he shouted back at her, "I'm making myself a drink, goddamn it!"

I remained at my desk a long time that night, thinking. How strange it was, I thought, that I had known for a long time everything my father told me and yet I knew, really, nothing at all. Two days before, when I told Charlie Dart about my encounter with Eileen Betz, Charlie had said, "That's fine pussy," and I had agreed with him. I often used the word myself, along with all the others I had known since I was a small boy. But in spite of the worldly airs I put on when I used such words, I did not actually know what I was talking about. Here I had been living fourteen years with "pussies" everywhere around me all my life—under Deedee Herrick's panties years ago when we played jacks together on the porch on Audubon Street, in seats next to me in grade school and high school, in the high-school corridors under those provocative swirling skirts, on benches at my side at basketball games and football games, on the streets, in movies, in church even—and yet I had never seen one. For several years, sex had been the most absorbing subject of conversations with my friends; it motivated almost everything I read, the news in the *Gazette* that I still delivered along Audubon Street, the advertisements that my father was at last resigned to illustrating, stories in magazines, in books, the lines I had to recite from *Macbeth* with Eileen Betz in English class, even in the Latin assignments in Miss Treen's room; and yet I had no firsthand knowledge of this universal theme. It was like being a blind person in the museum I had visited that afternoon. It was like being stone deaf at a symphony concert in Crescent City's "Coliseum," where I went as often as I could. As my father said, *c'était vraiment trop con!* I even knew what *con* meant now, or thought I did.

That night I decided to find out as soon as possible what it was all about, and remembering Charlie Dart's, "You've got it made!" I settled upon Eileen Betz as the source of my information. Everyone agreed that she was easy. She obviously liked me. It would be stupid of me to wait any longer.

But in the very moment that I made this decision I heard myself say aloud, *"Mais, au fond, je n'aime pas Eileen."*

And that was true. I did not like her. She was coarse. She was common. She wasn't really pretty, even. She was only "well-stacked," as boys said in those days. When they admired her "boobs," her "ass," her legs, I agreed with them. But I was only echoing an accepted opinion. She was not the type of girl who attracted me, *au fond*; she was too obvious, too full-blown, too big. I wished it could be somebody like Miss Treen, only young of course, a girl who stirred something more in me than a stiffness in my Levis. I did not want it to be Eileen Betz. But if what Charlie Dart and everyone else said about Eileen was true, Eileen was the most available, the only immediate, the quickest and perhaps the best solution to my problem. I had no choice, and I could not wait any longer.

The next day, at the hour when the last classes at the high school were dismissed, I was pacing nervously back and forth in front of the Crescent City Savings Bank on Seventh Street, having stationed myself there early, a discreet three blocks from the school building. Seventh Street, a noisy thoroughfare that became tawdry with secondhand stores and pawn shops on the other side of Main, was not the pleasantest route between the high school and Eileen Betz's home, but it was the shortest and therefore, because of the cold blackberry-winter drizzle that had been falling all day, the one she was sure to take.

There was a chance of course that she might ride the trolley home, and as I waited for her, alternating between periods of funk and excited moments of anticipation, I half hoped that she would. But I knew there was a very slim chance that she would. She would have to transfer from one trolley line to another in mid-journey, and at the end of her second trolley-ride she would still have to walk three blocks to her house in the rain. There was almost no chance at all that she would get a ride home in a car. Her mother, a divorcee, worked at the Gas and Electric Company and could not come and fetch her; and very few students owned cars in those days when the post-war age of affluence and adulation of youth had not yet begun.

While I was watching, fearfully and hopefully, for Eileen Betz to come along among the pedestrians on Seventh Street, I failed to give a second glance to a little woman in a red raincoat and raincap and was startled when she stopped before me and said, "Thomas! What are you doing standing here in the rain? You're sopping wet!"

It was Miss Treen. The rain gave a youthful freshness to her upturned face, garlanded by a crown of wet ringlets of chestnut hair creeping out around the cap's brim. The long raincoat covered her from her chin to the small black rubber boots that were planted in a puddle on the sidewalk. She held a purse close under one arm and carried a green cloth bag crammed with books and papers.

I was about to tell her that I was waiting for a trolley car when I remembered that no trolleys ran on Seventh Street.

"Hello, Miss Treen," I stammered.

"Are you waiting for someone?"

"Oh, no!" I said, as if her question were an accusation.

She smiled at me gently.

"I bet you are. But if you aren't, maybe you would like to come up and have a cup of tea with me. I'll light a fire and you can dry that jacket. It's going to stop raining soon."

"*Up—?*" I said.

"Yes, I live right here." She nodded toward a stairway entrance in the building next to the bank. "Come up and have a cup of tea."

"A cup of tea?" I said; and my voice sounded like Aunt's when Aunt said, "I never heard of such a thing!" Indeed I had not heard of such a thing in a long time. I probably had not tasted tea since my days with Cousin Claudia in Boston. In the Mid-dlewest, tea was for children and invalids and old ladies.

"Yes, Thomas, tea," Miss Treen said, still smiling at me in her gentle, mocking way. She nodded again toward the entrance next to the bank. Inside the door there were rows of mailboxes and polished brass bell buttons.

I glanced down the street. No high-school students were in sight.

"There is an assembly at school this afternoon," Miss Treen said. "But I didn't stay for it."

That settled it. If there was an assembly, Eileen would not be coming along for a while. Tea with Miss Treen would certainly be better than waiting in the rain.

"But of course if you are waiting for someone, Thomas—"

"Oh, no!" I protested again, guiltily.

While I held the bag of books and papers, Miss Treen searched for a key in her purse and finally unlocked the inner door of the apartment-building entrance; and after that we climbed four flights of carpeted stairs and entered a dark chilly room that she quickly made bright and warm by turning on lamps and setting a match to a gas grate. Afterward, she drew curtains across the rain-streaked window and shut out a dismal view of rooftops and chimneys. The room became cozy then as well as bright and warm, but suddenly it seemed very small.

I saw that it was crowded with furniture, not only a big comfortable sofa and several easy chairs and a low table, where Miss Treen set out an ironstone teapot and cups and saucers and plates of sandwiches and cookies, but also a collection of straight-backed antique chairs, an étagère with more ironstone on its shelves, and a grandfather's clock that reached to the ceiling.

When Miss Treen saw me admiring the clock, she said, "It really is a grandfather's clock. My grandfather made it. In Con-necticut. He made them, and so did his father and his grandfa-ther. I do need a larger place for all these things, don't I?"

"You have a lot of books," I said.

Bookshelves that reached from the floor to the ceiling on three of the four walls further reduced the size of the room. There were books also stacked on the floor, and others were piled on some of the antique chairs. I noticed that one whole section of the shelves was filled with yellow paperbacks with French titles.

"Do you read French?" Miss Treen asked, when I crossed the room to look at them. "I know you speak French but do you keep it alive by reading it too?"

"A little," I said. "But I have to use a dictionary a lot. There isn't much in the library. Victor Hugo and Dumas, but that's about all. Anyhow, I read them in English, because it's easier. They have some old copies of *Illustration,* but it's more fun to look at the pictures than to read the articles."

"I should think your father would have some French books."

"He does. But they're mostly about art." At that time, I took no interest in art, and I was surprised to hear myself saying so to her without embarrassment. "I don't know why," I said. "I like music. I go to the concerts when they come to the Coliseum. But pictures don't grab me."

"*Grab* you?"

"Interest me."

"Oh," she said. She smiled again. She had a tight little smile, lips closed, but her eyes sparkled merrily. "That's because your father is a painter, I bet." Her habit of saying "I bet" made me want to laugh. She said it pertly and with an air of finality, as if the words would clinch any argument. "Take me, for instance. Until recently I have never enjoyed cooking, and I am sure it was because my mother was an expert cook. When I was a little girl, she was always preparing one of her elaborate *spécialités.* She was French—like your mother. Only, she was a Creole —from the West Indies. Do you know Romain Rolland?"

It was hard to keep up with her. I wondered whether Romain Rolland was a West Indian or a painter or a famous cook.

She got up from her chair and took down from the shelves a book bound in white paper and handed it to me.

Vie de Beethoven stood out in red-and-black lettering against the white background above three letters in script: *NRF.* Under that was the name: *Romain Rolland.*

So Romain Rolland was an author. I admitted that I had never heard of him.

With the quick impetuous movements of a bird, Miss Treen had come and perched on the sofa beside me.

"These are mostly the books I used in college," she explained. "I majored in French. Sometimes I wish I taught French, instead of Latin. French grabs me more than Latin." Pleased that she had used my word, she paused and indulged in a little smile of accomplishment. "You may borrow this if you like. It is short and it's a good introduction to Rolland. To Beethoven too. If you enjoy it, you might want to start then on *Jean Christophe*. That's a novel—in ten volumes." She pointed up at the bookshelves. I must have looked daunted; for she laughed and said, "Oh, you would like it, I'm sure. But if there is something else you would rather borrow . . ."

"No, I'd like to read about Beethoven," I said. "The *Seventh* is my favorite symphony."

She nodded, as if it were hers too.

"But do you know any of Beethoven's even-numbered symphonies? The odd-numbered ones are the most famous, except of course the *Pastoral*. Do you know the *Pastoral*? "

I shook my head.

"The odd-numbered ones seem to be the ones they always play at our concerts. But, you know, last year I went down to Warren and Williams Music Store and bought all the even-numbered symphonies and learned them, and they're just as good, in a different way. Listen!"

She took flight from the sofa and put a record on the record-player on one of the bookshelves.

"The *Pastoral*, " she murmured, coming back to the sofa. "The last movement. It's something like a Courbet painting."

I was too young to realize she was being a bit precious—too young and too pleased, suddenly, to find myself on familiar ground at last. I had heard of Courbet, at least. My father had told me Courbet was one of the great ones before the Impressionists came along. Ingres and Delacroix and Courbet, he said. They were Cézanne's heroes. Cézanne, he told me, used to exclaim, *"Le reste, c'est de la friponnerie! "* I remembered the remark because I liked the word *friponnerie*. A *fripon* was a rascal, a cheat. I did not understand how a symphony could remind Miss Treen of a painting, but certainly Beethoven was not a *fripon*.

When the record ended, I got up reluctantly. To my surprise, I had been having a very good time.

As Miss Treen let me out the door, she said, "I hope you enjoy your little vacation, Thomas."

So she knew I had been suspended from school! I supposed she knew the reason too, and I blushed.

"That's the word my father used," I said. "He gave me five dollars to spend on my vacation."

"Good for him!" Miss Treen said. "I'm glad he believed you. But of course he would believe you. Everybody at school believes you, Thomas. In his heart, even that dreadful Mr. Haddon knows you're not guilty, I bet."

I was amazed that she dared to call the assistant principal dreadful. There was probably no other teacher in the school who would.

She gave me her hand. It was thin and had brown spots on it, but it was warm and soft.

"Will you come again?"

"Yes, ma'am," I said.

She drew back and looked at me quizzically.

"Yes, *what?*"

Her tone echoed the tone Aunt used when I left off the ma'am. I was puzzled.

"Yes, ma'am," I repeated.

Miss Treen shook her head.

"Just yes, Thomas. I know you're expected to say ma'am to teachers in classrooms. But outside, you mustn't. Ma'am is for children and servants." She took my hand again. "*Au revoir,* Thomas. *Donnez-vous du bon temps pendant vos vacances.*" Her French was prim and careful.

I laughed.

"*Entendu,*" I said. "*Au revoir et merci, mademoiselle.*"

After she closed the door, I went down the dark stairs, light-hearted, three steps at a time all the way; and when I emerged into the street, it was no longer raining.

On the sidewalk, I all but collided with Eileen Betz. I had forgotten about her.

I have never liked to think about the rest of that afternoon. I have tried to forget it. Indeed, until I met Eileen some twenty years later at my lecture at Crescent City's university, I thought I had forgotten it.

It was a mistake for me to go home with Eileen Betz that day in the afterglow of Miss Treen's spirit. If I had been older, I would have known better. But I was still a child, not yet fifteen. Maybe even at that age I would have known better if there had been only French blood in my veins. But half of me was Scot, in one sense more than half, for since my infancy in France I had lived with my Clayburn clan in Boston and Crescent City and I had been "filled" by Aunt with the Covenanter's faith of my Scottish ancestors. I had resolved to get myself seduced by Eileen Betz and here she was on Seventh Street, virtually in my arms, and so I had no choice, predestined Calvinist that I was. As some of my ancestors themselves must have learned at one time or another in their lives, John Knox's preaching can work for evil as well as good.

"*Well*—!" Eileen said, stepping back and giving me her cryptic smile and knowing nod. "Where did *you* come from?"

"I've been borrowing a book," I said, with some belligerence.

She glanced at the *Vie de Beethoven* in my hand.

"From Miss Treen, I bet."

I wished she had not said "I bet."

"Yes."

"Is it Latin?"

"French," I said.

She raised her brows and nodded more knowingly than ever, and I felt compelled to protect Miss Treen.

"I didn't know she lived there," I said. "I was waiting out here on the sidewalk when she came along. I was waiting for you."

That was the end of Eileen's interest in the book and Miss Treen. Her face lighted up with genuine pleasure.

"Were you really?"

"I had to come downtown anyhow," I said.

She smiled and nodded.

"Well—" I said blushing.

"Do you want to walk home with me today?"

"I might as well, I guess."

"Well, you certainly don't have to if you don't want to. Anyhow, I'm not sure I should let you. Not after you wrote my initials in the boys' room."

"I didn't do it, Eileen. You know I didn't."

"Who did, then?"

"I don't know."

"Was it Charlie Dart?"

I was so startled I could not answer.

"Because Charlie teased me about you yesterday morning,"

she said, "and that was before anybody knew about the initials. He's the only one who knows about us. *I* haven't told anybody."

Her "us" annoyed me. It took things for granted.

"Charlie doesn't know anything about us," I said, and immediately realized that I had put my own seal upon the word. "I mean—"

"Oh, I don't care who knows," Eileen said. "It's all right with me if everybody knows. I like you. Especially now that you've changed your mind and want to go home with me. You're sweet! You know it? I could have dates with any boy in school, but I like you best of all of them."

"I like you too," I said. I had to say it. It would have been impolite not to.

Eileen took my arm possessively, and we started down the street together.

As we walked out toward the East Side, I felt like a prisoner. At the same time, I was trembling with anticipation both fearful and eager. Eileen set our pace, walking fast, an impatience in her stride. She seemed intent upon something within herself, frighteningly confident, and was quiet most of the way. I could think of nothing to talk about. "It has stopped raining," I said once; and Eileen agreed with a nod that it had. "Was there an assembly at school this afternoon?" I asked, knowing that there was; and she said there was. "It wasn't much," she said. When we reached her house, she took it for granted that I would come in. "My mother won't be home from work for an hour," she said.

After Miss Treen's apartment, the Betz living room was sterile and unwelcoming. Blond wood gleamed everywhere. Each piece of furniture was carefully placed and seemed anchored where it stood. There were no books. Two movie magazines lay precisely edged on a glass-topped lowboy before an enormous divan that was upholstered in an aggressive shade of yellow. The drapes at the window were of the same material. In a corner, a collection of glass dogs was arranged symmetrically on a brass and marble whatnot, and on the walls there were two paintings. Both were reproductions, one a picture of an English setter with a dead bird in its mouth, the other a representation of a glass pitcher containing a stiff bundle of yellow roses. An airless smell of floor polish and yesterday's cooking pervaded the house.

We did not sit down in the living room. After I took off my jacket, Eileen said, "Come on back to my room," and led me down a long, empty, varnished hallway.

In her room at the end of the hall, I had only a fleeting glimpse of pillows and stuffed dogs piled on a bed and a framed photograph of a middle-aged man among an array of jars and bottles on a dresser, because as soon as we were inside the doorway Eileen threw her arms around my neck and began kissing me wetly. Her tongue tasted of spearmint and probed my mouth in a greedy agitation that threatened to choke me. All the while, she kept her pelvis locked against mine as securely as her lips.

After a time, breathing heavily, she leaned back and said, "You sweet baby! Oh, you sweet baby!" Then she began kissing me again, this time taking my hand and placing it against one of her breasts. Beneath her bra the breast was tight and hard, like a new softball.

When she disengaged her mouth from mine the second time, she looked levelly into my eyes and said, "You've never done it before, have you?"

Not only had I never done it before, I had never been kissed before in the fashion that Eileen had devised. She had been so diligent in the pursuit of her own pleasure that I felt excluded and stood rigid and resistant against the assault of her strong body. She did not seem to notice my state, however, and without waiting for an answer to her question about my virginity, began her attack again.

Finally, she seemed to achieve whatever end she had been working toward and stopped abruptly. This time, before I fully realized what was happening, she left me at the door empty-armed, and was across the room taking off her clothes.

I remained where I was, staring in amazement as her large breasts spilled from her bra. I saw next that the elastic of her panties left a red band on the flesh round her waist, and below it a splotch of hair streaked downward in an uneven smear that was more abundant than I had expected. She looked nothing at all like the naked women I had seen in posed photographs.

At the last, she threw herself on the bed among the pillows and stuffed dogs, stretched her arms out toward me, and spread her thighs in a shameless invitation; and at that point, seeing finally what the night before I had thought was so important for me to see, I no longer wanted to look. It was like a dark wound.

"Come here!" she commanded. "Come!"

I moved reluctantly toward her, and when I was at the bed-side she reached up and unbuttoned my shirt; then, loosening my belt, she unzipped my Levis.

"We can't do it with our clothes on, you know," she said, pretending to be cross with me, as if I were a child.

I felt like a child. It might be more accurate to say I felt like a patient in a hospital being undressed by a nurse. I certainly did not feel like a lover.

"We have to take off everything," she said, as she pulled at my pants, seeming to talk to herself now more than to me.

Standing foolishly by the bed with my Levis and shorts tangled about my feet, I dared not glance down at my exposed self. I knew that nothing was happening down there. I felt numb, as if I were paralyzed below the waist, as if my blood had stopped flowing. But I was embarrassed only by my nakedness, not my impotence.

"Do we have a thing?" she was saying now. "Where is it? Did we leave it in our jacket in the living room?"

I did not know what she was talking about.

"A rubber, silly boy!" she said. "A condom."

I was more shocked by her speaking out the word condom than I was by anything else she had said or done up to that moment, and I blushed.

When finally I shook my head, she looked disappointed and seemed on the verge of anger. But she recovered quickly, the knowing smile returning. "Okay," she said. "There are lots of other things we can do, the first time." She rose on an elbow and, cupping a hand around my buttocks, tried to draw me toward her. "Come on, silly! You have to get on the bed."

I knew that I was in danger then of fleeing naked from the room, from the house. I jerked loose from her grasp, stumbled back from the bed, and began clumsily pulling up my shorts and pants.

"I don't want to, Eileen," I stammered. "I'm sorry. I really don't want to. Some other time maybe. I'm awfully sorry. . . ."

I was standing on one leg of my pants and, as I yanked at them, I nearly tumbled over on the bed. When I got them up to my waist, I could not buckle the belt and let the two ends of it dangle while I struggled with the buttons of my shirt. My fingers were fumbling and weak.

"I guess I don't want to, Eileen, really," I kept saying. "I'm sorry. . . ."

Of a sudden, among the pillows and stuffed dogs, Eileen's whole body seemed to shrink, draw tight within itself like a spring. Her knees closed and her eyes narrowed. Even her breasts looked smaller.

"You mean you can't," she said. Her voice was cold and even at first. "That's what you mean. You can't. Do you think I'm blind? Do you think I don't know anything? I'm not dumb. You can't! Just because your name is Clayburn and you used to live on Audubon Street and Miss Treen gives you French books and stuff like that, you think you're smart. Well, you're not! You're stupid! And you can't get a hard-on. That's what's the matter with you! You can't! You rich, stupid, stuck-up—" She paused in search for a final insult. "Frog!" she said. "You rich, stupid, stuck-up French frog!" Her voice had risen to a yell—not a scream, but a yell—as if I were already out of the house and far down the street. "Frog! You dirty, rich, stupid French frog . . . !"

It seemed forever that I heard her voice echoing behind me down that long, empty, varnished hallway.

". . . frog . . . !"

Fortunately, I remembered to snatch up my jacket and the *Vie de Beethoven* from the chair where I had left them in the living room. Finally, I was outside in the cold fresh air.

As I ran down the front steps and out into the street, I was still trying to buckle my belt.

". . . frog . . . !"

". . . I'm Eileen Trautwein. I used to be Eileen Betz. . . ."

More than twenty years later, when Eileen Trautwein, née Betz, came up to me after my lecture at the university, the echo in the hallway returned.

". . . frog . . . !"

". . . Do you remember Eileen Betz . . . ?"

The knowing nod had not changed. Nor the smile either.

Except that the nod seemed, in that later time, to ask for confirmation, for reassurance, and the smile had become, with the
years, more of a smirk than a smile, mincing, plaintive perhaps,
and touched with a thin disdain that included herself as well as
others.

". . . Do you remember Eileen Betz . . . ?"

How could I ever forget her? How had I failed to recognize
her?

After Eileen Betz, I was technically still a virgin; only my
curiosity had been satisfied; nothing else. On that particular
road to manhood, I still had a long way to go. But considering
the kind of boy I was, perhaps I came away from that half-hour
in Eileen's bedroom more experienced than I would have been
had Eileen succeeded in initiating me in the physical exercise of
sex. That afternoon in May's blackberry winter of my fifteenth
year, if I did not yet know what I wanted, I was at least beginning to learn what I did not want.

That day in May moved me closer to the end of what I sometimes think of as the four-letter-word stage of life. I employ the
term figuratively of course. I do not believe that I used four-
letter words any more than most boys in that period, and I
certainly have not given them up entirely since, in extremis.
Such words serve a purpose. From time to time a man's mind
needs a purge; the error is to mistake the purgative for a pana-
cea, as American society seems to have been doing in recent
years by accepting hollow noises as substitutes for wisdom and
forthrightness. What I mean by four-letter words is not four-
letter words alone but all pretentious adolescent loudness that
tries, in any stage in life, to conceal frustration and fear. To
return to the figure of speech, for a grown man there are at all
times in the language words wiser and more honest than bullshit. He must must learn them or he remains an adolescent all
his life.

Of all people, it was Miss Treen who began to teach me some
of them. Again, not literally of course. She did not give me
lessons in specific synonyms for the vulgar words I had known
in both French and English since childhood. All I mean is that

Miss Treen taught me to think with more clarity and precision than I had achieved before I met her.

Her first effort in my education, however, was a failure. Romain Rolland's *Vie de Beethoven* did not grab me, and afterward *Jean Christophe* in ten volumes was too much for me. Its subtlety was beyond my understanding, its French too advanced for me to read with any pleasure. I did not finish Volume One. But Miss Treen was an incurable teacher. Recognizing her initial mistake, she loaned me *Le Grand Maulnes* next. After that, when a novel by Georges Simenon caught my fancy, she ordered a dozen of the Inspector Maigret stories from a bookstore in New York, and I devoured them. Because of his colloquial style, Simenon was easier reading for me than he was for Miss Treen, who spoke the language stiffly, the way she had learned it from college textbooks. On the other hand, her grammar and vocabulary were more sophisticated than the casual speech I had learned from my father. We were able to teach each other.

"My tongue is too old to learn," Miss Treen would say, despairing, when I tried to help her with pronunciation. "I wish I could have traveled in France when I was young. You must go back sometime, Thomas. You must. You will!"

"If I do," I said, "I won't be able to talk to anyone but children and bartenders."

Of course I was in love with Miss Treen. But I had the good fortune of not realizing it at the time. Or perhaps I should say that Miss Treen had the good sense not to let me realize it. I do not like to think what would have happened to me if she had taken me to bed with her, as she could so easily have done at the beginning of our relationship; for, virgin or no, she was a middle-aged lady and not the right person to educate me in that department of my growing up. What is more, if she had taken me to bed, I would have lost her much sooner than I did, and with her I would have lost the restraining influence that prevented my seeking out or being trapped by another girl, perhaps a girl like Eileen Betz, who would have held me captive longer in the four-letter-word stage of life.

Fortunately, I was not trapped by Miss Treen either. I was too fond of girls for that. Throughout our relationship I had more dates than the earnings from my paper route could pay for. During those remaining years in high school, I constantly dipped into my allowance and had to skimp on meals in the school cafeteria in order to go to movies and football games and dances. The cakes and sandwiches Miss Treen fed me in her apartment after school were a larger part of my daily sustenance than she ever suspected. Once or twice at school, I even stooped so low as to borrow from Cooper Cox, who always had more money in his pockets than he needed. But because I measured all my girls against an idealized Miss Treen and found them wanting, I was forever seeking out new ones and, in the end, escaped involvement with any of them.

Soon after that first cup of tea in Miss Treen's apartment, I found a book on Courbet in my father's library and studied the illustrations in search of one that would remind me of the final movement of Beethoven's *Pastoral Symphony*. I did not find one. I have never found such a picture by Courbet. I am sure Miss Treen was not on familiar ground that day. Maybe she was thinking of Constable, not Courbet. Out of loyalty, however, I pretended for a while that I saw resemblances between Courbet and Beethoven and I bought a reproduction of "The Funeral at Ornan" and, to Aunt's great disgust and my father's amazement, hung it in my room on Willow Street.

"What's pretty about that?" Aunt asked; and my father rubbed his moustache with his forefinger and remarked that it was a damn poor reproduction. "You can't cut down a ten-by-twenty-foot canvas," he said, "and make it into a bedroom wall decoration."

I paid no attention to either of them. For a while, I even considered ordering another copy of "The Funeral at Ornan" to give to Miss Treen. But it was too lugubrious a gift, and in the end I settled upon a recording of the Brahms Third Symphony instead. "The Funeral at Ornan" remained on my bedroom wall, however, and became a kind of symbol, a shrine, like the bullet hole on Audubon Street where I used to worship my ancestors. I suppose it was a substitute for Miss Treen herself there in my bedroom.

I was in love with Miss Treen and we wore much of the wardrobe of love without ever disrobing. Symbols. Mementos. A little language of our own. Music. Art. But no sex. No kisses. Seldom even the touch of hands. It was a situation that no man could have endured for long. But I was still a boy. When finally

Miss Treen asked me if I would like to call her Dorcas, it was too late. I could not think of her as anything but Miss Treen and told her so.

The best part of our intimacy was its complete frankness, and because of it I was able eventually to tell her about the afternoon with Eileen Betz.

It was an October day in my senior year in high school, and we were in her apartment again and we were talking about *Sister Carrie.* By persuading me to read in those high-school days many of the books that would be assigned to me later in college, she all but spoiled my first two college years. But perhaps she saved them for me too by making it easy for me to survive the neglect to which I treated them. That afternoon in her apartment she had been telling me about Dreiser's early difficulties as a writer, how he found it impossible to publish a second novel for a long time because publishers as well as the public thought his *Sister Carrie* was immoral.

"It seems ridiculous now, in the light of all that has been published since, doesn't it?" Miss Treen said. She was sitting on the sofa opposite me. She had learned by then that I did not like tea, and there was ginger ale on the table between us along with the sandwiches and tea. "Very puritanical and very quaint," she said, "because there is really nothing shocking in *Sister Carrie.* Not in the language, anyhow. Remember the first time Drouet sleeps with Carrie? Dreiser does not attempt to describe what happens. Instead, he takes us clear across Chicago that night to Carrie's sister's house and tells us about a dream the sister had, a dream of Carrie going down into an abandoned coal mine. That is how we learn that Carrie has lost her virginity. It's really rather funny when you stop to think about it."

I found myself wondering whether Miss Treen was still a virgin, and again I wondered whether my father had slept with her when they were in high school. But that afternoon I did not blush as I had blushed the day in her classroom when I first thought about them together.

"I almost went down in a coal mine myself that first afternoon I came up here," I said, without thinking; and I did blush then. The figure of speech was even more ridiculous than I had realized, and I had made it sound as if I had almost taken the subterranean journey with Miss Treen. "I mean after I left— with Eileen Betz."

I told her then about that rainy afternoon in May two years before. I told her almost everything, about my father's lecture on sex the night before and how I deliberately set out to get myself seduced by Eileen the next day. But I did not tell her everything of course. I did not describe how Eileen lay on the bed inviting me with her legs spread and how I discovered that I really did not want to look after all, or how I got tangled in my pants trying to pull them up. But I did tell her, unabashedly, that I found myself not only unwilling but incapable that afternoon and how Eileen yelled at me, calling me a "rich, stupid, stuck-up French frog." The absurdity of the encounter came out in the telling of it, and at the end of the story we were both laughing. I felt better about the experience then than I had ever felt before.

After a while, Miss Treen became serious and said, "Do you know why you didn't go through with it, Thomas?"

"I told you," I said. "I couldn't."

Miss Treen shook her head.

"No, that wasn't it. That was only a result, not a cause. You didn't want to. But Eileen didn't want to either."

I saw Eileen once more as she had been that day, naked on her bed of stuffed dogs and pillows.

"Oh, she was willing, all right!" I said.

Miss Treen shook her head again.

"No. She was as unwilling as you were. She was on her own precipice on the other side of the chasm that stretched between you, and it looked just as wide to her as it did to you."

"What chasm?" I said, and Miss Treen laughed.

"I sound like Theodore Dreiser, don't I? What I mean is that basically—*au fond,* as you said—Eileen disliked you as much as you disliked her. Don't you see? The night before, after your father gave you that lecture, although you admitted to yourself that, *au fond,* you did not like Eileen, you were going to use her to find out the things you wanted to learn. Maybe it was because you did not like her that you chose her. Well, Eileen did not like you either, Thomas, and that was part of the reason she took you home with her. It would mean a kind of victory over you and what you represented. Don't you see? She was on the defensive that afternoon as much as you were, and unconsciously she did just about everything she could to make you not want her. Eileen isn't really as bad a girl as all that, as vulgar, as crude, as stupid. In her own way she has a certain charm and knows something about sex that many women don't know and wish they did. In the end, when she had a different kind of victory from the one she expected, she called you a rich, stupid, stuck-up French frog, but don't you see it was because she knew what you thought of her, what you would have called her if you weren't a gentleman?"

"What would I have called her?" I said.

"I'm not sure. An ignorant, vulgar, lower-middle-class slut, probably."

Bitch, I thought. But I liked her word too. It was better than Aunt's hussy or my father's *con*. Bitch . . . hussy . . . *con* . . . slut . . .

"You didn't use any of those words," Miss Treen said, "for the simple reason that you are, after all, in a sense, what Eileen called you. People like you don't resort to name-calling. Don't you see?"

"No," I said. "Because that makes it sound like I—"

"—as if," Miss Treen corrected me, primly.

"—as if I thought I was better than she is."

"You do, don't you?"

"No," I protested. "I may be stupid and all the other things she said, but I don't think I am stuck-up."

"Fastidious, then," Miss Treen said. "Different. Not really rich, but more privileged than Eileen is. Not really stupid, but not very knowing in the matters that she thinks should make one wise. Not really French of course, but alien to her world. Not stuck-up, but fastidious, discriminating. Don't you see?"

"I guess so," I said.

"*Au fond*, Eileen did not want you any more than you wanted her. You were each on a precipice looking across a chasm at each other, and to come together each of you had to start building a bridge of love that neither of you was capable of building. If you had been in love in spite of your differences, it would have been all right for both of you and you could have done it. But you weren't in love, you were just pretending. Under those circumstances, if anything had happened that afternoon, it would have been a kind of rape, for both of you."

Miss Treen got up and went to a window and stood looking out at the chimneyed rooftops. A milky film of overcast was closing across the October sky. In the distance, toward the river, the top story of the New Century Hotel peered above the last low roof like a squatting cat ready to pounce. A red pennant, limp above one of the monumental cornices at its corners, was a ribbon tied in a bow above the cat's ear. I could not read the words on the pennant, but I knew what they said. "50 Years of Hospitality." It had been hanging there almost two years.

Finally, Miss Treen turned about and stood with her back to the window. Against its light I could not see her face.

"Love is the only thing that will bring people together," she said. "Why don't we learn that? All the good intentions and good deeds in the world, all the Eleanor Roosevelts and Harry Trumans and Father Divines, all the N.A.A.C.P.'s and Urban Leagues and United Nations, all the revolutions and laws cannot build the bridge, because they try to build it from one side only, sometimes with love maybe, but from only one side. It has to be built from both sides at once—with love."

She came and sat down opposite me again. Although she began to speak once more of Eileen, I had a feeling that she was talking about herself as well. She sounded intimate, involved, passionate, and yet despairing.

"The mistake you and Eileen made that afternoon was in believing it had to be sex. But at your age that was inevitable, I suppose—at any age, maybe. In the end, I guess, it always comes down to sex. But it has to start with love." She stopped and refilled my glass with ginger ale. Her hand shook a little. She appeared to be trying to get control of herself, and when she spoke again she sounded like the Miss Treen of the classroom; there was an impersonal jauntiness in her voice. "Yes, sex. You know, if white people could just forget about sex, they could love black people, I bet." She laughed. "But then think of all the things black people would have to forget in order to love white people."

I thought of Florence Taylor, my "Floor-ants." She had died the year before. Aunt had found her one morning slumped over in the rocking chair that she had insisted on bringing from her own home on Dove Creek because, she said, "nothing you got in this house fits my rump." There was a pan of half-peeled apples in her lap and a paring knife on the floor at her feet. Aunt gave her a fine funeral.

"Florence Taylor loved me," I said. "And I loved her."

Miss Treen looked at me sadly and shook her head.

"Don't be naive, Thomas. Of course you loved her, but not for the right reasons. You did not think of her as quite a fellow human being. You loved her because she entertained you and because she had no ultimate authority over you in that house where everybody else had authority. You looked upon her as another child, like yourself, not as a grown woman. Do you think she didn't know you regarded her as a child? Do you think she enjoyed playing that role?"

"*Mussoo*" Florence had called me, and I had laughed at her, I remembered. But she had laughed at me too.

"I think I just loved her. That's all," I said. "I'm sure she loved me."

"Of course she did. She was a woman. And you were a child, a lovable child. But she loved you also because you meant security to her, because an alliance with you was a hedge against your father and his wife. Even when she conspired with you against them, it was for her own pride as well as your happiness. Don't you see how that corrupted her love for you? You can't really love an insurance policy, money in the bank, something you use."

"But what about our two families?" I said. "Her great-grandfather and my great-great-grandfather, the Mayor, were friends." I had given Miss Treen my great-great-grandfather's book to read early in our friendship. "He said Goosehead was one of the few friends he could count on in Crescent City. They loved each other. Taylors and Clayburns have been friends for generations."

"*Goosehead!*" she exclaimed. "*Friends!* To Mayor Clayburn, Goosehead Taylor was a servant, a faithful old dog, and to him the Mayor was security, an insurance policy. Simple as that poor black man was and common as it may have been, back in those days, for blacks to have names like his, do you suppose he really liked being called Goosehead—*au fond?* Oh, Thomas!"

I remembered how disturbed I was when I first encountered

Goosehead's name in *The Fires of Anger* and how shocked I was
when I saw that there was no apology for the name in the
Mayor's mind when he used it.

"You're right," I said. "I've always felt that. Of course it was
another time. But people were callous, just the same. But maybe
we have learned something."

"It's not love," Miss Treen said. "It's only manners. Maybe in
some cases it's respect. But it's not love."

"Will we ever learn, then?"

She gave a little shrug of despair.

"I don't know."

For a long time she sat in silence, looking across the table
at me, her gray eyes speculative, her lips parted. Finally, she
said, "Thomas, I'm going to tell you something I've never
told anyone. I said once that my mother was a Creole. That
usually means a white person of French or Spanish descent
in America. Well, she was French, as I told you, and in the
West Indies where she lived when my father met her, she
was white. But up here in North America, in Connecticut,
where they lived for a while, and out here, where they came
when I was a child, she would have been a Negro, if anyone
had known, because she was an octoroon. They were always
afraid somebody would find out." She looked levelly into my
eyes for a long time. "Does that make any difference to you
now, Thomas?"

"No," I said without hesitation.

She smiled and reached across the table for my hand.

"Because we love each other," she said. "Because we built the
bridge first, from both sides. But most Negroes don't have the
advantage of a white skin that I have, although in the end it's
no advantage because if it's a marrying love, you have to tell, and
then . . ."

"I would marry you," I said.

"And maybe have a black child, a very black child?"

I lowered my eyes and did not answer.

She gave a little shrug and got up from the sofa.

"Let's play the Brahms," she said.

With the passage of the years, as all the good intentions of the time between that time and this have faltered, laws have been ignored and circumvented, and the revolutions and threats of revolution have only widened from both sides the chasm that Miss Treen saw, I have come to understand better that shrug of Miss Treen's that day and her despairing "I don't know." She would probably not lose her job in Crescent City today as she would have lost it then if the school authorities had learned that one-sixteenth of her blood was black. There are laws that would prevent it if she wanted to use them. But would there be love in the hearts of men like Mr. Haddon, say, or Vergil Waters. And if she wanted to marry . . . ?

Love . . . ?

There was no question of my marrying Miss Treen. When she asked me if I would risk having a black child, I could not answer "yes" because I was too young for such a question. Now I would answer "yes" without hesitation. But the question of love is not a question of blacks and whites only. It is much larger, a question of forgiveness, of charity, of humanity.

Can I ever learn to love the memory of Eileen Betz or she the memory of me?

"Do you remember Eileen Betz . . . ?"

How she wanted me to remember that afternoon in May more than twenty years before! How she wanted to make me suffer! And how painfully I remembered!

Love . . . ?

I don't know. . . .

What answer did Cromwell's pious Christians have when they captured John Clayburn under Doon Hill at Dunbar three hundred years ago and shipped him off to a strange land, virtually a slave? Did John Clayburn himself, the Covenanter, have an answer among his masters at the ironworks? Did Supply Clayburn find an answer in his eighteenth-century faith in perfectability, professing that all men are created equal and that every man is entitled to liberty, yet all the while closing his eyes to Negro slavery in the South? Oh, Supply, thou shouldst be living at this hour! Could his grandson, Mayor Henry Clayburn, indeed have loved Goosehead and still called him Goosehead? And how could Henry Clayburn have done anything but despise the redneck, Estol Sykes, when with a single shot Estol shattered the peace the mayor hoped to preserve in Crescent City while Morgan's men were there? Could he have loved the dandified, lascivious and vengeful major who took command when Colonel Stacey Morey, C.S.A., was murdered? Or Rodney L. Marvin, who sent him to jail when the war was over? Even my father, three generations later and thinking not of the Mayor but only of himself and Matilda, hated Rodney L. Marvin. *Him* . . . ! Never had his ass in a saddle . . . ! How could my father be expected to love the Germans who maimed him? *Je suis devenu Dadaiste.* . . . I too, *au fond.* Do you remember Eileen Betz? Do you remember Matilda . . . ? When I read in the Washington *Star,* years later, that Matilda Herrick was dead, I felt a guilty sense of deliverance, as if I had murdered her.

Love . . . ?

Love thine enemies . . . ?

I don't know. . . .

Matilda . . .

Matilda returned to Crescent City finally, unannounced. At least, she returned unannounced so far as I was concerned. I am sure that Aunt had no advance notice either; otherwise, she would have talked of nothing else. If my father knew, he gave no evidence of knowing, although I doubt that he would have cared much by then, one way or another. Surely, though, he would have given a sign that Aunt would have detected. I suppose old Mrs. Marvin—Mrs. Rodney L. Marvin—knew in advance that Matilda was coming back, and there was no reason why she should not have told me when I collected for the *Gazette* at the door of that Tuscan villa on Audubon Street, except that I never saw Mrs. Marvin on those occasions. For a long time she had been an invalid, restricted first to the upstairs of that old house and then to her room. Aunt said she was a hundred years old that spring. When I collected for the *Gazette,* I saw only the servants, a dour German woman whose speech I could hardly understand and a dour black man who never spoke at all when he handed me a dollar and waited in the doorway for the change.

Only them I saw at the door of the Tuscan villa until one fresh

April morning of my last year of high school when I rang the door bell beneath the tall, square, four-storied tower and neither the German woman nor the black man appeared, but Matilda herself.

"Tersh Clayburn!"

She was as beautiful as ever and as young! I remembered my father protesting, when Aunt called her "that Herrick woman," that Matilda Herrick was not a woman, but only a girl.

A girl she was still on that April day, dressed in the same pale shade of green that she had worn the first time I ever saw her. Her blue eyes, shining in a sudden happy recognition, were as wide and unclouded as ever; and when she came out on the stoop and impulsively took my hand, the sunlight striking her hair shimmered around it like a cloud of golden bees, as it had done that other time long before, when she went down the steps of my grandfather's house next door after she had kissed me. That April day the taste of violets came to my lips again in anticipation.

But she did not kiss me. After coming out on the doorstep, she stood looking up into my face intently for a moment, and afterward, as if suddenly distracted by the glory of the day, let go my hand and looked around her with wonder and joy.

"Oh—! How lovely!" she cried; and somehow she made me feel that I was included in her delight, as once before, when I was seven, she had made me feel like a man.

Everything was in bloom at once that year: forsythia, flowering quince, a pear tree, even a few daffodils still on the lawn, and violets, purple and white. Aunt had said it was because of the late snows. I remember that the last drops of magenta had not yet fallen from a redbud at Matilda's gate, although the dogwood beyond it was already past full bloom. Over our heads sunlight threaded through the new leaves of the maples and spilled, trembling, on the grass at our feet like dew.

Turning back to me, Matilda said, "Won't you come in, Tersh? Do come in and tell me all about yourself."

"I'm here for the *Gazette*, Mrs. Herrick," I told her solemnly. "It's forty cents."

It was then that she kissed me, lightly, on the mouth.

Afterward, she laughed at me, looking up into my face.

"I won't pay you your forty cents if you don't come in, Tersh

Clayburn!" she said. "And it's not Mrs. Herrick. It's Matilda. Who wants to be Mrs. Herrick on a day like this?"

If Aunt Beulah Cox, next door, had asked me to come into her house that morning, I would have said, "No, thank you, Aunt Beulah, I'm late," as I always did. I *was* late. I was always late. But I could not say no to Matilda.

As I looked down into her upturned face, I could think of nothing to say for a moment, except how beautiful she was, and I did not yet know how to tell her that. She still had the evanescent loveliness that I had remembered, the grace of a young tree in spring, the flowerlike fragrance. For me it was like our first meeting all over again, except that now I was looking at her in a way that I could not have looked at her before.

"Do come in, Tersh, won't you?" she pleaded, still laughing at my solemnity.

Of a sudden I found myself laughing with her.

"Of course, Matilda," I said.

I think now that in the next moment, when I followed her into the house, before anything else happened between us, I became a man by the simple act of crossing her threshold, for as I walked at her side down the deep-carpeted hallway under the white-balustraded stairs in that beautiful old house, I felt sure and calm, different from any way I had ever felt before in a woman's presence. It was as if the house were my own.

Like the Clayburn house, it was shadowed by many trees and hence cool and dark. But there the resemblance ended. Upstairs, old Mrs. Marvin might indeed be a hundred years old and dying, but the house did not speak to me of age and death, as my own, next door, had always done. It spoke only of Matilda. Its fragrance was hers, its whole ambience. As we passed the parlor, I saw long white curtains move softly in the breeze that came in through the windows, and outside the windows a cardinal sang. Cut branches of japonica stood in a green vase on the marble mantle, and on a table in the hall there were jonquils. Only Matilda could have put them there. Somewhere in the house music was playing quietly. I recognized Charles Trenet's jubilant Provençal voice. *Route Nationale Sept.* . . . It was a recording that I had thought once of giving to Miss Treen. I was glad I had not done so.

Matilda led me back to a small room that must originally have been Major Marvin's office. Sombre and solid, it was obviously a man's room still, although there had been only women in the house for years. But as soon as she entered the room, it was no longer the Major's and became hers.

She went at once to a walnut desk by one of the windows and, taking some change from her purse, came back to me and poured it into my hand.

"There's your forty cents," she said. "Now we can talk."

I sat in the chair she pointed to, and she dropped into another opposite me, looking very small in its depths, one leg crooked under the other, bare suntanned arms stretched above her head.

"I just got home last night," she said. "The place is still a mess."

As she spoke, she nodded toward an open traveling case on the floor beside the desk. Papers were strewn around it on the plum-colored rug. A tennis racket in a canvas cover lay beside it. On the back of the chair at the desk a light gray coat hung where she must have dropped it when she came in the night before with the bag and the racket.

"How is Deedee?" I asked, and realized as I spoke that I did not care how Deedee was, that Matilda was the only one who mattered to me in that house. "Did she come home with you?"

Matilda shook her head.

"She lives with her father now, in Rhode Island, a place called Wakefield. She may come to visit me before the summer is over, but I doubt it. She is fine."

"Then you've come to stay?"

There was such delight in my voice that Matilda responded by leaning forward in her big chair and giving me a quick smile. Her mouth did not have the pouting bee-stung look that Dee-dee's had. Instead, when she smiled, her lips drew thin and firm across fine white teeth, and then the smile vanished as instantly as it had come. In all moods there was something fine about her face that never completely surrendered to emotion. I suppose the word for it was patrician.

"Yes," she said. "I'm here to stay. Are you pleased?"

"Very," I said.

"So am I!"

Through one of the windows I saw the cardinal light on a branch of crape myrtle, dart away, a flash of red among green leaves, and dart back again. In a moment his song filled the room. We sat silent, listening till he stopped.

Matilda asked me then if I would like something to drink. "A Coke, coffee, wine . . . ?" she said. When she suggested the wine, the smile flashed again; but it was a bemused smile this time, lips closed. I said, "No, thanks," and she tossed her head and, brushing back a lock of hair from her eyes, gave me a look that was somehow defiant. "How is your father?" she said.

I laughed at her, and her eyes acknowledged the association of the wine in her thoughts with my father. But she made no comment. She took a cigarette from a box on the table at her side and, when I leaned forward to give her a light, offered me the box.

I shook my head.

"I'm in training."

"For what?"

"Baseball," I told her.

"Do you play tennis?"

"Yes," I said.

"Baseball," she said then, and laughed; and for a moment I was puzzled. "I was thinking of that ball game your father took you to years ago," she explained; but I did not understand until she continued. "I was out in the yard that afternoon when you and your father came home from the game. I was behind the crape myrtle, listening, eavesdropping. I couldn't see you, but from what Maude Ewbank said, you both must have been a sight."

"I had catsup on my shirt," I said, "and my father's sleeve had come unpinned. He'd had more beers at the game than he should have, I guess. He slept all the way home on the bus."

"And your pants were unzipped," Matilda said. " 'Just look at you!' Maude kept saying, although I am sure it was the last thing in the world she would have wanted anyone to do."

"Unbuttoned," I corrected her. "They were my proper Bostonian pants."

"Boston!" she said, making a little face. "You must have been a sight, both of you." Smoking her cigarette, she enjoyed the memory for a while; then she said, abruptly, "All right. How *is* your father?"

I told her I thought he was much better than he had been

when he came home from France, not so bitter, less rebellious, that he had become a commercial artist and was busy.

"Painting ads for the local beer," she said. "That's what he used to say."

I nodded.

"He tried to go back to his serious painting for a while," I said. "Maybe he didn't try hard enough. I don't know. Anyhow . . ." I struggled to think of something else to say about him. I was always startled to discover how little I really knew about him. "Oh," I said. "He has gone into politics lately, sort of." Enthusiasm for Adlai Stevenson had inspired him to run for precinct committeeman that spring. "Politics is in the Clayburn blood, you know. I think it has been good for him."

"As a Democrat, of course."

There was a light disdain in her voice. Those were the days of Joe McCarthy and Bill Jenner, and Republicans like Matilda's family believed what they said. If you were a Democrat, you were probably a Communist, a traitor of some kind, hardly an American. Certainly people like Matilda's friends believed that Democrats were below the salt.

"Of course," I said. "What else?"

Matilda laughed, not quite in disparagement, I thought, and yet not quite as if she were ready to admit that being a Democrat was respectable. I could hear the ghosts of Marvins stirring in the room, and I hoped the old feud between our families was not going to rise between us.

"And you too, I suppose?"

"A Democrat—? But of course," I said, stubbornly. "What else?"

"I like Ike," she said; but I saw that she was teasing me now. Her eyes danced with affection. The Marvin ghosts were quieted.

I like Ike was a slogan in those days. When I went to France four years later, when Eisenhower was running for his second term, there was a woman on the *Liberté* who wore an enormous button that read *J'aime Ike*. Reports came down from First Class that she wore it all the time, even at dinner at the captain's table. We Fulbrighters, who were in Tourist Third and almost unanimously for Adlai Stevenson, wondered whether she wore it to bed.

"Ike won't be too bad," I said, trying to be conciliatory. "But he has to get the nomination first."

"But I like Robert Taft too," Matilda teased.

I refused to rise to the challenge. She gave a shrug and, making a little face, said, "Let's talk about something else. Let's not spoil this beautiful day. Let's never talk about politics again."

"Entendu," I said; and she laughed.

In the next moment, with concern in her voice, she said, "Tell me about the draft. You're old enough, aren't you?"

I told her I would be eighteen in July.

"That's what I remembered. You look older, though, Tersh. I suppose everybody tells you that." She studied me through the smoke of her cigarette. "I hope they won't draft you. I don't want them to send you to Korea."

"I'll be exempt for a while," I said. "While I'm in college, at least. I may take Rotsy, but I'm not sure."

"What is Rotsy?"

"R.O.T.C. Actually it would be N.R.O.T.C. Navy officers training. That's what they have at Harvard."

"Harvard is where Cooper Cox is going," she said. "Is that good?" She laughed then at the way she had put it. "I don't mean Cooper of course. I imagine you couldn't care less where he goes. I mean Harvard."

"It's okay, I guess," I said. I was not half as pleased as Miss Treen had been when the notice came in February that I had been admitted to Harvard. There had been a lot of girls that spring. And baseball. The game had become a passion with me that year, mainly because it was a discovery for me. I was still amazed that I had made the varsity and was a reasonably good first baseman. I am sure now that it was only because I was the tallest boy on the team. I had never gone out for any kind of athletics before. Miss Treen complained that I was neglecting my studies. "I really haven't thought much about it," I said to Matilda. "There isn't any other place I'd rather go. Let's put it that way."

Matilda smiled reminiscently, with a certain wryness.

"You sound like a Harvard man already," she said. "At least, the way they used to sound when I was at Smith. Maybe Harvard indifference has gone out of style since then. I was at Smith only a year, and then I married a Harvard man." She ground out her cigarette in an ashtray on the table at her side. "You also sound like your father," she said. Her eyes widened, as if she had only at that moment thought of him. "I used to be in love with him, Tersh. Did you know? I followed him to Paris. I was just a girl. I had seen him only once. Here. In Crescent City. At my wedding, in fact. I was impetuous. People in Crescent City called me wicked. They said I was 'wild.' That was the word in those days, before the war. I followed him to Paris and I lived there almost a year, just to be near him, although I was married and so was he. I got a divorce in Paris. It's easier there. My husband . . . " She stopped and studied me for a moment. I suppose I looked embarrassed. I cannot remember how I felt. "Did you know all this?" she said.

"Most of it," I said.

"Because your aunt told you. I'm sure your father didn't."

I wanted to change the subject. Laughing nervously, I said, *"Elle n'est pas ma tante."*

Matilda replied promptly, *"Bien entendu. Je m'en souviens."* Then she said, "When you were children, you and Deedee, kids . . . " She broke off for a moment, frowning. "Aunt Bitch," she said, and laughed. "That was it. That's what Deedee said. I remember now. I heard that too. Not from behind the crape myrtle, though; I was in the house that day. I heard Deedee say it. 'Aunt Bitch!' And then you yelled at her from your porch, 'She is not my aunt!' It was the day your father came home from France, from England. 'She is not my aunt! She is *not* . . . !"

"I only call her that!" I mimicked myself after her, remembering.

Matilda lighted another cigarette.

"Deedee doesn't go to college for another two years. She's at Miss Wheeler's School now. That's in Providence. Maybe you will see her in the East. She is thinking about Radcliffe. She lives with her father in Rhode Island. But I told you that. . . . "

It was as banal as that, the first time. But for me, that day, every word we spoke was reverberant with overtones, promises, other meanings, portents. It was like that for her too, she told me afterward. "I knew it at once," she said. "As soon as I saw you out there on the doorstep something told me. It was inevitable. It needed no planning. I just took it for granted." I believe she spoke the truth.

I still believe that. I am sure she planned nothing. She did not seduce me. I also believe it was not because of my father that she let it happen—at least in the beginning. When I left her house that day, I said that I had never before liked being called Tersh until she used the name; and with an irrelevance that was at the same time a kind of relevance, she said, "What I told you about your father is all over now, Tersh. I want you never to think about it. . . . " and I think she really believed what she was saying. Maybe, like Hamlet's mother, the lady was protesting too much, but I don't think so. For that day at least, it was true —and for a while afterward.

Before I left, she kissed me once more, lightly, on the mouth; and that was as close as we came to each other that day. The other kiss, the laughing one, out on the doorstep a half-hour before, did not count. I was still a boy then. I had not yet crossed the threshold of that Tuscan villa.

In the beginning, baseball came between me and Matilda. Practice and the high school's game schedule took up every weekday afternoon and weekends during the remainder of April and throughout May, and for a while the only times I saw her were when I collected for the *Gazette* on Saturday mornings. Sometimes we went back into the Major's office as we had done the first day, but more often we only stood on her doorstep and chatted for a few minutes. We were never really alone. The German woman and the Negro man were always somewhere within the house. We said nothing significant, made no plans.

Then, one Sunday morning when I was delivering the newspaper just after dawn, Matilda came out on the doorstep in a white skirt and sweater and asked me to play tennis with her when I finished my route. I finished quickly, went home for my racket, and joined her at the city courts by the river. We played two sets and returned to her house and she fried bacon and scrambled eggs and we had breakfast together in the kitchen of the Tuscan villa, a big, square, high-ceilinged room with a fireplace. I sat in a rocker by the fireplace while she stood at the stove. After that morning, I carried my racket in my newspaper bag every Sunday, delivered Matilda's *Gazette* last on my route and, leaving my bicycle at her back door, walked over to the courts with her.

There was no blackberry winter that year, and those early mornings were very fine. I suppose early mornings are the best part of summer anywhere, but in Crescent City they seem especially so because along the Ohio River the days can become insufferably hot and humid by noontime, even in May. Walking down Audubon Street to the river just after sunrise we had the world to ourselves, except for the birds that sang in the bushes and trees all around us: cardinals, song sparrows, mourning doves, towhees, robins, catbirds, occasionally a woodthrush, and always, at the end of the street, just before we turned toward the river, a mockingbird on the roof peak of the John Ross house, high above a row of white Greek columns. The mockingbird seemed to put on a special performance when he saw us coming, teetering on his perch and fluttering his wings while he offered us a full repertoire of trills and throaty tremolos. We named him "Cooper." I don't know why. Sober and self-contained Cooper Cox was anything but a show-off, and I am sure he could not sing.

At that early hour there were never many people on the tennis courts, and those who came to play at that time were so serious about the game, so devoted to it that they paid little attention to us. Sometimes they were people we knew; sometimes not. In either case, they greeted us with a nod and a "good morning" or a wave of rackets across the courts; that was all. Anyone who gets up at dawn to play tennis regards it as a sport, not a social event. So, in a way, we had the courts to ourselves as well as Audubon Street.

Matilda played a good game; not brilliant, but steady. She had a strong serve and a dependable backhand. My best attack was to draw her down to the net, where she was erratic. But my backhand was not reliable, and she soon discovered that. We were so evenly matched that often we went to extra games to finish a set. Most mornings we were content with two sets, usually one for each of us, and went back to her house for breakfast feeling fine.

By the time we returned along Audubon Street people were beginning to stir in the big old houses, and the air was fragrant with breakfasts. Doors opened and shut and dogs scurried about in the yards, sniffing and wriggling along the hedges and under bushes, too excited by fresh morning smells to bark at us. In some of the houses radio broadcasters were giving the morning news. Under the iron-grilled galleries and the Greek Revival columns men in shirt sleeves were picking up the newspapers I had delivered earlier. If they saw us, they nodded and said "Good morning," whether they knew us or not. Several times between the tennis courts and Matilda's house we stopped and exchanged something more than greetings:

"Aren't you Tersh Clayburn? Haven't seen you in a long time."

"I deliver your paper, sir."

"How's your father?"

"Fine, thanks."

"Have you come home to stay, Mrs. Herrick? How is your grandmother?"

Then we had breakfast in Matilda's kitchen.

One Sunday in June, while we were finishing our coffee, Matilda asked me if I would like to take a shower before I went home. Without thinking, I started to point out to her that I would have to put my sweaty clothes back on afterward, but I glanced up at her in time and saw the steady look she was giving me across the table. "Yes, Matilda," I answered then, quietly.

We went upstairs together, our arms about each other. The servants were off on Sundays, and nothing prevented our going to bed in her room after our showers. It was as simple as that. I did wonder momentarily about old Mrs. Marvin in a room somewhere down the hall, but Matilda read my thoughts. "She sleeps late," she said. "I don't take her breakfast to her until eleven o'clock on Sundays."

From the first everything was right for both of us. There is nothing more that I can say about it. I mistrust people who write in detail about good sex experiences. I cannot believe they were really there. They are voyeurs, not participants. Even to myself, in my most private recollections, there is nothing I can say about that first morning with Matilda. It remains separate and distinct in my memory, apart from all the other times that followed, not blurred with the other times, as those other times have become; but that is all. It was not love, certainly. But it was not what it would have been with someone like Eileen Betz either. A timeless dissolution of myself in sensual delight. Nothing less. But nothing more. I believe it was like that for Matilda too, if such a thing is possible for a woman.

After that morning, we did not always have the will to go and play tennis, but we usually did; and those times, after tennis and after breakfast, were the best, I think. When summer vacation came, I gave up my paper route for a job as copy boy in the *Gazette* newsroom, and then I was able to go to Matilda's house at night. The servants went home after dinner. Sometimes I did not return to Willow Street until the first light of dawn.

During all that summer I was aware of old Mrs. Marvin's presence in the house only once.

One night she called out from her room.

"Matilda . . . "

"Yes, Grandmother."

A silence.

"Do you need me, Grandmother?"

"No."

Another silence; then, "Is that young man with you?"

"Yes, Grandmother."

I do not know how Mrs. Marvin knew of my presence in the house. She never left her bed, and I never saw her. Nor am I sure why Matilda admitted that I was in her room with her in the middle of the night. When I looked down at Matilda with that question in my eyes, she smiled up at me from the pillow and laid a finger lightly on my lips.

Once, in that summer, I scolded Matilda for stopping at the *Gazette* to ask me whether I was coming to her house that night after work.

"But everyone knows, Tersh!" she said. "Don't you realize that? People always know. So why should we be so secretive? That's the advantage of being Marvins and Clayburns. We don't have to care."

That may explain why she did not lie to her grandmother. Perhaps she had already told her grandmother about me. I have sometimes wondered if the old lady, confused about time, thought I was my father, long ago.

I suppose Matilda was right about everybody knowing. By the end of summer everyone in Crescent City probably knew. "The mailman too, Maude . . . ? Have you consulted the F.B.I. about me yet . . . ?" But in my bewitchment I did not care. I cared about nothing except what was happening to Matilda and me.

For example, that was the summer that Aunt Beulah and Uncle Jack were drowned, and although I was present when the police dragged their Rolls Royce out of the water with their bodies in it, I felt no horror. They were coming home late at night from a party, and Uncle Jack took a wrong turn in the complex of drives on the new levee at the foot of Main Street and drove straight into the river.

I can still see them sitting upright in the front seat of the Rolls when the police pulled them out of the river. Water ran off the stiff brush of Uncle Jack's moustache like spill over a dam, and Aunt Beulah at his side, erect and smiling her apologetic smile, was as proper as life. There was no doubt that Uncle Jack had a load on that night. He was a notorious boozer. As I watched, I felt nothing.

After the accident, when Aunt learned that negotiations were in progress for the sale of our old house to an undertaker, I felt no regret. I lost my interest in politics that summer and experienced no excitement when Adlai Stevenson finally got the Democratic nomination. At the *Gazette* my new work threw me into the vortex of the local maelstrom of intrigue, chicanery, and crime that until then I had not known existed; but I was undisturbed. I lived only for my nights with Matilda.

Certainly Aunt knew about Matilda and me long before anyone else. There was no way for me to account for my long hours away from the house on Willow Street, the extended time that my Saturday collections and my Sunday deliveries required, and my lack of interest in breakfast when I came home those first Sunday mornings. When I began staying on with Matilda after breakfast, Aunt was already off to church by the time I came home, and when she returned she could see that there were no dishes stacked in the sink. If she wondered whether I had washed them and put them away, which was unlikely, she was not above counting the eggs remaining in the refrigerator and measuring the level of the cereal in all the boxes in the pantry. Later, my night hours certainly made Aunt suspicious. But by that time, she had learned the truth, I am sure, from one of her many sources; by that time, she had consulted the milk- man and the F.B.I., figuratively, if not literally. Yet all that summer, Aunt never once mentioned Matilda in the house on Willow Street or asked me what I was up to. I do not know why.

She treated me to a trial of constant disapproval that summer, however, made a pariah of me in the house. When I did some- thing that she could openly disapprove of, like leaving the re- frigerator door open or neglecting to hang my clothes in my closet, she took an obvious delight in the opportunity such mis- deeds gave her for scolding me openly.

"You're two of a kind!" she would say significantly. "I can see you're following in his footsteps in every respect!"

If she could not take me to task directly for some mis- demeanor, she went about sighing in my presence, addressing an invisible third person.

"I've always done the best I can for him. I've done the best I can, and look what it has accomplished!"

Perhaps she was unwilling to bring my affair out into the open because she did not want my father to know about it.

"Nothing can come of it in the end," I often heard her reassur- ing herself, apropos of nothing that she had said before. "Abso- lutely nothing. People always get their come-uppance, one way or another."

She meant Matilda then, I am sure. It gave her pleasure to think that Matilda, who was twice my age and who she foolishly assumed would like to marry me, was bound to lose me in the end.

"Nothing can come of it. You'll see!" she said aloud to herself.

Sometimes, in her satisfaction that it was I this time and not my father who was involved in the Tuscan villa on Audubon Street, she contradicted herself.

"You're not at all like your father," she would say to me. "You'll always come out on top, no matter what. You've got that French blood in you. It's like ice water. I don't care what they say. Look at Napoleon and Marie Antoinette."

This, of course, was in the aftermath of some minor misdemeanor in the house on Willow Street, something she could scold me for openly.

To torment her, I would point out that Napoleon was not French, but a Corsican, and Marie Antoinette was Austrian.

But historical accuracy was of no concern to her.

"I don't care what they were. They were up to no good, I can tell you, neither of them, him and his Waterloos and her going about cutting off people's heads. They both got their comeuppance in the end."

"But, Aunt, Napoleon lost the Battle of Waterloo, and Marie Antoinette never cut off anybody's head. It was her own head that was cut off."

She would fix me then with that dark portentous gaze of hers, head aslant.

"Will you stop educating me, young man! That's exactly what I said, isn't it? Antoinette got her come-uppance in the end, just like Napoleon and his Waterloo. *I* know what I'm talking about!"

She was talking about Matilda and me of course.

Like Aunt, my father never spoke to me directly about Matilda that summer, but I suspect there was significance in the story about his boyhood that he told me one day in a sudden irrelevant seizure of reminiscence that was not natural to him.

I was watching him finish a drawing. It was painstaking work, and after it was done he laid the fine pen he had been using on the back of his drawing board and gave me an apologetic smile. I supposed that he was letting me know that he thought the commercial job he had just finished was not worthy of the skill he had put into it, but now I think he was apologizing for the intrusion on my affairs that was implied by what he was going to say.

"Do you remember those iron picket fences along Audubon Street, Coco?" He made it sound as if not only the fences but Audubon Street itself no longer existed.

"Yes, of course," I said.

"I suppose you've never painted one."

"No, sir."

"Well, I'd rather do a job like this any day than paint one of those fences. They took forever, and when you were through, all you had was a black fence that was already black when you started, unless it was rusty and you had to chip off the rust and give it a coat of red first. That was even worse."

He tipped his chair back, put his hand behind his head, and stretched.

"I ever tell you about the Audubon Street Improvement Society when I was a boy?"

He must have known he had not told me; he seldom told me anything about himself. Unlike most sons, I never had the experience of listening to a father's twice-told tales.

"No, sir," I said.

"Well, there was a boy named Sam Turner who lived back on Third Street. He and I used to mow lawns together, do odd jobs, trim hedges, things like that, the way you carried papers all those years. Kept us in pocket money. We called ourselves the Audubon Street Improvement Society. God knows, it needed improvement. But all we worked on was yards of course. I had a toy printing press and we printed cards and distributed them among the neighbors. 'Audubon Street Improvement Society. Reasonable Rates. Clayburn and Turner.'"

He stretched again and afterward, letting his body sag in the chair before the drawing board, snorted and said, "That old son of a bitch!"

I had no idea whom he meant.

Finally, he looked up at me out of a reverie, as if he had forgotten I was in the room, and explained, "Major Marvin."

"The one who got the Mayor sent to prison after the Civil War," I said.

He nodded.

"That one. 'Savior of Crescent City.' 'The Patriarch' is what that Audubon Street crowd used to call him. The old fraud! One morning the old son of a bitch was out in front of his house— next door to ours, you know—painting his iron fence. I've never seen anything so comical. I guess he was wearing what he would have called work clothes. Striped pants with a hole in the seat and a rusty morning coat. I can't remember ever seeing him in his shirt sleeves, even in the hottest weather. Probably went to bed with his coat on. And wearing an L. and N. railroadman's cap! Must have stolen it somewhere! Anyhow, there he was, making a mess of everything, the fence, the sidewalk, and himself, slapping paint around, splattering it all over. Even had some in his dundrearies."

"What are dundrearies?"

"Whiskers. Made him look like a goat."

"Oh," I said.

"When Sam Turner and I came along, we stood and watched him for a while, and finally I got up my courage to say, 'Major, why don't you let us do that for you?'

"I should have run into our house first and got one of our cards, but I didn't.

"The Major stopped painting and said, 'You want to, boys?'

" 'Sure,' Sam and I said. 'We do that kind of work. We'll be glad to.'

" 'You think you'd really enjoy doing it?' he said.

" 'Sure,' we said.

" 'Well, I kind of hate to stop, but if you really want to . . . ' the old son of a bitch said, and handed me his brush.

"Sam ran home and got another brush and we worked all day on that damned fence. The Major came out and watched us a couple of times, pointing out spots we'd missed and asking us if we were having a good time, saying maybe we weren't big enough for that kind of work, after all, and it was too hard for us. We assured him, hell, we'd done harder jobs than this one and we were having the time of our lives and would be through in a jiffy, although by that time we had blisters on our hands and were so tired we could hardly see the fence.

"At the end of the day, when we went up to the house to tell him we had finished, the old fart came to the door and just stood there behind the screen looking out at us, pulling on his dundrearies, and not saying anything, until finally he said, 'All right, boys. But it seems to me you've forgotten something, haven't you?'

"We supposed he meant our pay; so I said, 'Whatever you think it's worth, Major Marvin.'

"I'll never forget how he bellowed at us from behind the screen door then. He roared like a bull.

" '*Worth*—?' he said. '*Worth*—? What do you mean? You boys don't think I'd charge you for the fun you've had today, do you?

If you had a good time painting my fence, that's reward enough for me. Don't insult an old man by offering him money for a kindness, boys! *Worth*—? Why, I wouldn't think of accepting a cent from you! It's been my pleasure, boys. But I did expect you would at least say thank you.'

"That left us speechless. We didn't know what to say. We had never encountered anything like that before. Casuistry, I guess you'd call it.

" 'Aren't you going to thank me?' the old bastard kept insisting in a pitiful high voice.

" 'Thank you,' we said finally.

" 'Why, you're welcome, I'm sure,' he said then. 'If anything, I suppose I ought to give *you* a little something for the pleasure you've given me watching you have all that fun out there. But I'm not going to. No, sir! I don't intend to insult you the way you've just insulted me. No, sirree!'

"He disappeared back into the house then, and Sam and I stood on the doorstep a long time looking at each other in amazement. Finally, we thought we heard him laughing somewhere inside the house, and that made us feel better for a few minutes, because we decided it had all been some kind of a grownup joke and after he had enjoyed it for a while he would come back to the door and pay us. So we stood there a while longer, waiting, expecting him to come back to the door. But he never came back, and finally we dragged ourselves out to the street and went home.

"The next day, when I came home late in the afternoon from cutting someone's grass, your grandmother met me at the door and said, 'Major Marvin brought you a present this afternoon.' She was as pleased as punch. I hadn't told her what the old bastard had done to Sam and me the day before, and she supposed the present was some kind of a bonus for the good job we'd done."

"What was the present?" I asked.

"Can't you guess?" my father said.

I shook my head.

"A copy of *Tom Sawyer*."

"*Tom Sawyer*—?"

"Remember the fence-painting?"

"Oh," I said. "You mean that's all he ever gave you?"

My father nodded.

"I remember when I finally got around to reading it I liked it very much," he said. "But it was a long time before I saw the connection between the book and the way the old bastard tricked us into painting his fence."

Him . . . ! I thought, remembering the day my father and I sat on the library lawn under Major Marvin's equestrian statue. *Him,* on a horse . . . ! *Mens sibi conscia recti.* . . . I knew what the Latin meant by then. Miss Treen had found it for me in the *Aeneid.*

" 'A mind conscious of the right,' " I said.

"What?" my father said.

"That's the Latin on the statue," I said. "You told me once it meant 'A silly man conscious of his rectum.' It means 'a mind conscious of the right.' It's from the *Aeneid.* "

"Oh," my father said. "I like my translation better."

He slid a pad of paper toward himself across the drawing board and, picking up a pencil, made a quick sketch on it and handed it to me. The sketch was a mounted cavalryman who looked startlingly like the Major Marvin of the statue in front of the library. He was in Civil War uniform and was pointing a sword just the way the statue pointed its bronze sword toward the river and Kentucky. But in my father's sketch the cavalryman's mount was not a horse, majestically rearing on its hind legs like the bronze horse of the statue; it was a donkey, and the donkey's hind legs, not its forelegs, were in the air, and the Major's ass was in the air too, off the saddle, and he was about to vault over the donkey's long ears and plunge the sword into the ground.

"That was my revenge," my father said. "That picture appeared mysteriously on the alley-side of the Major's carriage house a few days later, life size. It gave me a lot of satisfaction. They were never able to paint over it completely, because I pretty much carved the whole damn outline of it into the stucco-covered bricks with a chisel before I painted it. I bet the outline is still there."

I felt a slight annoyance, such as I had felt, years before, when Aunt delayed a whole month after my arrival in Crescent City before she told me about the bullet hole in the doorway. When I was a boy I had never noticed the alley-side of the carriage house behind the Tuscan villa, because I had not known there was anything there to look for. And now I could not very well go out into Matilda's alley to look at it.

"They finally planted ivy to cover it," my father said.

That made some difference. But when I was boy I could have pulled the vines down to look at it.

Father was studying me above his glasses, rubbing his white moustache.

"But, you know, son," he said, "I still hurt when I think what that old son of a bitch did to me. Nobody likes to remember being outsmarted, I guess. I'd have done a lot better if I had read Mark Twain's book before I offered to paint the old bastard's fence, instead of getting it as a present from him afterward. It always pays to know what you are about before you get mixed up with people like that. They'll do you in every time, if they can. Of course, you have to learn everything you know from somebody, but they're hard people to learn from." He stroked his moustache in silence for a moment. "Just remember there are a lot of fences you can paint the rest of your life." he said finally.

The hint took no effect on me. Anyhow, it came too late. I continued to see Matilda as often as I could. I liked what I was learning from her, and it would be a long time before she gave me her equivalent of Major Marvin's copy of *Tom Sawyer*.

I am sure that Miss Treen knew about Matilda and me, and possibly she could have said something early in the summer that would have influenced me more than Aunt's obtuse attacks or my father's anecdote about the Major. But Miss Treen said nothing.

I suppose it was not in Miss Treen's nature or within the range of her talents to talk to me about Matilda Herrick as she had talked about Eileen Betz, for Matilda was a rival in a sense that Eileen was not. In the sexual armory of a woman like Miss Treen there were no weapons against a woman like Matilda Herrick. Or maybe Miss Treen concluded that Matilda was what I needed at that stage in my life, what I would find somewhere, no matter what she said, and since she had not taken me to bed herself, she thought she had no right to interfere with

Matilda's doing so. I don't know. Certainly Miss Treen had to admit to herself that Matilda was better for me than another Eileen would have been. Whatever her reasons, she said nothing.

One afternoon in late June, realizing that I had not seen Miss Treen for several weeks—not since the night of the high school commencement, in fact—I went dutifully but reluctantly to the entrance of her apartment building on Seventh Street and rang her bell, hoping she would not be at home. Her voice came promptly on the house-phone, however, and she told me to come upstairs. I climbed the four flights, heavy-footed, and when she let me into her apartment I stood tentatively inside the door, pretending I was on my way to the *Gazette* and late.

In contrast with Matilda's airy spacious house, the little apartment seemed more cluttered and crowded than ever. Miss Treen appeared to be nervous and embarrassed and apologized for a pile of dresses that was laid over the back of one of the antique chairs.

"I'm packing," she said. "I have decided to go to Connecticut for the summer."

"For the whole summer?" I asked her.

I tried to sound dismayed, but I am afraid I sounded hopeful.

"Yes, Thomas, for the whole summer," she said.

I am sure she saw a look of relief come into my eyes then. I was never a good dissembler.

"When do you leave?"

"Tomorrow."

I offered to drive her to her plane.

"Train," she corrected me. "I'm afraid to fly. I am taking the same train to Boston that you will take when you go to college in the fall with all your trunks and things. No, dear, I wouldn't think of letting you take me to the station. I wouldn't ask anybody to get up at the early hour I'm leaving. I have already ordered a taxi."

"I wouldn't mind getting up early," I said. Did I not get up early every morning and go home from Matilda's house? "I'm sure our old jalopy is reliable enough to get you to the station on time."

We still had the old Packard that had been my grandfather's. While I was in high school I had kept it in running order for my dates, but I had not taken it out of the garage all summer. The few times Matilda and I went anywhere we went in one of her cars. My father almost never drove the Packard because it was hard for him to steer and shift gears with only a left arm.

Miss Treen shook her head and said again, firmly, that she would not consider my offer. "Anyhow, I don't like goodbyes in public places," she said.

"Then this has to be goodbye," I said.

I tried to sound sorrowful but knew I had not succeeded.

"Yes, Thomas, this has to be goodbye."

There was a faint note of mockery in her voice and smile when she offered me her thin, spotted hand; and when I tried to say something gallant in French and linger over our farewells, she withdrew her hand from mine and said, "You're late to work, remember?"

I asked for her address, so that I could write to her, knowing that I probably would not; but she said she was not sure where she would be after she had spent a few days with cousins in Connecticut.

"Then you must write to me," I said; but she did not answer.

Afterward, in my freedom, I tried not to thump too joyously down the four flights of stairs for fear she would hear me.

That night—or, more precisely, the next morning, when I came home from Matilda's house—I took down Courbet's "The Funeral at Ornan" from my bedroom wall. It had been there almost three years, and it left a rectangle that was lighter than the rest of the wallpaper. Every morning for a week the rectangle was the first thing I saw when I woke up. Finally, unable to endure its blind accusing stare, I hung my first baseman's mitt on the picture hook to cover the space.

Aunt objected to the glove on the wall but admitted she liked it better than "that old cemetery picture."

When my father saw that a baseball glove had taken the place of "The Funeral at Ornan," he rubbed his moustache and said, "A collage. You've gone modern."

In September, just before I left for college, I stopped once more, dutiful and reluctant, at Miss Treen's apartment entrance, and I enjoyed a guilty sense of relief when I saw that the sub-lessor's name was still on her mailbox. I did not ring the bell.

I have never seen Miss Treen since.

Matilda . . . you bitch. . . .

. . . you quaint, archaic, superannuated bitch. . . .

. . . because something happened in America about that time that makes everyone who played a role in those Crescent City years not so very long ago seem archaic now—quaint, archaic and superannuated—like the antiquarian figures in the museum at the riverside.

Maybe what happened happened only to me. But I think not. Although I grew into manhood that summer with Matilda Herrick in her Tuscan villa on Audubon Street and nothing ever afterward could look quite the same to me, although I have traveled since then, made a happy marriage, fathered daughters, had a kind of success, and achieved a separate truce, if not peace, with the world I live in, I think that I too, along with Matilda and everyone else in America born before World War II, regardless of our ages or what has befallen us since, became, presto, in that summer of 1952, a single generation, a superannuated generation, outmoded before our time.

Age, wealth, the lack of it, blood, color, religion, philosophy, politics, spared none of us that superannuation. Being a Marvin who liked Ike, being young and beautiful, and excelling in her bed did not spare Matilda our common fate any more than being half-French, a Democrat, and at last a man of sorts spared me. My father's homemade brand of Dadaism, devised in the agony of his maiming, did not exclude him from our superannuated generation; nor did Aunt's platitudes, Eileen Betz's precocious knowing, Mrs. Rodney L. Marvin's century of living, or Miss Treen's secretly cherished one-sixteenth-of-blackness exclude them. All of us—black, white, young, old, rich, poor, bitter, hopeful, indifferent, good and bad—together became archaic.

I did not know this then. I did not yet know that Matilda Herrick was a bitch, much less archaic, although the knowledge of her bitchiness would come sooner than that other discovery.

I still had four years of Harvard College ahead of me, itself archaic, a fragile glass greenhouse for the isolated growing of young men, a place dedicated for three hundred years to the proposition that men are not created equal, that the elite among them should be thinking reeds and their careful cultivation is preferable to rank crops of weeds. And after those four years of Harvard I would have another year in France, then the most archaic of Western countries, where men still spoke solemnly of *La Gloire* and believed in its second coming, and aging heroes wore their faded ribbons with a pompous naive pride. I was to spend all those next five years an anachronism imprisoned in anachronisms without knowing it.

My father, playing prophet, tried to let light into my prison from time to time, but his efforts were not always to be trusted. After all, he was my father and a man with one arm, *un manchot*, as the French say, which is sometimes also their way of saying fool.

The day after the election of that year 1952, obviously stinging from defeat in his one small venture into politics, my father wrote to me that he believed we were headed for "the damnedest era of vulgarity this country has ever seen."

"It's going to make the age of Andrew Jackson look like the Glory that was Greece," he wrote, "and the age of Calvin Coolidge like the Grandeur that was Rome. That grinning hero they're sending to the White House is going to set the stage for us to lose everything he won for us in the war—our pride, our self-respect, our faith in ourselves and our friends' faith in us, and our hopes for the future. It's ironic that we have chosen that exhausted and befuddled hero to lead us down the road of defeat and degeneration. I think America has run out of luck. . . ."

My father was right about the era of vulgarity. After Ike came Jack, then Lyndon and Dick. Even in the free-and-easy 1920s we did not refer thus familiarly to our presidents. Who ever heard of Woodie or Warren? Cal sometimes perhaps, but jokingly, when he was wearing an Indian bonnet. But never Herb. Maybe, actually, it began with Frank and Harry. But before Ike, was there ever a President whose bowel movements were reported in the public press?

My father was wrong, however, about the blame. Ike no more led us down the road to vulgarity than Jack led us out of it eight

years later when we substituted his youthful smile and stammered simulation of aristocratic speech for Ike's grin and wob-
bly syntax and mistook winsome Jackie's new decor and string
ensembles in the White House for a cultural renaissance. Jack
did not have time enough to let us prove what we could do for
our country, but it is significant that, in his time, our country
proved what it could do to us with a mail-order rifle equipped
with telescopic sights. The point, however, is that grinning Ike
was no more responsible for our vulgarity than smiling Jack or
beetling Lyndon or scowling Dick. We were ourselves responsible, impelled by the same force that created the superannuated
generation in the year that I became a man.

Force could be the wrong word. Maybe it was not a force but
the absence of a force. Maybe, as we have been so often told, we
lost our illusions after World War II and were left with nothing
but the bleak discovery that we had been outsmarting ourselves
ever since the founding of the Republic. Maybe, as we have been
told, man has always been deluded; pride is only vanity; love was
never more than a four-letter word; friendship has always been
homosexuality in disguise when it was not the calculated practice of winning and influencing people for our own selfish ends;
good taste is timidity; art a hoax; liberty, like religion, the opium
of the people; equality a lie that needs only to be proclaimed by
enough laws to be forgotten; fraternity bullshit.

If so, America has indeed run out of luck.

In that profound pessimism, I think my father was wrong.
Luck changes. America is not dead. Nonetheless, I know that
something that seemed once to exist in my country seems now
no longer to exist, that the small world I lived in on Audubon
Street is gone and everyone who played a role in that earlier
time is now archaic. . . .

. . . Matilda Herrick included. . . .

I took Matilda with me when I left Crescent City for Cambridge that September—not the Matilda Herrick of that Tuscan
villa on Audubon Street of course, but a Matilda new and unfamiliar to me, a woman recreated in a dream by the abrupt end

of my nights with her in that old house. For a long time the dream haunted me day and night.

Sleepwalking, I rode the train to Boston with Cooper Cox and a hundred other young men and women who went East to college from the Middlewest that year, took a cab from South Station out to Harvard Square, found my room in Wigglesworth, met my roommate, exchanged with him the guarded pleasantries that all new roommates exchange with each other, registered for classes, bought books, ate three institutional meals a day and supplemented them with snacks in the bars and restaurants around the Square, made first ventures into the subway, got drunk once experimentally, sculled on the Charles, attended classes, explored new friendships. Dreamwalking, I saw Matilda in every girl I passed in the Yard and on the Square, found her image on every page of every book I tried to read, heard her voice on the street, on the river, in my rooms at night, at every lecture I tried to listen to. Obsessed by those abruptly ended nights in Crescent City, I was always alone and yet never alone.

Because of Matilda, Cambridge and Boston bored me at first. Perhaps it was because I was too young for them as well, too Middlewestern, too ill-prepared in American history and, in spite of Miss Treen, in music and literature and art; but certainly I was too lost in dreaming. Boston meant little more to me at first than Cousin Claudia's tall gloomy house on Beacon Hill, where I went every Sunday for dinner, encouraged to accept my cousin's invitations by Aunt's frequent letters— "Blood is thicker than water, I always say"—but compelled by the Gargantuan hunger that gnaws constantly at every college student's belly. I was probably homesick too; I loathed New England's climate.

As for Cambridge and the college, my studies occupied as little of my time as I thought it safe to give them. In fact, I cannot remember what I did with the long hours of my first year in Wigglesworth, or of my second, for that matter, in Eliot House. I went out for baseball but quit when I saw that I was not good enough to make the team. I thought of entering a competition for the *Crime* but did nothing about it. I was invited to join a club but declined. I cut classes. I loafed, but I did not invite my soul; for two years after my affair with Matilda I had none to invite. It is a wonder that I did not enter into the indiscriminate chase of girls, once the dream of Matilda was gone; but I didn't. I did nothing.

The dream began to vanish with the arrival of Matilda's letters. To put it bluntly, they were dull. I suppose I should have foreseen that they would be, but I did not. Looking back now, I find all my memories of her are associated with something physical: sex, tennis, even those hearty breakfasts in her kitchen. I cannot recall anything she ever said that was not banal. Her only distinctions were her beauty and her expertness in bed. For a while they were enough to sustain the dream, but it was soon feeding on nothing but itself.

"Dearest Tersh . . ." Matilda's letters invariably began, written in a large, square, college-girl calligraphy on large square sheets of expensive stationery. There were never more than a dozen widely spaced lines on a page. "Dearest Tersh. . . ." Never "Darling Tersh . . ." or "Dear Tersh. . . ." Never a "Dearest . . ." or a "Darling . . ." alone, never any of the little names she had called me in bed. Never even an inverted "Tersh dearest. . . ." Always the same. . . .

Lingering over the uniform introductions of her early letters, I sucked them dry of their thin endearment like a hot sun drinking dew, until finally they lost their meaning and became no more than what they were, complimentary salutations, invisible on the page, like her address above them, discreetly embossed without her name.

"I have been trying to get the house in order since you left. I neglected it so during the summer. . . ."

No mention of the reason she had neglected it. No suggestion of delight in the remembered cause of its disorder.

" . . . Saw Maude Ewbank downtown yesterday. Played tennis with Mr. Ross in the afternoon. Lost—6–0, 6–2, 6–4. . . ."

Should I rejoice that she had seen Aunt? Was I expected to be jealous of Mr. Ross? I remembered him vaguely; he was one of those men on the front porches of Audubon Street picking up their Sunday papers when we came home from tennis. He lived in the house where the mockingbird had sung. He was president of the First National Bank, married, the father of four children, an old man, fifty at least. Who cared about him? Who cared about their tennis scores?

"These bright October days are fine. . . ."

Ah, there was a kind of poetry in that!

But did she miss me on those bright October days? Did they remind her of our walks down to the courts at the riverside in the fresh early-morning air of summer? Did she remember the mockingbird we named Cooper, the breakfasts in her kitchen, and what ultimately we did afterward?

She did not say.

"I guess it's Indian Summer. . . ."

She sounded like Aunt and her blackberry winter.

"I'm glad you are enjoying Harvard. . . ."

I had not said I was enjoying anything. I was lonely, goddammit! I wanted her!

"Love. . . ."

Ah! "Love. . . ."

But that was the end of the letter. That "Love . . ." at the bottom of the last, stiff, square sheet of expensive stationery soon became a complimentary close as invariable and as meaningless as the complimentary salutation of the "Dearest Tersh . . ." at the beginning.

". . . Matilda."

A beautiful name!

Her own!

Written by her own hand!

But Eileen was a beautiful name too. So was Dorcas, Miss Treen's name. What was there in a name? I would have loved Matilda just as much if she had been named Maude!

Finally, in desperation, hoping to inspire her to greater heights of eloquence, I wrote her a letter in which I tried to express my passion. I mentioned her breasts, her soft white belly (my English instructor had said that "belly" was one of the most beautiful words in the language), her round buttocks (what other acceptable word is there for buttocks if you are only eighteen and trying to write with passion for the first time?), the fine golden hair on her mound of Venus (what *does* one call that part of the anatomy?), all with the wild surmise of one of stout Cortez's men at his first view of the Pacific. When I finished writing the letter I had an erection and, convinced that I had achieved only pornography, I tore the letter up. Then I wrote another almost as bad and mailed it.

"Dearest Tersh . . ." her answer began.

Had I failed?

"I was so glad to hear from you. I would have answered sooner but Grandmother has had several bad days. . . ."

It was like taking a cold shower.

But wait!

That "would have answered sooner" gave promise. It suggested eagerness. Maybe I had stirred her, after all, and further on in the letter . . .

But the promise was not fulfilled. In the three pages of large, square, widely spaced, college-girl calligraphy that followed there was nothing that I was looking for. Only details of Mrs. Rodney L. Marvin's indisposition. (What the hell was phlebitis, anyhow?) Another encounter downtown with Aunt. (Who cared?) Another tennis match with Mr. Ross. (Why didn't he drop dead?) Then: "Love, Matilda."

(Merde!)

By Thanksgiving, I was allowing a whole week to elapse before I answered a letter from Matilda, and I became as stilted as she was. ("Dearest Matilda: Yesterday my roommate and I— he's from Concord, Mass.—went to hear a talk by Charles Boyer at the Cercle Français. He—I mean, Boyer—is in Boston for the production of *Don Juan.* I'm learning to play squash. . . . Love, Tersh.")

Matilda's replies became less prompt. ("Dearest Tersh: I played tennis with John Ross yesterday in the new indoor court at the Country Club. Lost—6–0, 6–3, 6–1. It's quite cold here. . . . Love, Matilda.") I noticed that it was John Ross now; not Mr. Ross. Perhaps I should have been jealous, after all. But it was too late. I felt nothing.

A week before Christmas, my roommate suggested that I come home with him to Concord for the holdiays, and I accepted with alacrity.

"I am mailing my Christmas packages to you," I wrote to Aunt and my father. "I think it would be extravagant for me to come home for so short a visit after so short a time away. . . . Love, Tom."

A week or so after the Christmas vacation, I saw Cooper Cox coming out of Leavitt and Peirce. Cooper and I were on good terms, but our paths seldom crossed in Cambridge. He had done his last year of preparatory at Exeter and lived in Holworthy and had a different set of friends from mine. In her Christmas letter, Aunt reported that Cooper had come home for the holidays and was staying with the Rosses. "You'd think he would never want to see Crescent City again after what happened to his parents last summer," she wrote. "And that old house already being remodeled into a funeral home! But some people have thicker skins than others, I guess. . . ."

Cooper and I stopped in the press of students on the sidewalk and shook hands.

"Hi, Clayburn."

"Hi, Cox."

He had been loading a meerschaum pipe as he came out of the tobacco shop, and before he spoke again he struck a match and lighted the pipe lovingly.

"Didn't see you in Crescent City at Christmas," he said.

He was a pudgy boy, round-faced, not handsome, but very well turned out in the standard attire that Harvard men wore in those days: chinos, blue jacket, white shirt, narrow black tie, no hat, no overcoat.

The rich aroma of the pipe smoke lingered heavily in the cold January air.

"Looked for you at the Charity Ball at the club," he said.

"I went to Concord with my roommate," I told him.

"Adkins—?"

"Yes."

"Knew him at Exeter."

"He told me."

Another cloud of pipe smoke. Then: "Say—Deedee Herrick was in Crescent City for Christmas."

"Oh—?"

The wreath of smoke around his bare head made him look like Peter Pan, I thought. Peter Pan in thick-lensed glasses.

"Saw her at a party at the Rosses," he said. "She's a mere child of course. Only sixteen or so. But she's becoming quite a dish."

It was an opening for me to ask about Matilda. Perhaps Cooper expected me to. But I said nothing.

After adding a supplemental wisp of smoke to his wreath, Cooper said, "Hear you signed up for Rotsy, after all."

"Yes."

"How is it?"

"Not too bad," I said.

"Thought about it myself for a while, but decided to take my chances with the draft. Probably be 4-F anyhow, because of my eyes." He puffed at the pipe meditatively for several seconds. We had run out of conversation. Finally, he said: "Sorry. Have to run. Squash date. See you, Clayburn."

"See you, Cox."

Afterward, I thought he had sounded like one of Matilda's letters. Matilda and I had stopped writing to each other by that time.

When the spring recess came, I stayed in Cambridge.

"I hope you will understand," I wrote to my father. "I've got to study. I'm way behind. . . ."

When summer came, I took a job as a counsellor in a camp in New Hampshire and again did not go home. I did not want to run the risk of seeing Matilda.

In New Hampshire, I borrowed the camp's station wagon one weekend and drove down to the town of Dunbar to look up Supply Clayburn's house, and afterward I wrote my father a long letter about it. We had a snapshot of the house at home, taken in the 1930s, when, according to Aunt, my grandfather was thinking of buying it. I remembered she said the price was $2500 then, and in Dunbar, learning that the house was again for sale, I inquired at a real estate office about it. The price had increased to $25,000.

The place was badly run-down. Since the 1930s photograph, the ell at the back of the house had burned and had not been rebuilt, and the blackened cellar hole remained unfilled. Weeds grew tall beside the fanlighted front door, and the stone wall that ran beside the blacktop road was falling down. The land was no longer farmed, the pastures all gone to wild cherry and cedar trees and the woods behind them choked with undergrowth. The family who lived in the house kept a few straggling chickens. When I got out of the station wagon, a vicious-looking German shepherd strained at his heavy chain in the side yard and growled at me.

The family's name was Wenkowski or Wykowski, something like that. The woman who came out on the front stoop in answer to my knock pronounced the name only once and I did not like to ask her to repeat it. I gathered she disliked living in the house. It had a furnace and was warm enough in winter, she said, and the kids did not have to ride far on the school bus, but her husband commuted to work in Keene, twenty miles away. They were renting it, she said, till they could find something better.

When I told her that my great-etcetera-grandfather had built the house, she showed no interest and did not invite me in but remained on the stoop, hugging her elbows and blocking my view of the interior through the open door at her back.

"I've heard people in the village call it the old Clayton place," she said; and I did not correct her about the name.

While we talked, I heard the voices of quarreling children indoors above the blare of a radio.

"All very sad," I wrote in conclusion of the letter to my father. "*Sic transit gloria mundi.* Only the ghost of Rodney L. Marvin could have rejoiced in seeing the place."

"*On n'est jamais si heureux ni si malheureux qu'on s'imagine,*" my father wrote back.

I spent the Christmas holiday of my sophomore year in New Hampshire, this time with the family of my new roommate in Eliot House, Paul Winter; and the following summer I took my Rotsy cruise.

We were assigned to a light cruiser that sailed to the Mediterranean, but to my great dismay it stopped at no French ports. Also to my great dismay, we were in Naples longer than anywhere else. I still think the best way to see Naples is on a postcard. We put in at Beirut, and there I had a shore leave and looked up a Lebanese classmate who took me to dinner at a restaurant called Chez Lucullus where I ate octopus for the first time. I was supposed to have another shore leave at Casablanca, which the men called "Casa," the way they abbreviated Alexandria to "Alex" and Genoa to "Gen," but it was canceled at the last minute because of scuttlebutt that the enlisted men were planning one last glorious drunk. The midshipmen had to stay aboard to help hoist them back on the ship in nets, we were told. But the orgy did not take place. Joining the Navy, I decided, was a poor way to see the world.

The next Christmas, Paul Winter and I went to New Hampshire again, this time to ski, and once more I did not go home.

When the summer after my junior year came, however, I had a job on a ranch in Arizona, and there was no excuse then for not stopping over in Crescent City on the way West. I had not seen my father and Aunt for three years. I no longer felt the need to avoid a chance encounter with Matilda, and I spent an afternoon and evening with my father and Aunt on Willow Street.

By that time, Matilda played such a small role in my thoughts that when Aunt and I were alone together once on that visit and she said archly, "Your friend is making quite a name for herself," I had no idea whom she was talking about.

"My friend—?" I said.

Aunt tilted her head farther to one side, nodding.

"Next door."

I remained puzzled until I realized that she was speaking as if we still lived on Audubon Street.

"Oh," I said. "You mean Matilda Herrick."

Aunt sniffed.

"There's talk of a divorce in the Ross family."

So I should have been jealous of John Ross, after all! As Aunt might have said, I could not have cared less.

On that visit, Aunt looked the same to me, but my father had aged greatly in the three years of my absence. He was not yet fifty, and by that time I knew that fifty was not old; but he looked old and acted like an old man. His hair and moustache were snow white, with no traces of gray left, and his face was lined, the skin parched and cracked, like a badly preserved calf binding on a book. He had stopped smoking and was still nervous and jumpy from the effort to break the habit. At the same time, he was quieter, gentler, and that made him easier to get on with; but the new manner seemed like another surrender, sadder than his old retreat into cynicism and profanity.

With pathetic eagerness he asked about all the details of my life at Harvard. He had been a student there himself for a year in the 1920s before he went to New York and then to Paris to study painting, but I had never heard him talk sentimentally about the place. Now he did. He seemed to want to share with me, vicariously, an affection for Cambridge that he had not until recently known he had.

"Do they still yell 'Rinehart' from the windows on the Yard in the spring?" he asked. It was the old-grad's stock question. "Do they riot in the Square and march out Garden Street to Radcliffe in pajamas?"

Riot—! What innocent college days his were! And mine too! "Rioting" still meant marching over to Radcliffe in pajamas when I was there!

"I remember once somebody put a jock strap on the Discobolus in front of Hemenway."

"Hemenway—?" I asked.

"The gym."

"Oh," I said. "There's a new one now."

"I suppose everything has changed."

"The house plan has made a difference."

"No" he said; "I mean Max Keezer and Felix the Greek and J. August and the Waldorf. They're gone, I suppose. There used to be a restaurant—Armenian, I think—where you could get fig pie. Maybe even Billings and Stover is gone. Eh?"

I had heard of some of them.

"Leavitt and Peirce is still there," I said. "I buy pipe tobacco there, and I go in to their snack bar sometimes. You can get fishcakes or hash with a dropped egg for lunch."

"A snack bar in Leavitt and Peirce," he said, wonderingly. "I don't remember. I smoked their Cake Box Mixture." He struggled to remember something more about his Harvard days and finally said, "Codfish cakes. We used to have them for breakfast every Sunday morning in the dormitory. I lived in Smith Hall, the Persis Smith entry, above the carbarns. Blue lights flashed on my bedroom ceiling at night, from the trolleys."

"Yes, you've told me," I said.

That was cruel of me, and I regretted it. He was not often a father of twice-told tales.

"I guess I'm growing repetitious in my old age," he said, and rubbing his moustache with his forefinger, he fell silent.

In the few hours that I was at home, I left the house on Willow Street only once, briefly, to go to a liquor store for wine for our dinner. I did not drive around past Audubon Street to see the old house; so maybe I did dread an encounter with Matilda, after all. Instead of going to one of the big stores downtown, I went to a neighborhood store. The storekeeper had never heard of Pouilly-Fuissé or any of the other wines my father used to talk about; so I settled for two bottles of an American "Chablis," which was probably more appropriate anyhow, because Aunt was frying a chicken for dinner, Liggum County style.

At dinner, my father and I emptied both bottles, and after the first bottle he began to call me Coco and to swear a little and he seemed more like my father. On the second bottle we began to speak French, and Aunt, excluded then, sniffed and tapped her long thin fingers on the tablecloth the way she used to do.

"Have another piece of chicken, boy," she would interrupt from time to time. "You're as skinny as a rail. You look half-starved. Don't they feed you at that college?"

Then my father and I would speak French again.

After dinner, Aunt gave me a jar of her strawberry preserves to put in my suitcase and take to Arizona; and I was so ashamed then of the way my father and I had excluded her in our tippling at table that I kissed her, and she cried.

Later, with my taxi waiting at the curb to take me to the airport, my father laid his arm stiffly across my shoulders and said, "I love you, son," and then I damn near cried myself.

That was the last time I ever saw him. He was killed in the old Packard a few weeks later. I flew home from Arizona for his funeral, but I did not stay to see his stone put up in the cemetery: *Thomas Bradford Clayburn II, 1907–1955.*

Deedee had come to Radcliffe when I was a junior. Whenever I ran into Cooper Cox that year, he spoke of her, telling me each time, between contemplative puffs on his pipe, what a "dish" she was. But I did not look her up, and I never saw her until the

last semester of my senior year. I found myself sitting behind
her then, one cold February morning, at the first meeting of an
English class in Sever 11.

Her hair was what I saw first. In fact, because she wore it
straight and long over her shoulders to her waist, a bright cascade of gold was almost all I could see of her below the benchlike
desk where I was jotting my lecture notes in that tiered and
steep-floored lecture hall. I found the view very distracting; not,
I tried to assure myself, because it was feminine and beautiful
but because girls were still something of a novelty in Harvard
classes in those days and I thought of myself as a die-hard who
resented their intrusion into our male sanctuary. Several times
during the hour, when she tossed her head and a gossamer wisp
of her hair danced across my lecture notes like remembered
Arizona tumbleweed, I was tempted to give it a schoolboy's
yank; but I restrained myself and satisfied my pride by batting
at it angrily as if it were a mosquito and muttering to the man
at my left—one Claxton, whom I knew only by name although
he had sat at my left in almost every class since my freshman
year—"Goddamn women!"

She was an industrious note-taker, and I did not see her face
until the end of the lecture, although I tried to catch a glimpse
of it, always stealthily of course, by shifting on my bench, first
to the right and then to the left, and several times arching my
back and stretching my neck as if writer's cramp had attacked
my whole torso.

When the bell rang, she closed her notebook, clicked her ball-
point pen and put it in her purse, picked up a green bag—a
green-bagger yet!—and started to work her way toward the aisle
along the narrow row she was in. It was a silly, ineffectual,
feminine way of getting out of Sever 11, I thought, glancing
back at her. The male practice was to use the benchlike desks as
steps and leap upward, two at a time if the way was clear,
straight toward the exit at the back of the room; and that was
what I myself was doing until, catching a glimpse of her face at
last, I stopped on the third or fourth bench above the row where
I had been sitting and stood still with one foot in mid-air.

"Why, that's Deedee Herrick!" I said aloud, and nearly lost
my balance.

She heard me and, turning around, gave me an inquiring

smile, and there they were, the bee-stung mouth and the squeezed-shut eyes of my school days, and I knew that I was not mistaken. She looked as if she were about to cry.

If I had known what was good for me, I would have leaped at once the rest of the way up those benches to the door, shouting, *"Merde! Merde! Merde!"* as I had done once years before, running away from her across a schoolyard. But I didn't. In that startled moment of recognition I had no time even to guess what was good for me, and I remained standing foolishly on one leg like a crane. Anyhow, by that time I had already fallen in love with her.

"You *are* Deedee Herrick, aren't you?" I said.

"Yes."

She spoke with a hushed breathless diffidence, as if her being Deedee Herrick depended entirely upon my good will, as if, without the assurance of it, she would never dare to make such an admission to anyone again.

"I thought so," I said. "I suppose you don't remember me."

"You must be Tersh Clayburn."

"Tom."

"I mean Tom Clayburn," she said. "Why don't you ever go home for Christmas?"

"I didn't this year because I was in Stillman Infirmary," I said. "I had the flu."

"Oh, that's too bad!"

If I still had any doubts about what had happened to me, they vanished with the sympathetic smile she gave me then. In two leaps downward I was at her side.

The top of her head came just to my shoulder. She was nineteen, I computed, remembering what Cooper Cox had said three years before when I met him in front of Leavitt and Peirce, but she still looked like the "mere child" that Cooper had called her then; and she was certainly a "dish." Hardly a feast or a banquet; just a dish; but enough for any man; a small, exquisite, Epicurean dish that could never be duplicated.

"God's in His heaven," I said.

"What did you say?"

"I said, 'God's in His heaven.'"

"That's Browning."

"Herrick," I said.

She shook her head.

"I'm sure it's Browning. 'God's in His heaven—all's right with the world.' It's from *Pippa Passes.*"

"Herrick," I repeated. "Deedee passes, not Pippa. You put Him there. God, I mean. Just now. In His heaven. For me. I don't mean Robert Herrick, girl; I mean Deedee Herrick—of Audubon Street."

With the name of Audubon Street my voice trailed off weakly at the end, and my little speech echoed glib and foolish in my ears afterward. Audubon Street—! I had not been thinking when I said it. But I was thinking now. God was in His heaven, all right; but He was a vengeful God and all was not right with my world. Not at all. I had remembered Deedee's mother.

I heard Deedee say, "Oh—!" and after a moment I saw that she was blushing, and I wondered whether she knew about me and her mother. I could not remember when I had last seen a girl blush.

"You shouldn't say things like that," she said. "Even in fun. It's blasphemy. You might go to hell."

"Rest in peace," I said.

"What?"

"That's blasphemy too."

Hell was exactly where I would be going if I was not careful, I told myself. Still, I reasoned, a man could not walk off and leave a girl blushing in Sever 11, thinking he was going to hell, even if he was.

Knowing I shouldn't, I said, "How about coffee?"

"I'd like some. I haven't had breakfast."

I wondered whether she played tennis.

"Because you went to church this morning, I bet," I said.

I said it jokingly, because I was trying not to think about Matilda. To my surprise, Deedee nodded an affirmative.

"To confession, I bet," I said.

I was even more surprised when she nodded again. Deedee Herrick a Catholic? It was incredible.

"Black coffee then," I said. "You probably need it."

That was the poorest joke of all, I thought as I said it. A girl like this one would have nothing to confess. She looked like an angel; a very small angel; a very minor angel probably in the celestial order of things; but an angel nonetheless; with nothing to confess and no need of black coffee afterward. But she gave me another smile and afterward said, "Oh," again, this time without the blush.

"What?" I said.

"I forgot. I have another class."

"You, mean next hour?"

"Yes," she said.

"So do I," I said.

I should have left it at that. My avenue of escape was wide open. But I lacked the strength of will.

"So we'll both have to cut classes, won't we?" I said.

She nodded and took my arm.

I saw then that it had happened to her as it had happened to me. But she did not know about her mother and me. I saw that too.

I made myself remember Matilda all that month and the next, conscientiously and painfully. In spite of La Rochefoucauld's maxim, I am sure that I have never been so happy and so unhappy both at the same time.

I remembered Matilda, but I could not stay away from Deedee. I saw her every day—the three times a week that the class in Sever 11 met (at the next lecture, I deserted Claxton-on-my-left and moved down beside her), but on all of the other days of the week as well. We met for coffee, Cokes, had breakfast, lunch and dinner together, in all the restaurants and bars and delicatessens around the Square, in Elsie's at first, because that was where everyone went, but afterward in little holes-in-the-wall, because we wanted to be alone, and in Boston too, at Durgin Park's and Jakey Wirth's, the Union Oyster House, at Locke-Ober's more often than I could afford, because she ate the Lobster Savannah there with an unabashed greediness that delighted me.

I doubt that I had a dozen meals in those two months without her. If Cousin Claudia had not died the year before, I would probably have taken her to Sunday dinners on Beacon Hill. As it was, the ancient Pierce Arrow that Cousin Claudia left to me in her will served to take us to movies, to plays, the opera, the symphony, the museum, and transported us to Concord, Lexington, Salem, Marblehead, all the places where people go in New England. We were sightseers who saw nothing but each other.

Why did I love Deedee?

Why does anyone love a pretty girl of nineteen? Because she is pretty and nineteen, I suppose. Looking back upon that spring, I cannot remember anything she said that seems still to shake the spheres in their unalterable courses as she seemed to shake them for me then. Perhaps by the time Deedee was thirty she became as dull as her mother. It is hard to believe. But whatever she became in later years, in those days in Cambridge she possessed for me a cosmic talent; every motion of her small body, every gesture, every glance, every slightest word she spoke was cataclysmic.

It is six o'clock and already dark on a snowy afternoon in March, and I am at the telephone in my room in Eliot House although I have promised not to telephone her that day.

"Deedee—?"

"Yes."

"This is Tom."

"Yes."

"Have you finished studying *Hamlet* yet?

"No."

"Then you aren't ready for your exam tomorrow?"

"No."

"And so I can't see you tonight?"

"Yes."

"You mean I can see you, even so?"

"Yes."

Was I not thus, by one word, made more eloquent than Shakespeare, more persuasive than his most memorable dramatic achievement, more compelling than the academic requirements of a great university?

How did I love her?

In as many ways as a youth of twenty-one can count, which may not be all of them because in love as in all things, we are told, the best is always yet to be, and I loved her only briefly. But in the ways that I knew, I loved her well.

It is midnight and very cold, still the month of March and once more snowing. Deedee and I are at the door of her dormitory. We have just returned from Concord, where, at my first roommate's home, we have been celebrating her passing the exam on *Hamlet* in spite of the previous evening that she spent with me instead of studying.

"Goodnight, Deedee."

"Goodnight, Tom."

I want to kiss her, but I don't.

"Oh—!"

"What is it?"

She has been looking for something in the pocket of her coat.

"Nothing."

"You have lost something?"

"No."

"Yes you have. Tell me."

"It does not matter."

"What?"

"One of my earrings."

"Where?"

"In Concord, I think. I took them off while we were on the bridge, and I must have dropped one. There is only one in my pocket."

"I'll go back and look for it."

"Oh, no, Tom! Don't be foolish! It's not that important."

"I'll find it."

"No, Tom! It's midnight. And it's snowing."

"But they are the earrings your father gave you!"

"I know. But don't go now! Please! You mustn't. We can go together—tomorrow maybe."

"It's beginning to snow, Deedee. We would never find it tomorrow. It will be covered with snow tomorrow. If I go now—"

"Please, Tom! You mustn't! Not tonight. Don't . . ."

It is almost an hour's drive back to Concord in the old Pierce Arrow, but I go and, alone in the cold night, search with a flashlight around the spot where we stood on the rude bridge that arches the flood, and I continue searching until, at last, I find the earring gleaming in the thickening snow.

Sans reproche though Galahad was—as I, alas, was not—was ever Galahad more gallant or more perseverant?

Yet all that time in Cambridge I made myself remember Matilda.

I remembered Matilda because I loved Deedee, and because I loved Deedee and remembered Matilda I never spoke to Deedee of love. I knew what would happen if I did. So did Deedee. She wanted it to happen, and that made it more difficult for me. I marvel now at my will power; twenty-one is very young. I suppose Deedee deserves the credit. Although she wanted me to make love to her, she never let it become impossible for me not to.

What held her back, I think, was not a virginal instinct for self-preservation. I have no doubt that she was a virgin, but she loved me. Nor was it diffidence. Her diffidence was not timidity; rather, it was an innocent wonder at the world in which she found herself, and that world and the wonder included me. Nor her religion. Like most converts she was devout, but she would have been equal to the necessary casuistry. What held her back, I think, was her woman's intuition. She recognized something perilous and precarious in our relationship. She did not know what it was, but she knew that I knew what it was and she also knew it might be disastrous if she forced me to tell her about it prematurely.

How does one say to a girl like Deedee, "I have slept with your mother"?

Yet how does one love a girl like Deedee as I loved her and not say it?

Perhaps the code of honor that guided me then would seem archaic now. Perhaps such a predicament as mine would no longer be a predicament. We were of that super-annuated generation, both of us. We were what we were and I had no choice.

I could not say it. For two months we dined together and sometimes wined and rode about in Cousin Claudia's ancient car and saw movies and plays and listened to music and went to parties and stood on bridges and walked and talked and were silent together and loved each other, and by the end of March Matilda was probably the only secret that remained between us. But still I could not say it.

When the spring recess came that year, Deedee invited me to spend the first weekend of it, Easter weekend, at her father's house in Rhode Island. For the rest of the holiday she was going with her family to Bermuda.

On Friday afternoon we drove down from Cambridge in the Pierce Arrow through a gray spring rain, taking with us Deedee's half-brother Jack, who was a freshman at Harvard; and when we arrived at her father's house in Wakefield, the rest of her family and their guests had already convened. Besides Jack there were two other half-brothers and a half-sister, who had brought a roommate home from school. There were also two stepsisters, children of Mrs. Herrick's first marriage, who had come down from Providence with their husbands and small children. The first night at dinner, when Deedee's father "called the roll," there were sixteen people present or accounted for. The Herrick family was what we called in those days "a mixed bag."

Deedee's father was a tall, thin, ruggedly built man of fifty with iron-gray hair cut *en brosse* and a close-clipped moustache and beautiful gray eyes whose gaze reminded me of my father's. But Dr. Herrick was nothing like my father in other respects. He was unmistakably a happy man, and the second Mrs. Herrick and the houseful of children, stepchildren and grandchildren were unmistakably the reason for his happiness. Deedee had told me that he was a brain surgeon, that after his divorce from her mother he had gone back to Harvard Medical School and repreprared himself for the career that he had all but given up when he married her. As soon as I saw him, any pity I had been feeling for him because of Matilda vanished. When he shook my hand, his gray eyes searched my face steadily, and I knew at once how much he loved Deedee.

Mrs. Herrick, small and graceful at his side before the big fieldstone fireplace of the living room, greeted me with merry dark eyes that peered out at me above high cheekbones.

"You're just in time to help Bob and Ralph cut wood for the fireplaces," she said.

Bob and Ralph were the other half-brothers. When Deedee and Jack and I went out with them to the woodshed, it became obvious to me that everything with the Herricks was a family project and I was not going to have much time alone with

Deedee during the weekend. For that I was grateful. From the start I had wondered whether I should accept Deedee's invitation. I was afraid that going home with her might look like a commitment that I was not yet prepared to make but the intimacy of being with her in her home might be disastrous to my will power.

It was half-brother Ralph who robbed us of privacy more than any of the others. Ralph was eleven, fat, myopic, and precocious. While we were working together over the woodpile that afternoon he told me he had been looking forward all week to my coming because he was studying French at school and wanted someone to practice talking with.

"*Nous sommes des coupeurs de bois, n'est-ce pas?* " he said pedantically; and I laughed at him and told him that was the title of a song that Charles Trenet sang. I sang a verse of it as we worked and then, suddenly remembering that Matilda had often played the Trenet recording that included it, I stopped abruptly.

"Do you know *Frère Jacques?*" Ralph asked.

I was glad that I did. We sang it together, and I forgot Trenet.

Ralph was at my heels the rest of the weekend. The one time that Deedee and I deliberately eluded him and went off together for a walk in the rain through the woods, he turned up at the pond, waiting for us. Deedee tried to shoo him back to the house, but he would not be shooed.

"But you already speak French better than I do, Ralph," I said to him once.

"*D'accord,* " he agreed. "But I need practice."

He was not endowed with his sister's modesty, but he had his own kind of charm.

On Easter morning, the family's departure for a variety of churches created a hub-bub in the house. After much running up and down stairs at the last minute for forgotten gloves and prayerbooks, there was a debate at the door, with everyone talking at once, to decide who would go in which cars where.

Mrs. Herrick and her second brood of children were Unitarians. Deedee's stepsisters and their husbands were Episcopalians. The half-sister's roommate—a pretty flibbertigibbet, as Aunt would have said, with a heart-shaped face and enormous brown eyes—was a Baptist.

"I'll go to the Unitarian church with you all," she said. "Really, I don't mind," she kept saying; until finally Ralph said, "You'll mind when you get there. The Unitarian preacher will lecture about the United Nations. That's what he did last year. It takes him forever."

Deedee, of course, was going to the Roman Catholic church, and I expected to go with her; but she urged me to stay at home with her father, instead. When Ralph learned that I was going to stay at home, he announced that he would stay at home too.

"Tom and I can read *Tartarin de Tarascon* together," he said.

For a moment I thought I was trapped; but when I offered Cousin Claudia's ancient car for the transportation of the Unitarian contingent, Ralph changed his mind and rode off happily in the front seat of the Pierce Arrow beside his Harvard brother Jack, who was equally delighted by the opportunity to drive the old crate. Mrs. Herrick and half-brother Bob rode in the back seat, and half-sister Diana and her flibbertigibbet Baptist roommate followed in the flibbertigibbet's Volkswagen. Deedee and the stepsisters and their husbands and children combined forces in the two cars from Providence. When they were all gone, Dr. Herrick and I stood silent in the doorway enjoying the sudden churchlike silence for several minutes. Then he proposed a walk to the pond.

It was wet in the woods. Although the rain had stopped, the trees were still dripping and the paths were spongy underfoot. But the air was pungent with early spring. From time to time Dr. Herrick stopped to point out green plants coming up in the bogs or to turn over leaf mold and show me things that were beginning to grow. At the pond he laid his old Navy raincoat on a wet log and we sat there for a time before renewing our walk back toward the house.

We talked about the Navy and Harvard and baseball and politics, all the interests we shared in common, except Deedee and, of course, Matilda. Finally he asked me about my plans for the future, and I had to admit that, beyond a Fulbright scholarship to France that I had just received and the two years of Naval Reserve service that must follow it, I had none. If he was sizing me up as a prospective son-in-law, I thought, I must look very unpromising.

"You might consider teaching," he said dryly. "You've shown great patience with Ralph since you've been here."

I laughed and replied that I feared patience was the only virtue I could bring to the teaching profession. "I've made good enough grades, but I'm really a poor student," I told him. "I've thought sometimes that I'd like to try newspaper work of some kind. I enjoyed the writing course I took with Archibald Mac-Leish. But I guess it was hardly the right preparation for newspaper writing."

"Are you on the *Crimson*?" he asked.

I wasn't. I hadn't even tried out for it.

"I wish I had an all-consuming passion like my father's," I said. "He was an artist."

I regretted the slip at once. I should not have mentioned my father. But Dr. Herrick seemed undisturbed.

"Your father is dead?" he asked quietly.

"He died last summer, in an automobile accident."

Dr. Herrick was silent then for a few minutes, his elbows on his knees, his slender hands knotted between them.

"I think I don't put much stock in youthful ambitions," he said. "Or perhaps I should say I don't think it is very significant if a young man doesn't have any, doesn't find himself right away. Except, of course, in the case of artists—painters and writers, people like your father—and even so I've known a lot of youthful would-be artists who proved in the end to have no talent. My roommate in college was a fine arts major, and the Fogg Museum was full of dilettantes, I remember. I think it is better for a young man to take his time until he is sure what he wants. I suppose a brain surgeon is a kind of artist, but I must say I didn't really know what I wanted to do with my life until I was in my thirties." He was silent again for a while, and I was sure he was thinking of Matilda then. Finally he got up abruptly. "We'd better be going back, or the Unitarians will be there before we are. That lecture on the United Nations doesn't take as long as Ralph seems to remember."

We walked single file for a time, the doctor leading the way along a narrow path to the rutted wagon road by which we had come down through the woods. We were in sight of the house, walking side by side in the road, before he spoke again. He began this time in the fashion of a New England countryman, without relevance to anything that had been said before and not using Deedee's name when he spoke of her.

"I give a little cheer for her every time I think about her conversion to Catholicism," he said. "It was her declaration of independence in this hodge-podge of a family of ours."

"She takes her religion very seriously." I said.

"She takes everything she does seriously, Tom. She is an extremely loyal and selfless little girl. Consequently she can be easily hurt. Maybe she is too much of an idealist. But she is tough too. You have to remember that. When there is real trouble, she can take it. Don't be deceived by her size or that shy manner of hers. She is strong in a crisis." He paused and seemed to be arranging his next words carefully before he spoke them. "If ever you have anything you think you have to tell her, Tom, tell her. You will hurt her more by silence than by frankness."

I knew then why Deedee had not wanted me to go to church with her and why her father had taken me on the walk to the pond. Deedee had asked him for help, and this was it. And his gesture of help was his indirect way of letting me know that he had accepted me. For the first time since I had met Deedee in Sever 11 in February, I found the courage within myself to tell her about her mother and me, to tell her as much, at least, as seemed necessary when the time came; and for the first time I believed that Deedee and I would survive together.

"Thank you, sir," I said.

I probably sounded fatuous, but if Dr. Herrick thought so, he did not show it. He gave me a quick smile that was something like Deedee's. His eyes puckered into wrinkles, half-shut below the shaggy brows, and below the clipped moustache his lower lip thrust forward, not in a bee-stung pout like Deedee's but as if he could have said much more than he had said. He nodded then toward the house.

"I was right," he said. "The Unitarians are home first."

The old Pierce Arrow and the Volkswagen were just then rolling into the circular drive before the house.

"I'm afraid you're in for a few pages of *Tartarin de Tarascon*, after all," he said. "The Catholics and the Episcopalians take much longer."

That afternoon, as I was setting off alone on the return to Cambridge, Deedee stood in the driveway beside the Pierce Arrow with her hand on mine on the car door. It had begun to rain again, and the raindrops sparkled in her hair.

"I'll be at the airport when you come back from Bermuda," I told her. "Get a good rest from me while you are away, because when you return I may be hard to take for a while. Just remember that I love you. I love you, Deedee. I've never told you before, but I've loved you ever since that day in Sever."

She gave me her odd, half-crying little smile and leaned inside the car and kissed me.

"I love you, Tom," she said.

"God's in His heaven," I said.

She *was* crying then.

"Herrick," I said.

"No. Clayburn," she said; and as I drove off she was smiling again.

My roommate's message, printed in large letters on a laundry shirt board and propped against a pile of books on my desk, was the first thing I saw when I switched on the light in our room in Eliot House.

TOM

CALL OPERATOR 8

PAUL

Beneath his name Paul had scrawled: *Have gone to New York for the vac. See you next week.*

CALL OPERATOR 8. . . .

He must have got the long-distance call late in the afternoon, after I had started back from Wakefield; otherwise, he would have given the operator Deedee's number there.

As I dialed the phone on my desk, I could not think of anyone but Aunt, and it was hard to imagine her making a long-distance call unless there was an emergency. She had telephoned me only once before, the previous summer, when I was in Arizona, when my father died: "Your poor father has gone to his rest. . . ."

"You have a long-distance call for Thomas Clayburn," I said

into the phone; and soon I heard a remote voice say, "Crescent City Operator."

So it must be Aunt, I thought, unless she was sick or had died and someone was calling to tell me.

"Tersh—?"

I had never once thought of Matilda until I heard her voice.

"Yes," I said, finally.

"I called earlier and got your roommate."

"Yes," I said.

"He said you were in Wakefield."

"Yes."

For several seconds she did not speak again. I could hear music faintly. It was Charles Trenet singing *Route Nationale Sept.*

"Tersh—?"

"Yes."

"This is Matilda. Did I tell you?"

There was heavy breathing afterward. Was she drunk? I thought not. I had never seen her drunk. But why was she calling me, drunk or sober? What did she want? I had started doodling on Paul Winter's shirt board as soon as I recognized her voice, and I saw that I had written *"Merde!"*

"This is Matilda, Tersh."

"I know," I said.

"I saw Cooper Cox at a party this afternoon. He is home for the vacation."

Charles Trenet sang several bars of *Route Nationale Sept* before she spoke again.

"Cooper says you are seeing a lot of her."

I crossed out the French word on Paul Winter's shirt board and waited.

"You mustn't, Tersh." There was more of Charles Trenet. "I say you must not, Tersh Clayburn," she said.

"I heard you."

"Because—"

I heard her take a deep breath. *Route Nationale Sept* had come to an end, and I was trying to remember what the next song was on the record.

"Because she is your sister, Tersh. She is your half-sister. . . ."

Trenet had begun again. *"Trois hommes du nord. . . ."* But of course! *Les Coupeurs de Bois. . . .*

"What?" I heard myself shouting into the phone. "What did you say? Matilda . . . ! Matilda . . . !"

She had hung up.

I called back immediately.

There was no answer.

All that night I called back.

And all the next day.

And the day after that.

There was never an answer.

On Wednesday I bought a plane ticket to Crescent City and took a cab to the Boston Airport. But when I arrived there I turned the ticket in and went back to Cambridge. I was sure Matilda would not be in Crescent City when I got there. Even if she was in Crescent City and I succeeded in seeing her, or if she wasn't there and I set out in search of her and ultimately found her, she would only say it again; and I did not want to hear her say it again. In her face, beautiful and patrician and unmoved, there would be nothing to tell me whether she was lying or not. Only my father could tell me whether she was lying, and my father was dead.

By the time Deedee returned from Bermuda at the end of the week, I was gone from Cambridge, bag and baggage.

I have never returned.

I never returned to Crescent City either, until the day I gave my lecture in the new auditorium of the city's university and afterward attended the president's reception in the house on Audubon Street that had once been the John Ross home, the house where the mockingbird sang on the roof peak, the mockingbird that Matilda and I named Cooper. That return to Crescent City, that Halloween homecoming, was fifteen years after the Easter Day of Matilda's telephone call to Cambridge, and by that time Matilda had been dead ten of those years, to the day.

As I sat, that night of my return, in a room of the New Century Hotel looking down from the window upon the black void of the river where Uncle Jack and Aunt Beulah had drowned in their Rolls Royce and, before them, the high-school classmate with the field-corn teeth and the burnt-orange hair whose name I could not remember, there came to me among the multiple hallucinations of memory one more image from the past. Like the memory of that afternoon long ago in Eileen Betz's bedroom, it was a memory that I had tried always not to recall.

I was in Aix-en-Provence again, sitting in a hotel room as I sat that night, years later, in a room in Crescent City. But on that occasion in that hotel in Aix, in another time and another country, night had not yet fallen, and below me was not the black void of a river but a sun-drenched street named Frédéric Mistral. Across its narrow canyon drain pipes zigzagged over the face of the house opposite like a child's haphazard invention with a building toy. The sun of Provence had baked the house to the color of dust and honey and was etching black shadows on the wall behind the drain pipes. Although it was winter, my hotel window was open, for the sun provided more heat than the faint and intermittent fevers of the ancient radiator that stood in a corner of the room, and through the window I could hear from the Cours Mirabeau not far away the artillery of Vespas and *vélos* and Deux Chevaux, which made up most of France's traffic in that impoverished post-war time. Although I had already lived in Aix half the year's term of my Fulbright Scholarship, I was still aware of the splash of fountains, audible between bursts of traffic noises on the Cours, persistent and continuous, like a ceaseless fall of rain. But on that day, because of the letter that lay crumpled at my feet on the red tiles of the floor, there was no music for me in the fountains' splashing.

The letter was from Aunt.

"So you are in France, are you?" she had written. "So you have finally perched somewhere where a person can write to you! It's about time! What ever got into you last spring, Tertius Clayburn, leaving college like that before you got your diploma and tearing around the country in that crazy old car your Cousin Claudia left you? You never said what was the matter with you on any of the cards you sent. All those years and all that money spent on your education and nothing to show for it! I've never heard of such a thing! And then you having that accident in Colorado in the summer and being in a hospital and all and never letting me know till afterward! Don't you ever have any consideration for others? You're just like your father, only worse, God rest his soul! Well, I'm glad you've settled down somewhere at last, even if it is in a foreign country. At least I know where you are now. . . ."

There was much more, but in that letter Aunt had written only one short paragraph that mattered. It came at the end, characteristically delayed and roundabout, like a slow curve pitched high and inside by a left-hander.

"Remember that little Herrick girl who used to live next door on Audubon Street? Matilda Herrick's daughter. Well, several months ago you got a piece of mail from her that might interest you. I've gone and mislaid it, stuck it away somewhere to keep till I heard from you, and now I can't find it, or I'd send it on to you. But I can tell you what was in it, because I opened it. I could see it was an invitation of some kind and maybe needed answering. She was getting married. The wedding took place in the East somewhere, in Rhode Island, a place called Wickfield or Wakefield, something like that. Anyhow, she married that Cox boy—Cooper Cox."

After Aunt's signature there was a postscript, and there was an enclosure too, a long, legal-sized envelope, folded twice and certainly not the announcement of Deedee's marriage. I did not look at them and let the enclosure and Aunt's letter fall, crumpled together, to the floor, because as soon as I read about Deedee's marriage to Cooper Cox, Deedee's image appeared in the room and stood before me as if she were real, looking as she had looked on that Easter Day in Wakefield almost a year before, rain in her hair, eyes shining. I believed I could feel again the softness of her first and last kiss on my mouth; but this time it was a kiss of betrayal, not an acknowledgment of love, and I drew back and cried out at her.

"God's in His heaven!" I said; and it was blasphemy indeed this time, the way I said it. "God's in His heaven! Oh—Deedee!"

"Tersh . . ." I heard her say.

I got up and paced about the room, back and forth, from the bed with the lumpy mattress to the battered armoire with the mirrored door that would not close and back to the bed again. Outside, the traffic noises rose and fell and the fountains splashed on and two workmen in the street below the window began to quarrel. *"Je te casserai la gueule . . . !"*

I turned upon Deedee's apparition finally and shouted, *"Tom!* Don't call me Tersh! That's what *she* called me! My name is Tom!"

"I mean Tom," Deedee said gently, and smiled her bee-stung smile at me. I found myself hating her smile then as I had hated it when I was a small boy. "Why did you run away, Tom?" she asked. She was still smiling, and I said, *"Merde!"*

"What does that mean?"

I laughed, and she laughed with me, spittle forming at the corners of her mouth as it used to do when she was a child, and our joined laughter became an ugly sound in the ugly room. Then the room grew suddenly dark and we stopped laughing and I could hardly see her.

"I've lost something, Tom," she said.

"Of course you've lost something!" I shouted at her. "And don't tell me this time that it doesn't matter, because this time I can't go back and find it for you in the snow. This time I can't. I saved it for you once, one whole goddamn snowy winter, but now you've lost it for good! Oh—Deedee!"

"It's not important, Tom. Don't be foolish!"

"Oh, yes, it is! To me it's important! Or *was!* Christ, what a sanctimonious boob I was!"

"Don't, Tom! You mustn't."

"That oaf! That Peter Pan in thick-lensed glasses! That rich, stupid, stuck-up, Audubon-Street—!"

"Tom!"

"Why didn't she tell you he's your cousin? *Him . . .* ! I wish he was the one who fell and broke his neck! Why didn't she tell you? If I'm your brother, then he's your cousin. Did you know I am your brother, Deedee? Your half-brother, your half-assed brother."

"Tom, that's blasphemy."

"Rest in peace."

"Please, Tom."

"Merde!" I cried, *"Merde, merde, merde!"*

And she was gone.

I paced the room again, bed to armoire and back, across the red-tiled floor, until finally, my anger waned and I grew numb.

Like a man who needs another drink, I picked up Aunt's letter and read the last paragraph again; and this time I read the postscript too.

"I found the enclosed last summer in your father's blue suit when I was getting ready to send it to the Salvation Army. There's 'Coco' written in pencil on the envelope, and since that's what he called you sometimes, I suppose he intended it for you. You can see I haven't opened it, so I don't know what's in it or when he wrote it. Just think, your father has been gone to his reward a year and eight months now, on the 16th. Why, that's tomorrow! My, how time flies!"

I picked up the folded envelope and tore it open.

My father had written on three sides of two sheets of paper in a bold and angular scrawl that, like Matilda's square and careful college-girl calligraphy, allowed only a few lines on a page. At the top of the first page, the date was June 14, 1955. If Aunt's memory was correct, that was two days before he drove out into the country in the old Packard and struck a tree.

"Dear Son,

"The doctors told me today I've got a growth in my lungs. So now I don't know whether I'll still be around when you stop here in the fall on your way back from Arizona, as you said you might, and there is something I have wanted to say to you for a long time but have never known how. Maybe I'll make a botch of it now, but I want to try. It's about your mother and, in a way, about . . ."

I turned the first sheet over.

". . . Matilda.

"Your mother was a simple, uneducated woman, son, a country girl, a peasant really, from Brittany, as you know. She was an artists' model in Paris when I met her. At the end of her life she lost her mind, went mad. But she was a good woman and I loved her. Maude thinks Matilda broke up our marriage when she followed me to Paris because that is what everybody in that Audubon Street crowd was saying. But this is not true. I loved your mother and I cared for her, looked after her and you, and I was faithful to her to the end. Matilda did not break up my marriage. I won't say that I didn't try my luck with Matilda Herrick afterward, after your mother died and I came back to Crescent City and Matilda was living next door to us on Audubon Street. Nothing mattered to me then. Yes, I tried then. But Matilda, who was willing enough in Paris, wouldn't have me when I came home to Crescent City, because she couldn't stand the thought of my arm, my red-white-and-blue stump. I think she might have come around if I had kept on trying because I think she loved me, so far as a woman like Matilda is capable of love. But the point is . . ."

I dropped the first sheet on the floor beside Aunt's letter and read the rest on the second sheet.

". . . in Paris I had nothing to do with Matilda and was as good a husband as I knew how to be, because I loved your mother and I knew that what I felt for Matilda was something else.

"I am not sure why I am telling you this, Coco, unless it is because, as I look back on my life, it seems to me it's about the only thing I ever did right and I want you to think as well of me as you can."

I dropped the second page of the letter beside the other and beside Aunt's and ran out of the room.

For three days I left the letters on the red-tiled floor of my hotel room in Aix. Three days—? Four. A week maybe. I don't know. For when I departed from that room, I departed also from myself, went out of myself and the hotel into the street called Frédéric Mistral, past the quarreling workmen *("Plouc! Marteau! Espèce d'anguille . . . !")*, along the narrow sidewalk, skittering once, I remember, one foot high in the air, on a fresh turd dropped by one of the pampered dogs of Aix, toward the Cours Mirabeau, under its arching plane trees and across, beyond the statue of Roi René, dodging the Vespas and the *vélos* and the Deux Chevaux, and under the blotched branches of the trees again, amongst parked bicycles and whining gypsy children with palms outstretched, into the *terrasse* of the Deux Garçons, bumping against tables *("Attention, monsieur . . . !")*, and on, without stopping, without apology, into the green-and-gold interior of the Deux G's and its ambience of dark mirrors and old men with gnarled hands like Cézanne's card players *("Jeune homme, je vous en prie . . . !")*, to the back of the mirrored room, to the very back, to the farthest table at the back, next to the phone booth *("Consultez le Bottin . . .")*, and the w.c. *("Fermez la porte s.v.p.")*, where Léon, best of the Deux G's waiters, sat tugging at his black moustache,

bored by his day of duty indoors, back to the table nearest
Léon and the bar. . . .

"*Une fine*, Léon."

"*Ça va*, Monsieur Clayburn?"

"*Ça ne va pas.*"

After Léon finally refused to bring the brandy bottle to my
glass another time and refused to sell me the bottle and discreetly guided me out through a door at the rear, admonishing
gently, "*Soyez sage, monsieur,*" and after I staggered across the
street and into the narrow, covered alley that was called the
Passage Agard and stopped in the reek of a pissoir for an eternity of frantic fumbling at my fly and another eternity of helpless waiting for the splashing at my feet to stop and then stumbled on through the alley's dingy darkness to the Place du Palais
de Justice, a *quartier* that had never been among my haunts till
then, I remember nothing, until three days later—four, a week
—I found myself back where I had started, in my hotel room on
the rue Frédéric Mistral, where I threw myself on the lumpy
bed and lay exhausted, *pompé*, staring at Aunt's letter and my
father's still lying crumpled on the red-tiled floor.

Years later, as I sat by the window of the New Century in
Crescent City, remembering that other time in that other hotel
in that other country, I discovered why I had cherished a wrong
image of Cooper Cox for so many years and failed to recognize
him when I saw him that night at the president's reception on
Audubon Street. It was because in those three days in Aix, a clot
of anger formed in my brain and, heated by the brandy I consumed in the Deux Garçons and in the bistros and houses behind the Place du Palais de Justice, swelled to a point of bursting
and melted the images of Matilda Herrick and Cooper Cox in
my memory into one, as if Cooper as well as Matilda had been
in a conspiracy against me from the beginning. Surely, that time
in Aix, among all my memories of Cooper there had been the
.pudgy, curly-haired boy behind the closed window above the
cornice of the house on Audubon Street thumbing his nose at
his brother shut outside, the homunculus in Sunday clothes that
I saw later on the upper gallery the day the brother died, the sly
youth who lurked in the corridors of Crescent City's high school

with too much money in his pockets, the Peter Pan in thick-lensed glasses coming out of Leavitt and Peirce on Harvard Square attired in Harvard man's chinos, dark jacket, white shirt and narrow black tie; but I needed, that time in Aix, a different Cooper Cox from all the Coopers I could remember, a Cooper worthy of my anger, one I could despise, as I despised Matilda Herrick, and so I forged from the clot of anger in my brain against Matilda the Cooper Cox, sinister and supercilious, that I looked for at the reception in Crescent City fifteen years later and failed to find.

As I sat by the window of the New Century, there came to me also, out of nowhere, the name of the boy who had drowned in the Ohio River.

Rob Grills.

I had never known Rob Grills well. All I could remember of him besides the field-corn teeth and the burnt-orange hair was that he had sat next to me in a history class and came to high school in a bus from the country.

Rob Grills . . . Robbe-Grillet. . . . Robbe-Grillet was one of the authors in the list the pale-shanked girl at the reception had reeled off so glibly. "Mr. Clayburn, tell me, what do you think of the anti-novel in France—like, you know, I mean Robbe-Grillet and . . . ?"

Robbe-Grillet . . . Rob Grills. . . . was that why I had thought of Rob Grills when I first looked down from my hotel window at the dark void of the river?

Rob Grills . . . Robbe-Grillet. . . . It was like Maude Ewbank and Modigliani.

What was it the pale-shanked girl had said afterward? "Reality is seen only when you strip away the personal point of view. . . ." But could you ever strip away the personal point of view? Quoting La Rochefoucauld, my father used to say: "One is never so happy nor so unhappy as one imagines. . . ." My father was a great translator of aphorisms. *Mens sibi conscia recti*. . . . It meant a man conscious of the right, but I liked my father's translation better: a silly man conscious of his rectum. You could never be conscious of anything without always being conscious of your rectum at the same time. One was always conscious of one's rectum. So maybe Ike's bowel movements were newsworthy, after all.

But could you strip away the personal point of view if, at the same time, you could never be sure how happy or unhappy you were? In my reconstructions of the past that evening, had I stripped away the personal point of view completely and seen reality, the truth? Had I seen truly the Aunt who never knew me although she did the best she could? The father I had never known until that day in Aix, almost two years after he died? The Major Rodney L. Marvin I learned in boyhood to despise and the Mayor, my great-great-grandfather, at whose bullet-hole shrine on Audubon Street I worshipped when I was a boy? The Eileen Betz I fled from and the Miss Treen I fled to? And the Matilda—that quaint, archaic, superannuated bitch—whose death brought me a guilty sense of deliverance, almost as if I had murdered her? Was the Deedee I loved any more truly seen than the Cooper Cox I hated and misconceived in Aix and failed to recognize in Crescent City? If my wife should ask me, when she telephoned, whether I had seen the girl I used to be in love with —"that rich, beautiful, little blond girl you used to be in love with"—should I answer yes or no?

"Tersh—?"

It was Deedee once more. She was there beside me in the New Century, and I heard her voice as distinctly as I had heard it that day long ago in Aix-en-Provence, as truly as I might have heard it only a little while before if I had allowed the phone on River Hill Drive to ring long enough for her to answer. Although the room was dark, I could see her clearly: not the *Cox, Mrs. Dorothy H.*, whose number I had called on River Hill Drive, but the Deedee I had loved when we were young.

"*Tom*, Deedee," I said gently.

"I mean Tom. Why did you run away after that day in Rhode Island? God was in His heaven for us that day."

"Because I learned—or thought I learned—He was not the God we believed He was."

"Were you ever sorry you ran away?"

"In France, I was. In Aix. In Aix, when I learned that you had married Cooper Cox and then, in the same moment almost, learned that you were not my sister after all, I went out of my mind for a while."

"Are you still sorry, Tom? Are you sorry now?"

At that moment, the telephone on the bedside table rang and I was on my feet at once.

But I sat down again and let it ring.

"No, Deedee," I said.

And she was gone.

The telephone rang a long time.

If it was Deedee who was calling, from River Hill Drive, I had no need now to answer. If it was my wife, calling from Washington, she would call again. God was in His Heaven for her and me. Of that, at least, I was sure.